W9-CCD-920

365 Stories for Boys

PaRragon

Bath · New York · Singapore · Hong Kong · Cologne · Delhi
Melbourne · Amsterdam · Johannesburg · Shenzhen

This edition published by Parragon in 2012

Parragon
Queen Street House
4 Queen Street
Bath BA1 1HE, UK
www.parragon.com

ISBN 978-1-4454-6478-7

Printed in China

New Year's Day

It was the first day of the new year, and Pongo and Perdita were out for a walk with their pets, Roger and Anita. The morning fog was beginning to part, and the air was clear and cold. "Oh, Pongo." Perdita sighed happily. "What a wonderful year we've just had – 15 puppies to be thankful for!"

"Yes, darling, and think of all we have to look forward to this year," said Pongo.

"Can you believe they all stayed up till midnight last night to ring in the new year?" Perdita cried. "And still awake when we left! I do hope they don't tire out dear, poor Nanny."

"Yes, that was quite a party we had at the flat last night," Pongo agreed. "And Lucky would have spent the whole night watching television if we had allowed him to."

"Perhaps we should be getting home now," said Perdita. "I am so afraid that Cruella De Vil may come around while we're out. I dread the way she looks at our puppies."

"I suppose we should," said Pongo. "But I'm sure Nanny has been taking good care of them." Pongo and Perdita gently pulled on their leads to let Roger and Anita know it was time to go home. The four of them walked towards home just as a new sprinkling of rain began to gently fall.

"Nanny! Puppies! We're home!" called Roger as he and Anita took off their muddy boots and Pongo and Perdy brushed off their paws on the mat in the hall. But no one answered.

"Pongo!" exclaimed Perdita, her panic rising. "Where are the puppies?"

Pongo raced up the stairs and began searching the rooms one by one. Perdita went to check the kitchen. Roger and Anita exchanged concerned looks, but tried to remain calm.

Pongo hurried into the sitting room to rejoin Perdita, who was on the brink of tears. "Oh, Pongo!" she cried. "Where can . . ."

"Hush, darling," said Pongo, his ears pricked intently. The two dogs fell silent. Then they both heard it: a tiny snore coming from the direction of the couch. There, nestled among the cushions, the puppies were sound asleep!

"I found Nanny!" Roger called. "She fell asleep in her chair!"

Perdita was busy counting the sleeping puppies. ". . . 12, 13, 14 . . . Oh, Pongo! One of the puppies isn't here!"

But Pongo had trotted into the next room. "Here he is, darling!" he called. "It's Lucky, of course. He's watching the New Year's Day celebration on television."

Aladdin
Three Cheesy Wishes

Long ago, before there was an Aladdin, a Jasmine, or even a Sultan, the magic lamp was making its way towards the Cave of Wonders, where Aladdin would one day find it. A travelling merchant had bought the lamp, along with some other 'junk.' Not knowing its value, he sold it to a cheese seller for some lunch.

Hassan the cheese seller looked at the lamp sceptically. He sighed, and began to shine it up. In a puff of smoke, the Genie appeared.

"Hello there! I'm the one and only magical Genie!" the big blue spirit announced.

"Excuse me?" said Hassan.

"Nice to meet you," said the Genie. "And what do you do here in Agrabah?"

"My name is Hassan, and I'm a – "

"Wait!" cried the Genie. "Let me guess! They say I'm a little psychic, you know!"

The Genie put his hand over his brow as he secretly looked around the man's shop. "You sell . . . cheese! Am I right or am I right?"

"You are right," said Hassan. "But that's an easy guess. Not very magical."

"You're very observant, Hassan," said the Genie. "So I'll give you three wishes."

"Three wishes, eh?" Hassan thought for a few minutes. Then he said, "It's hard to get enough good milk to make the best cheese. I wish I had many, many goats so I would always have enough milk."

Poof! In a flash, thousands of goats filled the streets of Agrabah. Goats were everywhere! They crowded the little shop, and knocked over the stalls in the market.

"Goodness!" Hassan cried. "I would have to wish for the biggest cheese shop in the world to sell the cheese from so many goats."

Poof! All of a sudden, Hassan's store began to grow and grow! His cheese shop was even taller than the highest sand dunes outside the city.

"This is terrible!" Hassan cried. Far below, the people looked like tiny ants. "I can't live and work in such a monstrosity. All I wanted was to make the finest cheese in Agrabah."

Hassan turned to the Genie. "I wish I'd never met you!" he cried.

Poof! Suddenly, the Genie was gone. Hassan found his shop back to normal. Outside, the marketplace was completely goat free.

Hassan searched high and low for the lamp, but it was already tucked into a little boy's pocket. Where would it end up next?

"It must have all been a crazy dream," said Hassan.

But, from that day, everyone said Hassan's cheese was the finest in all of Agrabah!

HANDY MANNY

The Best Repairman

Manny ran to answer the phone. "Handy Manny's Repair Shop. You break it, we fix it!"

"Manny? It's Jasmine Chung from the Sheet Rock Hills Herald. I'm calling to let you know you've been picked as the county's best repairman!"

Manny couldn't believe it. Jasmine wanted to interview Manny at his next repair job. He was going to fix Sparrow Fountain at the park. It had been broken in the big storm last night.

"A reporter is coming to interview me at the park!" Manny told the tools.

"Wow, will we get our picture in the paper, Manny?" shrieked Dusty.

"Maybe," answered Manny.

Once they got to the park, Manny inspected the damage to the water fountain. All the pipes inside were broken and the fountain was empty, so the birds had nothing to drink. Just then, a woman raced over.

"Manny! Jasmine Chung here," she said quickly. "Ready for the interview? Yes? Okay, then. Take a seat!"

Manny was unsure. He thought he should fix the fountain first. But Jasmine talked so fast. "So, did you always want to be a repairman?"

"Oh, yes." Manny grinned. "My parents tell me that 'fix' was my very first word!"

"That's a great quote," Jasmine said. "I may even put that under your picture!"

"Picture?!" shouted Dusty, as she and the other tools gathered around. Manny decided it was time to start fixing the fountain. Jasmine got her camera ready. Not wanting to miss out, the tools began practising their best poses. Soon they were all hopping around Jasmine.

"Tools—STOP!" Manny ordered. "I know you want your pictures in the paper, but you're forgetting why Jasmine wants our picture to begin with – because we help others by fixing things. But we can't help anyone if you're all too busy posing. This fountain is broken, and the birds can't get a drink on a hot day like today," said Manny. "So, let's think about why we're really here."

"To help others!" cheered Dusty. "Let's get going and fix it right!"

So, Manny and the tools worked together to fix the fountain.

"Wow, Manny, you really are the county's best repairman!" raved Jasmine.

The following week, all of the tools appeared in the paper. "I may be the county's best repairman," Manny said. "But you're the county's best tools!"

Disney
**MICKEY MOUSE
CLUBHOUSE**

A Rainy Day Adventure

A clap of thunder suddenly shook the Clubhouse. *BOOM!*

"Aw, phooey. I didn't think it was going to rain," said Donald. "Now we'll be stuck indoors with nothing to do!"

"There must be things we can do," said Mickey. "And we can get help from some Mouseketools! Oh, Toodles!"

The Mouseketools are: Four ceramic frogs, some striped napkins, a toy pirate ship and the Mystery Mouseketool.

"What is that noise?" said Mickey.

"Oh, pickle juice!" said Donald. "It's water dripping through a leak in the roof!"

"We need a Mouseketool," said Mickey. "Let's use the ceramic frogs to catch the drops of water in their open mouths. We've got ears! Say cheers!" said Mickey. Everyone grabbed a ceramic frog and placed it under a leak.

"Let's go to the kitchen and get a snack!" said Goofy. Everyone hurried to the kitchen. Dirty bowls and baking trays were everywhere. Donald carried dirty dishes to the sink. Daisy put away ingredients. Mickey turned on the water to start washing the dishes.

"Gee, with all the rain and the water from washing the dishes, it feels like we've had a boatload of water today!" said Mickey.

"Being on a boat would be fun," said Goofy. "Or a pirate ship!" said Minnie.

"That's it!" said Donald. "Let's be PIRATES!"

The friends tied the striped napkins around their heads.

"Let's head for the high seas!" said Daisy.

"I think we need another Mouseketool," said Mickey. "The toy pirate ship. We've got ears! Say cheers!" said Mickey.

Mickey flipped the Silly Switch and the bath tub appeared. Everyone took a turn sailing the toy pirate ship.

"We're looking for sunken treasure!" said Donald.

"It's time for the Mystery Mouseketool!" said Mickey. "It's gold coins. Super cheers!" said Mickey. "I'm going to hide these coins throughout the Clubhouse. Each one of you has to find a coin and bring it back."

The friends played and played.

"Let's drink root beer and eat popcorn!" said Mickey.

"And sing pirate songs!" said Minnie.

"Who cares about the rain!" said Daisy. "We pirates know how to have fun no matter where we are!"

Mickey passed around the popcorn, and no one even realized that the rain had stopped.

Disney·PIXAR
MONSTERS, INC.

Relaxopolis

It was another cold blustery day in Monstropolis. Sulley and Mike were on their way to work. Mike sighed heavily.

"What's wrong, little buddy?" asked Sulley.

"I'm sick and tired of winter!" Mike replied. "It's cold, it's windy and it gets dark early." He thought for a moment. "Sulley, I think I have the winter blues!"

"Sure sounds like it," said Sulley. "Only a month or so to go, though."

Mike sighed again. A month or two more of winter sounded like an eternity! But a big smile spread across his face when he looked up and saw an advertising board. On it was a big pink monster sitting in a lounge chair on the beach, wearing sunglasses and sipping what looked like an ice-cold booberry slushie. In big letters it said: BEAT THOSE WINTER BLUES IN RELAXOPOLIS!

Mike stopped in his tracks and grabbed Sulley's furry arm. He pointed at the sign, too excited to say a word.

"That's a great idea!" Sulley cheered. "A week on a tropical island is just what we need!"

As soon as he and Sulley got to work, Mike filled in their holiday forms. They would be on their way to Relaxopolis first thing Saturday morning!

When they arrived, they didn't even unpack their bags. They went right to the beach where they each ordered an ice-cold booberry slushie.

As they lay down on their deck chairs on the sunniest part of the beach, Mike said, "This is the life!"

"You bet," said Sulley. "Do you think you need some of this Monster Tropic sunscream? You'd better be careful. You don't want to get too much sun on your first day!"

"I'll just soak up the rays for a little while first," said Mike happily. "My winter blues are just melting away." He slipped a big mirrored sunglass over his eye and put his arms behind his head. This was paradise!

After a while Sulley got bored with sunbathing and decided to go for a swim. Then he joined in a game of beach monsterball. Then he let some little monsters bury him in the sand up to his neck. A couple of hours later, he returned to the deck chairs, where Mike was sound asleep. Sulley took a closer look. His little green friend had not changed position since Sulley had left. Mike had burned himself in the sun!

Sulley covered Mike with a towel and ran over to get him a refreshing booberry slushie. When he returned to the deck chairs, Mike was just waking up.

"Hey, little buddy," said Sulley. "Guess you chased those winter blues away, huh?"

Mike just looked at Sulley sleepily.

"You aren't blue any more," Sully explained. "Now you're bright red!"

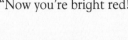

THE INCREDIBLES

A Super Summer Barbecue

One hot summer afternoon, Helen Parr stood in the kitchen frosting a cake. It was almost time to leave for the barbecue.

"Hey, Mum," said Helen's eldest son Dash, running into the room at Super speed. "Why do we have to go to some silly neighbourhood barbecue?"

"Dashiell Robert Parr," said Helen. "We're lucky to have been invited. You know we're doing our best to fit in here. And remember: no Super powers outside the house."

A while later, the Parrs walked around the block to their first neighbourhood party. Helen placed her cake on the dessert table. Her husband Bob headed over to the grill to help out. Her daughter Violet looked around for someone to talk to and Dash watched some children compete in a sack race. He couldn't join in because it might reveal his Super speed.

"Are you too chicken to play?" A boy teased. Dash scowled. When the mean boy hopped by, he mysteriously tripped and fell. Dash smiled to himself and brushed off his sneaker. His speed had come in handy, after all.

Meanwhile, out of the corner of her eye, Helen saw Jack-Jack atop a high brick wall. He was about to topple off! In a flash, she shot her arm all the way across the yard and caught him. She sighed with relief and cuddled Jack-Jack. The other mother just rubbed her eyes and mumbled something about not sleeping much the night before. Oops, Helen thought to herself.

A while later, Helen saw the neighbours enjoying her cake. She looked around the yard and spotted Dash telling a story. Violet was eating an ice cream cone with a girl her age. Wow, it looks like we really fit in here, Helen thought. But just then, she overheard one of the neighbours.

"There's something strange about those Parrs," he said.

Had someone discovered them? Were their Super powers about to be revealed?

"All that may be true," someone else added, "but that Helen sure makes a terrific cake!" Everyone agreed, and the conversation ended.

The Parrs chuckled to themselves. Their cover wasn't blown after all! Maybe they were a little strange compared to the average family, but they were doing their best to act normal.

Bob and Helen rounded up their children and headed for home, pleased with the way things had gone. As they reached their house, Helen gave Bob a great big kiss, which the kids did their best to ignore.

The Arrival of a Space Ranger

Andy was a young boy with a big imagination. He loved playing with all his toys, but his all-time favourite was Woody, a pull-string cowboy doll.

"C'mon Woody!" Andy called. Andy took Woody everywhere. Just then, Andy's mother called out that his friends were about to arrive.

"It's party time!" Andy shouted happily. He dropped Woody off and headed downstairs. After Andy left, the room was quiet for a moment. Then, Woody sat up. "Okay everybody, coast is clear!" he shouted.

One by one, all the toys peeked out of the closet, from beneath the bed and out of the toy chest. Mr Potato Head, Hamm, Slinky, RC, Rex and Bo Beep all stretched and chatted as they came out – just as they did every time there were no humans around to see them.

Woody gathered the toys for a special meeting. First, he reminded them that only one week remained before Andy and his family would move to a new house. Then he blurted out the big news: "Andy's birthday party has been moved to today."

All the toys started squeaking and shouting! The toys dreaded Andy's birthday, because they feared some newer toy might replace them. This year, the party was being held earlier than usual because of the move.

"They're here!" Hamm shouted suddenly. Out the window, Andy's guests were arriving with lots of presents!

Woody sent the Green Army Men downstairs to spy on Andy's party. Using a jump rope, the soldiers scrambled down to the first floor, then set up a baby monitor inside a potted plant. Hidden, the soldiers described each present as it was unwrapped, sending the news back to Andy's room. Luckily, nothing sounded too threatening... until the last package. All the kids gasped as they saw –

Just then, the baby monitor cut out. The toys were frantic! What was that last present?

Suddenly, Andy and his friends burst into the bedroom. They ran around happily, then rushed out again – leaving the mystery toy on the bed. In the excitement, Woody had fallen on the floor. All the toys watched anxiously as he climbed back up onto the bed.

The new toy turned and blinked. He was white and green and stood with his hands on his hips.

"I am Buzz Lightyear, Space Ranger," he declared. He claimed to be a space hero who had just landed on Earth!

Woody sighed. He knew this newcomer was going to be trouble.

Disney · PIXAR

WALL·E

A New Friend

If you lived back in the 29th Century, you would live off in space with all the other people from Earth.

Long ago, Earth had been evacuated because it was too polluted. No one could live there until someone cleaned up the planet. And there was someone left behind to do that work.

WALL•E was a Waste Allocation Load Lifter, Earth-Class. He didn't mind his lonely job of compacting rubbish. He looked at it as a sort of treasure hunt. He never knew what he would find each day in the trash.

But WALL•E wanted more in life. He didn't ask for much, he just wanted to hold hands with someone – someone he loved. He had seen this watching his favourite movie over and over. It was his dream.

One day, WALL•E was out compacting and cubing trash when he found something special. It was a plant. His pet cockroach chirped, knowing that his friend would be really interested in this green thing. Neither one of them had ever seen anything like it before. WALL•E took it home to keep with his other treasures.

Soon afterwards, another robot landed on Earth. WALL•E was very excited to have some company! WALL•E fell in love with the sleek new robot at first sight. Her name was EVE, and WALL•E watched her in awe.

Over time, WALL•E figured out that EVE was looking for something. But she wouldn't tell him what it was.

WALL•E took her to his home and showed her all the treasures he had collected from the trash. He was very proud of the things he had found.

But when WALL•E showed EVE the plant, she immediately grabbed it from him and stored it in a secret compartment in her chest! Then she shut down. She slept and slept, no matter how hard WALL•E tried to wake her up.

Before long, EVE's ship returned to take her away.

No! WALL•E loved her. He didn't want her to leave.

As the ship prepared to fly away with EVE inside, WALL•E decided he couldn't let her go. He latched onto the outside of the ship.

WALL•E had finally found someone he wanted to hold hands with, and he was not going to let her leave without him.

And so, WALL•E followed EVE into space . . .

HERCULES

A True Hero

"Hercules! Slow down!" Amphitryon yelled to his son, who was pulling their cart to the market. His son was headed straight for a marble archway that was under construction. Because Hercules didn't understand how strong he really was, his attempts to be helpful often turned into disaster.

Later, Amphitryon and his wife, Alcmene, decided to tell Hercules the truth: they weren't his real parents. They'd discovered him when he was a baby and raised him as their own.

Amphitryon handed Hercules a medallion. "This was around your neck when we found you," he said. It had a thunderbolt on it – the symbol of the gods.

Hercules wanted to know more, so the next morning, he left for Zeus. Once he arrived, he stood before the giant statue of Zeus. Suddenly, a great stone hand reached down. "My boy. My little Hercules," Zeus said.

Hercules' eyes widened. Zeus, the most powerful of all gods, was his father! Zeus explained that as a baby Hercules had been stolen and turned into a human. Hercules' superstrength was the only godlike quality he still had.

"If you can prove yourself a true hero on Earth, your godhood will be restored," Zeus told him. "Seek out Philoctetes, the trainer of heroes." With that, Zeus whistled and a winged horse, Pegasus, flew into the temple.

That night, Hercules and Pegasus flew to Philoctetes' home. Phil, as Hercules called him, started training him. Hercules succeeded with all of his hero lessons and grew into a strong man.

Finally, Hercules felt he was ready to test his strength in the real world. Phil took him to Thebes, where Hercules heard that two boys were trapped in a rockslide! He and Pegasus flew to the boys. Hercules lifted a giant boulder and freed the trapped children.

There was no time to celebrate, though. A terrible monster called the Hydra was emerging from a nearby cave... and it was hungry. With a massive head and sharp claws, it went after Hercules. Hercules slashed at the monster with his sword. But when he cut off its head, more grew back. The more heads he chopped off, the more appeared!

Then the Hydra trapped Hercules in one of its claws. Hercules slammed his arms against a cliff wall with all his might. Within seconds, the wall broke apart. Huge boulders tumbled down, killing the monster. Hercules was overjoyed. He was well on his way to becoming a true hero.

DUMBO

An Elephant Lullaby

Mrs Jumbo was very sad. More than anything else in the world, she had been longing for a baby elephant of her own. Many other animals in the circus had babies and, as she watched the mothers with their infants, she grew sadder and sadder. Then one day, a stork delivered a baby elephant to Mrs Jumbo! The tiny elephant was the most beautiful creature she had ever seen, and she was the happiest animal in the circus. But then it happened: her baby sneezed, causing his ears to unfold.

They were extremely large ears, and the other elephants laughed at him in a way that was not nice at all.

"Instead of calling him Jumbo Junior," one elephant said drily, "he ought to be called Dumbo!" The others laughed loudly at this.

Mrs Jumbo ignored their taunts and curled her trunk around her beloved baby.

As the days went by, Mrs Jumbo grew to love her baby more and more. She played hide-and-seek with him, pretending to be surprised when he hid behind her legs. She played peeka-boo with him. She sang him lullabies at bedtime, and danced around with him when he woke up.

One evening, Mrs Jumbo found her precious baby looking terribly sad. She guessed that the other elephants had been taunting him again, and her eyes flashed with indignation.

But she tenderly put him to bed, tucking his large ears around him to keep him warm. "Don't mind what the others say," she whispered softly. "You are going to grow up to be a fine elephant! Shall I sing you a lullaby, darling?"

As Dumbo nodded, Mrs Jumbo heard the other elephants talking in low tones in the next stall. "Honestly!" one of them was saying. "You'd think he was the only elephant left on earth, the way she pampers him! She spoils him terribly, she does!"

But Mrs Jumbo ignored their whispers and began to sing:

Hush, little baby, don't you cry.
Mama's gonna sing you a lullaby.
And if someone should laugh at your ears,
Mama's gonna be here to dry your tears.
And if your tears can't be extinguished,
Mama thinks that large ears are really
    distinguished.

Then she continued to hum and rock her son until his eyelids grew heavier and heavier, and he fell asleep.

Mrs Jumbo hummed for a little while longer, then stood up. But wait – why was it so quiet?

All along the elephant stalls, soft snoring could be heard. Mrs Jumbo's lullaby had put all the elephants to sleep!

12

Disney·PIXAR
FINDING
NEMO

Marlin's Story

"P. Sherman, 42 Wallaby Way, Sydney . . . P. Sherman, 42 Wallaby Way, Sydney." Dory kept muttering the address. She and Marlin were searching for Marlin's missing son, Nemo. They had just escaped an angry anglerfish, and now they were trying to find someone who could give them directions to Sydney. That's where Nemo probably was.

"P. Sherman, 42 Wallaby Way, Sydney . . . P. Sherman, 42 Wallaby Way, Sydney," Dory continued to chant.

Marlin had the address memorized and thought he would go crazy if he had to hear it again. "Dory!" he said with a sigh. "I know you just want to be helpful, but do you really need to keep talking?"

"I love to talk," said Dory. "I'm pretty good at it. Hmm . . . what were we talking about?"

"I just want to find Nemo," Marlin said.

"That's right, Chico," said Dory.

"One time, Nemo and I . . ." Marlin began.

"Go on," Dory said. "Is this going to be exciting?"

"Yes, it's an exciting story," said Marlin, relieved that he had got her to stop reciting the address. "Well," Marlin began, "one time, I took Nemo to the other side of the reef, to visit a relative of mine who was known as the fastest swimmer of all the clownfish, in his day. But when we visited him, he was getting on in years."

Dory yawned. "When's the good part?"

Marlin sighed. "I was just about to get to it!" he said. "So, anyway, on the way back home, guess what we ran into?"

"What?" asked Dory, confused.

"A huge jellyfish! It was hovering in the water, blocking our way through two big tufts of sea grass."

"Uh-huh," said Dory. She seemed to be trying to remember something. "P. Sherman . . ." she muttered softly.

"For a moment there I thought we were goners," said Marlin. "But then . . . a huge sea turtle swam up and swallowed the jellyfish in one gulp!"

"Did you say thank you to the sea turtle?" asked Dory, who seemed back on track.

"Well, no," Marlin replied. "I was afraid he would eat us, too, so Nemo and I hurried on our way. But, ever since then, I have been fascinated with sea turtles. And I hope I never have to meet another jellyfish!"

"Say, I've got a story too!" said Dory excitedly. "It takes place at 42 Wallaby Way, Sydney. At P. Sherman. Now, at P. Sherman, 42 Wallaby Way, Sydney, there was this, um, fish . . . and . . . well . . ."

Marlin just groaned and kept swimming.

Disney

THE
LION KING

Scaredy Cats

"**N**ala!" Simba whispered. "Are you awake?"

"Yes," Nala whispered back, stepping out of the dark cave where she slept with her mother. "Why are you here? You're gonna get us in trouble . . . again."

Earlier, Simba and Nala had gone to explore the forbidden Elephant's Graveyard, where they'd been trapped by hyenas. Simba's father, Mufasa, had rescued them.

"Come on," Simba hissed. "Follow me."

Soon the two cubs were on the dark savannah near the base of Pride Rock.

"What do you want, anyway?" Nala asked.

"I just wanted to make sure you weren't still scared," Simba said.

Nala scowled at him. "Scared?" she exclaimed. "*I'm* not the one who was scared!"

"What?" Simba cried. "You're not saying *I* was scared, are you? Because there's no way I'd be scared of a few stupid hyenas. I wouldn't have been scared even if we ran into *ten* hyenas."

"Well, I wouldn't have been scared even if we found *20* hyenas and an angry water buffalo," said Nala.

"Oh yeah?" Simba said. "Well, I wouldn't have been scared of *30* hyenas, an angry water buffalo and a – "

"FURIOUS HORNBILL?" a new voice squawked from the darkness.

"Ahhhhhh!" Simba and Nala cried, jumping straight up in the air.

Just then, a brightly coloured bird stepped out of the shadows. It was Zazu, Mufasa's most trusted adviser.

"Zazu!" Simba cried. "You scared us!"

"I wasn't scared," Nala put in indignantly.

"Me neither!" Simba added quickly.

Zazu glared at both of them over his long beak. "Not scared, were you?" he said drily. "That certainly explains the shrieking."

"You just startled us," Nala mumbled.

Zazu fluffed his feathers. "Listen up, you two," he said. "There's no shame in admitting you're scared. Even King Mufasa wouldn't deny that he was terrified when he found out you were missing. And, if it's good enough for him, it's good enough for a pair of scrawny cubs like you. Right?"

"I guess so," Simba said as Nala shrugged.

"Everyone gets scared," Zazu went on. "It's how you respond to it that counts. That's where *true* bravery lies. Get it?"

"Got it," Simba and Nala said.

"Good." Zazu marched towards Pride Rock. The sun was coming up and it was time for breakfast. "Now let's get you back home posthaste . . . or I'll *really* give you something to be scared of!"

Disney
Lilo & Stitch

Friends Forever

Experiment 626 was a blue creature from a distant planet, who was punished for being very naughty and destroying everything around him. One day, he escaped his planet in a police cruiser and headed straight for the tiny island of Kauai, on Earth!

On the island of Kauai was a little girl named Lilo. She found it hard to make friends and was very lonely. Lilo lived with her big sister, Nani, who was learning how to be a good parent. One night, the sisters had a big fight. Lilo went to her room and slammed the door shut. Out of her window, Lilo saw a falling star and made a wish. "I wish for someone to be my friend," she whispered.

The star that Lilo had seen was Experiment 626's ship crashing on the island. A truck driver found him and took him to an animal shelter. All the other animals were scared of 626, but he didn't care. He scrunched two of his four arms in towards his torso so he would look more like a dog. That way, he'd be adopted and have a place to hide from the aliens who were chasing him.

The next day, Nani decided to take Lilo to the shelter to pick a new pet.

"Hi!" Lilo said when she saw 626.

"Hi," the creature replied and then gave her a hug. Lilo went to the front room and told

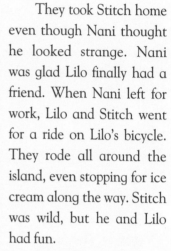

Nani she'd found the dog she wanted.

"He's good," she said. "I can tell. His name is . . . Stitch."

They took Stitch home even though Nani thought he looked strange. Nani was glad Lilo finally had a friend. When Nani left for work, Lilo and Stitch went for a ride on Lilo's bicycle. They rode all around the island, even stopping for ice cream along the way. Stitch was wild, but he and Lilo had fun.

At home, however, Stitch began to tear things apart and cause trouble for Nani.

"We have to take him back," Nani said.

"We adopted him!" Lilo cried. "What about 'ohana'? Dad said ohana means family! Family means –"

"Nobody gets left behind," Nani finished. "I know."

She remembered how welcoming her parents had been and how important family was to them. She changed her mind. She would give Stitch another chance – for Lilo's sake.

From then on, Lilo and Stitch stuck together through anything that came their way. Lilo helped Stitch learn how to behave, and Stitch became the friend that Lilo had wished for on a falling star.

Spaghetti and Meatballs

Tramp had just escaped from the dogcatcher – again. He'd taught that dogcatcher who was boss!

Tramp could smell wood burning in fireplaces, dinner cooking . . . his stomach suddenly rumbled. Escaping from the dogcatcher always made him work up quite an appetite!

But where would he go for dinner tonight? He usually stopped by the Schultzes for some Wiener schnitzel on Monday, he had corned beef and cabbage with the O'Briens on Tuesday . . . but what he was really craving was some spaghetti and meatballs.

So, Tramp headed to Tony's Restaurant. He scratched at the back door, as was his custom.

"I'm coming! I'm coming!" Tony shouted. He appeared at the door wiping his hands on a towel. He pretended not to see Tramp, as he always did.

"Hey, nobody's here!" Tony shouted. "It must be April Fools' Day!" He pretended to think for a moment. "No, it's not the first! It's not even April! It's January!"

Tramp couldn't take it any more. He was so hungry! He barked.

"Oh, there you are, Butch my friend," said Tony. Tramp, aka Butch, jumped up and down. "I'll get your dinner," said Tony. "Relax, enjoy yourself."

Tramp sat down and looked around the cluttered alleyway. This was the life!

Just then Tony appeared with a plateful of pasta. He had given Tramp two, no make that three meatballs! This was quite a special night.

Tony stood and chatted with Tramp as he ate his meal, telling him about his day – the late delivery of fish, the customer who had complained that the tomato sauce was too garlicky, the trip that he and his wife were planning to take . . . .

Tramp finished eating and gave the plate one last lick. It was sparkling clean.

"That reminds me," said Tony. "There's something I've been meaning to talk to you about. It's time you settled down and got a wife of your own."

Tramp gave Tony a horrified look and began to back out of the alleyway.

Tony laughed so hard his sides shook. "Goodbye, Butch!" he called. "But mark my words, one of these days, you're going to meet the dog you can't resist! And, when you do, I have a good idea – you bring her to Tony's for a nice romantic dinner!"

Tramp barked his thanks to Tony. He walked down the block, shaking his head. He was footloose and collar free! Settle down? That was never going to happen!

A Never Land Story

It was a cold winter night, and John and Michael just couldn't get to sleep. They climbed onto the bed of their older sister, Wendy.

"Oh, tell us a story, Wendy!" said Michael.

"Yes, please. A Peter Pan story!" pleaded John.

"Certainly," said Wendy. "Have I told you about the time that Peter Pan out-smarted the evil Captain Hook?"

"Yes!" said Michael eagerly. "And we want to hear it again!"

Wendy laughed and began her story. "Well, one night, Captain Hook moored his ship in a secret cove close to the island of Never Land. He and his men rowed ashore quietly, for he was intent on discovering the hiding place of Peter and the Lost Boys. Captain Hook hated Peter Pan because the boy had cut off his hand in a duel and fed it to a large crocodile. And now that crocodile was determined to swallow up the rest of him. Luckily for Captain Hook, however, this crocodile had also swallowed a clock, so the pirate would always be alerted to the crocodile's presence by the sound of the ticking clock.

"Fortunately for Peter Pan," Wendy continued, "his dear friend Tinker Bell learned of Captain Hook's evil plan ahead of time.

She flew to Peter and warned him that the pirate was coming. 'Oh-ho!' laughed Peter. 'Well, we shall be ready for him then!' He found a clock just like the one the crocodile had swallowed. He whistled up into the trees, and a group of his monkey friends appeared. 'Here's a new toy for you!' Peter shouted, and tossed the clock up to them. 'Stay out of sight, now!' Peter told the monkeys, and then he and the Lost Boys hurried to their hiding places.

"When Hook came to the clearing, the first thing he heard was the ticking clock. The sound seemed to be coming at him from all sides! The monkeys were having a grand time, tossing the clock back and forth, and creeping up behind Hook. Seized with terror, Hook and his men raced to their boat and rowed madly back to their ship."

Just then, the Darling children's parents came in to check on them. "You're not telling more of these poppycock stories about Peter Pan, are you, Wendy?" their father asked.

"Peter Pan is real, Father!" cried the children. "We know he is!"

As the parents kissed their children good night, they didn't see that a boy in green was crouching just outside the nursery window. He had been listening to the story, and he would be back again – soon.

A Rookie Racecar

Rookie racer, Lightning McQueen, was waiting for the biggest race of the year to begin. The winner would receive the Piston Cup and a sponsorship deal with Dinoco.

"Speed. I am speed," Lightning repeated. When he roared onto the track, the crowd went wild!

Lightning was fast – but could he beat the King, who had won the most Piston Cups in history, or ruthless Chick Hicks, who always finished second?

The race was on! Lightning and Chick sped around the track side by

side. Suddenly, Chick slammed into Lightning, sending him skidding off the track. Lightning raced to catch up.

"Dinoco is mine!" Chick shouted. He veered and caused a pile-up! In seconds, wrecked cars littered the track. Lightning dodged and leaped over wrecks. To Chick's fury, Lightning took the lead!

But then Lightning made a huge mistake. He refused to let his pit crew put on fresh tyres. On the last lap – *BANG! BANG!* – Lightning's old tyres blew out! As he limped towards the finish line, the King and Chick caught up. It was impossible to tell who had come in first.

"Ka-chow!" Lightning posed for reporters with cameras. "I'm a one-man show!"

"We quit!" His pit crew stormed away.

Lightning didn't care. He thought he could win without anyone's help. He was daydreaming about fame and fortune when, suddenly, he heard a loud announcement: The race was a three-way tie! A deciding race would be held in California in one week.

Lightning wanted to leave for California immediately. But his driver, Mack, reminded Lightning that he had to make an appearance for his sponsor, Rust-Eze. Lightning reluctantly greeted the old rusty cars that were his fans. As soon as he was finished, he raced into Mack's trailer. Mack was tired and needed to get some sleep, but Lightning insisted. "We're driving all night."

As Mack struggled to stay awake, four flashy cars pulled alongside and shoved him back and forth across the road. Startled, Mack swerved. Inside the trailer, a trophy fell and landed on the ramp button. The back of the trailer lowered, and a sleeping Lightning rolled out! Lightning woke up in the middle of oncoming traffic – with giant trucks coming straight at him!

Because he'd forced Mack to drive, even though he was too tired, Lightning was now lost in the middle of nowhere! Would the rookie ever learn to listen to his friends?

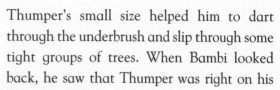

Bambi

The Race

"**G**ood morning, young Prince," Thumper greeted Bambi one bright winter day.

"Good morning, Thumper," Bambi said.

"I have a great idea, Bambi. Let's have a race," Thumper said. "We'll start from here." He drew a line in the dirt. "And whoever makes it to that big pine tree over there first, wins the race."

"But it would be silly for us to race," Bambi told his friend.

"Why's that?" Thumper asked, confused.

"Because I'll win," Bambi said.

"What makes you so sure?" Thumper challenged, puffing up his chest.

"Because I'm bigger and faster than you," Bambi explained.

"If you're so sure you'll win," Thumper said, "why are you afraid to race me?"

Bambi paused to think about this. He didn't want to hurt the little rabbit's feelings. "Fine," he said at last. "Let's race!"

"Great!" Thumper exclaimed. "Ready?"

"Ready!" Bambi said.

"Okay," Thumper said, crouching down. Bambi crouched down too. "On your mark. Get set. Go!" cried Thumper. They both took off as fast as they could.

Bambi, with his long legs and big, wide stride, immediately took the lead. But Thumper's small size helped him to dart through the underbrush and slip through some tight groups of trees. When Bambi looked back, he saw that Thumper was right on his heels. Thumper took the opportunity to hop past Bambi. Bambi paused to jump over a tree that had been knocked down, blocking the path. Thumper was able to wriggle under it. He popped up in front of Bambi and took the lead.

Bambi took longer and longer strides, running faster and faster. Soon he had passed Thumper. But, in his hurry to go as fast as he could, he got tangled up in a bush. As Bambi struggled to free himself, Thumper hopped past him again.

They were quickly approaching the big pine tree. Bambi was running as fast as he could, jumping over logs and bushes. Thumper hopped as quickly as his bunny legs would carry him, ducking and weaving through whatever obstacles were in his way. As they crossed the finish line, they were in a neck-and-neck tie.

"See!" Thumper said, panting. "Little guys can keep up!"

"You are absolutely right!" Bambi said, also panting.

And the two friends, both winners, sat down together to catch their breath.

Stuck in Radiator Springs

Lightning McQueen had just raced in the last race of the Piston Cup championship, and it had been a three-way tie. He could have won if he had listened to his team. But instead, he decided to go it alone and ended up sacking them.

Eager to get to California for the tie-breaker, Lightning had forced Mack to drive all night. As Mack struggled to stay awake, some flashy cars had shoved him. Startled, Mack had swerved, and Lightning rolled out of the trailer!

Lightning, feeling terrified, searched for Mack – but he couldn't find him! Lightning was completely lost. Suddenly he heard a siren blaring and saw red lights flashing. A sheriff cruiser was after him!

Panicked, Lightning crashed through a fence, got tangled in fencing wire and roared through a sleepy little town, destroying its main street. He ended up dangling from a telephone pole! "You're in a heap of trouble," Sheriff said just before Lightning passed out.

When Lightning woke up, he was inside an impound lot and saw a rusty old tow truck named Tow-Mater grinning at him.

"Where am I?" Lightning asked.

"Radiator Springs," Mater answered.

Later in court, Doc Hudson, the judge of the sleepy little town, rolled slowly into the room. Doc didn't like racecars.

"Throw him out of here!" Doc ordered. "I want him out of our town!"

That's when the town attorney, a sleek blue sports car named Sally, arrived. She didn't want Doc to let Lightning go. "Make him fix the road," she insisted.

So Doc told Mater to hook Lightning up to Bessie, the road-paving machine. Lightning was furious. But if he wanted to leave, he had to do the job.

While Lightning worked, a couple came down the broken road through town. "Customers!" Sally cried. The townsfolk rushed up to them. But the couple just wanted directions to the Interstate.

"I'm Lightning McQueen," Lightning told the couple, hoping they would help him. But they looked at Lightning as if he were crazy and sped off. There went his last hope of rescue! Lightning hauled Bessie down the road as fast as he could.

"The road looks awful," Sally said.

"Now it matches the rest of the town," Lightning replied grumpily. He was still only thinking of himself, and didn't care about Radiator Springs and the cars that lived there. If he carried on this way, he'd never be allowed to leave for California!

Disney · PIXAR

TOY STORY

Stranded

A new toy called Buzz Lightyear had just arrived in Andy's room. He claimed he could fly, then he tried to prove it, by bouncing off a ball and shouting, "To infinity and beyond!"

The other toys were impressed, but Woody rolled his eyes.

"That's just falling with style," he complained.

Poor Woody. Now that Buzz had arrived in Andy's room, nothing was the same.

The cowboy posters on the wall were replaced with space posters. Andy stopped wearing his cowboy hat, and started running through the house in a space costume. Buzz was a hit with the other toys, too. Everyone wanted to spend time with him.

But the biggest shock was at bedtime. When Andy climbed under the covers, he took Buzz with him. Woody was left in the toy chest, awkward, alone and forgotten.

One evening, Andy's mum suggested a trip to Pizza Planet. Andy could take only one toy along, and Woody wanted to make sure he was chosen. Woody's plan was to knock Buzz behind the desk, where Andy couldn't find him. But instead, Buzz fell out the window!

"It was an accident!" Woody tried to explain to the other toys.

"Didn't want to face the fact that Buzz just might be Andy's new favourite toy, so you got rid of him!" Mr Potato Head said.

Before the toys could gang up on Woody, however, Andy ran into the room. He searched high and low for Buzz, but couldn't find the space ranger anywhere.

Finally, he grabbed Woody, ran downstairs and hopped into the car with Molly and his mum, heading for Pizza Planet. As the car started up, a small figure leapt onto the car's bumper. It was Buzz!

When Andy's mum stopped at a petrol station, Buzz jumped into the back seat with Woody.

"Buzz! You're alive!" Woody exclaimed in relief.

But Buzz wasn't so pleased to see Woody. "Even though you tried to terminate me, revenge is not an idea we promote on my planet," Buzz said. Then his eyes narrowed. "But we're not on my planet, are we?"

Buzz leapt onto Woody, and the two began pummeling each other. As they wrestled angrily, they tumbled out of the car and onto the pavement.

Suddenly, Andy's mum drove off – without them!

Woody and Buzz were stranded at the petrol station. How were they ever going to get home?

RATATOUILLE
(rat·a·too·ee)

Discovering Paris

Deep in the French countryside, a colony of rats was busy sifting through a compost pile for food. It was one rat's job to make sure the scraps of food were safe to eat. That rat's name was Remy. Remy had a highly developed sense of taste and smell and was the 'poison checker' for the rest of the rat colony.

Emile, his younger (but bigger) brother, ate anything in sight. He was always impressed by Remy's gift. Secretly, Remy had much bigger dreams. He wanted to be a great chef, like his idol, the great chef Auguste Gusteau. In fact, Remy had even learned to read Gusteau's cookbook... *Anyone Can Cook!*

The cookbook and the compost pile belonged to an old woman named Mabel. Her attic was home to the entire rat colony, though she didn't know it. One day, Remy and Emile sneaked into her kitchen together. Remy always enjoyed looking for spices in her cupboards. The nervous Emile did not. Their father, Django, always said humans were dangerous.

Suddenly, Remy raced from the kitchen to the TV. He saw his idol Gusteau on the news! Remy learned that Gusteau had died from a broken heart when his restaurant lost its five-star status. Remy was so shocked by the news about Gusteau that he didn't notice Mabel waking up! He and Emile had to scramble to escape as Mabel chased them! In the chaos, the ceiling cracked and the entire rat colony fell to the floor!

"Evacuate!" Django shouted to the rats.

As the others headed out of the door, Remy went back into the kitchen for the cookbook. He couldn't leave it behind. But it was Remy who got left behind, as all the other rats made it to the evacuation boats.

Separated from his family, Remy used his cookbook as a raft. He got swept down the sewer currents. Remy finally found a landing place and started drying out the pages of his cookbook.

Suddenly, Gusteau seemed to come to life on one of the pages! "If you are hungry, go up and look around," said Gusteau. "If you focus on what you've left behind, you will never be able to see what lies ahead."

So Remy climbed up and up until he saw... Paris! "All this time I've been underneath Paris? Wow! It's beautiful!" he said.

Remy looked to his left. His jaw dropped. There was the sign for Gusteau's restaurant! To Remy, this was a dream come true, and he knew his adventures were only just beginning.

Out for a Spin

One day, Princess Kida was showing Milo and the rest of the explorers the wonders of Atlantis. Vinny found an ancient gold medallion. Everyone was impressed, and they all decided to search for more treasure.

Milo, however, decided to go exploring with Kida instead. The Princess led him up the staircase of a huge pyramid. When they reached the top, they found a shark-shaped vehicle.

"It's an Aktirak," Kida told him.

"Aktirak must mean shark, because this flyer is shaped like a hammerhead," said Milo. "Can we take it for a spin?"

"If you wish," Kida said. "But you must not wreck this flyer as you did the last!"

Milo blushed. "Sorry about that," he said.

Kida used her crystal to start the engine. Then she and Milo climbed on.

Milo pushed a button and the Aktirak blasted into the sky!

"Wow! This machine looks like a shark but flies like an eagle!" cried Milo. They dived low over the water, skimming the waves.

Suddenly, a school of flying fish burst out of the water and surrounded the flyer. One flapped in Milo's face and he nearly lost control.

"We've got to get back to land!" he exclaimed. The Aktirak shot up into the sky.

"Beware of the cliffs ahead!" Kida warned.

Milo tried, but the Aktirak could not fly high enough. They were about to crash!

"The cave!" Kida cried, pointing to a hole in the side of the mountain.

Milo steered the Aktirak through the entrance. Now they were racing inside a large cavern.

Twisting the flyer, Milo dodged stalactites hanging from the cavern roof. Then he saw the head of a huge stone fish in the cave wall. Its mouth was open, and daylight streamed through it. He twisted the controls, and the Aktirak flew right though the fish's gaping mouth.

"Like threading a needle!" Milo declared.

Just then, the tail of the flyer scraped the stone fish and the Aktirak flew out of control.

"Hang on!" Milo cried.

The flyer hit the side of the pyramid, then bounced. It landed at the exact spot where Kida and Milo first found it.

The others heard the crash and rushed over. They found Milo and Kida standing next to the wrecked flyer.

"What happened?" Audrey cried.

"We went out for a spin," Milo said.

"Are you saying you actually *flew* this wreck?" Audrey demanded.

"I did!" said Milo. "But it's pretty obvious I need to sign up for Atlantean driver's ed!"

A Race Against Doc

Lightning McQueen was lost in a sleepy town called Radiator Springs. All he wanted to do was get to California for a tie-breaker race – the last race in the Piston Cup championship had ended in a three-way tie – but Lightning couldn't leave because he'd ruined the town's main road. The judge, Doc, had ordered him to resurface the road, but selfish Lightning had done a bad job.

"Scrape the road and start again," Doc ordered.

"I'm not a bulldozer – I'm a racecar," Lightning argued.

So Doc challenged him to a race. "If you win, you go. If I win, you do the road my way."

Lightning agreed. He was sure he could beat the old car.

When the race flag dropped, Lightning roared off. But on a sharp left turn, Lightning lost control. He skidded off the road and plunged into a cactus patch.

That night, muttering angrily, Lightning scraped the road. When the rest of the cars awoke, they saw Mater – the town's tow-truck – driving on a perfectly smooth road. Even Doc was impressed. But where was Lightning? Doc thought he knew.

Sure enough, the stubborn racecar was out on the dirt track, trying again and again to make that tricky sharp left turn – and spinning out of control every time.

"You've got to turn right to go left," Doc told Lightning. As usual, Lightning scoffed. What did Doc know about racing?

Later, Lightning finished repaving the road. It looked great! Luigi, who ran the town's tyre shop, even offered Lightning a great deal on new tyres. Everyone in town was happy, except Lightning. He was hot, tired and grumpy!

Suddenly, Red the fire engine blasted Lightning with water. "Do you want to stay at the Cozy Cone?" Sally asked. "If you do, you have to be clean." She was beginning to like Lightning, and he realized he liked her, too.

That night, Mater took Lightning tractor-tipping. Mater sneaked up on a sleeping tractor and beeped. The startled tractor woke up and fell over! Then Lightning revved his engine so loudly, all the tractors keeled over at once. Mater and Lightning could not stop laughing.

As they returned to the Cozy Cone Motel, Mater showed off his amazing backwards-driving tricks. Lightning was impressed.

"Maybe I'll use it in my big race," Lightning said thoughtfully. He was starting to enjoy himself in Radiator Springs, but had he learned to appreciate the help of others?

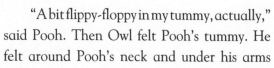

Say Ahhh, Pooh!

"Christopher Robin says it's time for my animal checkout," said Pooh.

"Checkout!" cried Piglet. "Oh p-p-poor P-P-Pooh – you're sick!"

"Sick?" asked Pooh. "No – I'm fine. Though I must say I am feeling a bit rumbly in my tumbly."

"Let's go together," said Piglet. "It's so much more friendly with two." So, Pooh and Piglet climbed the ladder up to Owl's house.

"Christopher Robin, why do I need an animal checkout, anyway?" asked Pooh once they had arrived at Owl's house.

"Silly old bear," said Christopher Robin. "Not an animal checkout – an annual checkup. We need to make sure you are healthy and strong. And this time, Owl will give you a special injection to help keep you well." Pooh's tummy flopped and flipped.

"It's okay," said Christopher Robin. "It will only hurt for a few seconds, and the medicine in the injection will keep you from getting mumps and measles and things like that."

Rabbit called for Pooh to go into Owl's room. Piglet wished him good luck. Once Pooh and Christopher Robin were inside, Owl entered with a flourish. "Well, if it isn't Winnie the Pooh!" he exclaimed. "Splendid day for a checkup, isn't it? I say, how are you feeling?"

"A bit flippy-floppy in my tummy, actually," said Pooh. Then Owl felt Pooh's tummy. He felt around Pooh's neck and under his arms and said that everything seemed to be right where it should be. Pooh was glad. Then Owl pulled a small rubber hammer from his bag. "Reflex-checking time!" he said grandly.

"What's a reflex?" asked Pooh. Owl tapped Pooh's knee – and his leg gave a little kick. "Oh do that again," said Pooh. "That was fun." So Owl tapped Pooh's other knee, and that leg gave a little kick, too. And it didn't bother Pooh in the least when Owl said… "Sit right here in Christopher Robin's lap. It is time for your injection."

"I know it will only hurt for a moment, and it will keep me from getting bumps and weasels," Pooh said bravely.

"That's mumps and measles, Pooh," said Owl.

Piglet came in and sat right next to Pooh while he had his injection. When Owl was done, Rabbit popped back in with a plaster.

"Wow," said Piglet. "You didn't even cry!"

"An annual checkup is no problem for a brave bear like Pooh," said Christopher Robin.

I'm just that sort of bear, thought Pooh with a smile.

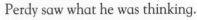

101 DALMATIANS

Pongo Carries a Tune

"**I** don't know what we're going to do," Roger Radcliffe told his wife, Anita. "We have all these puppies to feed, and I don't have *one* song to sell!"

"Don't worry," Anita told him. "I'm sure you'll be inspired soon."

"I'm glad *you're* sure!" said Roger. "Because all I've got is a bunch of used paper." He pointed to the overflowing wastebasket.

"Don't give up," said Anita. "I know that you can do it."

After Anita left, Pongo watched his pet pace in front of his piano.

"Pongo, old boy, I must have written ten songs in ten days. But they're all terrible," said Roger, pointing to the wastebasket. "What am I going to do?"

Pongo wanted to help his pet, but he didn't know how.

That night, Pongo talked to Perdy about Roger's dilemma. They sat in the middle of the living room, surrounded by puppies.

"Roger has already written ten songs," explained Pongo. "He just doesn't think they're good enough to sell. But I know they are – I've heard him play them, and you don't have a songwriter for a pet without developing a good ear for hit songs. The songs are right upstairs, stuffed inside his wastebasket."

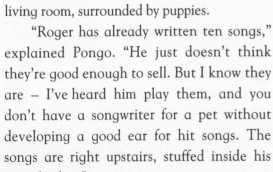

Perdy saw what he was thinking.

"Do you know the way to the music publisher?" she asked.

Pongo nodded. "I've taken Roger for walks there dozens of times."

"I think you should try it," said Perdy.

After Roger and Anita had gone to sleep, Pongo padded into the music room and gathered up the sheet music from the wastebasket. Then he sneaked out of the house, carrying the music to the publisher's office. Pongo pushed all the pages under the door, then trotted back home.

The next day, the phone rang. Roger answered.

"You what?" Roger said into the receiver. "You did . . . ? But how did you . . . ? Oh, I see . . . well, thank you. Thank you!"

Anita rushed over. "Who was that?"

"My music publisher," said Roger. "He's buying ten of my songs."

"Ten songs!" cried Anita. "I thought you didn't even have *one* to sell."

Roger scratched his head in confusion. "I didn't think I did."

"So, what happened?" asked Anita.

Perdy looked at Pongo and barked. Her husband could carry a tune too – all the way across town to Roger's publisher!

Mango Hunting

Once upon a time, long before Mowgli came to the jungle, Bagheera the panther met Baloo the bear for the first time.

This is how it happened.

Bagheera was younger then, but no less grave. He took himself very seriously indeed. When Bagheera hunted, he moved silently, with grace and speed. He never tripped, and he certainly never fell. When he slept, he kept one eye open. When he spoke, he chose his words carefully. And he never, ever laughed.

One day, Bagheera was edging along the branch of a mango tree leaning out over a river. There was one perfectly ripe mango right at the end of the branch, and Bagheera loved mangoes. The only problem was, the branch was slender, and, when Bagheera moved towards the end of it, it began to creak and bend alarmingly. The last thing Bagheera wanted was to break the branch and go for an unplanned swim in the river. His dignity would never allow such a thing.

So Bagheera, crouched on the middle of the branch, was just coming up with a clever plan, when he heard a "harrumph." He looked down and saw a great big grey bear. "It looks like you could use a hand," said the bear.

"No, thank you," said Bagheera politely. "I prefer to work on my own." But the bear paid him no heed, and began climbing up the tree.

"I'll tell you what," huffed the bear. "I'll just sit at the base of that branch and grab your tail. You can climb out and grab the mango, and I'll keep a hold of you in case the end of the branch breaks off. Then we can share the mango!"

"No, I don't think that's a very good idea," said Bagheera impatiently. "I doubt this branch can hold both of us any – "

Snap!

The bear had, of course, ignored Bagheera and climbed out onto the branch. And the branch had, of course, snapped under their combined weight. And now a very wet, very unhappy panther sat in the river next to a very wet, very amused bear.

"Oh, ha-ha-ha-ha!" hooted Baloo (for it was Baloo, of course). "Oh me, oh my, that was an adventure! Oh, come now," he said, seeing how angry Bagheera was, "it's not a total loss, you know." And Baloo held up the broken branch, with that perfect mango still hanging from the end of it.

"I'll tell you what," said the bear, "let's go climb onto that rock and dry off in the sun while we eat this mango. I'm Baloo. What's your name?"

"Bagheera," said the panther, as they climbed up onto the warm, flat rock. And then, almost despite himself, he smiled. And then, very much despite himself, he laughed. And Baloo laughed right along with him.

Disney
Lilo & Stitch

Show-and-tell

"Please?" pleaded Lilo.

"No way, Lilo!" Nani replied.

"He'll be good. I promise!" Lilo said.

"Oh, all right!" Nani said crossly.

Lilo had been pestering her big sister all morning, begging Nani to let her take their pet, Stitch, to dance class for "show-and-tell." Nani was worried it could cause a lot of trouble. The girls her age were not kind to Lilo, who had a lot of trouble fitting in. As a result, Lilo tended to lash out at them and get herself into trouble. And the problem was, her strange pet, Stitch, was just like her. Nani was convinced that the awful-looking creature they picked up at the pound wasn't even a real dog. Just like Lilo, Stitch didn't seem to fit in very well, either. The other dogs at the pound had certainly shunned him.

When they arrived at dance class, Nani gave her little sister a quick hug. "You behave yourselves!" she said.

"You'll behave yourself," Lilo said to Stitch. "I know you will."

Some of the girls sniggered as Lilo and Stitch walked in and sat down.

"All right," said the dance teacher. "What have you brought today, Lilo?"

Lilo stood up. "This is my dog. His name is Stitch. I got him at the pound."

"He sure is ugly!" said Myrtle.

"Now, Myrtle, be nice," the teacher said.

"Can he fetch?" Myrtle asked. She threw a water balloon that she had brought for show-and-tell right at Stitch!

Stitch caught the balloon neatly, then threw it back at Myrtle. "No!" yelled Lilo, and threw herself in front of Myrtle, accidentally knocking the other girl over. The water balloon hit Lilo and broke, sending water flying everywhere!

"Oh, Lilo," said the teacher, "I think it's time for your pet to go home." Lilo picked up Stitch and ran outside.

Lilo sat down at the kerb. Stitch sat down too. "You got us in trouble today," Lilo said to him. "Why did you hit Myrtle with that water balloon?"

Stitch growled.

"Oh, that's right," said Lilo, "you don't *do* fetch. How could I have forgotten?" She looked thoughtful. "How about we play catch, instead? That's almost the same thing as fetch, but there's an important difference. Fetch is something you play with a pet, and catch is something you play with a friend. I think you're more my friend than my pet, Stitch."

Stitch nodded eagerly and held up a ball. Lilo smiled, and the two friends spent a lovely afternoon together playing catch.

Geppetto's Gift

One day, Geppetto was in his workshop painting a clock, when he had an idea. "I know what I will do with that pine log I just found," he told his little cat, Figaro. "I will make a splendid puppet!"

He put down the clock and got to work. When he had finished making the puppet, he got out his jars of paint and some fabric. "Now," he said to Figaro, "should my puppet's eyes be blue or green? Should her hair be yellow or brown or black? Should her dress be red or purple?"

Suddenly, Geppetto heard a noise outside. He went to the window and looked out. He saw groups of children on their way home from school. Geppetto watched them skip past, laughing and shouting and swinging their schoolbooks. He sighed sadly. "How I wish I had a child of my own," he said.

Just then, he noticed a little girl walking quietly with her mother. Like the other girls, she carried a schoolbook under her arm. When a group of girls skipped by her, she looked at them shyly.

"That little girl must be new in town. She looks like she could use a friend," Geppetto said. Suddenly, he had an idea.

"Excuse me, young miss," he called from the window. "I wonder if you could lend me a hand?"

The girl hurried over, tugging her mother after her. Why, an invitation to Geppetto's workshop – how grand!

"As you can see, my friend here needs some eyes," Geppetto said, pointing to the puppet. "But I don't know what colour her eyes should be."

The girl thought hard. "Green," she decided.

Geppetto picked up his pot of green paint and painted two big green eyes onto the wooden face.

"Now, what colour do you suppose her hair should be?" Geppetto asked.

"Brown," the little girl said with a smile.

Carefully, Geppetto painted brown curls on the puppet's head. "She'll need a dress," he said next. "What do you think? Red? Green?"

The girl looked down at her own blue dress. "Blue," she told Geppetto.

So Geppetto made a little blue dress for the little puppet. Then he added a smiling red mouth to the puppet's face.

"Now there's just one last thing," Geppetto said. "I'm busy in my shop all day long, and I'm afraid this little lady might be lonely. Could you take care of her for me?"

The girl's face lit up with delight. "Thank you!" she cried. Hugging the puppet in her arms, she carried her out of the workshop.

"Thank you," the girl's mother said. "You know, you'd be a wonderful father."

Gepetto smiled. If only! he thought.

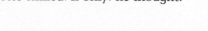

More to Life

Lightning was in a sleepy town called Radiator Springs. He'd crashed there on his way to California, and had ruined the main street. The judge, Doc, had ordered him to fix the road – and he wasn't allowed to leave until he'd done it.

Doc even challenged Lightning to a race – and won! Lightning couldn't understand how the old car had beaten him.

Lightning eventually did a good job fixing the road, and the residents of the town were grateful. Sally offered him a place to stay and Mater took him tractor-tipping.

Lightning told Mater that winning the Dinoco 400 tie-breaker race in California meant getting a new sponsor with private helicopters. Mater asked if he could ride in a helicopter some day! Lightning said yes.

"I knew I made a good choice for my best friend," Mater said.

Sally overheard their conversation. "Did you mean it?" she asked. Sally was worried that Lightning didn't understand the importance of keeping his promise to Mater.

The next morning, Lightning wandered into Doc's shop and noticed something on a shelf. A Piston Cup! Then he saw two more. Lightning was amazed. Doc Hudson was the "Hudson Hornet" – a racing legend!

Doc was furious when he found Lightning in his shop. "All I see is a bunch of empty cups." He pushed Lightning out.

Lightning rushed over to Flo's Café to tell everyone that Doc was a famous racecar. But no one believed him. While the other cars were laughing, Sally filled Lightning's tank. Sheriff worried that Lightning would escape, but Sally surprised everyone – including Lightning.

"I trust him," she said.

"Let's go for a drive," Sally suggested.

As the two cars zoomed up a winding mountain road, Lightning realized he was actually racing just for fun for the very first time.

Sally told Lightning how she'd found Radiator Springs. "I was an attorney in L.A., living life in the fast lane – but I never felt happy. So I left California, just drove and drove and finally broke down right here."

"I fell in love – with this," Sally continued, leading Lightning to view point. Far below lay a gorgeous valley surrounded by mountains. In the distance, Lightning saw cars speeding past on the Interstate.

"They don't even know what they're missing," he murmured. Lightning was finally beginning to understand that there was more to life than winning.

Elliot Minds the Store

One morning, Manny and the tools headed to Kelly's Hardware Store to buy some supplies. When they arrived, Kelly was teaching a nervous Elliot how to serve customers.

"Excellent!" Manny said. "We need a strong hook for our bulletin board."

"No problem!" said Kelly. "I'm sure Elliot could help you with that."

"Me? Oh, I d-d-don't know," Elliot sputtered.

Kelly assured Elliot he would do fine, and went out of the front door. Elliot stood for a while and looked at Manny nervously. He tried to serve Manny but made a lot of mistakes. Elliot dropped the parts catalogue on his foot. He forgot to ring up the purchase on the cash register, and then he caught his sleeve in the till. "I'm so totally bad at this!" he cried.

"Está bien! It's all right, Elliot," assured Manny. "Everybody makes mistakes when they're learning something new. The important thing is to learn from your mistakes…so you can be ready the next time," said Manny.

"Aw, it's no use. I can't do this! If it's not a skateboard or a drum set, I'm completely useless," Elliot said with a sigh.

Stretch had an idea. "You know, I always heard that if you do something that you're good at, confidence is sure to follow. So why don't you go get your skateboard?"

Manny looked nervous. "Um, I don't think skateboarding in Kelly's shop is such a good idea…" Manny was interrupted by a huge CRASH! Elliot had collided with the new shop display!

Elliot couldn't believe his eyes. He started to panic. "Oh, no!" he cried.

"Hang on, Elliot," said Manny. "You know, the balance you use on your skateboard might come in handy for piecing that display back together! And that drumming of yours is perfect for using a hammer."

"Really?" Elliot was shocked. "Are you saying that I could actually fix the shelf before Kelly gets back? ME?"

"Well, with a little help, I don't see why not," said Manny. "You just have to believe in yourself."

So, using a shelf like a skateboard, Elliot rounded up all of the spray paints. Then he put his drumming skills to work and hammered the shelves back into place.

"Muy bien, Elliot," said Manny. "Very good! See? You have more talents than you thought you did!"

"You're right. I should have believed in myself all along," said Elliot. "Thanks, Manny. Thanks, tools."

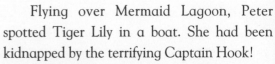

The Story of Peter Pan

One evening, Mr and Mrs Darling were getting ready to spend the evening in town. Before leaving, Mrs Darling popped into the bedroom of her children, Michael, John and Wendy, to wish them goodnight.

Soon after, Peter Pan and Tinker Bell landed on the roof. They'd come for Peter's shadow, which he'd left behind when he last visited!

Tinker Bell gave Peter a signal. He had barely opened the drawer when his shadow escaped. He chased it all over the room and the children were woken up by the noise.

"Peter! When are you going to take us to Never Land?" asked Wendy.

"I will," replied Peter Pan. "But first you must learn to fly. A little pixie dust should do the trick."

Tinker Bell sprinkled the children with pixie dust and soon, the children arrived in Never Land. Peter introduced Michael and John to his friends, the Lost Boys. They went off to play Indians in the forest. But all of a sudden, the real Indians came out from behind the trees and captured the children!

"My daughter Tiger Lily has been kidnapped!" shouted the Indian Chief. He thought the Lost Boys had done it, and wouldn't let them go.

Flying over Mermaid Lagoon, Peter spotted Tiger Lily in a boat. She had been kidnapped by the terrifying Captain Hook!

Peter confronted the pirate. They fought until the crocodile that ate the Captain's hand emerged from the water. The Captain ran away as fast as he could!

Back at the Indian village, the Chief held a banquet to celebrate the return of his daughter. All the children were set free!

But Captain Hook was not defeated yet. To get his revenge, he convinced Tinker Bell, who was jealous of Wendy, to tell him where Peter's hide-out was. Then he sent Peter a booby-trapped gift. It was a bomb! Then he kidnapped the Lost Boys and the Darling children!

Luckily, Tinker Bell, feeling very bad for betraying her friend, managed to warn Peter and save him from Hook's trap! In no time, Peter rushed to Hook's boat and freed his friends. After a mighty battle, the defeated Hook disappeared into the mouth of that waiting crocodile...

With a sprinkle of pixie dust, Hook's boat was transformed into a flying ship! Destination? The Darlings' home. The exciting journey to Never Land had taken barely any time at all... the equivalent of just one evening in the human world.

Leo's Baton

The Little Einsteins were inside their clubhouse. Suddenly Rocket's antenna lit up. "We have a mission!" exclaimed Leo. The team quickly headed to Rocket's Look-and-Listen Scope to discover their mission.

"I think it's a flower trying to push its way through the snow," guessed Quincy.

"Ooh, it's a crocus – the first sign of spring!" June exclaimed.

"Our mission must be to help spring arrive!" Leo said excitedly. "And to do that, we'll need to get the crocus to bloom."

Suddenly Leo realized something was wrong. "My baton is missing!" shouted Leo.

"Oh, dear!" exclaimed Annie. "You'll need it to conduct the crocus. We have to go back to the clubhouse and find it!"

Quincy was puzzled. "There has to be a clue around here somewhere."

"What do all these pictures mean?" asked Annie. Quincy looked intently at them, "Hmm, maybe it's a code we need to crack."

June had an idea. "Let's write down the first letter of each pictured word to see if it spells out a sentence."

"Let's see," said Leo. "If we write in an F for frog, an I for ice cream, an N for nail and a D for dog, we have the word FIND!"

"Awesome job, Leo!" said June. "Let's look at the next word: a Y for yo-yo, an O for owl, a U for umbrella and an R for rabbit – YOUR!"

"The final word is FOOTPRINTS!" shouted Quincy. "Find your footprints – that's the secret message!"

"Leo just needs to track down his footprints to find his baton," said June.

"Leo, didn't you have it on our last mission, in Vermont?" asked Annie.

"You're right, Annie!" exclaimed Leo. "And my footprints should be easy to find in the snow – let's go!"

Once they reached Vermont, the team quickly found Leo's footprints and followed them to a tree.

"Here it is!" June called, picking up Leo's baton.

"Following our footprints really worked!" exclaimed Quincy. "We found Leo's baton and now we're ready to wake up spring."

"Look!" exclaimed Annie. "The snow is melting, and leaves and flowers are popping up everywhere!"

"We followed our footprints, found Leo's baton and helped the crocus to spring into action," said Quincy.

"Great job, team!" exclaimed Leo. "Mission completion!"

Palindrome-mania!

"Hey, Atta," Flik said. "Did you know that your name is a palindrome?"

Atta gave him a strange look. "What's a palindrome?" she asked.

"It's a word that reads the same forwards and backwards," Flik replied. "Spelled forwards, your name is A-T-T-A. Spelled backwards, your name is also A-T-T-A. See?"

"Oh," Atta said. "That's neat. I've never heard of palindromes before."

"Really?" said Flik. "I love them. There are other names that are palindromes, like *Bob*."

"Or *Lil*?" tried Atta.

"Right!" said Flik. "And *Otto*."

"And *Nan*!" added Atta. "This is fun!"

"What's fun?" said Dot, who had just run over to them.

"Thinking of palindromes," Atta replied.

"Huh?" said Dot.

"Exactly!" said Flik. "*Huh* is a palindrome!" Together, Flik and Atta explained to Dot what a palindrome was.

"Oh!" said Dot. "Wait! Let me see if I can think of another one." Dot looked around, hoping that something she saw would spark an idea. She spotted her mother, the Queen, off in the distance, lounging in the shade.

"*Mum!*" cried Dot. "That's one, isn't it?"

"Not bad," said Atta with a wink, "for a tot like you!" Atta giggled, pleased that she had got another palindrome into her sentence.

"Oh, yeah?" replied Dot with a mischievous grin. "Well, you ain't seen nothin' yet, *sis*!"

Taking turns, Dot and Atta challenged one another to think of more and more palindromes. Dot came up with *eye*, *pop* and *toot*. Atta countered with *gag*, *noon*, *did* and *redder*.

"Yes," Flik interjected, "*redder* is a nice, long one! It's harder to think of palindromes that have more than four letters. Believe me, I've spent hours on that. But there's always *Aidemedia* – that's a type of bird, you know. And *Allenella*, of course, which is a category of mollusc . . . ." Flik went on to list a longer palindrome for just about every letter of the alphabet – most of them sciencey words that Atta and Dot had never heard before. As he droned on and on and on, Dot and Atta looked at each other and rolled their eyes. Now they were both thinking of the same word, and it wasn't a palindrome: B-O-R-I-N-G.

When Flik had finally finished with his list, he looked up at Dot and Atta with a self-satisfied smile. Each of them had a palindrome ready.

"*Wow*," said Atta flatly, sounding more bored than impressed.

"*Zzz*," snored Dot, who had drifted off somewhere between *V* and *W*.

34

Disney · PIXAR

TOY STORY

Captured by Sid

Oh dear! Woody and Andy's brand-new toy, Buzz Lightyear, were stranded at a petrol station. They had been in Andy's mum's car, on the way to Pizza Planet, but because they'd been fighting with each other, they'd fallen out onto the ground! Andy's mum had driven away without them!

Luckily, Woody spotted a Pizza Planet delivery truck. The truck could take him to Andy! But Woody knew he couldn't face the other toys without Buzz.

Woody had knocked Buzz out of Andy's window, and the other toys thought he'd done it on purpose. So, Woody tricked Buzz, telling him the truck was a shuttle that could return him to his home planet – you see, Buzz didn't realize he was just a toy.

At Pizza Planet, Woody quickly spotted Andy. With a little luck, he figured, they could jump into Molly's pushchair.

"Okay, Buzz, get ready and.... Buzz?" Woody turned around to see Buzz striding towards the Rocket Ship Crane Game. The space ranger thought it was a real spaceship!

Buzz climbed into the Rocket Ship Crane Game. Woody followed, still hoping he could make Buzz return to Andy.

Suddenly, the machine started whirring. Then the claw dropped – right on Buzz.

Woody grabbed Buzz and tried to drag him back down. But it was no use. Both toys were pulled into the air and dropped into the prize slot.

"All right! Double prizes!" shouted the kid, seeing the two toys.

To Woody's horror, he saw that the boy was Sid, Andy's nasty neighbour!

All the toys in Andy's room knew Sid. He lived next door and was the cruellest kid on the block. Many times, Andy's toys had watched Sid in his backyard as he tortured toys. Sometimes he even blew them up, just for fun!

Now Sid looked at Buzz and Woody with evil glee. "Let's go home and... play!" he said with a wicked laugh. Woody knew they were doomed.

Sid carried Woody and Buzz home and up to his bedroom. The room was dark and eerie, and Sid had lots of scary tools that he used for toy 'operations'.

Then, Woody and Buzz heard strange rustling sounds – distorted toys were creeping out of the darkness. Sid had modified his once-normal toys, turning them into terrifying mutants!

Woody and Buzz clung on to each other in fear – how would they escape...?

35

RATATOUILLE
(rat·a·too·ee)

Anyone Can Cook

Remy the rat was in Paris – he had just discovered he had been living underneath the city his whole life! He made his way to a skylight in the roof of his favourite chef's restaurant. He peered down and saw an awkward young man. The man's name was Linguini and he was hoping to get a job at the restaurant.

Linguini's mother, like Gusteau, had recently died. She had been a good friend of Gusteau's. The ill-tempered chef named Skinner had no choice but to hire the ungainly Linguini. He would work in the kitchen as a garbage boy. Linguini went right to work, but he was very clumsy. Remy watched in horror from the skylight as Linguini accidentally spilled a pot of soup and began trying to fix it. "Oh no!" Remy shouted. "He's ruining the soup!"

Then, suddenly, the skylight fell open, and Remy tumbled downwards, landing in the kitchen! Quickly, he scrambled across the kitchen floor. Then he smelled Linguini's horrible soup – and stopped short. This was Remy's chance. He could fix the soup! He jumped to the stovetop and started carefully choosing ingredients to put into the pot.

Suddenly, Linguini was staring right at Remy, and Skinner was right behind them! Linguini quickly hid Remy under a colander.

"How dare you cook in my kitchen!" shouted Skinner, and fired Linguini on the spot. But worse things were happening. While Skinner was yelling the waiter whisked a bowl of the soup off to the dining room to an important food critic!

Word came back from the waiter. The soup was delicious! The critic loved it! Colette, one of the cooks, looked at Linguini. "You can't fire him!" she said to Skinner. "Wasn't Gusteau's motto that anyone can cook? Linguini should be given a chance to cook in the kitchen."

Angrily, Skinner gave in. Remy made a move for the window, but Skinner spotted him. He made Linguini catch the rat in a jar. But poor Linguini didn't have the heart to throw Remy out. He started talking to him instead. When Remy nodded, Linguini realised Remy understood what he was saying!

"Wait. You can cook, right?" asked Linguini, and he made a deal with Remy. Linguini would let Remy out if he promised to help him cook. But when the jar was open, Remy ran away!

Then, Remy stopped and turned back. This could be his big chance to cook in a real gourmet kitchen! The little rat decided to trust Linguini and give the partnership a try.

Disney · PIXAR

Cars

Lightning's New Friends

Rookie racecar Lightning McQueen was beginning to understand that there was more to life than winning. He had been stranded in a sleepy town called Radiator Springs after getting lost on his way to a tie-breaker race in California. Sally, the town's attorney, was explaining to Lightning why Radiator Springs wasn't the busy place it once was.

"Forty years ago that Interstate didn't exist," Sally explained, looking at the busy highway. "Folks here never had to travel because the world came to them."

"What happened?" asked Lightning.

"The town got bypassed just to save ten minutes of driving," Sally replied.

Later that day, as Lightning worked on the town's main street – which he had ruined when he arrived – a herd of escaped tractors stampeded through town! When Lightning followed a stray into the desert, he saw Doc roaring around the dirt racetrack.

"You're amazing!" Lightning told the old pro. But Doc raced off. Lightning had just found out that Doc, the town's judge, had once been a famous racecar.

Lightning followed Doc to his office. "How could you quit at the top of your game?" he asked.

Doc showed Lightning a newspaper article about a wreck he had been in. After he was repaired, Doc wanted to return to racing. But he had been replaced – by a rookie. That was why Doc didn't like Lightning when he first arrived!

The next morning, the road was finished. But where was Lightning? Had he left for California? Everyone felt sad. But then Lightning rolled up. He hadn't left!

"I knew you wouldn't go without saying goodbye!" Mater exclaimed.

Lightning said before leaving he wanted to say thank you for the way the town's residents had treated him. "I'm not sure these tyres can get me all the way to California," he said. In a flash, Guido and Luigi proudly fitted Lightning with four shiny new tyres!

And that was just the beginning. Before long, Lightning made his way to every shop in town. He filled up on Fillmore's organic fuel, tried out night vision goggles at Sarge's Surplus, picked out a bumper sticker at Lizzie's and got a new paint job at Ramone's body shop. Lightning liked helping the town's small businesses.

It was one of the first times Lightning had put others before himself, and he liked teaming up with his new friends.

Disney · PIXAR

TOY STORY

Just a Toy

After losing Andy and his mum at Pizza Planet, Woody and Buzz had found themselves in nasty neighbour Sid's house! Sid had modified his once-normal toys, turning them into terrifying mutants. Trying to escape, Buzz and Woody ran into the hall – and straight into Scud, Sid's vicious dog!

Buzz ducked through an open door. Inside, he heard, "Calling Buzz Lightyear! This is Star Command!" Then the voice continued: "The world's greatest superhero, now the world's greatest toy!" It was a TV advert for Buzz Lightyear toys! At the end of the ad, a voice added: "Not a flying toy."

Buzz was stunned. Was the ad true? He walked to the stairs and saw blue sky through the hall window. He knew he could fly... couldn't he? Wasn't he a space ranger? Gathering courage, he climbed to the top of the stair railing – and leapt. "To infinity and beyond!" he cried.

For a moment, Buzz seemed to hang in the air. Then, he fell CRASH! onto the stair landing, and his left arm broke off.

Buzz Lightyear finally understood the truth: He was a toy.

Upstairs, Woody searched for Buzz. He peeked into a room and saw Sid's little sister,

Hannah, playing with her dolls. Woody stared as he realized: one of the dolls was Buzz!

Hannah had found the space ranger and added him to her tea party. Woody waited until Hannah left, then ran to help Buzz. But Buzz didn't want to move. He was upset because he wasn't a real space ranger. "Look at me," he moaned. "I can't even fly out the window."

The window? With wide eyes, Woody turned around towards Sid's bedroom. Sid's window was directly opposite Andy's bedroom window! Woody picked up a Christmas decoration from the floor and ran into Sid's room, pushing Buzz in front of him. He climbed up onto the desk, where he could look out of the window. On the other side of the garden he saw Andy's window! On top of the desk inside Andy's room, Hamm and Mr Potato Head were playing battleships and, as usual, Hamm was winning. Woody opened Sid's bedroom window.

"Hey there, guys! It's me!" Woody called out to them, full of hope. The two toys turned to look, amazed.

"Woody's in nasty Sid's bedroom!" exclaimed Hamm. "Hey, guys, come and look, it's Woody!"

All of Andy's toys rushed to the window. Surely now Woody and Buzz were saved?

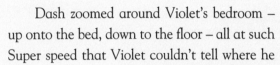

THE INCREDIBLES

Super Annoying!

Dashiell Robert Parr was bored. It was Saturday afternoon and he had nothing to do. He had already taken a twenty-mile run, but that had only taken about two minutes thanks to his Super speed.

"You know, you could do your maths homework," his mother Helen said.

Homework, now? Dash thought. I'll do that tomorrow. Right now I want to do something fun.

Brrrng! The telephone rang and Dash's sister, Violet, raced out of her bedroom to answer it. Dash had spotted his target. He grinned slyly and hurried into Violet's room.

Five minutes later, Violet returned. Things were not as she had left them. Her whole room was re-arranged! Only one person could have done it.

"Mum!" Violet yelled. "Dash messed up my room!"

As Helen walked down the hall, a breeze whipped through Violet's room. Helen looked inside. "It looks fine to me, honey. Now I've got to get dinner ready," she said. Violet looked at her room again and saw that everything was back in place. Then her eyes fell on the closet door, which was slightly ajar.

"Dash!" Violet exclaimed. "Get out of here, you little insect!"

Dash zoomed around Violet's bedroom – up onto the bed, down to the floor – all at such Super speed that Violet couldn't tell where he was. Dash only came to a halt when he spotted Violet's diary, which had fallen open on her bed.

"Ooooh," Dash said, picking up the diary. "What have we here?"

That was it. Violet had had enough of Dash. "Give that back!" she yelled. Dash tried to race out of the room, but Violet threw a force field in front of the door. Dash ran into it head-on and was knocked to the floor. Violet grabbed her diary, but before she knew it Dash had taken it again. Violet turned invisible and lunged at her brother.

Dash and Violet continued to chase each other around Violet's room in a blur of Super powers, until they heard their mum calling.

"Time for dinner!" she cried.

Dash froze. Then, in the blink of an eye, he zipped out through the bedroom door and down the hall to the kitchen table.

"Dash," Helen asked, "did you finish your homework?"

Then Violet appeared at the table. Her hair was all mussed.

"Nah," Dash replied with a smile. "I found something much better to do."

Lady *and the* TRAMP

A Lady's Touch

Late one night, Lady's ears perked up and her eyes flew open with a start. The baby was crying! Lady had grown to love the new baby in the house, and she was very protective of him. If he was crying, she was going to find out why. She climbed out of her basket, pushed open the swinging door with her nose and tiptoed up the front stairs.

Meanwhile, Jim Dear and Darling were trying to calm the baby. "Oh, Jim, I just don't know what's the matter with him!" said Darling. She was holding the baby in her arms, trying to rock him and soothe him, but his little face was a deep red and covered with tears. Jim Dear sat groggily at the edge of the bed and looked at his wife helplessly.

"Well, we know he isn't hungry," said Jim Dear, "since we've just given him a bottle." He massaged his temples as though they hurt. Then he noticed Lady, who had walked tentatively into the bedroom. "Hello, Lady," he said to her.

Lady took a few steps closer to the cradle, where Darling was laying the baby down. His little fists were closed tight, and his shrieks had turned to loud sobs.

"We just don't know what's the matter with the little guy," Jim Dear said wearily to Lady. "We've fed him and changed him, and I've sung him every lullaby I know. Maybe you can figure out what's bothering him!"

That was all the invitation Lady needed. She jumped up onto the bed and peered into the cradle. The baby's eyes were squeezed shut and his cheeks were wet with tears. His little legs were kicking the covers. Lady reached in and tugged at the covers to smooth them out. The baby opened his eyes and looked at Lady. His cries dropped to a whimper, and he reached out to touch her. His tiny hand grabbed hold of her ear and tugged. Lady winced but held still. With her chin, she began to rock the cradle and, with her furry tail, she beat a rhythmic *thump, thump, thump* on the bedcover.

"Ga!" said the baby as he broke into a gummy smile, his big blue eyes looking like wet forget-me-nots. Still holding Lady's ear, the baby giggled.

"Oh, look, Jim Dear!" cried Darling delightedly. "Lady has got him to stop crying!"

"I just don't know what we'd do without you, Lady!" Jim Dear said gratefully.

Rock, rock, rock went the cradle. *Thump, thump, thump* went Lady's tail. Soon the baby's eyelids grew heavy, and then his eyes closed. Tears still streaking his little round cheeks, he relaxed his grip on Lady's ear, smiled and fell asleep.

Winnie
the
Pooh

Roo's New Baby-sitter

"I don't want to be baby-sitted!" cried Roo. Roo's mama, Kanga, was going shopping and Pooh was going to baby-sit.

"I want to go shopping!" cried Roo. He had a large bag and was filling it when Pooh arrived.

"Hello, Pooh," said Roo. "I'm shopping!" He put more tins in his bag, partly because he didn't want his mama to see how much he minded being left behind.

Roo and Pooh said goodbye to Kanga. Then Pooh gave Roo a hug and tried to feed him a nice smackerel of honey.

"I want to go shopping," squeaked Roo. "I don't want to eat."

"Hmmmm," said Pooh. "NOW what do I do?"

"You don't know how to baby-sit?" asked Roo. "I'm good at baby-sitting. I'll tell you how. The first thing a baby-sitter does is climb!"

Pooh, who was starting to think there was not much SITTING involved in baby-sitting, said, "Okay, let's find a good climbing tree."

They climbed the old apple tree in Roo's back garden. Roo hopped from branch to branch, and Pooh climbed up behind him.

"Mmmm," said Roo. "Look at those apples. Baby-sitters always pick apples for supper."

So Pooh climbed up to the highest branch, picked four bright red apples and then inched back down using one arm. They sat side by side and swung their feet and ate the sweet apples.

"This is the best supper ever!" cried Roo.

Next, Roo showed Pooh how babysitters pour a whole bottle of bubble bath into the bathwater. Roo disappeared under the bubbles. *Wffffff.* Pooh blew on the bubbles but he couldn't see Roo!

"Look at me jumping," squeaked a little voice. Roo was jumping on his bed, all wet! Pooh dried Roo off, then helped put on his pyjamas.

"Time for your Strengthening Medicine," said Pooh, a little more sternly than when poohs usually say such things. But Roo didn't want it. He folded his arms across his chest.

"Oh well," said Pooh, slumping in a chair. "Why don't you give ME a spoonful? I think I could do with it!"

"Now, Pooh, dear, here's your medicine," said Roo in a cheerful, grown-up sort of voice.

"Ahhh!" said Pooh. "Thank you, Roo. You are a good baby-sitter."

Just then, Kanga opened the door and saw Roo and Pooh snuggled together in the chair.

"Mama!" cried Roo. "I'm babysitting Pooh!"

"Of course you are, dear," said Kanga.

THE LION KING

Simba's Secret

Simba and Nala were best friends. They liked to tell each other secrets.

"I'm scared of mice," Nala told Simba one day. "Don't tell anybody."

"Don't worry, I won't," Simba said.

One day, Simba and his father, Mufasa, were out for a walk. "Look at that mouse stuffing her cheeks with seeds," said Mufasa.

"That's so funny!" said Simba. "I don't know why Nala's scared of mice."

Nala had heard Simba talking with his dad, and she got really mad with Simba.

A few weeks later, Nala said, "I'm going to tell you a secret but it's a really big one. If you tell this time, I'll be so mad at you."

"I promise I won't say anything!" said Simba.

"Okay," said Nala. "Here's the secret: I found a huge cave yesterday, down in the red cliffs. I'm going back to explore it today."

Simba played all day without Nala. Before dinner he began to wonder when she was coming back. Nala's mother was worried. "Simba," she asked, "do you know where Nala is?"

"No," he answered. He'd made a promise to Nala, and he didn't want to break it. The sun went down and the moon shone in the sky.

Sarabi, Simba's mother, went to her son. "Do you know where Nala is?" she asked.

"I can't tell," said Simba. "It's a secret. I can't tell, no matter what!"

"Simba," said his mother, "you're a good friend to try not to tell Nala's secret. But there are some secrets that are good to keep and others that are important to tell."

Simba thought about what his mother had said. He decided that he had to tell everyone where Nala was.

The whole pride hurried to the red cliffs. At last, they heard a small voice. "M-mother?" It was Nala!

The lions rushed to the entrance of a cave, but it was almost completely blocked. A rock slide had trapped the little cub! The lions dug and dug, and finally they had cleared the rocks away. Nala rushed out of the cave and ran to her mother.

A few minutes later, Simba walked over and hung his head. "I'm sorry I told your secret, Nala," he said.

"If you hadn't said anything, I'd still be here. It was a stupid secret!" said Nala.

When they got home, it was time for bed. Nala and Simba snuggled together. "I'm happy you're home," said Simba. "And that's not a secret!"

101 DALMATIANS

Rolly's Midnight Snack

"Time for bed!" called Pongo.

"Aw, Dad," complained Patch, "we're not tired!"

"No arguments," said Pongo. "Little puppies need their rest."

With a sigh, Patch joined the line of puppies climbing the staircase.

"I'm hungry," Rolly complained as the puppies settled down for the night.

"You're always hungry," said Patch.

"And you always want to stay awake and have adventures," said Rolly.

Patch sighed. "Too bad we never get what we want."

Hours later, Rolly felt a tap on his shoulder. "Is it morning?" he asked with a yawn.

"No," said Patch. "It's midnight. Wanna explore? I'll get you a snack."

"A snack!" cried Rolly excitedly.

"Shhhhh!" said Patch. "Come on."

Rolly followed Patch to the kitchen.

Patch nodded towards the table. "After dinner, I saw Nanny put some juicy bones up there. She's saving them for tomorrow's soup."

"Soup!" cried Rolly. "What a waste! Bones are for chewing on!"

So, Patch and Rolly came up with a plan.

First, Patch climbed onto Rolly's shoulders to reach the table.

Everything went fine until Patch threw down the first bone and it landed in the dustbin. Rolly took off after it and leaped inside!

Rolly was stuck. Patch tried hard not to panic. He thought and thought until he came up with another plan – a Rescue Rolly Plan!

Patch went upstairs and woke Lucky and Pepper. The two puppies followed Patch into the kitchen. Then Patch found his father's long lead and tossed one end into the dustbin.

"Take hold of the leash!" Patch told Rolly.

"Okay," said Rolly.

Patch turned to the other puppies and said, "Now, let's all pull on this end of the leash, on the count of three."

The three puppies pulled. The dustbin fell over and Rolly tumbled out onto the kitchen floor.

"Thanks!" said Rolly.

The puppies licked their brother, and they all returned to bed.

Before Rolly drifted off to sleep, he whispered to Patch, "Guess you finally got your adventure."

"Yeah," said Patch. "But I'm sorry you didn't get your snack."

"Sure, I did," said Rolly. "While I was waiting for you to rescue me, what do you think I was doing? I was eating that juicy bone. And, boy, was it good!"

DUMBO

Hide-and-seek

For quite a while, Dumbo was the newest baby in the circus. But then, one day, the stork arrived with a brand-new delivery – a baby girl giraffe.

"You know, Dumbo," said his friend, Timothy Q. Mouse, "I think we should ask that new baby to play with us."

Dumbo nodded. He loved making new friends!

So together, Timothy and Dumbo made their way to the giraffes' pen.

"Hello, Mrs Giraffe," Timothy said. "Can your lovely new baby come out and play?"

Dumbo gave Mrs Giraffe a big, hopeful smile. "Well . . . I suppose so," she said.

She gave her baby a kiss, and sent her off in the care of Timothy Mouse – and Dumbo.

"Okay, kids," said Timothy, standing before the two, "what do you feel like playing?"

Dumbo and the baby giraffe stared back at him blankly.

"Hmm . . . I see," said Timothy. "You don't know that many games. May I suggest hide-and-seek?"

Dumbo and the giraffe nodded happily, as Timothy closed his eyes and counted.

"Ready or not," he said finally, opening his eyes, "here I – hang on! Don't you guys know you're supposed to hide?"

No, actually, they did not.

"Okay," Timothy sighed. "Let's take it from the top. When I close my eyes, you guys hide. You find a place where you can't see me and I can't see you. Like this . . ." Timothy ducked behind a popcorn tub. "Get it?"

Dumbo and the giraffe slowly nodded.

"Okay then, let's try this again. One, two, three . . ." Timothy counted to 20, then opened his eyes. "No, no, no!" he groaned. "You can't hide behind the popcorn. You're too big. Let's try this one more time."

Again, he closed his eyes and counted. Then, very slowly, he opened them and looked around. "Much better!" he said, surprised. Of course, it didn't take him long to find Dumbo's wide body behind a narrow tent pole, or the giraffe's tall neck sticking up from behind the clowns' trunk. But they were getting closer!

"This time, guys, try to find a place for your whole body to hide," Timothy said.

So, Dumbo and the giraffe waited for Timothy to close his eyes once more, then they quietly sneaked behind the pole and trunk again. This time, the tall, skinny giraffe hid behind the tall, skinny pole. And short, wide Dumbo hid behind the short, wide trunk. And do you know what? They were hidden so well, Timothy Q. Mouse may still be looking for them to this very day!

Disney · PIXAR
FINDING
NEMO

The Induction

Nemo still had a satisfied smile on his face from the previous night's induction ceremony. I'm part of the club! he thought.

"So, Shark Bait, what did you think of that ceremony last night?" Gill asked.

"It was the best!" Nemo exclaimed.

"If only we could get Flo to be part of the ceremony," Deb mused. "But she never seems to want to come out at night."

"So, kid, what was your favourite part?" Jacques wanted to know.

"I think my favourite part was swimming to the top of Mount Wanna ... wannaha ... ha ..." Nemo tried unsuccessfully to pronounce it.

"Wannahockaloogie," Bloat said.

"Yeah," Peach reminisced. "I have a soft spot for my first climb too."

"I wonder," Nemo said. "Who came up with that name?"

Bubbles pointed at Gurgle, who pointed at Bloat, who pointed at Peach, who pointed at Deb, who pointed at Flo.

Deb shrugged. "I guess we came up with it together," she said.

"Why do they call it the Ring of Fire if there's no fire?" Nemo asked.

"Well, you see, it's like this – I don't know," Peach had to admit.

"But who made it up, then?" Nemo asked, confused. "Didn't you guys *invent* the ceremony?"

"I think Bubbles came up with the Ring of Fire," Gurgle offered.

"Aren't they beautiful?" Bubbles mused.

"I find it very unsanitary to swim through others' bubbles," Gurgle complained. "Which is why I came up with the chanting part of the ceremony. It's very cleansing both for the body and the mind, and circulates carbon dioxide through the gills."

"That makes sense," Nemo agreed, although it really didn't.

"Don't forget about the kelp fronds," Peach piped up.

"Oh, there's no big secret there," Deb confided. "I just like giving a good whack with the old kelp fronds every now and then." And she demonstrated by whacking Bloat, who immediately began to swell up.

"Was that really necessary?" Bloat asked as he floated away.

"What can I do in the next ceremony?" Nemo asked eagerly.

"Hopefully, we won't have another one. Not if we break out of here first, Shark Bait," Gill answered.

"Well, you never know," Deb said forlornly. "Maybe Flo will come around."

Everyone rolled their eyes, including Nemo.

Disney
THE
LION KING
Tag!

Early one morning, Simba woke up ready to find Nala and continue their game of Tag. The night before, when their mothers had made them stop ("Time for bed, Simba!" "Time for bed, Nala!"), Simba had been It – which is a terrible way to go to bed! – and he was eager to tag Nala and make *her* It as soon as possible. But, when he arrived at the pride's meeting place, everyone, it seemed, was there except for Nala.

"Where's Nala?" he asked his mother.

"Oh, I heard her mother say she wasn't feeling well," she replied. "So they're staying in the cave and resting until she's better."

"But she has to come out," protested Simba. "I'm It and I have to tag somebody!"

His mother smiled. "I'm afraid you'll just have to wait, little Simba," she said.

"But that's so boring!" Simba groaned.

"You can play by yourself, Simba," she reminded him.

"Aw, all right." Simba sighed. First, he tried hunting grasshoppers. But they jumped so high and so far – and so fast! – he soon grew tired and frustrated.

Then he tried climbing trees. But the birds didn't much like a lion cub messing around among their branches and shooed him away.

Finally, he tried just lying down and finding pictures in the clouds. But that was Nala's favourite game, and it made him miss her.

He rolled over and swatted a bright wildflower with his paw. "Tag, you're It," he said half-heartedly. Then, suddenly, an idea popped into his head. What if he picked some wildflowers and took them to his sick friend? It might even make her feel better!

With newfound energy, Simba picked as many flowers as he could carry in his mouth and made his way back to the pride's cave.

"Dees ah fur Nana," he said, dropping the flowers at Nala's mother's feet. "These are for Nala," he repeated. "I hope she feels better really soon."

"Oh, thank you, Simba," the lioness said. "But why don't you give them to her yourself? She seems to be feeling much better. Nala!" she called. And out came Simba's friend, smiling and looking very glad to see him.

She sniffed at the pretty flowers. "Are these for me? Gee, thanks, Simba." Then she turned to her mother. "Can I go out and play with Simba now, Mama?"

"I don't see why not," said her mother.

"Grrreat!" said Nala.

"Yeah, grrreat!" said Simba. Then he reached out and gently tapped her with his paw. "Tag! You're It!"

Mowgli Finds a Friend

Bagheera the panther found Mowgli in the jungle when he was just a baby, and decided to take the boy to a wolf family that lived nearby.

The mother wolf agreed to take care of him, and for ten years she raised him as one of her own. Mowgli was a very happy Man-cub.

One day, bad news arrived in the jungle. Shere Khan the tiger had returned after a long absence. The tiger was mean and hated everything. More than anything though, Shere Khan hated Man. This meant that it was no longer safe for Mowgli to live in the jungle. The wolves decided that he should go to a Man-village at once.

Bagheera had kept watch over Mowgli through the years and volunteered to take him. Later that night, the boy rode on the panther's back as they made their way through the jungle.

But Mowgli did not want to leave the jungle. It was his home. "I don't want to go to the Man-village!" he shouted. Then he added, "I can take care of myself."

Although Bagheera cared a lot for Mowgli, he eventually became tired of the Man-Cub's fighting, and he walked off into the jungle, leaving Mowgli alone.

Mowgli began to worry that maybe he couldn't take care of himself.

Before long, a bear named Baloo walked out of the jungle and spotted Mowgli. The bear tried to be friendly, but Mowgli told Baloo to go away and leave him alone. But Baloo did not listen. He decided the little Man-cub needed to have some fun.

"Hey, kid, Baloo's gonna learn you to fight like a bear," he said, jumping around. The bear's silly behaviour made Mowgli laugh and soon he was dancing and boxing just like Baloo. When they finished, Mowgli jumped up on his new friend's stomach and tickled him. "You're all right, kid," Baloo said gently.

Just then, Bagheera walked over to them. He had returned to make sure Mowgli was okay. The panther told Baloo that he thought Mowgli should go to the Man-village so he'd be safe from Shere Khan.

Baloo didn't want his little buddy to go to a Man-village. "They'll ruin him. They'll make a man out of him," the bear said.

Bagheera sighed. He knew it would be hard to persuade Mowgli to leave now that he had made friends with Baloo. The panther watched as the pair jumped into the river and floated lazily away.

Peter Pan

Peter Pan's Visit

John and Michael Darling sat, silent and still, on Michael's bed, listening intently as their big sister, Wendy, told them yet another story about their favourite hero, Peter Pan.

Meanwhile, their dog and nursemaid, Nana, dozed peacefully under the open window of the Darling nursery.

"...And then," Wendy was saying, "with a quick slash of his sword, Peter Pan cut the evil Captain Hook's hand right off!"

Michael and John gasped. Nana started too, and jumped to her feet. But Nana wasn't alarmed by Wendy's story. She had heard a strange noise coming from just outside the window. Nana faced the window, listening carefully for the sound to repeat itself.

There it was again!

Unnoticed by the children, who were caught up in their story, Nana scurried over to the window and poked her head outside.

And there, just to one side of the window and crouched on a narrow ledge, was a red-headed boy dressed in green from head to toe.

Nana froze, then leaned towards the boy slowly, growling a low warning growl.

"There, there, Nana," the boy whispered softly. "Please, don't bark."

At the sound of her name, Nana froze again, then tilted her head to one side, as if trying to figure something out.

"You're wondering how I know your name," the boy whispered. "Well, I know a lot about you and Wendy and John and Michael. You see, I've been coming here, now and again, for quite a while to listen to Wendy's stories – stories about me!" He stood up straight and puffed his chest out proudly. "I'm Peter Pan, you know!"

Now, Nana was not a mean dog. But there was one thing – well, three things, really – that she was very protective of, and they were the three children inside that nursery. Nana knew it was up to her to make sure they were safe and sound. She also knew that strange boys crouching outside the nursery window – Peter Pan or not – were not to be tolerated.

And so, with another low growl, Nana suddenly lunged further out of the window and snapped her teeth at Peter Pan. The boy flew out of the way just in time, but his shadow was not quite so fast. It struggled to get loose, but it was held tight in Nana's mouth!

Startled, Peter Pan flew off into the darkness and began his journey home to Never Land. But he knew he had to get his shadow back. He would have to return to the Darling nursery – and soon! And *this* time, he would need to go inside....

THE JUNGLE Book

Go Fish!

"Okay, small fry," said Baloo the bear. "Today I'm going to teach you to fish like a bear!"

Mowgli was delighted. He loved his new friend Baloo. Unlike Bagheera the panther, who kept insisting that Mowgli should live in the Man-village for his own protection, Baloo made no such demands on Mowgli. Baloo was much more interested in having a good time living in the jungle, and so was Mowgli.

"Now, watch this, kid," said Baloo as they arrived at the riverbank. "All ya gotta do is wait for a fish to swim by and then . . ."

Whoosh! Quick as a flash, Baloo held a wriggling silver fish in his paw. "Now you try it!" he said to Mowgli.

Mowgli sat very still, waiting for a fish to swim by. Then – *splash!* – he toppled headfirst into the water.

"Hmm," said Baloo after he had fished Mowgli out and set him down, dripping. "Now I'll show you my second technique."

Baloo and Mowgli walked towards another part of the river. This time, the fish could be seen occasionally leaping out of the water as they swam down a little waterfall. Baloo waded a few steps into the water, waited for a fish to jump, then – *whoosh!* – he swiped a fish right out of the air. "Now you try, buddy."

Mowgli waded in just as Baloo had done. He waited for the fish to jump and then leaped for it. *Splash!*

"Okay, plan C," said Baloo, after he had fished Mowgli out a second time. "I'll take you to the big waterfall. The fish literally fall into your paws. All ya gotta do is reach out and catch one!"

Mowgli followed Baloo to the big waterfall. Sure enough, silvery fish were jumping all the way down the fall. Catching one would be easy!

In the blink of an eye Baloo held up a fish for Mowgli to admire.

"I'm going to do it this time, you watch me, Baloo!" said Mowgli excitedly. He scrunched up his face with concentration. Then – *flash!* – for an instant, Mowgli actually had a silvery fish in his hands. But, a second later, the fish shot out of his grasp and jumped into the water again. Mowgli looked down at his empty hands with a sigh.

"You know what, kid?" said Baloo, clapping a huge paw on Mowgli's skinny shoulders. "I think you're working too hard. That's not how life in the jungle should be! It should be fun, happy and carefree. So, come on. Let's go shake a banana tree instead!"

And Mowgli cheerfully agreed.

Good Luck in California

In the sleepy town of Radiator Springs, rookie racecar Lightning McQueen had found some great new friends. He had ended up there by accident, while on his way to the tie-breaker race for the Piston Cup in California. At first, he had just wanted to leave, but now he was beginning to realize what it meant to help others – maybe there was more to life than winning races after all.

Lightning had spent the day helping all the town's small businesses, and now the evening was drawing in.

"Is it getting dark out?" he called loudly when Sally, a shiny blue sports car he had become friends with, drove up.

Suddenly Radiator Springs lit up in glowing neon colours, and music played. It was time to cruise! But as the townsfolk drove in pairs together, a helicopter searchlight swept over them.

"We have found Lightning McQueen!" boomed a voice from a loudspeaker.

News vans swarmed into town. Reporters surrounded Lightning, shouting questions. He couldn't see Sally or reach his friends.

"Where are you?" Lightning's agent, Harve, shouted over the speaker phone in the back of Mack's trailer. Lighting tried to tell Harve how great Radiator Springs was, but the fast-talking agent wasn't interested.

"Get out of 'Radiation Stinks' now, or Dinoco is history!" he yelled. Dinoco was the sponsor Lightning would get if he won the tie-breaker race.

As Mack urged Lightning to get into the trailer, Lightning and Sally gazed at each other. Neither of them knew what to say.

"Good luck in California." Sally said at last. "I hope you find what you're looking for."

Sally was heading back to her hotel when she heard a reporter thank Doc for letting the press know Lightning's location. How could Doc do such a thing?

"It's best for everyone, Sally," Doc said.

"Best for everyone? Or best for you?" Sally replied in shock.

Doc didn't like young racecars. He used to be a famous racecar and, when he got older and was involved in a big crash, a rookie had taken his place.

Slowly, Lightning's friends went to their homes and shops. Soon, the street was empty. Doc idled alone. Behind him the neon lights blinked off until Radiator Springs was dark and quiet once more.

Doc sighed sadly. Had he been wrong about Lightning?

The Importance of Being a Toy

Woody and Buzz were trapped at Andy's nasty neighbour Sid's house, and Buzz had just discovered he wasn't a real space ranger. He was feeling hopeless, but Woody had an idea. He ran to Sid's bedroom window and waved out towards Andy's house. "Hey, guys!"

Looking outside from their own window, Andy's toys were surprised to see Woody. The cowboy threw them a string of Christmas lights – an escape line from Sid's bedroom. But the toys still didn't trust Woody, because he'd pushed Buzz out of Andy's window. He'd only meant to push him behind the desk, so Andy would pay attention to Woody again, but the plan had gone wrong.

Buzz refused to come to the window to prove he was okay. So, using Buzz's broken arm, Woody tried to show everything was fine – but the trick made it look like he'd hurt Buzz!

Andy's toys dropped the lights and walked away from the window. Woody felt terrible. And when he turned back into Sid's room, things seemed to be getting even worse – Sid's mutant toys had surrounded Buzz!

Woody tried to fight them off but they grabbed Buzz's arm and pushed Woody away. Then, after a moment, the mutants stepped away. Buzz sat up in surprise, flexing his left arm, which was now attached and working perfectly. Sid's mutant toys had fixed his arm! Although they looked scary, it turned out Sid's toys were friendly.

Suddenly, the toys heard Sid racing up the stairs. Everyone scattered – except for Buzz, who wouldn't move. He was still sad because he was just a toy. When Sid burst into the room, he strapped a rocket onto Buzz's back! Blast-off was the next morning!

All night, Woody pleaded with Buzz to escape. "Over in that house is a kid who thinks you are the greatest. And it's not because you're a space ranger. It's because you're a toy. You are his toy," Woody said.

Woody nearly lost hope, but Buzz finally realized Woody was right. Being a toy was important! Buzz ran over to Woody, to help the cowboy break free, too. But suddenly, the alarm clock started ringing and Sid jumped out of bed. "Time for lift off!" he yelled, grabbing Buzz and running outside.

Woody knew he had to do something fast. As soon as Sid left, Woody gathered the mutant toys and laid out a rescue plan. Buzz was a good toy, he explained, and they couldn't let him get blown up. "We'll have to break a few rules," he told the mutants. "But if it works, it'll help everyone."

HERCULES
Destructo-boy

"Hercules!" Amphitryon called. "This hay pile is about to fall over. Could you hold it up while I go to get the cart?"

"Sure, Pop!" Hercules told his father.

Hercules was the strongest boy in his village. He could easily hold up the enormous stack of hay bales with one hand.

Soon, another farmer approached, struggling to hold onto a team of six disobedient mules.

"Need any help?" Hercules asked.

"Hercules!" the farmer gasped. "If you'll hold these mules, I can go get my sons to help me get them home."

"Be glad to!" Hercules took the mules' leads with his free hand.

Just then, a woman came by dragging a cart filled with pottery. She was panting.

"Good day, ma'am," Hercules said politely. "Could I give you a hand with that?"

"Why, thank you," the woman replied. "But it looks like you have your hands full!"

"Oh, I'll be finished here in a second," Hercules said. "Then I can . . ."

His voice trailed off. He'd just noticed some children his own age running down the road, laughing and shouting as they tossed a discus.

Hercules gazed at them longingly. For some reason, he'd never seemed to fit in with the other village children. Perhaps it was because they didn't understand him. Or perhaps it was because Hercules had once challenged them to a 50-yard dash – and beaten them all by 49 yards.

"Hey, guys!" he called as the discus sailed towards him. "I've got it!"

He lunged towards the discus. The mules' leads went flying. The haystack teetered.

"Uh-oh," Hercules said.

He tried to grab the hay and the mules at the same time, but he accidentally tripped one of the mules, which crashed into the haystack, which fell right onto the woman's cart, and all over the boys.

Hercules winced at the sounds of breaking pottery and shouting boys. The mules were already running off towards the horizon.

"My pottery!" the woman wailed.

"What's the big idea?" one of the other children demanded, standing and brushing himself off.

"Yeah." Another boy grabbed the discus from Hercules. "Stay out of our way from now on . . . Destructo-Boy!"

Hercules' shoulders slumped. Why did this sort of thing always happen to him? Whenever he tried to help, he only made things worse. But he knew that, one day, his strength would help him be a hero. He just hoped that day would come soon. There was only so much unbroken pottery left in Greece!

Bambi

Practice Doesn't Always Make Perfect

One day, Bambi and Thumper were playing in the meadow.

"Look, Bambi!" exclaimed Thumper.

A herd of stags was thundering towards them.

"I wish I could be a stag!" Bambi exclaimed.

"Well, you know what my father always says," said Thumper.

"I know," said Bambi. "'Eating greens is a special treat. It makes long ears and great big feet.'"

"No, not that!" said Thumper. "I mean, he does say that, but he also says, 'If you want to hop well, but your hop is all wrong, then you have to practise all day long!'"

"I have to hop all day long?" asked Bambi.

"No!" cried Thumper. "If you want to become a stag, you have to practise!"

Bambi glanced back at two big deer. They suddenly ran towards each other, locking horns to test their strength. They looked so powerful and majestic. Bambi wanted to be just like them!

"Okay," Bambi told Thumper.

"Okay," said Thumper. "Follow me."

Thumper hopped to the edge of the meadow. He stopped by a big oak tree. "Lower your head," he told Bambi.

Bambi lowered his head. "Now what?" he asked, staring at the ground.

"Run straight ahead," said Thumper.

Bambi ran straight ahead – towards the trunk of the old oak tree! But, before he got there, a voice cried, "Stop!" Bambi did, skidding to a halt only a few inches from the tree trunk.

Thumper and Bambi looked up. Friend Owl looked down at them with big curious eyes. "Bambi, why were you going to butt my tree trunk with your head?" asked Friend Owl.

"I'm practising to become a big stag," said Bambi. "Stags butt heads to show their strength."

Friend Owl laughed and said, "Bambi, the stags have antlers to protect their heads! And becoming a stag is not something you can practise. It's something that will happen to you with the passing of time."

"It will?" said Bambi.

"Of course!" Friend Owl assured him. "Next summer, you'll see. You'll be bigger and stronger. You'll also have antlers – and, I hope, enough sense not to butt heads with an oak tree!"

"Yes, sir," said Bambi.

"Now go on, you two," said Friend Owl. "And don't be in too much of a hurry to grow up. You'll get there soon enough, I promise you!"

"Okay," said Bambi and Thumper. Then the two friends returned to the snowy meadow to play.

Disney · PIXAR

TOY STORY

Scaring Sid

Andy's nasty neighbour Sid had taken Buzz Lightyear prisoner, and had strapped a firework to his back! The boy was planning to blast Buzz into space!

Woody knew he had to do something fast. As soon as Sid left, Woody gathered Sid's mutant toys and laid out a rescue plan. Buzz was a good toy, he explained, and they couldn't let him get blown up. "We'll have to break a few rules," he told the mutants. "But if it works, it'll help everyone."

The toys started by sending Legs and Ducky through the air ducts. Arriving above the front door, they unscrewed the socket of the porch light bulb and then Ducky, hanging from the hook of Legs' crane, slipped through the hole, dangled down and managed to swing himself to ring the doorbell.

While Sid's little sister, Hannah, rushed to open the door, the other toys unbolted Sid's bedroom door, allowing Wind-up Frog, the speediest toy in the house, to slip out onto the landing. Sid's dog Scud immediately jumped up and chased Wind-up Frog all the way to the garden, allowing Woody and the others, piled up on Roller Bob's skateboard, to leave the room unnoticed. They hurtled down the stairs and swept into the kitchen, aiming for the cat flap.

Everything went like clockwork and in a matter of minutes they were outside!

In the backyard, Sid was preparing to launch Buzz into outer space.

With a cruel grin, Sid leaned over to light the big rocket's fuse as he began the countdown. "Ten, nine, eight, seven..."

Suddenly, he heard – "Reach for the sky!"

It was Woody, lying nearby. Sid turned and picked Woody up. How did the cowboy doll get outside? And was something wrong with its pull string?

Then, one by one, the mutant toys stood up and staggered out of the sandbox... splashed out of the mud puddle... and crawled from under the dog dish! Together, slowly and steadily, they surrounded the astonished human boy.

But Woody wasn't done with Sid. "From now on, you must take good care of your toys. Because if you don't, we'll find out," Woody warned. And then he leaned in very close and looked Sid right in the eye. "So play nice!"

"AAAHH!" Sid threw up his arms and shrieked in terror. Screaming, he ran into the house and slammed the door.

The toys cheered – their plan had worked! Buzz was saved! And best of all, Sid's days of torturing toys were over.

Stitch Upon a Time

"Once upon a time," read Lilo.

"Wait," said Stitch.

"Wait for what?" asked Lilo.

"Snacks," said Stitch. He climbed off the bed and scampered to the bedroom door.

"You better not let Nani hear you," warned Lilo. "She thinks we went to bed."

Stitch crept into the hall, lifted his big ears and listened.

"No Nani," he whispered. Then he dashed downstairs and into the kitchen.

"Soda, pineapple, pickles, coleslaw," recited Stitch, peering into the fridge. "Hmm . . . pineapple-pickle-coleslaw sandwich . . ."

Lilo tiptoed up behind him. "You can't put all that in a sandwich," she whispered.

"*Yaaaaahhhhh!*" shouted Stitch.

"Sorry," whispered Lilo. "I didn't mean to startle you."

"*What* is going on in here?" demanded Nani, storming into the kitchen.

"Stitch wants a snack," Lilo explained.

"It's not time for snacks," Nani said. She shut the refrigerator door and marched them both back up the stairs. "It's time for bed."

"*Story*," said Stitch as he climbed into bed and held up the book. "Time for story."

"Please?" Lilo asked. She and Stitch both blinked their big dark eyes at Nani.

Nani sighed and said, "Oh, all right. But it had better be a short one."

"Goody!" cried Stitch as Nani climbed into bed too.

After Nani settled in between Lilo and Stitch, Lilo opened the book and began to read, "Once upon a time, there was a sad little puppy named – "

"Stitch!" cried Stitch.

Lilo continued, "There was a sad little puppy named . . . *Stitch*. He was sad because he was lost."

"Lost," repeated Stitch.

Lilo passed the book to Nani and said, "Your turn."

Then Nani began to read, "But one day, he met a little girl named – "

"Lilo," whispered Lilo.

Nani smiled. "He met a little girl named . . . Lilo."

Then Nani continued reading the story, until she reached the very end.

". . . and they lived happily ever after," Nani finished, shutting the book.

"Ever after," murmured Stitch, closing his eyes.

"Ever after," echoed Lilo, closing her eyes.

Nani waited until they were both sound asleep, then headed downstairs for a snack. Maybe she'd have a pineapple-pickle-coleslaw sandwich!

Disney
Pinocchio

Follow Your Star

Jiminy Cricket was a wanderer. He loved the independence, the excitement and the simplicity of his way of life. For many a season, he had roamed the countryside, stopping to rest in towns along the way, and moving on when he grew restless.

But lately, Jiminy Cricket had noticed that there was one thing missing from his vagabond lifestyle: a purpose. Camping one night by the side of the road, he sat on his sleeping bag and gazed into his campfire.

"I wonder what it would feel like to be really helpful to someone," he said.

Jiminy lay on his sleeping bag and tried to get comfortable on the hard ground as he gazed up into the starry night sky. As his eyes scanned the many tiny points of light, one star to the south jumped out at him and seemed to shine brighter than all the rest.

"Say, is that a Wishing Star?" he wondered aloud. Since he couldn't know for certain, he decided it would be best to make a wish on it, just in case. "Wishing Star," he said, "I wish to find a place where I can make a difference and do a bit of good."

Then, his wish made, Jiminy Cricket suddenly felt a strange impulse: an urge to get up, gather his things and follow that star – the Wishing Star. He couldn't quite explain the feeling, but he felt it just the same.

So do you know what Jiminy Cricket did?

He put out the campfire. He gathered his things. And he took to the road. He followed that star all through the night. He walked for miles along highways and byways, across fields and over hills. He walked until the sun came up and he could no longer see the star to follow it. Then he made camp and he slept.

He did the same thing for several more nights and several more days.

Then, one night, he came to a village. Looking up at the Wishing Star, Jiminy Cricket noticed that it seemed to hang directly overhead.

It was very late at night as Jiminy Cricket walked into the village and looked around. Every window of every house was dark – except for one window in a shop at the end of a street. So Jiminy Cricket hopped over to the window. Peering inside, he saw that it was a woodcarver's workshop, dimly lit by the embers of a fire dying in the fireplace. It seemed a warm and pleasant place to stop for the night.

Little did Jiminy Cricket know that it was the home of Geppetto, a kind old woodcarver who had just finished work on a puppet he called Pinocchio.

And little did he know that he had just found a place where he would do more than just a bit of good.

The Hero of the Race

In a packed stadium in California, the tie-breaker race for the Piston Cup had started. But Lightning couldn't concentrate. He kept remembering the new friends he'd met in Radiator Springs. Somehow, winning was no longer that important.

Lightning had ruined the town's road when he crashed there, and been forced to stay and fix it. He'd learned how good it felt to help others. But the town's judge, Doc, had let the press know where Lightning was. Doc used to be a racing champion and didn't like young racecars like Lightning, because one had replaced him. But Doc had started to change his mind about the young racing star.

Just then, as Lightning was feeling like giving up, Doc's voice came over the radio: "I didn't come all this way to see you quit."

Lightning saw his Radiator Springs friends in his pit – with Doc as his crew chief!

"If you can drive as good as you can fix a road, then you can win this race with your eyes shut," Doc said.

Inspired by his friends, Lightning tore around the track, closing the gap. Chick Hicks tried his usual dirty tricks, but Lightning remembered what his friends had taught him. He drove backwards like Mater had taught

him; he took Doc's advice and turned right to go left. And when he blew a tyre, Guido performed a super-fast tyre change!

Lightning was winning! Chick and The King – a veteran racecar racing his final race – were fighting for second place.

Then, Chick rammed the The King! The veteran hit a wall. When Lightning saw The King's crumpled body, he remembered Doc's final crash. Lightning screeched to a stop inches from the finish line. Chick won the race.

"What are you doing, kid?" Doc asked.

"I think The King should finish his last race," Lightning answered. As he pushed The King over the finish line, the crowd erupted in cheers. Chick may have won the Piston Cup, but Lightning was the hero of the race!

Lightning was offered a great new sponsorship deal, but he politely refused, deciding to stay loyal to his original sponsor. He did ask for one favour, however....

Later, Lightning found Sally in Radiator Springs. They heard someone wildly yelling, "Wooo-hoo!" Lightning had promised his new best friend, Mater, that he'd arrange for him to fly in a helicopter, and he had done just that. Sally smiled. It looked as if the rookie racecar had found a new home.

Winnie
the
Pooh

The Mysterious Backson

One morning, Winnie the Pooh woke up to his tummy rumbling. He was certain a walk in the Hundred-Acre Wood would turn up some honey.

On his journey, Pooh passed by Eeyore and noticed that his tail was missing! The friends decided to hold a contest to find a new tail.

"It's okay," said Eeyore sadly. "I'll learn to live without it."

Pooh then stopped by Christopher Robin's house and he found a note.

Pooh brought it to Owl. "It says, 'gone out, busy Backson.'" Owl looked horrified. "Christopher Robin has been captured by a creature called the Backson!" Luckily, Rabbit came up with a clever plan to capture the Backson. Pooh and Piglet got straight to work digging a pit. Tigger decided to track the Backson on his own.

Meanwhile Pooh's tummy craved honey. He started having strange dreams. Pooh woke from his daydream in a puddle of mud!

The rest of Pooh's friends were looking everywhere for Pooh. Suddenly, they heard a loud THUD! "The plan worked!" Rabbit exclaimed. "We caught the Backson!" The friends peered into the pit, only to discover that it was Pooh! The friends tried to throw the anchor in so Pooh could climb up, but instead

they all fell in – apart from Piglet! Now Piglet had to save everyone. A terrified Piglet made his way through the Wood – until he saw a red-eyed monster glaring down at him! He realized the monster was only B'loon stuck in a tree and tugged him free.

Suddenly, an enormous shadow fell over him! "B-B-B-BACKSON!" he shouted. Holding on tight to B'loon, he ran off. But it was only Tigger dressed as a Backson. B'loon lifted Piglet up and away. As he floated down nearer the pit, he crashed into Tigger. Everyone in the pit was relieved to see Piglet and Tigger, and not the Backson. Luckily the friends were finally able to climb out. Back above ground, Christopher Robin had appeared. Pooh handed him the note. Christopher Robin explained he had written that he would be "back soon"– not "Backson"!

Relieved, the friends went on their way. Pooh was hungry for honey still. He got to Owl's front door and pulled the bell rope... and realized that it was Eeyore's tail! Pooh decided that returning Eeyore's tail was more important than satisfying his tummy.

Pooh was declared the winner of the tail contest and was presented with a big pot of honey. All his honey dreams had come true, after all!

Monster Moneymaker

As Mike and Sulley walked through the lobby of Monsters, Inc., to the Scare Floor, they passed the Scarer of the Month photos of Sulley hanging on the wall.

Mike suddenly turned to his big blue friend. "Sulley," he said, "do you ever think that we deserve a little more?"

"More?" Sulley asked.

"Oh, you know," Mike continued. "You're the top Scarer month after month. All you get is a lousy picture in the hallway, and I get nothin'. We should be famous!"

"What have you got in mind?" Sulley asked.

"A marketing campaign," Mike told him.

"How would we do that?" Sulley asked.

"Well, for starters, we'll get you some new head shots, and not just any old head shots but autographed head shots. And we won't stop there." Mike was on a roll. "We'll make mugs, posters – T-shirts even – with all your best poses." Mike demonstrated a few of his friend's Scarer poses for Sulley, including Sulley's personal favourite – the ol' Waternoose Jump and Growl. "We can set up a gift shop right here in the building featuring 'Sulley the Super Scarer' memorabilia."

"Why would we want to bother with all that?" Sulley wondered.

"Money!" Mike exclaimed, rolling his eye.

"I don't know, Mike," Sulley said. "It just doesn't seem right, us making money off these things. But what if we . . . that's it!" Sulley jumped up, nearly knocking Mike over. "We'll donate the money to charity!"

"Who said anything about donations?" Mike asked.

"That's a great idea!" Sulley said, ignoring Mike.

"How will we bask in any glory if we give the money away?" Mike asked.

"Well, we will, sort of," Sulley explained. "We'll make the donation on behalf of Monsters, Inc."

"I don't know about that," Mike said.

"It's a wonderful idea!" Sulley replied. "And when we help the company make a generous donation, Mr Waternoose will be very proud of us!"

Mike was suddenly warming to the idea. "And we'll get lots of press!" he added.

"Sure, why not?" Sulley said with a shrug.

"It's a great idea!" Mike cheered.

"I agree!" Sulley said.

"I'm glad I thought of it!" Mike gave his best friend a huge smile.

"You always have such good ideas," Sulley agreed with a grin.

"It's like I always say," Mike added. "Scaring's important, but it's the brains behind the monster that matter most!"

Making it Home

Woody, along with Sid's mutant toys, had just terrified the cruel boy by coming to life! It was all a plan to save Buzz from being blasted into space with a rocket strapped to him.

But Woody and Buzz couldn't hang around – a moving van was in front of Andy's house! If they didn't hurry, Andy would leave without them.

The two toys ran towards Andy's house. But Buzz couldn't fit through the fence because the rocket was still attached to his back. "Just go, I'll catch up," he assured Woody.

But Woody wouldn't leave without his new friend. By the time Woody helped Buzz through the fence, though, it was too late. Andy's van had driven away.

Woody and Buzz raced after the moving van. Buzz grabbed a loose strap, then climbed up onto the rear of the truck. He tried to help Woody up, too. But Sid's mean dog, Scud, raced right after them. He leapt up and dragged Woody off the van.

"Nooooo!" Buzz yelled. He jumped onto Scud's head to save Woody. Now Woody was safe, but Buzz was left behind!

Woody rummaged through the boxes in the back of the van and found RC Car. Using the remote, he sent RC back to pick up Buzz.

But Andy's toys didn't understand, and angrily threw Woody off the van! Luckily, Buzz and RC picked up Woody as they came speeding back. Finally, the other toys tried to help... but RC's batteries ran out!

Woody watched as the moving van chugged further away. Then they realized – Buzz still had the rocket on his back! Once the fuse was lit, Woody whooped.

As the rocket began to burn, RC picked up speed, zooming down the street. Buzz and Woody hung on tight as they got near the moving van. But by now, RC car was whizzing so fast, they began to lift off the ground! As they rose upwards, Woody let go of RC, who landed in the van. Buzz and Woody whooshed into the sky. Just before the rocket exploded, Buzz snapped open his space wings.

"Buzz, you're flying!" Woody exclaimed.

"This isn't flying," Buzz replied. "This is falling with style!"

Buzz and Woody glided down towards Andy's car and dropped unnoticed through the open sunroof, landing safely on the back seat. Hearing a thump, Andy looked over.

"Woody! Buzz!" Andy shouted. He hugged them close, thrilled to have his two favourite toys back.

Albatross Taxi Service

Orville the albatross was feeling low. His maintenance job at the Central Park Zoo (hours: 9–3; duties: eating all the popcorn, pretzels and half-finished hot dogs that the little children dropped) had just ended for the season. What would he do next?

Orville sighed and leaned against a lamppost at the busy junction of 45th and Broadway. He liked to watch the cars zoom back and forth. Just then there was a tap on his wing. He looked down to see an elderly mouse couple. "Excuse me, sonny," said the grandfather mouse. "Would it be possible for you to help us cross this busy street?"

Orville looked confused. "You want me to go in the middle of the street and stop traffic?"

"Perhaps you could give us a lift . . . *over* the traffic," the grandmother mouse suggested. "We'll buy you a hot dog as payment."

Mmmmm! Orville couldn't say no to the promise of a tasty hot dog with mustard and sauerkraut, so he readily agreed. Besides, it was the right thing to do, lending another animal a helping wing. "It's a deal!" he said.

Just then, the grandmother mouse whistled to a group of mice standing nearby. "Harvey, Mildred, Polly, Carl – let's go. We have a ride!"

"Wait!" Orville said. "I can't give *all* of you a ride. Just how strong do you think I am?"

"Think about it this way," said the grandfather mouse. "The more mice, the more hot dogs."

Well that was certainly true. With that in mind, Orville agreed to help all the mice across the road. It took three trips. The mice held on just a bit too tightly to Orville's feathers, and Orville's landings left something to be desired, that was certain, but soon everyone was across the road, safe and sound.

"Here are your hot dogs!" the mice said. Orville was disappointed to see that they were offering him hot dogs from the mouse hot-dog stand, which were considerably smaller than the human kind. Still, a deal was a deal, and Orville was not one to look a gift horse – or mouse – in the mouth.

Orville then found a discarded sardine tin, which he used for seats, and thus began the Albatross Taxi Service for Mice. Word spread, and soon Orville couldn't keep up with the demand! He was a very successful businessbird.

Then one day it hit him – he was selling himself short! Forget about Albatross Taxi Service – it was time to think bigger. He'd get himself a scarf and goggles and start Albatross Airlines! He sold his taxi business to an entrepreneurial pigeon and set up shop at the airport.

Now, if he could only learn how to land, everything would be perfect!

Disney
MICKEY MOUSE
Leaping Leap Year

It was a sunny morning, and Mickey and Pluto were outside playing catch. Mickey threw Pluto a ball. Pluto took a deep breath, did a fancy spin and leaped into the air to catch it.

"Nice job," Mickey said, cheering him on. "Great catch! Great leap!"

Great leap? Mickey's words echoed in his head. "Oh, my goodness, do you know what today is?" he asked Pluto.

Pluto leaped into the air again and again. He wanted Mickey to take the ball from him and toss it again.

"I almost forgot. Today is leap year!" Mickey exclaimed.

Pluto dropped the ball at Mickey's feet.

"I mean, today's not actually a year – it's a day," Mickey continued, talking to himself.

Pluto wasn't sure Mickey understood him. He wanted to play! So he leaped into the air again and again.

Leap! Leap! Leap!

Leap! Leap! Leap!

"That's the spirit!" Mickey encouraged him. "Leap year is something to be excited about! After all, it happens only once every four years. Well, almost every four years."

Mickey took a pad and pencil out of his back pocket and started working out figures. "There's a mathematical equation to figure this out if you really want to be exact." He scribbled some notes. "That's zero divided by . . . hmm, let me see here . . . carry the . . ." Mickey started blushing. "Maths is not really my thing." He put the pad back in his pocket. "Let's just say once every four years! Imagine if your birthday were on 29 February – 29 February only comes once every four years. So instead of being 12, you'd be three!" He laughed. "Just kidding . . . I think!"

Pluto sat down, panting with exhaustion, as Mickey continued explaining it to him. "Every four years, there's an extra day in the calendar – 29 February – and that's today!

"Do you know why we have leap year?" Mickey asked. "Because we have 365 days in a year, but it actually takes the earth a little longer to orbit the sun. So we have to make up for lost time!"

The excitement in Mickey's voice got Pluto excited again. He was back on his feet, tail wagging, ball in his mouth, leaping up and down.

"That's right," Mickey agreed, and joined Pluto in his leaping.

Leap! Leap! Leap!

Leap! Leap! Leap!

"Hooray!" shouted Mickey. "It's leap year!"

Winnie the Pooh

March Comes in Like a Lion

"Oh dear," said Pooh as the wind whipped around him. "It's very windy. Are you sure this is a good idea, Tigger?" He and Tigger were carrying Pooh's kite out into a clearing in the middle of the Hundred-Acre Wood.

"Don't be silly, Pooh Boy," Tigger responded. "Today is the perfect day to fly your kite. After all, what else is wind for?"

"Yes," Pooh replied. "I suppose you're right." He leaned into a particularly strong gust to keep it from blowing him over as they walked on. Winter was on its way out of the Wood, and spring was on its way in – and it seemed the wind was rushing in to fill the space in between, for it was one of the blusteriest days Pooh could remember.

At last, struggling against the wind, Pooh and Tigger reached the middle of the clearing and got ready to launch the kite. Pooh unrolled some kite string while Tigger held the kite.

"Okay, Pooh," said Tigger. "Get ready! You hold on to the string, and I'll toss the kite up into the wind. One . . . two . . . THREE!"

With that, Tigger tossed the kite and it was immediately seized by the strong wind and carried high into the air where it danced and darted this way and that.

Meanwhile, Pooh struggled to hold on to the roll of kite string.

"Let out some more string, Pooh!" Tigger suggested. "Let's see how high we can fly it!"

So Pooh let out some more string. The kite sailed higher into the air and, blown around by stronger and stronger gusts, it tugged harder and harder on Pooh's end of the line.

"Fly it higher, Pooh!" exclaimed Tigger.

So Pooh let out more and more string until he had let it all out. He clung tightly to the end of the line as the kite soared, seeming almost to touch the low clouds.

Then, all of a sudden, a tremendous gust of wind blew through the clearing. At the end of the kite string, Pooh felt his feet leave the ground as the wind grabbed hold of the kite and carried it sharply upward.

"My goodness!" said Pooh, realizing that he was being lifted up. Then, before he could be carried too high, he let go of the kite string and tumbled gently to the ground.

But the kite sailed on – up and away, dancing on the breeze for what seemed like forever, until it came to rest at last in the high branches of a very tall tree at the edge of the clearing. Pooh wondered how he would ever get it down.

"Oh well," said Tigger, patting his friend sympathetically on the back. "Guess you flew it just a little too high there, Pooh Boy."

HUNNY

Friday Night Fun

Mater looked out at all the sleeping tractors. Then, as Lightning watched, he quietly drove up to one and honked. *Beep!* The startled tractor woke up, tipped over and moaned as its wheels spun helplessly in the air.

Suddenly, headlights shone in the two friends' faces as Sheriff pulled up. "You should know better. I'll see you both in traffic court tomorrow."

The next morning at court, they were sentenced to community service.

"Why don't you help Ramone clean his shop?" Sheriff suggested.

Lightning and Mater drove over to Ramone's House of Body Art. "Well, here's the job," Ramone said as he showed them the back room. It was a mess.

"You bet," answered Lightning. A few minutes later, Mater accidentally knocked over a can of pink paint. The lid flew off, and the paint splattered Lightning.

"You sure do look purty in pink," said Mater.

"Let's see how you look in it!" shouted Lightning. He threw an open can of paint at Mater. After a few minutes, they were covered in paint! When Ramone peeked in, he got splattered, too. "Look at my shop! Out!" The friends left the shop and drove to Doc's garage.

"Boys, boys..." Doc sighed when he heard what they'd done. He gave them one last chance. "Go find Bessie and surprise Flo with a new paving job."

"This sure is a nice surprise," Flo said, when she saw Mater and Lightning. The two friends spent hours scraping up the old pavement in the hot sun.

"I'm pooped," said Lightning. "Would anyone mind if we took a little break and zipped out to the butte?"

"Wee-hoo!" shouted Mater, driving off at top speed. The friends had so much fun that they forgot all about the paving job at Flo's. By the time they remembered, it was dark.

The next morning, Mater and Lightning drove over to Flo's. Just about everyone in Radiator Springs was hard at work, trying to finish the paving job. No one had been able to drive in for their breakfast fill-up!

Mater and Lightning were embarrassed. "Sorry, everyone," the race car said. "We'll take it from here."

A couple of hours later, they were done. The V8 Café looked fantastic. Everything finally went back to normal – until Friday night rolled around again....

"Hey, buddy," whispered Mater to Lightning. "How 'bout a little tractor-tipping fun ternight?"

There's No Place Like Home

"I see you guys are getting excited about the production of *The Wizard of Oz*," said Manny.

"I think the whole town will be coming, especially since it's for a good cause," Stretch added.

"The show is a fund-raiser to pay for a swimming pool at the community centre," Rusty explained.

Just then, Mrs Hillary arrived. "Hi, Manny! Hi, tools! I brought the props for Friday's show."

"Terrific!" said Manny. "We'll install hooks in them, attach wires and then hang them over the stage for you before tonight's rehearsal."

"Wow," marvelled Dusty. "What pretty scenery you'll have for the show."

Mrs Hillary explained that the kids from the community centre had done all the work themselves.

Manny and the tools had just finished hanging up the rainbow and the clouds. Suddenly, all the lights went off. The theatre was so dark, everyone had to go outside!

"I just spoke with the electric company. We had a major power outage," Mayor Rosa announced. "Sheet Rock Hills probably won't have electricity until Sunday."

Everyone was disappointed, particularly Mrs Hillary.

"That means we can't put on the musical tomorrow!" she said.

"I'm sure we can find a way to make this work," said Manny.

"Since it's summer," said Stretch. "Why not move the show outside?"

"That's a great idea!" said Mrs Hillary. "We could stage it in the park!"

While it was still light, Manny and the tools drove around town looking for items they would need for the outdoor performance.

Soon, the park was ready. Before the show started, Mayor Rosa spoke. "If it weren't for quick thinking on the part of Manny Garcia and his tools, tonight's performance would not have been possible. Please give a round of applause to the 'wizard' of Sheet Rock Hills!"

Manny blushed as the crowd cheered.

Mayor Rosa also announced that work could now start on the new swimming pool very soon. When the show was over, the crowd cheered again.

"I'm impressed with the townspeople – they really have heart," said Turner.

"It took a lot of courage to go on without electricity," said Rusty.

Manny smiled at the tools. "Well, as Dorothy from *The Wizard of Oz* said, 'There's no place like home!'"

Disney

Lady and the TRAMP

Don't Mock Jock

Aunt Sarah had only just arrived to look after the baby while Jim Dear and Darling were away, but already her Siamese cats, Si and Am, had caused nothing but trouble. When they made a huge mess in the living room, Lady had been blamed for it, and Aunt Sarah had taken Lady to be fitted with a muzzle!

Meanwhile, left alone in the house, Si and Am had discovered the doggy door that led out to the garden.

"What works for doggies, works for kitties, too," hissed Si.

They slunk out to the garden. They dug in the flower beds, scared the birds at the birdbath and chased a squirrel up a tree.

Then they found a small hole in the garden fence. They poked their heads through the hole and spied Jock snoozing by his kennel.

"Time for a wake-up call?" said Am.

Si smiled and nodded. They squirmed through the hole and stole silently across the yard until they were sitting on either side of the sleeping Jock. Then, at the same moment, they let loose a shrill, ear-splitting yowl.

Jock awoke with a start. By the time he had identified the culprits, Si and Am were halfway across the lawn, heading for the fence.

Jock tore after them, barking. But, in a flash, the cats squirmed through the small hole and were out of Jock's reach. The opening was too small for Jock. He had to be content with sticking his head through and barking at the cats as they strolled casually up the back steps of Lady's house and through the doggy door. Then they collapsed in a laughing fit on the kitchen floor.

"Dogs are so dim-witted." Si cackled.

They waited a while, then crept out through the doggy door again, itching to try their trick once more. Peeking through the hole in the fence, they spied Jock, eyes closed, lying in front of his kennel. They squirmed through the hole and crept towards him.

But, this time, Jock was ready for them. When the cats got within five feet of him, the feisty Scottie leaped to his feet and growled. The cats gave a start, wheeled around and raced for the fence, only to find the way blocked by Jock's friend, Trusty the bloodhound, who stood, growling, between the cats and the hole.

Jock and Trusty chased Si and Am around Jock's garden until Jock was confident they had learned their lesson. Then they allowed the cats to retreat through the hole in the fence.

This time, they didn't stop running until they were up the back steps, through the doggy door, and safely inside.

And inside is where they stayed.

THE INCREDIBLES

The Parr Family

During the golden age of the Supers, Mr Incredible was the world's greatest hero. With the power of Super strength, he caught criminals, stopped disasters and protected the public from harm.

Mr Incredible's greatest fan was a boy called Buddy. He wanted to be a Super like his hero. Buddy decided to change his name to Incrediboy, and he even invented some rocket boots that allowed him to fly. He asked Mr Incredible if he could be his sidekick, but Mr Incredible told Buddy that fancy boots didn't make someone a Super. Supers were born, not made.

Mr Incredible married another Super, Elastigirl. They loved each other and the future seemed bright... until disaster struck.

People started to sue the Supers and claim they hadn't wanted to be saved! The government told the Supers to stop being heroes. They had to go into hiding and live like normal people.

So Mr Incredible became boring, average Bob Parr, and Elastigirl became Helen. They had a shy daughter, Violet, who could turn invisible and create force fields, a Super-fast son named Dash, and a baby called Jack-Jack who seemed to have no Super powers at all.

With all these Super powers, family meals could get chaotic. Controlling Super kids was tough. Helen adjusted very well to normal life and focused all her efforts on the kids. Bob worked in a boring job at an insurance company and desperately missed being a Super.

Bob couldn't stop dreaming of the past. He would occasionally give himself away by using his powers. Then the whole family had to be relocated!

One night, Bob went out with his friend Lucius. Lucius Best was known as Frozone, literally the coolest Super of all! They were tuned into the police radio, listening to reports of crimes in progress. He was hoping to save someone – just like in the good old days. When he heard about a fire at a nearby block of flats, Bob convinced Lucius they should go and help.

"We're gonna get caught," said Lucius.

The two Supers saved several people – but in order to escape the fire, they had to break into the jeweller's next door. A policeman thought they were thieves! Lucius had to use his Super powers to freeze the policeman, and the two Supers escaped.

Nearby, a mysterious woman watched them from her car... but Bob wouldn't find out who she was just yet.

Disney Bambi

Spring Has Sprung!

Spring had come at last to the forest. *Sniff, sniff* – Bambi could smell the change in the air. The days were growing longer. The nights were getting shorter. The ice and snow were quickly melting away. Crocuses and daffodils were pushing new green shoots out of the ground.

And the forest didn't feel quite as lonely as it had during the cold weather. In just the last few days, Bambi had noticed that there were more animals peeking their heads out of their holes and burrows and dens.

As he took a walk through the forest very early one morning on the first day of spring, Bambi came upon Mrs Possum and her children hanging upside down by their tails from a tree branch. She and Bambi had not seen one another in a long while. But Mrs Possum recognized him just the same.

"Well, hello, Bambi," said Mrs Possum.

"Hello, Mrs Possum," Bambi replied. "I haven't seen you since autumn. Where have you and your family been all winter long?"

"Oh, we like to spend most of our winter indoors," Mrs Possum replied. "But now that spring is here, it's so nice to be out in the fresh air again." Then Mrs Possum and the rest of her family closed their eyes and dozed off, because they liked to spend most of their days sleeping, you know.

Walking on through the forest, Bambi stopped by a tree filled with twittering birds.

"Hello, Bambi," said one of the birds.

"Hello," Bambi replied. "And where have you birds been all winter long?"

"Oh, we fly south for the winter, to warmer places where we can find more food," the bird explained. "But we are so happy it is spring once more. It is lovely to be back in the forest."

Then the bird joined her voice with her friends' twittering tunes. After so many months without it, the chirps and tweets were sweet music to Bambi's ears.

Bambi walked further, meeting old friends at every turn. He came upon mice moving from their winter quarters back into their spring and summer homes. He noticed the squirrels and chipmunks snacking leisurely on nuts, no longer storing them away in their winter stockpiles. He heard a woodpecker rapping at a pine tree. And he spotted the ducks out for a swim on the pond.

Yes, thought Bambi, it had been a long, cold, difficult winter. But somehow the arrival of spring made him feel that everything would be all right. Everywhere he looked there was life, there were new beginnings . . . and, most importantly, there was hope.

Potion Commotion

Emperor Kuzco's royal adviser, Yzma, was down in her secret laboratory, mixing potions. She had enlisted her enthusiastic but dim-witted right-hand man, Kronk, to help her in her work.

"Kronk, I need spider legs, one eye of newt and elderberry juice . . . and quickly!" Yzma directed.

"Legs, eye, juice," Kronk repeated. "Right." He hurried across the laboratory to the cupboard that contained all of Yzma's potion ingredients. Inside were hundreds of glass jars, some filled with coloured liquids and powders, others holding creepy-looking body parts of various insects and lizards.

"Let's see," Kronk said to himself as he pored over the containers. "Legs, eye, juice. Legs, eye, juice." He found the 'legs' section. "Newt legs! Check!" Kronk said to himself, confusing Yzma's instructions.

Then he found the 'eye' section. "Spider eyes! Got it!" he said, grabbing the jar. He hurried back to Yzma with the two containers.

"Kronk!" shouted Yzma. "I said spider legs and newt eye! Not newt legs and spider eye! And where's the elderberry juice? Hurry, hurry!"

Kronk hurried back to the cupboard. "Spider legs . . . newt eye . . . spider legs . . . newt eye," he recited as he went. This time, he managed to remember them and took down the right containers from the cupboard. But what was that third ingredient? "Juice!" Kronk cried. "Berry juice." He found a small vial of blueberry juice and took everything to Yzma.

"Not blueberry juice, you numbskull!" Yzma screamed. "ELDERBERRY!"

"Right," Kronk said.

He hurried back across the laboratory and quickly located the 'juice' section. "Boysenberry . . . cranberry . . ." he read, moving alphabetically through the containers.

"ELDERBERRY!" Yzma shouted at him. "Get it over here! *And step on it!*"

Kronk finally located the right bottle. "Got it!" He rushed it across the laboratory. Yzma reached out to take the bottle from him.

But Kronk didn't hand it to her. Instead, he gently placed the bottle on the floor.

Then he lifted his right foot and stomped on it – hard – shattering the bottle and splattering juice everywhere.

"KRONK!" Yzma screamed in surprise. "What are you doing?"

Kronk was confused. "I did just what you said," he explained. "I got the elderberry juice. And I stepped on it."

Yzma let loose a hair-raising scream of frustration and collapsed in a heap on the laboratory floor.

THE JUNGLE Book

The Den of Doom

"Where are we going, Baloo?" Mowgli asked. He and Baloo had been travelling through the jungle for a while now.

"Have you ever heard of the Den of Doom, Man-cub?" replied Baloo in a hushed voice.

Mowgli gasped. "The Den of Doom? They say that the Den of Doom is a giant cave filled with bears who will eat anything – or anyone! They say that those bears can hear for miles and see in the dark! They say that even Shere Khan is afraid of them!" he exclaimed.

"Mmm-hmm," said Baloo. "They do say that. They *also* say that all of the bears in the Den of Doom are over eight feet tall, that their teeth are green and razor-sharp, and that their battle cry is so loud that the whales in the ocean hear it and shake with fright. They say all that, and much, much more."

"And we're *going* there?" Mowgli squeaked. "We can't! Baloo, those bears aren't like you! They're dangerous!"

"Too late, Man-cub," Baloo said with a grin. "We're already there!" He picked up Mowgli, whose knees were knocking together so hard he could barely stand, and strode right into a thicket. The bear ducked under a huge palm frond and emerged into a large, sunlit clearing in front of an enormous cave. Baloo put Mowgli down. The boy looked around in complete and utter surprise.

Mowgli had expected to see hundreds of fierce, angry bears. Instead, he saw hundreds of relaxed, happy bears having a really good time. Bears were swimming in a small pond, splashing and laughing. Bears were resting in the cool shadows of the cave. Bears were playing tag out in the clearing and chomping on piles of ripe, delicious fruit. It was, in short, a bear party.

"I don't understand," Mowgli said to Baloo. "This is the Den of Doom?"

"Yep," Baloo said happily, grabbing a palm frond and fanning himself with it. "It used to be called the Den of Delights, but we had to change the name. See, everyone in the jungle knew that the Den of Delights was the most fun place around. We bears never turned anyone away from our party. But then it got so crowded that it just wasn't any fun any more. So we spread a few rumours, changed the name, and presto – it's the Den of Doom! Now no one bothers us bears any more."

"But what about me?" Mowgli said anxiously. "I'm not a bear."

"You're an honorary bear, Mowgli," Baloo replied with a smile. "You sure have enough fun to be one!"

DUMBO

Float Like a Butterfly

One day, Dumbo's best friend, Timothy Q. Mouse, found Dumbo looking sad. "What's the matter, little guy?" the mouse asked the elephant. "Have people been teasing you about your ears again?"

Dumbo nodded. The little elephant looked totally miserable.

Timothy shook his head. The two were very good friends and did everything together. He didn't mind one bit that Dumbo had large ears. In fact, he thought they were great.

Timothy was trying to think of a way to cheer up his dear friend. And then he saw something. "Look, Dumbo!" he cried, racing over to a nearby fence post. Hanging from the fence was a large cocoon. "It's a butterfly cocoon!" Timothy said excitedly.

Dumbo came over to examine it.

"And look – it's about to hatch into a butterfly," said Timothy. He looked thoughtful for a moment, and then he turned to Dumbo. "You know what? You are a lot like the little caterpillar that made this cocoon."

Dumbo looked at Timothy quizzically.

"Yep, it's true. You see, a caterpillar is something nobody really wants around much. They think it's kind of plain looking, and it can't really do anything very interesting. But then one day, the caterpillar turns into a beautiful butterfly, and everyone loves it. And you know what? I think you're going to be that way, too. When you get older, everyone is going to admire you rather than tease you!"

Dumbo smiled gratefully at his friend, and wiped away a tear with one of his long ears.

Suddenly, it started to rain. "Oh no!" cried Timothy. "The butterfly is going to get its new wings all wet. It won't be able to fly if it gets rained on. What'll we do? We need an umbrella!"

As Timothy looked this way and that for an umbrella, Dumbo smiled and unfurled his long ears. He draped them over the fence post so that they made a lovely roof for the insect, protecting it from the falling droplets of rain.

"Great idea!" said Timothy admiringly. The two friends stood there during the downpour, which didn't last very long. While they waited, they watched the beautiful new butterfly emerge from its cocoon and unfurl its colourful wings. When the rain stopped, the butterfly spread its wings (which were quite dry, thanks to Dumbo) and flew away.

"You know, my friend," said Timothy as they watched it fly away, "I think someday you're going to be a big success. You'll be like that butterfly – happy, carefree and floating along. Well, not floating for real, that's impossible. Imagine that, a flying elephant!"

Homesick

Nemo still couldn't believe everything that had happened to him. First, he'd been snatched up by a scuba diver in the ocean. Then, he'd travelled a long way in a big water cooler. Finally, he'd been dumped in a fish tank in a dentist's office. The other fish in the tank seemed nice, but Nemo missed his dad and his old home. He couldn't think about anything except getting back to the ocean. But would their plan to escape really work? It seemed hopeless . . . .

"Hey, kid," Bloat the blowfish swam over to him. "Are you okay? You look a little down in the gills."

"I'll say," said Nigel the seagull.

Peach the starfish glanced over from her spot on the tank wall. "He's just upset," she said. "It's only natural." She smiled kindly at Nemo. "It's okay, hon. We know how you feel."

"How could you know?" he muttered, feeling sorry for himself. "You weren't grabbed out of the ocean, away from your dad."

"Well, no," a fish named Gurgle admitted. "But we all had families back where we came from. We all miss them."

"Really?" Nemo blinked in surprise. He hadn't thought about that.

"Sure," Peach said. "The lady who sold me over the Internet kept lots of us starfish in her basement." She sighed sadly. "I still wonder where all my brothers and sisters ended up. I'd give two or three of my arms to see them again."

"I hear you," Bloat agreed. "I was hatched in somebody's garage. They sold me and a whole school of my brothers and sisters and cousins to Bob's Fish Mart. Just when we made friends with the other fish there, he came in and bought me." He waved a fin towards the dentist in the office outside the tank. "It could be worse, though," Bloat continued. "You guys are the best friends I've ever had."

A fish named Deb nodded. "I'm lucky he bought me and my sister together. Right, Flo?" She smiled at her own reflection in the glass of the tank. When the reflection didn't answer, Deb shrugged. "I guess Flo is too choked up to talk right now. But I can tell by her smile that she agrees. We don't know what we'd do without each other. But we still miss the rest of our family."

"Wow," Nemo said, looking around at his new tankmates. "I guess you guys *do* know how I feel."

Even though he was sad that the other fish had been taken from their families, it made Nemo feel a little less alone. At least they understood how much he wanted to find his way back to his father. Now, a little braver and more determined than ever, Nemo was ready to escape from the tank – no matter what.

THE LION KING

Just Like Dad

"Dad, when I grow up, I want to be just like you," Simba said to his father.

Mufasa nuzzled his son's head gently. "All in good time, son," he said.

Just then, Simba's friend Nala bounded up to them. "Come on, Simba!" she called. "Let's go play by the river!"

On their way, Simba stopped abruptly. "Listen to this," he said. He threw back his head and roared as loudly as he could. Then he looked at her expectantly. "Do I sound like my dad?"

Nala tried unsuccessfully to suppress a giggle. "Not quite," she said.

Soon they reached the river. The waters were high as a result of the recent rains. Simba found a quiet pool at the side and stared down at his reflection. "Do you think my mane is starting to grow?" he asked Nala.

Nala sighed. "Maybe a little," she replied. "But, Simba, what's the big rush? Let's just have fun being young!"

Simba was eyeing a tree branch that extended over the raging river. "Well, I may not be as big as my dad yet, but at least I'm as brave as he is!" he shouted, and raced up to the tree. Climbing its gnarled trunk, he began walking along the branch over the water.

Nala hurried over. She heard a loud crack. "Simba!" she yelled. "Come back here! The branch is going to break!"

But Simba couldn't hear her over the loud waters. Nala bounded away to get help.

Simba felt the branch begin to sag. "Uh-oh," he said to himself. Suddenly the whole thing broke off and Simba tumbled into the water. The current was strong, and he struggled to swim towards the shore. He was running out of strength, and he realized he might not make it.

Then he felt himself being lifted out of the water and tossed onto the bank. Dripping and coughing, he looked up – right into the angry eyes of his father.

"Simba!" thundered Mufasa. "There's a big difference between being brave and being foolish! The sooner you learn that, the better chance you will have of growing old!"

Simba hung his head. Out of the corner of his eye, he saw Nala, pretending not to overhear. "I'm . . . sorry, Dad," he said softly. "I just wanted to be brave like you."

His father's gaze softened. "Well," he said. "As long as we're soaking wet, why don't we go to a quieter part of the river and do some swimming?" He looked over to where Nala was sitting. "Come on, Nala!" he called. "Come with us!"

"Yippee!" cried the cubs, and they all went off together.

Disney

Peter Pan

Pixie Play

"What do you say, Tink? Can you get it?" asked Peter Pan.

Peter and Tinker Bell were floating high above the streets of London, right outside a large open window. Inside, three children were sleeping soundly.

Tinker Bell made a confident, jingling sound.

"All right, then. In you go!" said Peter.

Tink darted through the window. Then, leaving behind a trail of pixie dust, she flitted around the nursery searching for Peter's missing shadow.

When Peter had last visited this house, the children's nurse, Nana, had spied him outside the nursery window. She tried to grab him, but all she got was his shadow. Tonight, Peter had come to get his shadow back. He knew it wouldn't be easy, because Nana was a Saint Bernard dog. And Peter knew it was easy to fool children but hard to fool a dog. So, for this job, he needed a fairy's help.

Peter watched as Tinker Bell flew around the nursery. First, she flew over the eldest child, Wendy Darling, and then her two younger brothers, John and Michael. All three kept right on sleeping.

But, when Tinker Bell flew over Nana, the dog awoke with a sneeze! Tinker Bell's pixie dust had tickled Nana's nose.

"Woof! Woof!" barked Nana, trying to grab the fairy. All of a sudden the poor dog's feet couldn't find the floor. The pixie-dust magic had lifted her up. Now Nana was floating around the room!

When Peter heard Nana bark, he raced inside. Then he saw Nana floating and started to laugh.

Suddenly, the pixie dust wore off, and Nana's paws hit the floor again. With an angry growl, the dog charged at Peter Pan!

"Yikes!" Peter cried, darting through the window with Tinker Bell right behind him.

"Back to Never Land, Tink!" said Peter. "We'll get my shadow back tomorrow night."

On a twinkling trail of light, Peter and Tinker Bell soared into the sky and vanished.

Back inside the nursery, Wendy suddenly woke up. "What's this!" she cried, touching the window. Her hand sparkled with pixie dust.

"Peter Pan must have come back, looking for his shadow. I'm sorry I missed him," Wendy told Nana with a frown of disappointment.

"Woof! Woof!" said Nana.

"Yes, I know," Wendy replied. "Time for me to go back to bed."

But, as Nana licked Wendy's cheek good night, Wendy promised herself that she would be ready to meet the remarkable Peter Pan the next time he paid her a visit!

THE JUNGLE BOOK

Bagheera Bears Up

Mowgli danced around, humming happily to himself.

"What are you doing, Mowgli?" Bagheera asked from his perch in a nearby tree.

"Practising being a bear," Mowgli told him. "You should try it."

"Me?" Bagheera said, stunned. "I couldn't possibly do such a thing."

"Why not?" Mowgli wanted to know.

"Well, I'm a panther and I happen to like being one," Bagheera replied. "Why on earth would I want to be a bear?"

"Are you kidding?" Mowgli exclaimed. "Bears have the life! They hang out all day long, and they eat ants!"

"Eat ants?" Bagheera asked. "And that's a good thing?"

"Sure!" Mowgli said. "Well, truthfully, they tickle your throat at first. But you get used to it soon enough."

"Have you?" Bagheera asked.

"Not yet," Mowgli confessed. "But I will!"

"Whatever you say, Mowgli," said Bagheera.

Mowgli thought for a moment. "And if you were a bear, you would eat fruit and drink coconut juice, and you would relax, just like us!"

"If you ask me," Bagheera said. "I don't see anything so bad about being a panther. In fact, I like it very much."

"I think you're scared," Mowgli told him.

"Absolutely not!" Bagheera protested. "What on earth would I have to be scared of?" He stood up, stretched and gracefully jumped out of the tree and onto the ground.

"Exactly," Mowgli said. "So, why not try it?"

"You've got to be kidding me!" Bagheera said.

"You know what your problem is?" Mowgli said.

"I'm afraid to ask," Bagheera said.

"You're like a beehive," Mowgli told him. "You work too hard." He stared at Bagheera. "Come on, dance with me!" he cried, grabbing Bagheera's paw and prancing around the panther. After a bit, Bagheera began to dance too, moving his feet and twitching his tail.

"That's it!" Mowgli cheered.

"You know what?" Bagheera admitted. "This isn't so bad after all."

"Now you're getting it!" Mowgli exclaimed. "Now you see why being a bear is so great!" The Man-cub stopped dancing and threw himself on a soft patch of moss. "It's not so bad, is it?"

"Actually," Bagheera said, scratching his back against a rock, "it's sort of fun!"

"One more time!" Mowgli cheered, and they began dancing again.

Red's Tune-Up Blues

One morning, Red the fire engine thought it was the perfect day to plant a garden. He started his engine. *Rrrrrr.* Red's engine sounded funny. *Pop! Pop! Pop!* Now loud noises were coming out of his tailpipe.

As his engine sputtered, Red tried to shrug it off. Hopefully, whatever was wrong would go away, because Red did not want to go to Doc's clinic. He sure didn't like the idea of being poked and prodded. Instead, he headed into town to work on his garden, and soon passed Lightning McQueen.

"Hey, Red!" Lightning greeted him. "How's it going?"

"Fine," Red replied shyly. *Bang! Bang!*

"Whoa!" exclaimed Lightning. "That can't feel good. You okay?"

"Mmm-hmm," said Red.

Pop! Red continued driving towards town. Lightning headed into town, too, to find his friends. They wouldn't want Red to be sick. Lightning found the others at Flo's V8 Café, filling up on breakfast.

"Red's not running right," Lightning explained as he pointed to the fire engine, who was starting to plant a garden across the street. "But he's afraid to go to the clinic."

"Aw, shucks," said Mater the tow truck. "I know how the poor fella feels. I was scared my first time, too! But Doc's a pro. He'll have Red fixed up before he knows what hit him!"

The friends tried to convince Red to visit Doc. Ramone offered a new coat of paint at his House of Body Art, but nothing would convince Red to go.

"We had better get over there," Lightning said to Sally, who had just rolled up. The two cars sped over. Mater, Luigi, Guido, Fillmore and Flo followed.

Bang! Pop, pop, pop! Red's engine gurgled and more loud noises came out of his tailpipe.

Sally inched forwards. "Listen, Red. We all know going to get a tune-up for the first time can be scary. But whatever is wrong could be easy to fix. If you don't go now, it could turn into a bigger problem later. None of us wants you to need a complete overhaul. We care too much about you."

Red looked back at his friends. He knew what Sally said was true "Will you go with me?" he asked Sally.

"Of course I will," she replied.

Later that day, Red rolled out of the clinic and all his friends were waiting for him. Red revved his engine. *Vroom!* It sounded smooth as silk. It was great to be running on all cylinders again!

GREAT MOUSE DETECTIVE

Basil Saves the Day

It was Olivia Flaversham's birthday, and she was celebrating with her father. Suddenly, there was a knock on the door. It was late, and Mr Flaversham felt uneasy. He told Olivia to stay in a cabinet. Olivia peeked out and saw a scary bat. Soon she heard a commotion and ran out. But Olivia's father had been kidnapped!

Meanwhile, Dr David Q Dawson had just travelled to London. He heard someone weeping.

"Are you all right, my dear?" asked Dawson. Olivia explained she was looking for Basil, the great mouse detective.

"Come with me," said Dawson. "We'll find him together." The two mice soon found Basil and explained that Olivia needed help finding her father. Basil knew that the bat, named Fidget, was employed by his arch enemy, Professor Ratigan!

Later that evening, Basil paced back and forth. Just then, Olivia screamed! Fidget had appeared in the window. Basil, Olivia and Dawson raced outside and followed him to a toyshop. Basil noticed that mechanical parts were missing from many of the toys. Olivia wandered over to a pretty doll cradle. Curious, she peeked inside. Suddenly, Fidget jumped out and stuffed her into a bag and flew away! Now they had to save Olivia and her father!

Dawson showed him a piece of paper that Fidget had left behind. He discovered it came from the riverfront. They went there, spotted Fidget and followed the bat all the way to Ratigan's secret lair.

But Basil had walked right into a trap! Ratigan tied Basil and Dawson to a mousetrap. Ratigan left. He was sure the mice wouldn't escape.

Basil thought hard. He calculated the timing of the trap and came up with a brilliant idea that would save them.

"Ready… steady… now!" yelled Basil to Dawson. They escaped!

Basil and Dawson found Olivia and raced to Buckingham Palace. There they discovered what Ratigan was up to: he had forced Olivia's father to build a robot replica of the queen. Then Ratigan had replaced Queen Moustoria with the robot.

A huge crowd was listening to the robot queen. It was announcing that Professor Ratigan was her new royal consort! The crowd gasped in horror.

Offstage, Basil and Dawson finally took control of the robot queen. Ratigan's plan was foiled!

Basil rushed onstage and yelled, "Arrest that fiend!" Ratigan was defeated. Best of all, Olivia and her father were reunited.

Buzz's Backpack Adventure

It was space day at school, and Andy couldn't wait to get there. He put Buzz in his backpack and set off for school.

In class, the teacher taught Andy and the other students about the solar system. *Brring!* The lunch bell rang. Andy and his friends went to eat lunch. Once they were gone, Buzz stepped out of the backpack. He saw models of the stars and planets hanging from the ceiling. Then he spotted a large cage. A hamster was inside, but Buzz hadn't seen one before. "Greetings, strange creature," he said. When the hamster didn't reply, Buzz lifted the lid off the cage so he could go inside.

Just then, the hamster jumped out of the cage! It ran into Buzz and sent him flying. Luckily, Buzz noticed some planets dangling in the air above him. He quickly grabbed onto one so he wouldn't fall. Then, all of a sudden, Buzz lost his grip – and fell into a jug of water!

Once Buzz had climbed out of the jug and dried off, he looked inside the students' desks. He found old chewing gum, broken yo-yos and mouldy sandwiches but no sign of the hamster. He put down the desktop and made his way over to a table. There, he spotted some creatures from space! Or at least, he thought they were from space. They were actually aliens that Andy and his friends had made from clay.

"Greetings," Buzz said. "Have you seen a strange, furry creature?" When the clay aliens didn't answer, Buzz shook hands with one of them to show that he was friendly. Its arm fell off.

"Sorry about that!" Buzz cried. He set the arm down and jumped off the table... straight onto a tower of blocks! Oops, Buzz thought as it wobbled back and forth. Then – *crash!* – the tower came tumbling down.

Buzz noticed that the classroom was a mess. Paint and blocks were all over the place, and the hamster was still on the loose. Buzz knew he had to clean up – and fast!

Brring! The bell rang just as he was stepping back into Andy's backpack. Buzz looked at the cleaned-up classroom. No one will ever know what happened, he thought.

When the class returned, it was time for show-and-tell. "This is Buzz," Andy said. "He's the best space ranger ever!"

Suddenly, Andy's classmates pointed at the chalkboard ledge. The hamster was sitting on it. "How did you get out?" the teacher asked as she brought it back to its cage. The hamster smiled at Buzz. He smiled back. He couldn't wait to tell Woody and the others about his exciting day....

St Patrick's Day Switcheroo!

Huey, Dewey and Louie were getting dressed one morning when Louie had an idea.

"Hey," he said to his brothers, "are you two wearing green for St Patrick's Day?"

"Yes, of course," said Dewey.

"Me too," said Huey.

"Well," replied Louie, gesturing at the green shirt and hat that he wore every day, "then I bet we could really confuse our Unca Donald!"

Huey and Dewey both smiled as they contemplated Louie's sneaky idea.

"He's so used to seeing me wearing red . . ." said Huey.

"And me wearing blue . . ." said Dewey.

"That if he doesn't look closely," said Louie, "he'll be totally confused!"

The three of them chuckled as they headed towards the kitchen. Then, while Huey and Dewey hid in the hallway, Louie walked in and sat down next to Donald Duck, who was reading the newspaper at the breakfast table.

"Morning, Unca Donald," said Louie.

"Morning, Louie," Donald replied. "Will you go get your brothers? Breakfast is ready."

"Okay," Louie replied, leaving the room.

Next, Dewey walked into the kitchen and sat down. "Morning, Unca Donald," he said.

Donald looked up only briefly from his paper. "I thought I told you to go get your brothers, Louie," he said.

"No, you didn't," Dewey replied. "And I'm not Louie."

Donald looked up and scrutinized Dewey's face. "Oh," he said. "I'm sorry, Dewey. Go get your brothers, would you?"

"Okay," Dewey replied.

A few minutes later, Huey walked into the kitchen and sat down at the table.

Donald glanced up from the newspaper. "Well, where are they?" he asked Huey impatiently.

"Where are who?" said Huey.

"Your brothers," Donald replied. "I asked you to go get them."

"No, you didn't," said Huey.

"Yes, I – " Donald looked up from the paper and stared at Huey hard. "Oh . . . Huey," he said, realizing his mistake. "I thought you were . . . hey!" Donald looked at Huey suspiciously. "Are you three trying to confuse me? Is that why you're all wearing the same thing?"

Huey looked up at Donald with a blank stare. "Whatever do you mean, Unca Donald?"

"It's St Patrick's Day," said Louie, coming in from the hallway.

"Yeah," said Dewey, following Louie into the kitchen. "That's why we're all wearing green. Happy St Patrick's Day, Unca Donald!"

Happy Mother's Day!

One fine May day, Roo hopped over to Winnie the Pooh's house.

"I have a problem," Roo told Pooh. "Mother's Day is almost here, and I don't know what to give my mama. Do you have any ideas?"

"Let me think," said Pooh. He thought very hard (or at least as hard as a bear of very little brain can think). "Think, think, think. A gift for Mother's Day . . . ."

Luckily, Pooh spotted a big pot of honey sitting in his cupboard. "That's it!" he cried. "Mothers like *honey*!"

"They do?" asked Roo.

"Doesn't everybody?" Pooh asked.

So Pooh gave Roo a small pot of honey. Roo bounced over to Rabbit's house next.

As usual, Rabbit was working in his garden. "Hello, Roo," he said. "What's in the pot?"

"It's honey," Roo explained. "To give to my mama on Mother's Day."

Rabbit frowned. "No, no, no," he said. "Mothers don't like honey. If there's one thing a mother wants to get on Mother's Day, it's a big bunch of fresh carrots."

"They do?" Roo said doubtfully.

"Oh, yes," said Rabbit. He reached into his wheelbarrow and pulled out a bunch of freshly picked carrots.

"Thanks, Rabbit," said Roo. Then he hopped to Eeyore's house of sticks.

"What do you have there, Roo?" Eeyore asked.

"Some gifts for my mama for Mother's Day," said Roo.

"I suppose some mothers might like carrots," Eeyore said. "And maybe others might like honey. But, in my opinion, you can't go wrong with prickly thistles."

"Prickly thistles?" asked Roo.

"Yes," replied Eeyore. "Here, take these. Then Kanga will be sure to have a happy Mother's Day. If that's what she wants."

"Well, thank you," said Roo, tucking the prickly thistles into his pocket and heading for home. He thought about his gifts as he ate his dinner. He wondered which gift to give his mother as he put on his pajamas and brushed his teeth.

The next morning, bright and early, Roo bounded into the living room. "Happy Mother's Day, Mama!" he shouted.

"Why, thank you, dear," said Kanga.

"I thought and thought about what to give you," Roo explained. "Pooh said honey. Rabbit said carrots. And Eeyore said thistles. But I decided to give you this," he said, throwing his arms around his mama.

Kanga smiled. "Thank you, Roo. That's the best Mother's Day gift of all."

The Sweetest Songs of All

"Why is Quasimodo so sad?" asked Hugo. "Judge Frollo has commanded that he never leave Notre Dame Cathedral," answered Victor. "He's lonely because he has no friends."

"But I'm his pal. And so are you," Hugo said.

"We're made of stone," Victor said. "Quasimodo needs living friends."

"But gargoyles make great friends!" Hugo exclaimed. "We're always there, and you can't break our hearts, because they're hard as rock!"

"Hush! Here he comes now," said Victor.

"Good morning, Quasi!" Hugo cried. "Nice day for ringing bells."

"I guess so," Quasimodo replied, staring at the people far below.

"Cheer up! What do they have down there that we don't have up here?" Hugo asked.

Quasimodo frowned. "I don't know, because I've never been there. But I hear people laughing and singing."

Then Victor spoke. "The sweetest songs of all can be heard in this tower, if you do what I tell you to."

"I will!" Quasimodo cried.

"It will take a long time, so you must be patient," warned Victor.

"I will! I will!" Quasimodo promised.

"Then fetch a piece of firewood and a knife from the kitchen," Victor commanded.

Quasimodo quickly returned with both.

"I want you to carve a statue of a dove," said Victor.

Quasimodo nodded. For two days, he worked. On the third day, he showed Hugo his first carving.

"Wow, that really looks like a dove," said Hugo.

"I'm going to carve a finch tomorrow," Quasimodo vowed.

For many weeks, Quasimodo carved hundreds of birds out of wood. Larks and thrushes and robins and sparrows. Each statue was better than the last. He worked so hard that he nearly forgot he was lonely.

Finally, he showed Victor and Hugo a carving of a beautiful nightingale.

"It is your best work of all," said Victor.

Quasimodo was so proud that he set his bird on the highest tower so they could all admire it.

The next morning, he was surprised to see two real birds perched next to his statue. More birds soon arrived. Some even built nests. Soon, hundreds and hundreds of birds lived in Notre Dame. They woke Quasimodo with their songs in the morning. They sang him to sleep at night.

As Victor said, the sweetest songs of all had come to Notre Dame. Since that day, birds have always lived in Notre Dame Cathedral.

Yard Sale

"Hey, Woody! Ready to go to Cowboy Camp?" Andy shouted, bursting into the bedroom.

Woody the cowboy doll was very excited about cowboy camp, though he couldn't show his feelings to Andy. Toys were supposed to stay very still whenever people could see them.

Andy had a few spare minutes before he had to leave for camp, so he grabbed Woody and Buzz, his two favourite toys, for a quick adventure.

"Never tangle with the unstoppable duo of Woody and Buzz Lightyear!" he proclaimed, linking the toys' arms together.

Suddenly, there was a loud *RIIIPPPP!*

Woody's shoulder had ripped open!

Andy's mum suggested fixing Woody on the way to camp, but Andy shook his head and sighed. "No, just leave him."

"I'm sorry," his mum replied. "But you know toys don't last forever."

Woody sat on the shelf and watched sadly as Andy left for cowboy camp without him. He couldn't believe it.

Woody didn't feel any better when he found Wheezy, an old toy penguin who'd been sitting broken and forgotten on the shelf for months.

Was that Woody's future, too?

Suddenly, the toys spotted something truly terrifying – Andy's mum was putting up a sign outside: YARD SALE!

Andy's mum came into Andy's bedroom looking for some items to sell. And she chose Wheezy as one of the sale items!

Thinking quickly, Woody waited until Andy's mum was out of sight, then whistled loudly for Buster, Andy's friendly – and helpful – puppy.

Together, Woody and Buster sneaked outside, grabbed Wheezy, and headed back to safety. But because his arm was injured, Woody lost his grip and tumbled to the ground!

Just then, a strange man noticed Woody, picked him up... and stole him! From their upstairs window, the other toys watched in horror as the man threw Woody into the boot of his car.

Buzz couldn't let Woody be taken away so easily, so he jumped out of the window and slid down the drainpipe, racing to rescue his friend – but he was too late. All Buzz saw was the car's license plate, LZTYBRN, and a few feathers floating in the air.

Buzz was horrified. He decided there and then, he would do everything he could to rescue his friend and bring him back home.

Smitten

Robin Hood straightened his hat and smoothed his whiskers. "How do I look, Little John?" he asked.

"You look like you always do," John replied with a wave of his hand. "Like a regular Casanova."

Robin grinned. "Let's hope Maid Marian agrees with you." He put a hand over his heart. "I just hope she still remembers me."

"Quit mooning and get going, Rob," Little John said. "The day isn't getting any longer."

"Right, right," Robin agreed. But the truth was, he felt a little nervous. Maid Marian was the cleverest and most beautiful maid in the land. And she'd been in London for several years. What if she didn't remember her childhood sweetheart?

"Get going," Little John repeated.

Robin nodded and set off through the forest. He had to be careful, because Prince John had declared him an outlaw. If he or any of his men saw him, Robin would be thrown into jail. Or worse.

"She's worth it," Robin told himself as he hurried towards the castle.

Soon Robin was outside the castle gate. He could hear voices – female voices – laughing and talking. Maybe one of them was Marian's!

Robin's heart pounded in his chest. He had to see! He looked around and spotted a large tree with branches that reached inside the castle grounds. Perfect!

Robin leaped gracefully up to the first branch, grabbed hold and began to climb. When he was nice and high, he worked his way out on a branch. Now he was inside the castle grounds. And, if he moved a few leafy branches aside . . . .

Robin moved a branch and leaned forwards to see who was talking. It was Marian! She was playing badminton with Lady Cluck. And she was a good shot!

"Nice one, Maid Marian," Lady Cluck said, as Marian won a point.

Robin gazed down at the sight below. Marian was so lovely, and so talented!

"Oops!" Marian said as the shuttlecock sailed off the court completely.

Robin saw it fly towards his hiding place. It landed in the tree just above him! Determined to get it for Marian, he got to his feet and reached up. But he lost his balance and fell just as the shuttlecock came loose. The two landed on the ground at the same time.

"Ooof!" Robin didn't mean to make an entrance like this!

"What was that?" Lady Cluck asked as Robin scrambled away and leaped over the fence.

"I do believe it was an outlaw," Maid Marian said with a smile.

Bird Trouble

It was the height of the rainy season, and the roof of the ant colony had sprung a leak. "Bucket brigade!" shouted Princess Atta. The ants obediently lined up and began catching the water in cupped leaves, passing them along the length of the line and dumping them into the stream. It was exhausting, but the ants were used to hard work.

"There's got to be an easier way," Flik said. "Tomorrow I'm going to invent a way to fix the roof!"

"What are you doing, Flik?" Dot asked the next morning. The rain had let up for a moment, and the two were outside. Flik had arranged dozens of torn pieces of leaves along one side of the sloping roof.

"I'm fixing the leak," he said cheerfully. "See, these leaves act as rain deflectors. Then the water will run into these hollowed-out flower stems that will act as gutters."

"Wow," said Dot. She was the only ant who thought Flik's inventions were worthwhile.

"The only thing I'm missing is some sort of deflection device for the ant hole itself," he said. "Aha!" he shouted a moment later. He had spotted a buttercup. "That flower should work perfectly. Come on, Dot. Give me a hand. Boy, oh, boy, is this invention ever going to impress the Princess!"

Together, the two ants dragged the buttercup to the top of the anthill.

"What on earth are you two doing?" It was Princess Atta.

"Flik figured out a way to fix the leak!" shouted Dot triumphantly.

Flik shrugged modestly. "It's very simple, really. See, what I did was . . ."

Suddenly, the ant lookout began shouting, "Bird! Bird! Bird coming!"

Flik, Atta and Dot ran for cover. Sure enough, a hummingbird was hovering just above the anthill.

"It's going for the flower!" shouted an ant. The hummingbird pressed its long beak into the buttercup Flik had dragged over the anthill.

"Avalanche!" shouted the ants. The delicately built anthill began to collapse. Ants scrambled to get out of the way. The bird flew off.

"Nice work, Flik," said Princess Atta. "This is going to take weeks to rebuild."

Flik sighed and hung his head.

"Don't worry, Flik," whispered Dot. "Someday you'll do great things."

"Oh, you're sweet, Dot," Flik said sadly. "If only it hadn't been for that bird. I should have known it would like the flower. Birds are so predictable." Now Flik looked thoughtful. "Maybe someday I could use that to my advantage."

Flik smiled at Dot. "Imagine that," he said. "An ant using a bird in his plan!"

Aladdin

Monkey See, Monkey Do

"Come on, Abu!" Aladdin called across the busy Agrabah marketplace.

From his perch on top of the basket-seller's cart, Abu barely heard the call. He was captivated by the monkey he had just spotted peeking out at him from behind the fruit-seller's cart. Abu jumped off the basket cart and darted over to say hello.

But the other monkey scurried away and hid behind a wheel. From his new hiding place, he peeked out at Abu.

Abu looked around, trying to think of a way to draw out the monkey. The fruit seller was distracted, talking to a customer, so Abu hopped up onto the cart and picked up an apple. He balanced it on top of his head. Then he scurried over to the edge of the cart and peered down, hoping to attract the monkey's attention.

But he was gone.

Abu heard monkey chatter behind him. He turned around to find the monkey standing at the other end of the fruit cart, balancing an apple on *his* head, just like Abu.

Abu laughed and picked up a pear and an orange. He began juggling them in the air, hoping to amuse the other monkey.

But the other monkey didn't look amused. He looked annoyed! He thought Abu was trying to show him up. Not to be outdone, the

monkey also picked up a pear and an orange and began to juggle them, just like Abu.

Abu put the fruit down. He did a handstand on the cart railing.

The other monkey did a handstand too.

Abu grabbed hold of the cart awning, then flipped over and swung from the awning by his tail.

The other monkey did the same.

Abu laughed again. He thought this game was fun. But now he wanted to find a stunt that the other monkey couldn't copy. Abu looked around. He spotted Aladdin coming his way.

Abu had an idea. He jumped off the fruit cart, darted over to Aladdin and scrambled up the length of his friend's body until he was lounging comfortably on top of Aladdin's head.

The other monkey stared in amazement. He didn't know that Aladdin was Abu's friend. How could he copy that stunt? He looked around. The closest human was the fruit seller. Throwing caution to the wind, the other monkey scurried over to him – but he'd only climbed as high as the fruit-seller's shoulder before the man chased him away.

Then, from behind the basket cart, the other monkey crossed his arms, pouted and watched that sneaky Abu laugh and wave good-bye as he was carried away on top of Aladdin's head.

Woody's Roundup Gang

Woody had tried to save Wheezy from being sold at Andy's mum's yard sale, but had ended up being stolen by a stranger!

The man brought Woody to a high-rise flat, and posed him inside a glass case. Then, to Woody's surprise, the toy-napper put on a chicken suit! He spoke to someone on the phone, then glanced at Woody and chuckled. "You, my little cowboy friend, are gonna make me big buck-buck-bucks!" he laughed.

Once he was alone, Woody ran to the door to escape. But it was no use. He was trapped.

POP! A cardboard box suddenly burst open, and Woody was knocked off his feet by a galloping toy horse.

"Yee-haw! It's really you!" shouted a cowgirl, squeezing Woody in a big hug. The cowgirl said her name was Jessie, and the horse was Bullseye. Then she introduced the Prospector, a mint condition toy who had never been out of his box.

"We've waited countless years for this day," said the Prospector.

Woody couldn't understand how the other toys recognized him. "How do you know my name?" he asked.

Bullseye dimmed the lights to reveal that the room was filled with items showing Woody's picture: posters, magazines and toys. Woody couldn't believe it! Then Jessie showed him an old TV show, *Woody's Roundup* – Woody was the star!

Woody laughed as he, Jessie and Bullseye looked at all the *Woody's Roundup* things.

"Now it's on to the museum!" the Prospector exclaimed.

"What museum?" Woody was confused.

The Prospector explained that the *Roundup* toys had become valuable. Al planned to sell the them, as a set, to a Japanese museum for a lot of money.

Woody told Jessie he couldn't go to the museum because he had to get back to Andy.

Jessie sadly explained that she had had an owner once, too – a little girl named Emily, who used to play with her all the time. But as Emily grew up, she played with Jessie less and less. Finally, she abandoned Jessie.

"You never forget kids like Emily or Andy," said Jessie. "But they forget you."

Woody began to worry that Andy would forget about him one day, too. Should he take his chance? Should he let Al take him to the museum? Perhaps he should....

Ka-choww!

"I am speed!" Lightning McQueen chanted as he focused on the dirt track stretched out in front of him. "Is my pit crew ready?"

"Standing by," said Luigi. "Tyres ready!"

VAAA-ROOOOM! Lightning revved his engine – and took off!

"Woo-hooo!" he shouted. "It sure is great to zip around this dirt track after all that fancy stadium stuff. Out here, it's just me and –" *WHOOSH!* Lightning lost control!

"I give you the best tyres, but look – you still wipe out," Luigi remarked.

"Yeah, thanks," Lightning replied. "Ouch! My turns work perfectly on a real racetrack. Why can't I handle the dirt? I can't wait till my racing stadium is built. I'll be cruising then! Ka-chOWW! Ow-ow-OW!"

"I told ya to steer right to go left. Can't you remember anything, hotshot?" It was Doc. He had been watching the whole time. "Mater, tow your rookie friend out of this mess!"

Mater got Lightning out of the patch in a jiffy. "I'm going back to town," he grumbled.

"Now, wait just a second, rookie!" Doc challenged. "If I'm crew chief, you gotta do things my way. Plus you're on my turf!"

"Whatever," Lightning said. "But first can I get cleaned up and take some of these prickles out of my tyres? I think I scratched my paint job."

"No!" interrupted Doc. "Try that turn again – unless it's too much for you." Reluctantly, Lightning stayed.

"New rules," lectured Doc. "No more worrying about your silly paint job. No more whining about a few cactus prickles. And no more rest until you make that turn look easy!"

Lightning tried the turn again and again. Sometimes he made it, and sometimes he didn't. "Ow-ow-OW!" he shouted each time he hit another cactus.

"I can do this, I know I can," Lightning said. Slowly, he returned to the starting line. Then, more determined than ever, he roared down the dirt track, concentrating on Doc's advice. And when he came to the curve, he glided around the corner – and stayed on the track!

"Ka-chow!" he hooted as he headed towards the finish line.

"Wahoo!" cried Mater. "You did it, buddy!"

"Congratulations," said Doc. "You finally listened to some good advice."

Lightning turned to Doc. "Feel like taking a little spin around the track?"

"Sure, rookie." Doc smiled and sped off. The race was on!

Annie's Solo Mission

Leo was giving Annie flying lessons!

"Today you'll learn the three most important tricks for flying Rocket," said Leo. "Are you ready?"

"Ready!" Annie said excitedly.

"Okay, here's the first lesson – the Up-and-Down Trick," said Leo. "If you want to make Rocket jump over something, you need to reach your arms up really high and then bring them down really fast."

"I think I've got it!" exclaimed Annie.

"Great job, Pilot Annie!" Leo said, beaming. "Next, you'll need to know the Squeeze Trick," explained Leo. "It comes in handy when you need to fly Rocket through a really tight space."

"That sounds hard!" said Annie.

"It's actually easy," said Leo. "Just cross your arms and pat your shoulders."

"This is fun!" Annie shouted.

"Okay, this next one is a bit difficult," cautioned Leo. "To make Rocket do big roller-coaster loops in the air, you need to clap your hands in a circle." Annie joined in and made big clapping circles in the air with him.

After Annie's flying lesson, the team decided to blow some superbubbles. The Little Einsteins blew their superbubbles into some pretty wild shapes! Annie ran to find her camera. She wanted to take pictures before they all popped.

June, Quincy and Leo blew a superbubble so big that it carried all three of them away!

Annie raced back, but her friends were nowhere to be found.

"Hey, where did they go?" Annie wondered aloud. "I wanted to take a picture!"

"Up here, Annie!" shouted Quincy.

"We need you to rescue us," said June. "If you fly Rocket up here, you can catch our bubble in his Bubble Wand."

Annie was nervous. "Me? But I've never flown Rocket by myself before!"

"You can do it, Annie," Leo assured her.

Inside Rocket, Annie prepared for her solo mission.

"According to this flight plan, I need to do the Up-and-Down Trick over the mountains, then perform the Squeeze Trick to fly through a small opening between two rocky cliffs and finally do a Loop-de-Loop Manoeuvre to get to the superbubble."

Annie was nervous but she knew the others were counting on her. She took off and followed the flight plan perfectly. "We're so proud of you, Pilot Annie!" exclaimed June.

"Way to go, sis!" Leo beamed. "I'm bubbling over with pride!"

Miss Bianca's First Rescue

The headquarters of the Rescue Aid Society was buzzing with activity. Mice from all over the world had gathered together for an emergency meeting. The Chairman of the Society had to shout to be heard over the hubbub.

"Attention, delegates!" he cried. "I have called this meeting because a canine urgently needs our help." He clapped his hands. "Mice scouts, bring in the distressed doggie!"

Two mice workers hurried into the room, leading a small dog with a long body and short little legs. His head was stuck inside a dog food can.

"*Mama mia!*" cried the mouse from Italy.

"Arooooo!" howled the dog.

The mouse from Yemen suggested pulling the can off the dog. Four muscular mice set to work, pulling and tugging. But it held fast.

The mice finally decided that the can would have to be removed by mechanical means. The Zambian delegate suggested using a can opener.

Suddenly the door to the meeting room flew open. There stood a pretty little mouse. She wore a fashionable coat and expensive perfume.

"Oh, excuse me," she said. "I seem to be in the wrong place. I'm looking for Micey's Department Store?

"Dear me," she said, noticing the delegate with the can opener, "what are you doing to that poor dog?"

"The dog is quite stuck, I'm afraid," the Chairman told her. "But the situation is under control."

The glamorous mouse pushed up her sleeves and marched over to the dog.

She kicked the top of the can three times. Then she gave it a swift twist to the left. And the can popped off!

"Hooray!" the mice all cheered happily.

The little mouse smiled. "That's how I open pickle jars at home," she explained. "Well, I'd best be on my way."

"Ah, Mr Chairman?" a voice piped up from the corner of the room. It was the Zambian delegate.

"Yes?" said the Chairman.

"I'd like to nominate Miss . . . uh, Miss . . ." The delegate looked at the pretty mouse.

"Miss Bianca," she told him.

"I'd like to nominate Miss Bianca for membership in the Rescue Aid Society," he said.

The Chairman turned to the rest of the mice delegates. "All in favour say, 'Aye!'"

"Aye!" all the mice cried.

"Woof!" the dog barked happily.

Miss Bianca smiled. "Well," she said, "I suppose Micey's can wait for another day."

A Royal Pain

"Sir Hiss, wake up! Wake UP!" Prince John shouted into the face of his slumbering royal adviser. Sir Hiss awoke with a start and sat bolt upright in his tiny cradle at the foot of Prince John's bed.

"Wha-what is it, Your Highness?" Hiss replied. He shook his head and tried to shake off his sleepiness. "Is everything all right?"

"No, everything is NOT all right!" Prince John snapped. He sat on his bed, crossed his arms and pouted. "I don't know how you can sleep while I lie here wide awake, tossing and turning!"

It was very late. All of Nottingham was quiet and still. No other candles were burning in the kingdom. Since the greedy Prince overtaxed all the poor people of Nottingham, he had every comfort, including the largest and softest bed in all the land. Yet, that night, Prince John could not get to sleep.

And Sir Hiss realized that he would not sleep until Prince John fell asleep. So he sprang into action, trying everything *he* could think of to send the Prince off to dreamland.

First, he brought the Prince something to drink from the castle kitchen.

"*Ugh!*"Prince John spat out his first mouthful. "This milk is WARM!"

"Well, yes, Your Majesty," replied Hiss. "Warm milk will help you get to sleep."

"Take it away!" the Prince ordered.

Next, Sir Hiss tried singing a lullaby. He crooned, "*Go to s-s-s-s-sleep, little prince-s-s-s-s . . .*"

But Prince John scrunched up his face, wiped it with the back of his hand, and yelled, "Say it! Don't spray it!"

Sir Hiss was annoyed. But he had one more idea. "Why don't you try counting sheep?" he suggested.

Prince John did as he was told. But, before he had counted to ten, he had lost his patience.

"Oh, I don't CARE how many sheep there are!" he thundered.

Sir Hiss was at the end of his tether. And he was completely out of ideas. Then he spotted the Prince's money bags, piled high in one corner of the bedroom . . . and he knew what to do.

"Okay, sire," said Sir Hiss. "Then how about counting your money?"

Sir Hiss opened one of the money bags and pulled out a handful of gold coins. As he dropped a coin back into the bag, it made a soft clinking sound. He dropped another, and then another . . . and Prince John closed his eyes and began to count each clink.

"One . . . two . . . three . . ."

Before he got to ten, Prince John was fast asleep . . . wearing a huge grin.

A Rescue Mission to Al's Toy Barn

Woody had been stolen! In Andy's room, Buzz and the other toys held an urgent meeting. They were trying to solve the mystery: Who took Woody?

Buzz thought about the clues – the license plate, the chicken feather – and finally figured out the man must be from Al's Toy Barn, a toy shop they'd seen on TV. He had to be Al, the owner who dressed in a chicken suit!

But now that they knew who the culprit was, what could the toys do?

"Woody once risked his life to save me," Buzz told the others. "I couldn't call myself his friend if I weren't willing to do the same."

Buzz decided to lead a rescue party to the toy store, to see if they could find Woody. Together, with a little help from Slinky, they jumped off the roof. "To Al's Toy Barn and beyond!" Buzz cried.

By early morning, Buzz and his rescue team had almost reached Al's Toy Barn. They just needed to cross one last, very busy, street. Luckily, Buzz noticed a pile of orange traffic cones. He told everyone to grab one and then, slowly, they ventured across the street, hiding under the cones.

Soon, the street was filled with skidding, honking, crashing cars, all trying to avoid the strange, moving traffic cones. But the toys didn't notice. They'd arrived at Al's Toy Barn.

Inside, aisles of shiny new toys seemed to stretch into the distance. Everyone looked up in awe – how would they ever find Woody here?

The only one who didn't seem worried was Rex, who had picked up a strategy book on how to defeat the evil Emperor Zurg in the Buzz Lightyear videogame. Rex loved playing the videogame, and desperately wanted to beat Zurg. Rex couldn't stop reading, even as the toys spread out to search for Woody.

Buzz discovered an aisle full of brand-new, updated Buzz Lightyear toys! He gasped when he saw each figure's fancy new utility belt.

He reached out to touch the belt – suddenly, a hand clamped onto his wrist. It was a new Buzz Lightyear, who believed he'd caught an escaped space ranger! Quickly, he tied Buzz into a box. Then New Buzz ran to join Andy's toys – and not one of them realized they'd left the real Buzz behind.

Buzz struggled free from his box just in time to see his friends head out the front door, inside Al's bag! Racing to catch up, he crashed – *SMACK!* – into the automatic doors as they slid shut. How was he ever going to catch up with his friends?

Dance, Daddy-o!

Deep in the jungle at the temple ruins, the monkeys and their ruler, King Louie, were always looking to have a swingin' time.

"Let's have a dance-off!" King Louie suggested to the monkeys one evening.

"Hooray!" the monkeys cheered.

"What's a dance-off?" one monkey asked.

"You know, a contest," said King Louie. "An opportunity for everyone to get down, strut their stuff, cut a rug! And whoever lays down the smoothest moves is the winner!"

"Hooray!" cheered the monkeys.

King Louie rubbed his chin. "The first thing we need is some music," he said, pointing at the monkey musicians. "Hit it, fellas!"

The musicians blasted out a jazzy tune, blowing through their hands like horns, knocking out a beat on some coconuts and drumming on a hollow log. Soon, all the monkeys were gathered around the musicians, tapping their toes and shaking their tails.

"Now," said King Louie, "who will dance?"

All the monkeys raised their hands. King Louie looked around. "Let's see," he said scratching his head, "I choose . . . me!"

"Hooray!" the monkeys cheered. They were disappointed not to be chosen. But, after all, King Louie *was* their King.

So King Louie moved his hips from side to side. He waved his arms in the air. He closed his eyes so he could really feel the beat.

"Dance, Daddy-o!" one monkey cried.

King Louie boogied and bopped like he had never boogied and bopped before. Then, when the song was over, King Louie stopped dancing and scrambled onto his throne. "Now it's time to choose the winner!" he said.

"But King Louie . . ." one monkey began to object. All the other monkeys were thinking the same thing: didn't you need more than one dancer to have a dance-off?

"Oh, silly me," said King Louie with a chuckle. The monkeys looked at each other and smiled, expecting that the King had realized his mistake. But, King Louie said, "Of course, we need a judge! Who will judge?"

Everyone raised their hands. King Louie looked around, then said, "I choose . . . me!"

"Hooray!" the monkeys cheered.

"And as the judge, I will now choose the winner of the dance-off," King Louie continued. He looked around at all the monkeys. "Now, let's see. I choose . . . me! Let's hear it for the winner!"

"Hooray!" the monkeys cheered, because, after all, King Louie was their King – and a pretty swingin' dancer, too!

Disney Pinocchio

A Helping Hand

"Oh, Pinocchio!" cried Geppetto. "I can hardly believe that my little puppet is alive!" It was the morning after the Blue Fairy had visited Geppetto's house and brought Pinocchio to life. "You must get ready for school, my boy," said Geppetto.

Pinocchio was full of curiosity. "Why must I go to school, Father?" he asked.

"Why, so that you can learn!" Geppetto replied. "Now be a good boy and go make the bed while I clear away these dishes."

Ever eager to help, Pinocchio sprang up from the breakfast table and ran over to Geppetto's workbench. He found a hammer, a nail and a piece of wood, and began to pound loudly with the hammer.

"Pinocchio! Whatever are you doing?" cried Geppetto.

"Well, you asked me to make the bed," said Pinocchio. "So I was starting to make one."

With a little smile, Geppetto patted him on the head and said, "Perhaps it would be better for you to put the cat out."

As Geppetto turned back to the breakfast table, Pinocchio jumped up and grabbed a pitcher of water. Hurrying over to Figaro, Pinocchio threw the water onto the cat.

"*YEEEEOOWWWW!*" shrieked Figaro.

"Pinocchio!" shouted Geppetto. "Why did you do that?"

"You . . . you told me to put the cat out. I thought he had caught fire," said Pinocchio in a small voice.

"Oh, my dear boy, you have much to learn!" Geppetto sighed as he dried off Figaro. "Okay, you can be a helpful boy by helping me to pick up the house a bit before you leave for school."

"All right, Father!" said Pinocchio, and he raced out the front door.

"Where in the world is he going?" Geppetto wondered aloud, as he followed Pinocchio outside.

Pinocchio was crouching at the base of the house, trying with all his might to lift it.

"What are you doing, son?" asked Geppetto with a twinkle in his eye.

"Trying to pick up the house, Father," said Pinocchio, his voice straining with effort.

Geppetto chuckled and gently guided Pinocchio back inside. "My boy, the sooner you go to school and learn about the world, the better for us both," he said. He collected Pinocchio's hat, his schoolbook and an apple for the teacher, and sent him on his way.

As Geppetto watched his new son walk off to school, he shook his head worriedly. "I hope he manages to stay out of trouble today," he said to himself. "My little boy has much to learn about the world."

Who's Fooling Whom?

Lilo had only had her new dog, Stitch, for a little while. Already he had managed to break just about everything he touched, and got Lilo's sister Nani dismissed from her new job.

Then April Fools' Day rolled around, and Lilo decided that, for one day, she was allowed to be a pain in the neck *back*.

Lilo got started first thing in the morning. She left a whoopee cushion on Stitch's chair at the breakfast table. When he came in to eat and sat down, a very loud and very rude noise reverberated around the kitchen.

Lilo laughed and shouted, "April Fools'!"

Stitch shrugged. He made rude noises all the time, so he wasn't embarrassed one bit.

After lunch that day, Lilo handed Stitch a cream-filled cookie. She had replaced the filling with toothpaste mixed with pickle juice.

Stitch took a bite.

"April Fools'!" cried Lilo.

Stitch took another bite . . . and another . . . and another, until he finished the cookie. Then he licked his lips. Ugh! thought Lilo. Stitch would eat anything!

Later that day Lilo smeared some of Nani's eyeliner around the eyepieces of her binoculars. She pretended to see something interesting out on the water. "Check out that huge wave," she said. Lilo held the binoculars up to Stitch's eyes so he could look through them. When she pulled the binoculars away, Stitch had a dark ring around each of his eyes.

"April Fools'!" cried Lilo.

Stitch had no idea that he looked so silly and even if he had, he wouldn't have cared.

Stitch also didn't seem to notice the fake blood dripping from Lilo's mouth before dinner, the ping-pong balls that rained down when he opened the bedroom door, or the arrow-through-the-head hat Lilo put on at bedtime.

"You're no fun to fool, Stitch," said Lilo.

Then she pulled back the covers on her bed and climbed in. But, for some reason, she couldn't extend her legs all the way.

"Hey!" Lilo exclaimed. "Someone short-sheeted my bed! Nani!"

Nani poked her head into Lilo's room.

"Very funny," Lilo said to her.

Nani looked at Lilo with a blank stare. "What's very funny?"

Nani looked as if she didn't know what Lilo was talking about. But that only left . . .

No way, thought Lilo. Stitch was just a dog. Lilo looked at him, sitting at the foot of her bed, wagging his tail. There was no way he could have short-sheeted her bed.

Was there?

101
DALMATIANS

The Good Thing About Rain

"Rise and shine!" cried Pongo. One by one, he nudged each of his 15 Dalmatian puppies with his nose.

The puppies yawned and stretched.

But Rolly just rolled over and slept on.

"Aw, come on, Rolly," Pongo whispered in the pup's ear. "It's morning! Don't you want to go out?"

At the mention of the word 'out,' Rolly was instantly wide awake!

Rolly was not alone. As if by magic, the sleepy group had become a pack of jumping, barking puppies. They raced together through the kitchen to the back door, where they jumped up and down, waiting for Nanny to let them out into the garden.

"Okay, here I come," said Nanny, as she made her way across the kitchen. Then she flung the door open wide and stepped out of the way to let the puppies race past.

But they didn't move. It was raining!

"Oh, go on," said Perdita, trying to nudge the pups out the door. "It's only a little water."

But they wouldn't budge.

The next morning, Patch awoke with a start. With a few sharp barks, he helped Pongo wake the other puppies. Within seconds, all 15 were crowding around the back door.

Nanny rushed to open the door again.

And once again, the puppies were very disappointed to see raindrops falling.

"Well," said Pongo with a sigh, "April showers bring May flowers!"

The next morning, the puppies weren't in any hurry to go outside. After all, it was probably still raining. They thought that all they had to look forward to was another whole day spent inside.

So, when Nanny opened the door on a sunny morning, the puppies were so surprised that they didn't know what to do.

Then, springing into action, they tumbled over one another in their rush to get out the door. They raced off in different directions, ready to sniff, dig, roll and explore.

But then, almost at once, all 15 puppies froze in their tracks. They looked around at each other, then down at themselves. What was this stuff getting all over their spotted white coats? It was brown. It was wet. It was squishy. It was mud! And it was FUN!

From the doorway, Pongo and Perdita looked out at their muddy puppies and laughed.

"You know what this means, don't you?" Pongo asked Perdita.

Perdy nodded. "Baths."

Pongo smiled, watching the frolicking puppies. "Let's not tell them – just yet," he said.

You're Gonna Be Huge!

Dumbo sat in the corner with a big frown on his face.

"What's the matter, kid?" Timothy asked.

Dumbo just shook his head.

"You've got nothing to be sad about," Timothy continued.

Dumbo didn't say anything.

"Well, if you're not going to tell me what's bugging ya, I guess I'll just have to figure it out for myself," Timothy said. "I know!" he exclaimed. "You're hungry?"

Dumbo shook his head.

"Thirsty?" Timothy asked.

Dumbo shook his head again.

"Concerned about the June-bug population in Saskatchewan?" Timothy suggested.

Dumbo shook his head doubly hard.

"Well, then," Timothy concluded. "It can only be one thing. It pains me to say it, but I think you have a case of 'feeling sorry for myself-itis'."

Dumbo's large ears pricked up.

"Yes," Timothy continued. "It's a dangerous disease that has affected many of us. Even the strongest cannot avoid it."

Dumbo looked to his left and to his right, then pointed to himself.

"Yes, that's right – you!" Timothy said. "I bet I know what's got you down – your above-average ear size."

Dumbo nodded.

"And the fact that people make fun of you," Timothy continued.

Dumbo nodded even more.

"And, on top of all that," Timothy said, "you've been separated from your mother."

A tear started to form in Dumbo's eye.

"Don't feel sorry for yourself!" Timothy ordered.

Dumbo looked up, surprised.

"You know why?" Timothy asked. "Because one day you're gonna be huge!"

Dumbo blinked in disbelief.

"We're talking autographs, your name in lights. They're gonna eat their hats for the way they treated you," Timothy predicted.

Dumbo looked nervous.

"I don't mean eat their hats for real," Timothy explained. "It's just a figure of speech. Not that some of them wouldn't deserve having to eat their hats. But that's not what we're talking about. They're gonna be really sorry they treated you so bad, understand?"

Dumbo nodded his head.

"All right then," Timothy said. "Feeling better?"

And Dumbo nodded doubly hard as visions of success, happiness – and being with his mother again – filled his head.

A Change of Scenery

Dr Sherman had left for the day when Gill called everyone together for a Tank Gang meeting.

"We need to make some changes around here," Gill began. "We've all been living in this glass box for how long now? And every day we stare at the same scenery – the same volcano, the same sunken ship, the same treasure chest and tiki hut. Well, seeing as how we can't change what's in our tank, I propose we rearrange things a little. Who's with me?"

"Great idea!" cried Peach the starfish.

"I'm with you," said Deb. "And Flo is too," she added, pointing at her reflection.

Everyone agreed it sounded like a good idea. "We can completely transform the place," said Bloat.

"All right!" said Gill. "Then how about we start with the tiki hut? Bloat, you hoist it up. Gurgle and I will help you move it. The rest of you guys tell us where you think it should go."

Gill, Bloat and Gurgle swam over to the tiki hut. Bloat wriggled his body underneath it and blew himself up, hoisting the hut a few inches off the gravel. Meanwhile, Gill and Gurgle stationed themselves on either side of the hut and prepared to push.

"Let's try it over there," said Peach, pointing to a far corner of the tank.

With blown-up Bloat acting as a cart underneath the hut, Gill and Gurgle pushed the tiki hut into the corner.

"Oh, no," said Deb, "that's all wrong. Can we see what it looks like over there?" She pointed to the opposite corner of the tank.

So Gill, Gurgle and Bloat worked together to move the tiki hut again.

"That's a disaster!" exclaimed Jacques.

"Yeah, he's right," said Nemo.

Gill, Gurgle and Bloat were getting worn out by all the moving. "Can we all just agree on where it should go?" said Gill. "And quickly?"

"Ooh! I know!" said Deb. "Bring it over this way." She led Gill, Gurgle and Bloat over to a shady spot next to some plastic plants. "Put it down here," she said. So they did.

"I like it!" exclaimed Peach.

"The perfect spot," said Jacques.

"Mmm-hmm," said Bubbles.

Gill stepped back and looked around. "Guys, this is where it was in the first place!"

"Is it?" asked Peach.

Deb giggled. "Well, no wonder it just seems to fit here!"

The other fish nodded – except for Gill, who sighed in frustration.

And that was the end of the tank redecoration for the evening.

Disney·PIXAR
MONSTERS, INC.

A Monstrous Mix-up

One morning at work, Mike Wazowski opened the door to his locker to find a note taped inside. It said:

Mike,
Roses are red.
Violets are blue.
I have got my eye on you!
Sealed with a kiss from . . .
Your Secret Admirer

Mike's mouth fell open. He showed the note to his best friend, Sulley.

"Who do you think it could be?" Sulley asked.

"I have no idea!" Mike replied. "Hey, you don't think it could be that six-armed cutie down in Purchasing, do you? Or that sassy, one-eyed receptionist, Celia, with the pretty hair?"

"I guess it could be anyone," Sulley said. "But, hey, it's time to get to work."

On the way to the Scare Floor, Mike's mind was racing. Who could his admirer be? Then Mike heard his least favourite voice.

"Wazowski!"

It was Roz, the humourless and strict Dispatch Manager, sliding up behind them. "You owe me some paperwork!" she said.

"Oh . . . right," said Mike. "I'll get that to you ASAP, Roz. See ya." He and Sulley turned on their heels and hurried on down the hallway.

"All right, Wazowski," Roz called out to Mike, shaking her finger. "But remember: I've got my eye on you. I'm always watching . . . ."

Mike and Sulley froze in their tracks and stared at each other.

"Did she just say . . . ?" Sulley began.

"'My *eye* on you?'" Mike said, recalling the wording in the note from his secret admirer.

Sulley gulped. "Your secret admirer is *Roz?*"

"NOOOOOOOO!" Mike's scream filled the hallway just as Celia came sauntering around the corner.

"Hey, Mike," she said batting her eye at him. "Rough morning?"

"Oh. Hey, Celia," Mike replied sullenly, still traumatized by the idea that Roz liked him.

"Gee," said Celia, "I thought my note would make your day."

Mike stared at her. "*Your* note?" he said, stunned. "Celia, you're my secret admirer?"

She sighed. "Wasn't it obvious? 'I have got my eye on you'? As in, I have one eye, just like you?"

A wave of relief swept across Mike's face.

"I was going to ask you if you wanted to go out sometime," Celia continued. "But if you don't want to . . ."

Without a word, Mike leaped into Celia's arms and clung to her. "Thank you, thank you, THANK YOU!" he exclaimed.

Celia giggled. "So . . . I guess that's a yes?"

Tony and the Tramp

Tramp licked the last of the tomato sauce from his chin. "So, what do you think, Pidge?" he asked Lady.

"That was the most wonderful meal I've ever had," Lady gushed.

"What did I tell ya?" Tramp boasted. "There's no one in the world who can cook up a meal like Tony!"

"I couldn't agree with you more," Lady said. "Can I ask you a question?"

"Sure thing," Tramp said. "Ask away!"

"I was just wondering," Lady began, "how you and Tony met."

"How I met Tony?" Tramp laughed. "Now that's a story!"

"I bet!" Lady said.

"Well, see, it goes like this," Tramp began. "It was a cold and snowy night. I don't think it had ever been that cold before, and I know it hasn't been since. I had been walking uphill for miles. Icicles were hanging from the tip of my nose."

"Wait a minute!" Lady interrupted. "You were walking for miles – uphill? In this town?"

"That's right!" Tramp said. "You've never seen the likes of it."

"Exactly!" Lady told him. "You know why?" Tramp shook his head.

"Because it isn't possible! There are no big hills around here!" Lady said.

"Not possible?" Tramp said. "Okay, you're right," he confessed.

"So, then, what's the truth?" Lady asked.

"The truth is," Tramp began, "I wasn't always the slick, handsome devil you see before you."

"Is that right?" Lady was amused.

"And this one afternoon I was being harassed by a group of mangy mutts who outnumbered me ten to one. So, I took off as fast as my paws could carry me. And as they were chasing me, along came this dogcatcher!"

"Oh, no!" Lady exclaimed.

"Exactly!" Tramp continued. "The mutts scattered out of sight, so I didn't have *them* to worry about any more. But now the dogcatcher was closing in! I thought I was a goner!"

"What happened?" Lady asked.

"Then Tony came running out with a bowl of steaming hot pasta," Tramp explained. "He told the dogcatcher I was his dog. The dogcatcher didn't believe him. But, when Tony put the bowl of pasta down in front of me, he had no choice. Let me tell you, I thought I'd died and gone to heaven."

"I can relate to that," Lady said, recalling the meal.

"And the rest," Tramp said, "as they say, is history!"

"And a tasty one at that!" Lady concluded.

WET CEMENT

Blue Ramone

"Dum-da-dee-dum," Ramone hummed to himself in his body shop.

"Hey there, buddy! Are you painting yourself again?" It was Lightning, with Mater.

"Yeah, blue is Flo's favourite colour. It's for her birthday party," Ramone replied. "And I plan on staying this colour for an entire week!"

"Gee whiz!" said Mater. "I've never seen you stay one colour for a whole week!"

That night, the town gathered for a cruise down Main Street for Flo's birthday. Suddenly, the door of Ramone's body shop popped open, and a very blue Ramone emerged, driving low and slow.

"Oh, Ramone!" Flo exclaimed. "You painted yourself blue! Now, are you going to take me on a birthday cruise or what?"

Ramone and Flo slowly cruised down Main Street together as the rest of the cars watched.

Then Mater said, "Hey, Ramone, do you think you can keep that promise you made today?"

Ramone stopped. "Hey, everybody! I've got an announcement to make!" he shouted. "In honour of Flo's birthday, I promise to stay blue for one full week!" Everyone gasped.

The next day, Ramone got up early and started cleaning his shop. But after a couple of hours, he was finished. He was tempted to paint himself a new colour. Then he remembered his promise, so he went over to Flo's instead.

"Hey, baby, you want a quart of oil?" Flo asked.

"Yeah, thanks," Ramone said. Then he added, "Do you want me to give you a new paint job?"

"Oh, honey, thanks, but no," said Flo. "I have all this work to do."

Ramone stayed blue the next day and the next. He kept asking all the cars in town if they wanted paint jobs, but they didn't. Ramone had to paint something!

"Ramone! What's wrong with you, baby?" Flo said. "Listen to me. If you want to paint yourself a new colour, just go right ahead and do it."

"But I made a promise," Ramone said sadly.

"No. A happy, freshly painted Ramone made that promise," Flo said with a sigh. "I miss that Ramone. Just be yourself."

"Yeah," said Mater. "Just be yourself. We like ya that way."

Ramone turned around. It seemed as if the whole town was there to encourage him.

So, Ramone happily went to work painting himself every colour he could find!

Lilo&Stitch

Easter Egg Hunt!

The Easter holiday was quickly approaching, which meant one thing: the annual Pelekai Easter egg hunt! Lilo couldn't wait to begin painting eggs. First she asked Nani to help make some hard-boiled eggs. Then Lilo found Stitch, Jumba and Pleakley, and everyone took turns painting the eggs.

"This is my favourite part," Lilo said. "I'm going to paint one pink with purple polka dots!"

"I'm going to draw mosquitoes on mine," said Pleakley, grabbing a crayon.

"Blue!" cried Stitch, dunking his egg violently in the cup of blue dye.

While everyone cleared up, Nani went down to the beach to hide the eggs. When everyone got to the beach, Nani announced the rules. "There are twenty-five eggs hidden on this beach. Whoever finds the most eggs will win the prize."

"What's the prize?" Lilo asked.

"Oh, you'll see," Nani replied with a smile. "On your mark . . . get set . . . go!"

The sun shone on the brilliant white sand as Lilo, Stitch, Jumba and Pleakley searched high and low for the eggs. They found one buried under a sand castle, another hidden under a beach blanket, and even one atop the belly of a man snoring on the beach!

As the afternoon sun began to sink, everyone gathered to count the eggs. Jumba had six eggs, and so did Pleakley. Stitch had six too. Then they finished counting Lilo's eggs, ". . . four, five and six!" But that added up to only 24. There must be one more egg hidden somewhere on the beach.

So they split up and went looking for the last egg. Finally, Lilo spotted something under a palm tree. "Everybody, come quick!" she cried. "I think I've found the last egg!"

Nani, Jumba and Pleakley came running. "Look," said Lilo, "it's a huge foil egg. The biggest chocolate egg I've ever seen!"

"It sure is," said Nani. "This is the prize, Lilo, and since you all found the same number of eggs, it looks like you all get to share it!"

"But where's Stitch?" said Lilo. Just then, the huge chocolate egg began to twitch. It rattled and shook, and then –

Stitch popped out of it, yelling, "Ta-daaa!" Bits of chocolate scattered everywhere.

"Wow!" cried Lilo. "Did you guys plan that?"

"No, Lilo," said Nani, looking completely confused and a little disturbed. "I have no idea how Stitch got in there without breaking the foil."

"My secret!" said Stitch cheerfully. He began munching on a piece of the chocolate egg.

Nani and Lilo smiled and shrugged, and then they all sat down and ate bits of chocolate egg while they watched the sun set over the water.

THE INCREDIBLES

A Mission for Bob

Bob Parr had a boring job. Nobody knew that he was actually Mr Incredible – a Super who used to save people from disaster. Being a Super had been banned many years ago, and Bob was trying to live a normal life with his wife, Helen – or Elastigirl, as she was once known!

One day at work, Bob wanted to help someone who was being mugged outside, but his boss wouldn't let him go. Bob was so frustrated at not being allowed to help that he gave his boss a tiny push, but it carried all of Bob's Super strength.

WHAM! Bob's boss crashed through five walls, and Bob lost his job. Bob was worried. He didn't want to tell Helen he was fired, but what could he do without a job?

At home, Bob was clearing out his briefcase. Suddenly, a computer fell out! On the screen was a woman who had secretly watched Bob save people from a fire the night before. Helen didn't know, but Bob had started using his Super powers again.

"My name is Mirage. I represent a top-secret division of the government," she said. "A highly experimental robot has escaped our control..." She had a very special top-secret mission for Mr Incredible!

Mirage told Bob that if he could stop the malfunctioning Omnidroid battle robot before it caused any damage, he'd be paid three times his yearly salary! Bob accepted. He needed the money – but more importantly he needed the adventure.

Bob knew Helen wouldn't approve, so he told her he was going on a business trip. He was taken to the island of Nomanisan, where Mirage told him to shut the robot down, and do it quickly. "And don't die," she added.

Mr Incredible soon met the robot, and the fight began. The Omnidroid was a fast learner when it came to defending itself, but in the end Mr Incredible tricked it into destroying itself.

Mirage and her boss watched the robot's defeat. "Surprising," said her boss.

After a celebration dinner with Mirage, Bob flew home. He was excited about getting back into Super work. He began to lose weight, bought a new car and even played with the kids more! Things were looking up. But he'd ripped his suit, so he decided to visit Edna Mode – the former fashion designer for the Supers. She agreed to mend the old suit for sentimental reasons, but insisted on making him a new bold, dramatic outfit!

Bob was excited about what the future might hold....

Woody's Decision

Buzz had led a rescue mission to Al's Toy Barn to save Woody – the cowboy doll had been stolen by the shop's owner. Al wanted to sell the whole *Woody's Roundup* gang to a Japanese museum, for a lot of money!

Buzz had just been accidentally left behind by the rest of the toys. A brand-new Buzz Lightyear toy had come to life and caught Andy's Buzz, and tied him inside a box before joining the rest of the toys!

Old Buzz struggled free from his box just in time to see his friends head out the front door, inside Al's bag! Racing to catch up, he crashed into the automatic doors as they slid shut.

To make the doors re-open, Buzz knocked a nearby pile of toy boxes onto the sensor mat. One box remained stuck between the doors. Opening and closing, the doors hit the box over and over. At last, the box popped open, and a dark figure rose up. It was the evil Emperor Zurg! He took one look at Buzz and growled, "Destroy Buzz Lightyear!"

Outside, the toys had hoped to hitch a ride in Al's bag to wherever Woody was being kept. But at his building, Al jumped out of the car, leaving his bag – and the toys – behind.

"No time to lose!" New Buzz shouted. Quickly, he led everyone into the building through an air vent. Then, because he thought he was a real space ranger, he tried to fly up to the top floor! Luckily, the lift came by just in time and carried everyone up instead.

Sneaking through the vents, the toys reached Al's flat. They charged into the room, knocking down Jessie and Bullseye, then grabbed Woody and ran. Everything was very chaotic – especially when the real Buzz showed up as well!

Finally, things got sorted out, and everyone figured out who was who. But that still left one problem.

"Woody, you're in danger here," said real Buzz. He knew that Al wanted to send Woody to Japan. "We need to leave now."

But Woody didn't want to leave. The *Roundup* gang needed him to make a complete set for the museum. Besides, what if Andy didn't want Woody anymore? Al had fixed Woody's arm when his shoulder had ripped, but what if he broke again?

"You're a toy!" Buzz said. "Life's only worth living if you're being loved by a kid."

"This is my only chance," Woody said.

"To do what?" Buzz replied. "To watch kids from behind glass and never be loved again? Some life."

Sadly, Buzz had to leave Woody behind.

Disney Bambi

First Impressions

Bambi was just discovering the wonders of the forest. His mother had brought him to a little clearing in the woods. The sudden sunshine and bright green grass surprised and pleased him, and he bounded around on his still-wobbly legs, feeling the warm sun on his back and the soft grass under his hooves. While his mother grazed nearby, Bambi began to explore.

He found a patch of green grass and clover, and he bent down to eat. This was not an easy feat, as his long legs made it difficult for his little neck to reach the ground. When his nose was just a few inches from the tips of the grass, he suddenly leaped backwards in alarm. A leaf had just sprung up from the patch of grass and had landed a few feet away. A hopping leaf? he wondered. He followed it and, as soon as he drew close, the leaf hopped away from him again! Bambi looked around at where his mother stood, still grazing. She seemed to think they were in no great danger. So, he followed the leaf all the way to the edge of the clearing, where a wide brook babbled over craggy rocks.

Bambi's fascination with the hopping leaf faded as he approached the brook. Water cascaded smoothly over the rocks, bubbling and frothing in shallow pools. He took a step closer and felt his foot touch a rock at the edge of the water. Suddenly, the rock moved! It shuffled towards the water and then – *plop!* – jumped right in and swam away. Bambi was dumbfounded as he watched it dive beneath the surface and vanish. He stared at the spot where the rock had been for a moment, and then stooped down to have a drink, widening his stance in order to do so.

Suddenly, he jumped back in alarm. There in the water, staring right back up at him, was a little deer! Cautiously he approached again, and there it was!

Bambi turned and bounded back across the clearing to his mother. "Mama! Mama!" he cried breathlessly. "You will never guess what I have seen!"

His mother lifted her head and gazed at him with her clear, bright eyes.

"First," he said, "first I saw a jumping leaf. Then, I saw a rock with legs that walked right into the water and swam away! And then," he continued in amazement, "and then I saw a little deer who lives right in the water! He's right over there, Mama!"

His mother nuzzled her son, thinking over what he had said. Then she laughed gently. "Darling," she said. "I think you have just seen your first grasshopper, your first turtle and your very own reflection!"

HERCULES

Bring a Friend

Hercules was training to be a hero, and it was a lot of work. One day, Phil, his coach, set up a practice course for Hercules and then tied his student's hands behind his back. Herc had to run the course with no hands!

Phil had put a doll at the end of the course. He said it was a "practice damsel in distress," and Hercules was supposed to rescue it. So the hero-in-training rushed into the first section of the course – a darkened cave. Herc plunged into darkness and fell headlong into stagnant water.

"Yech!" Hercules spat out the putrid water and scowled. He wanted to be a hero more than anything. But sometimes Phil made things a little more difficult than necessary.

Feeling his way in the darkness with his feet, Herc noticed something slithery slipping around his ankles. Snakes!

Herc shook several of the water snakes out of his sandals. He hurried towards the other end of the cave and dived into the daylight, shaking the last snake off his feet. Panting, Herc lay down on the grass to rest for a moment.

"Rest later!" Phil shouted.

Herc rolled slowly over. The doll had to be around here somewhere. Behind him Hercules heard more stamping hooves and turned around. A huge ox was thundering towards him!

Herc jumped to his feet. He dodged the ox, but another was on his heels. Spotting the damsel at last, Herc leaped over the second ox. The doll was sitting 20 feet above him on the edge of a steep cliff.

At least Phil had left him a rope. In fact, it looked as though Phil had left two. Gripping the first rope in his jaws, Herc inched steadily upward. He was about halfway up when Phil lit the end of the second rope, which was soaked with oil! The fire raced up the rope towards a stack of dry wood under Herc's damsel.

Hercules threw himself the last few feet. He tackled the damsel, rolling away from the stack of wood, which was now blazing merrily away.

Breathing hard, Hercules finally relaxed.

"And another thing . . ." Phil's gruff voice echoed up to him from the base of the cliff. Hercules held his breath, but not because he was waiting for Phil's next words. Herc was holding his breath because he had spotted a scorpion next to his foot. The insect was poised to sting!

Crunch. Hercules' winged horse Pegasus used his hoof to flatten the creature.

Hercules smiled at Pegasus as Phil's final words of advice reached his ears. It was the best tip yet: "Always bring a friend!"

Mike's Worst Nightmare

"AAAAAAIEEEE-AHHHH!" Sulley sat bolt upright in bed. The anguished yell was coming from his friend Mike's bedroom. Sulley raced out of his bedroom and threw open Mike's door.

"Hi," said Mike in a shaky voice. "I guess I must have had a bad dream." He swallowed hard, then sat up in bed and gave Sulley a sheepish grin. "I haven't had one since I was little."

Sulley nodded. "Okay, well, good night, Mike."

"Uh, Sulley, don't you want to hear about it?" Mike asked with a hopeful grin.

Sulley came over and sat down on the edge of his friend's bed. "Okay," he said.

"I dreamed . . ." Mike began. "This is going to sound really, really crazy, I know, but . . . I dreamed that there was a kid, a human kid, in my closet over there!" He pointed across the room and laughed nervously.

"Now, now," said Sulley good-naturedly. "Maybe it was the movie you watched tonight."

"*Kidzilla?*" Mike scoffed. "Nah. I've seen it a dozen times and it's never bothered me before."

"Well, why don't you try to go back to sleep?" said Sulley, suppressing a yawn.

Mike cleared his throat shyly. "I remember when I was little, my mum would bring me a sludgesicle when I had a bad dream," he said.

Sulley sighed patiently, then went to get Mike a sludgesicle from the kitchen.

"She would sing me a little lullaby too," said Mike.

In his low, scratchy voice, Sulley began to sing:

> Rock-a-bye, Mikey, Googley-Bear,
> With sharp little fangs and shiny green hair!
> Morning will come when the sun starts to rise,
> You'll wake up and open those googley eyes!

"Googley *eye*," Mike corrected his friend, snuggling under his blanket. "Uh, my mum also always checked the closet."

With another patient sigh, Sulley opened Mike's wardrobe door and stepped inside. "Nope. Nothing in here!" he called. Suddenly, there was a loud clatter and a landslide of junk spilled out of the wardrobe door. A yellow mop fell out. It looked just like blond hair!

"AHHHH!" shrieked Mike, leaping out from under the covers. Then he relaxed. "Oh, sorry, pal. In this dim light, I thought that mop was, you know, a human child!" He shuddered and gave Sulley another sheepish smile.

Sulley chuckled at the idea. "Don't be silly, Mike," he said. "A kid will never get loose in Monstropolis – what a disaster that would be!"

"No, you have a point," Mike agreed sleepily. "Good night, Sulley."

"Good night, Mike."

Abracadabra!

Manny was not at his best. Gypsy could tell. Already that day, he had lost two magic wands and stepped on his turban.

And with the matinee show at P.T. Flea's World's Greatest Circus about to begin, Gypsy knew she had to be on her toes. Manny was going to debut his new trick: the Levitating, Flaming and Disappearing Water Torture Chamber of Death.

"Ladies and gentlemen," Manny announced, "prepare to be stunned and amazed by the Levitating, Flaming and Disappearing Water Torture Chamber of Death. You will watch as my lovely and talented assistant, Gypsy, climbs inside this chamber" – Manny motioned towards the empty sardine can at his side – "where I will bind her hands and feet. Then I will fill the chamber with water, seal it, levitate it five inches off the ground and set it ablaze. And, finally, you will watch in awe as the chamber disappears before your very eyes!"

Manny and Gypsy had rehearsed the act thoroughly. Everything was planned down to the last detail. But, if one little thing went wrong with the trick, Gypsy could be in big trouble.

As it turned out, one little thing didn't go wrong – three big things went wrong!

Manny made his first mistake when he tied Gypsy's hands and feet together. He was supposed to leave the strings loose so that Gypsy could wriggle out of them once she was inside. But Manny accidentally tied them too tight!

Then Manny filled the chamber too high with water. In rehearsals, he had left a bit of space at the top so that Gypsy had some air inside. But, this time, he forgot!

Manny's third mistake was locking the trapdoor. Together, he and Gypsy had rigged an escape hatch in the back side of the sardine can. Once Manny sealed her inside, Gypsy wriggled out of her bonds, opened the trapdoor, and, unseen by the audience, escaped from the chamber before Manny levitated it, set it on fire and made it disappear. But, this time, Manny accidentally nudged the latch that secured the trapdoor from the outside. Gypsy was locked inside.

Luckily, Gypsy hadn't left anything to chance: she had stowed a sharp shard of glass inside the sardine can. She had learned to hold her breath for ten minutes. And she had put a release latch on the inside of the trapdoor.

She was safely out of the chamber in one minute flat.

At the end of the trick, Manny called Gypsy in front of the audience. "How did you do it, my dear?" he asked dramatically.

"It was magic!" she replied, with a smile and a sigh of relief.

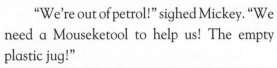

Let's Get Goofy

Everyone was gathered at the Clubhouse, ready for a day of fun! Everyone except Goofy. "Where is he?" asked Minnie.

"Maybe he's inside already," said Mickey. "Let's go see!"

"Goofy?" everyone called. The Clubhouse was quiet.

"Let's go up to the roof top and see if we can spot him!" said Mickey.

But there was no sign of Goofy. Then Mickey looked through the Mousekespotter towards the west and chuckled. "I know where Goofy is!" he said.

"Where?" asked Daisy.

"He's at home!" said Mickey. "He's still asleep! Come on, let's get him!"

But first, they needed some Mouseketools; a compass, an empty plastic jug, the Mystery Mouseketool and a yellow feather. Then everyone got into the Toon Car and Mickey drove off.

When they reached a crossroads, they were unsure which way to go.

"It's time for a Mouseketool," said Mickey. He held out the compass and the arrow pointed north. Now Mickey knew which way was west!

As they continued, the car moved slower and slower until, finally, it stopped.

"We're out of petrol!" sighed Mickey. "We need a Mouseketool to help us! The empty plastic jug!"

He and Minnie took the jug and went to the petrol station. They filled the car with petrol and were on their way again.

But up ahead, in the middle of the road, was a large hog. The hog wouldn't move out of the way. "It's time for the Mystery Mouseketool," Mickey said.

"What is it?" Minnie asked.

"Two ears of corn!" said Mickey.

Donald took the corn, then laid them on the grass. The hog walked onto the grass and started munching it.

"Enjoy the corn!" said Minnie.

They finally arrived at Goofy's house, but he was still asleep. Goofy wouldn't wake up!

"Let's try the feather Mouseketool!" said Mickey.

Mickey tickled Goofy's foot with the feather. Goofy opened his eyes and sat up.

"Hiya, Goofy!" said Mickey.

Goofy removed ear plugs from his ears.

"But, Goofy," said Minnie, "how could you hear your alarm if you were wearing ear plugs?"

"My new alarm clock kept going off every hour. If I hadn't worn the ear plugs, I wouldn't have got any sleep!"

The Prospector

Buzz had organized a rescue mission to Al's Toy Barn to save Woody – the cowboy doll had been stolen! Al wanted to sell the whole *Woody's Roundup* gang to a Japanese museum, for a lot of money!

But after meeting the rest of the *Woody's Roundup* gang, Woody had started to think that maybe he'd be better off at the museum. Soon, Andy might stop loving him and playing with him. Sadly, Buzz and Andy's other toys were forced to leave Woody behind.

Soon after, though, Woody realized Buzz was right – he belonged with Andy. He ran to the vent and called for his friends to return. Then he turned to the *Roundup* gang.

"Come with me," he said. "Andy will play with all of us, I know it!"

Jessie and Bullseye were excited... but the Prospector blocked their path! After a lifetime in his box, he was determined to go to the museum. "And no hand-me-down cowboy doll is gonna mess it up for me now!" he shouted.

Suddenly, they heard footsteps – Al was coming! The toys stopped moving.

Al packed Woody and the *Roundup* gang into a case, and dashed out of the door. He was late for his flight to Japan.

"Quick! To the elevator!" Buzz shouted,

hoping to catch up. But on the roof of the lift, Emperor Zurg refused to let them pass! As Zurg attacked the group with his blaster, Rex turned away, terrified – and knocked Zurg off the lift with his tail!

"I did it! I finally defeated Zurg!" Rex cried happily.

The moment Zurg was gone, the toys rushed to the lift's emergency hatch. Looking down, they saw Al, still inside the lift.

While Buzz held onto his legs, Slinky stretched down to Al's case. Swinging closer, he undid the latches and grabbed hold of Woody's arms.

But then the Prospector popped up – and yanked Woody back down again! A moment later, the elevator doors opened at ground floor. Al hurried outside, with the *Roundup* gang still in his case.

Andy's toys sprinted into the car park, but Al had already jumped into his car and driven off. How would they rescue Woody now?

New Buzz had just discovered that Zurg was his father, so he decided to stay behind with his dad. But everyone else hopped into an empty Pizza Planet delivery van that was nearby. Real Buzz handled the steering while Rex navigated and Slinky accelerated.

Soon they were swerving through traffic, hot on the trail of Al's car!

A Party of Three

The Widow Tweed hummed cheerfully as she decorated her cottage. Tod, the little fox she had adopted not long ago, watched with excitement. This was his first birthday in his new home!

"Now, Tod," said the widow, "who shall we invite to your party?"

Tod jumped on the windowsill and looked over at Amos Slade's farm. The Widow Tweed knew what that meant: Tod wanted his friend Copper the hound dog to share in the celebration. "I know Copper is your friend," she said, "but what if Amos catches him over here? There's no telling what that old coot might do!"

Tod jumped on the kind woman's lap and gazed up at her with big, sad eyes. "Oh, Tod! Stop looking at me like that. Well – all right! You can ask Copper over just this once!"

"I'm not supposed to leave the yard," Copper explained when Tod invited him. "I'll get in trouble with my master."

"Don't worry," Tod said. "I've got it all figured out." He lifted up one of the hound dog's enormous, floppy ears and whispered his plan.

Soon Tod showed up in Amos Slade's chicken yard. He ran among the birds, causing them to flap their wings and cluck in panic. That was Copper's signal to bark as loudly as he could. Amos burst out of the cabin just in time to see Copper chasing Tod into the woods.

"Follow me!" yelled Tod to Copper. He led his friend through a series of hollow logs, and then through a long, underground burrow. When the two pals emerged above ground, they were right outside Tod's back door. The Widow Tweed was waiting.

"Quick, scoot!" she said, shooing the two into the cottage.

While Amos Slade wandered around the woods trying to find Tod and Copper, the party festivities at the Widow Tweed's were just beginning. The three played hide-and-seek, pin-the-tail-on-the-donkey and drop-the-clothespin-in-the-jug. Tod won every game. Finally, it was time to cut the cake. After everyone had seconds, the widow spied Slade coming out of the woods. She let Copper out through the back door, where he stood barking ferociously.

"Good tracking, Copper!" Slade cried. "Did you chase that no-good fox all the way through the woods?" Copper looked up at his master and wagged his tail. "Copper," Slade said, "what's that on your face?" The hound turned his head and quickly licked the cake crumbs off his muzzle. "Hmmm," said Slade. "Must be seeing things. Let's go home then."

Inside the cosy cottage, Tod smiled. It had been a wonderful birthday – and sharing it with his best friend had definitely been the icing on the cake!

Pictures in the Stars

Ever since Mufasa had died and Simba had left the Pride Lands, Timon and Pumbaa had been Simba's only friends – but what fun the three of them had together. One of their favourite things to do after their evening meal was to lie on their backs in the tall grass and gaze up at the night sky, looking for shapes in the stars.

"Okay, okay, I got one," said Pumbaa, lifting a foreleg to point to one area of the sky. "See, over there, that long, thin, curving outline? It's a big, juicy, delicious slug!" Pumbaa licked and smacked his lips, imagining the taste of a slug snack. "Mmm-mmm!"

Simba chuckled. "Pumbaa, how can you still be hungry? We just ate!"

Pumbaa shrugged. "It's a gift," he said.

Timon cleared his throat. "I hate to disagree with you, Pumbaa my friend, but that's no slug you see up there. That's an elephant's trunk. If you follow that curving line of stars, you see it connects with the elephant's head at one end. And there are the ears," Timon said, tracing it all out with his finger, "and there are the tusks."

Simba chuckled again. "Somebody still has his mind on that elephant stampede we almost got flattened by this afternoon," he said.

"Hey . . ." Timon said defensively, "what's that supposed to mean?"

"Oh, no offence, Timon," Simba replied. "I just think it's funny that the things you and Pumbaa see in the stars just happen to be the same things that are on your mind at the time."

"Ooh! Ooh! I've got another one!" Pumbaa interrupted. "A big bunch of tasty berries right over there," he said, pointing at a grouping of stars. "Don't they look good?"

"See what I mean?" Simba said to Timon, gesturing at Pumbaa.

"All right, all right, Mr Smarty-Pants," Timon replied. "So what do you see in the stars?"

"Well, now, let's see," said Simba, gazing intently at the tons of tiny points of light twinkling down at them. There were so many that you could see practically any shape in them that you wanted to. It all depended on how you looked at them. But just to get Timon's goat, Simba wanted to find something really bright – something really clear. Something Timon couldn't deny that he saw too.

Just at that moment, a shooting star streaked the entire length of the night sky.

"I see a bright streak of light rocketing across the sky!" exclaimed Simba.

"Ooh! Me, too!" said Pumbaa. "Timon, do you see it?"

Timon had to admit that he did. "Yeah, yeah, I see it," he muttered grudgingly. "Ha-ha. Very funny, Simba."

Should I Stay or Should I Go?

Wendy sat watching Michael and John play with Peter Pan and the rest of the Lost Boys.

"John and Michael seem so happy," Wendy said to herself. "And why wouldn't they? Never Land is such a beautiful place, and the flying is so much fun!

"Still," she had to admit, "it is also dangerous. Who knows what sort of trouble we could get into, especially with Captain Hook running about?

"And," Wendy continued, "I don't think that Tinker Bell likes me very much."

Wendy considered this, then burst out, "What am I talking about? I'm making it sound like it's an awful place, but the truth is, Never Land is the most wonderful place on earth!

"Perhaps that explains it!" Wendy suddenly realized. "Maybe I really want to stay in Never Land, but in my heart of hearts I know I shouldn't. After all, Mother and Father must miss us terribly. And we miss them too! Oh, and what about Nana?" Wendy began to fret. "She must worry about us endlessly!

"That settles it!" Wendy stood up abruptly. "We must leave for home immediately.

"But if I stay – " Wendy stopped herself. "I'll never have to grow up!"

Wendy thought about the pros and cons of never getting old. "Then again, I always wanted to be an adult someday," she concluded.

Just then, Peter Pan swooped down beside her. "What are you doing, Wendy?" Peter asked. "Oh, nothing," Wendy told him.

"Then why don't you come join us?" he suggested.

"I will," Wendy told him. "In a minute."

"All right! But last one there is a rotten – " Peter took off before he could finish his sentence.

"How can I ever leave Peter and the Lost Boys?" Wendy wondered. "They need me so much.

"But so do our parents," she quickly reminded herself.

"Should I stay?" she wondered aloud. "Or should I go?"

Wendy's eyes fell upon a daisy. She bent over and pulled it out of the ground. "Should I stay?" she asked as she pulled a petal from the daisy. "Or should I go?" she asked as she pulled a second petal from the daisy.

Wendy did this over and over again until there was only one petal remaining on the daisy. "Well," she said, "this flower says we should go back home. And I suppose it's right. We'll go back . . . but maybe not just this minute."

Wendy stood up. "Hey, Peter, wait up!" And with that, she flew off after Peter, her mind at ease at last.

Al's Sky High Adventure

Al Oft, the Lightyear blimp, was hovering over the big stadium when he witnessed an amazing sight: superstar rookie Lightning McQueen was pushing a broken-down race car – The King himself! – across the finish line.

Everyone knew who Al was. The fans always cheered when he flew over. But he was lonely up in the sky all by himself. Al couldn't help admiring Lightning's pit crew. It was filled with the rookie's close friends. They had come all the way from Radiator Springs to support Lightning at his big race.

After the race season, Al decided to fly over the countryside, just enjoying the ride. Sometimes he even helped lost travellers. He had a good view from above and could guide the cars to their destinations.

One day, Al saw a town below him that looked like the place Lightning had described. He flew low – and spotted Lightning himself!

"Hey, Lightning!" shouted a rusty old truck. "Lookee there! It's that Lightyear blimp from your big race!"

"Al, it's you! How are you doing, buddy? Welcome to Radiator Springs!"

"My name's Mater!" said the rusty truck. "Wanna help us round up a stray tractor that busted loose, Mr. Blimp?"

"Yeah," said Lightning. "We can't see where the lost tractor went. But I'll bet you can from up there!"

Sure enough, from high in the sky, Al soon found the lost tractor.

"Hey, that's great, Al, but we can't get over those big rocks!" Lightning shouted. "Can you see a way for us to get around them?"

Al looked down and all around. He soon found a path the two cars could take to reach the lost tractor. Within minutes, Mater and Lightning were guiding the tractor home.

"Now, this calls for a celebration, Al!" Lightning shouted. "We're having one of our neon cruises tonight. Why don't you join us?"

But Al just looked sadly at Lightning. "I can't cruise," he replied. "I'm too big and too high up."

"Sure you can!" said Lightning. "Just turn on your neon and fly low."

As the cars in Radiator Springs looked up at Al, Lightning introduced him.

"That's my friend Al Oft, the Lightyear blimp. Just look at him. He's got the best neon you've ever seen."

Al smiled. He was having the most fun he'd ever had. And with all his new friends, he knew he'd never be lonely again.

Win Some, Lose Some

Sulley and his assistant, Mike, were in a race to become the Top Scare Team. But Randall and Fungus were right behind them. So it was lucky that Sulley and Mike were racking up the scares!

"We'll beat Randall easily," said Mike, giving Sulley a high five.

"Just keep that paperwork in order," Sulley warned. "You know how Roz hates when it's late!"

Suddenly, the Scare Floor exploded in panic. George Sanderson had returned from his cupboard with a ball stuck to his foot with chewing gum. Now, special teams from the CDA, the Child Detection Agency, swarmed into the factory to decontaminate George.

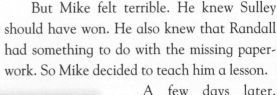

During the excitement, Randall crept over to Sulley's workstation. He stole Mike's paperwork and tossed it into a shredder.

After George had been cleaned – and shaved! – the Scare Teams got back to work.

"My paperwork is gone!" Mike cried, his eye blinking in confusion.

"Oh, no!" cried Sulley. "Without that paperwork, none of today's work will count."

"Too bad," said Randall, chuckling. "That makes me today's Top Scarer."

Mike was sad, but Sulley wasn't upset in the least. "Cheer up," said Sulley. "You win some, you lose some. Tomorrow is another day."

But Mike felt terrible. He knew Sulley should have won. He also knew that Randall had something to do with the missing paperwork. So Mike decided to teach him a lesson.

A few days later, Randall was ahead of everyone else in scares.

"This is my best day ever!" Randall crowed to the other Scarers. "Pretty soon I'll be Scarer of the Month!"

But, just then, the alarm went off. George had come back with a lollipop stuck to his ear.

As the teams rushed to decontaminate George, Mike sprang into action. When no one was looking, he hurried over to Randall's and Fungus's workstations and grabbed all their paperwork.

"This is contaminated, too!" Mike cried as he tossed the papers to the floor.

"Burn it!" commanded the CDA decontamination team leader.

With a *whoosh*, a flamethrower burned all of the papers to ashes.

"Where's the paperwork?" Randall cried when he returned to the scare floor.

"Yikes!" Fungus yelped. "Where did it go? It was right here!"

"Well, this is just great," Randall said. "Now my points don't count."

"Looks like you're cooked. Just like your paperwork," Mike said with a chuckle.

Howling at the Moon

Lady had been having a really bad day. First, she'd had a run-in with two nasty cats. Then, she'd been put in a horrible muzzle. But, because of Tramp, everything had changed.

"It's amazing how a day can start off terribly but end wonderfully," Lady told Tramp as they trotted through the moonlit park. "Thank you for helping me escape that terrible muzzle – and for dinner at Tony's."

"Aw, shucks, don't mention it!" said Tramp. "Hey, you wanna have some real fun?"

"I don't know," Lady said cautiously.

While she was very fond of Tramp, she also knew they were very different dogs. Tramp was used to life on the streets. So his idea of 'fun' might be very different from hers.

"Don't worry," Tramp teased. "This is something I think you'll enjoy."

"What is it?" asked Lady.

"Well, for starters, you have to look up," said Tramp.

Lady did. The sky was filled with stars and a big, bright moon.

"What am I looking for?" she asked.

"The moon, of course!" cried Tramp. "Haven't you ever howled at the moon?"

Lady laughed at Tramp's suggestion.

"What's so funny?" asked Tramp.

"I'm a practical dog," explained Lady. "I bark politely when the situation calls for it, but I don't see any point in howling at the moon."

"Why not?" asked Tramp.

"Well," said Lady, "what's the use of it?"

"You know, Lady," said Tramp, "a thing doesn't have to be useful to be fun. You like to chase a ball, right?"

"Right," said Lady.

"So, there you go," said Tramp. "Sometimes it's good to chase a ball. And sometimes it's good to just let go and howl at the moon, even for no reason."

Lady thought it over. "Okay," she said. "What do I do?"

"First, sit up real straight," said Tramp. "Then, look up at the moon, take a deep breath, and just let all the troubles of your day disappear in one gigantic howl!" He demonstrated: "Ow-ow-OWWWWWWW!"

Lady joined Tramp and howled as loudly as she could.

"You're right!" she cried. "It does feel good to howl at the moon!"

"Stick with me, kid," said Tramp. "I know what's what."

Lady suspected Tramp did know what was what, but there was an even better reason for her to stick with him. He'd become the very best friend she'd ever had.

WET CEMENT

Don't Be Alarmed

"CUT!" yelled Felipe from behind a video camera. "This film just doesn't have the razzle-dazzle I'm looking for. We need costumes, glitter, music – perhaps a few dancing nuts and bolts?"

"Or maybe all your film really needs is a new director!" Turner sneered.

"This is serious, Turner!" cried Felipe. "If we're going to be on the *Sheet Rock Hills Today* show tomorrow, we have to be prepared!"

The next morning, Manny and the tools arrived on the set of Sheet Rock Hills Today. All the tools were excited, except for Rusty – he was a bit nervous.

The presenter of the show, Dwayne Bouffant, spoke into the camera. "Good morning, Sheet Rock Hills! Today, Manny Garcia and his tools are here to show us how to change the batteries in a smoke alarm."

"Thanks for having us here, Dwayne," said Manny. "We're here to remind everyone to test your smoke alarm each month."

"Press this button, like so," Pat said, tapping the button on the alarm. "If it beeps, it means your batteries are working!"

"You should change the batteries in your alarm the same time each year," added Dusty.

"First, unscrew the top of your smoke-alarm cover," Turner explained.

"Next, remove the old battery," Squeeze continued. "Place it in a sealed bag before throwing it in the bin."

All the tools looked at Felipe. It was his turn to show everyone how to put the new battery in the smoke alarm, but he just stared at the camera. He didn't talk or move.

Rusty knew what to do. He picked up the new battery and explained how to insert it.

"Wow! Great job, tools. Thanks for teaching us an important safety lesson," said Dwayne.

"Our pleasure, Dwayne, and we'd also like to remind everyone to come down to the fire station this Saturday for a special fire-prevention demonstration," Manny said into the television camera.

After the show, Dwayne shook Manny's hand. "Thanks again, Manny. That was a great segment!"

When Dwayne left, Manny and the tools gathered around Felipe. They could tell he was upset.

"Aw, cheer up, Felipe," Squeeze said brightly. "I don't think anyone noticed."

"Do you really think so?" asked Felipe.

Squeeze nodded. "Besides, Rusty came to the rescue and put out the fire – so to speak!"

An Airport Rescue

Driving wildly in a Pizza Planet delivery van, Buzz and the gang were following the owner of Al's Toy Barn, who was taking Woody and the *Roundup* gang to the airport! Al wanted to sell them to a museum in Japan.

At the airport, Buzz spotted a pet carrier. The toys piled inside, sticking their legs through the bottom. Moving as quickly as they could, they followed Al and his green case, and climbed onto the luggage conveyer belt.

"Once we go through, we just need to find that case," Buzz explained, nodding at the door to the baggage area.

The toys gasped as they entered a huge room full of conveyer belts and chutes. Buzz finally found Al's case, but when he opened it – the Prospector jumped out and punched Buzz!

"Hey! No one does that to my friend," Woody yelled, tackling the Prospector.

With his pickax, the Prospector started to rip open Woody's shoulder! He was about to drag Woody back into the case, but the rest of Andy's toys arrived just in time. Bullseye also kicked free as a conveyer belt carried them outside, but Jessie was stuck!

"Ride like the wind, Bullseye!" Woody yelled as he and Buzz jumped on the little horse's back. They chased the baggage truck.

Woody finally scrambled onto it, but by then, the green case was already being loaded into a plane! Woody hid inside another bag and was tossed onto the plane, too. He found the scared cowgirl. "C'mon, Jess," he said. "It's time to take you home."

Just then, the plane's doors closed! They crawled through a hatch, down to the wheels. The plane was already speeding down the runway – and Woody slipped! Jessie caught him, but his arm was starting to rip again. Woody lassoed his pull string onto the wheels. Then he held Jessie's hand and, together, they swung down and landed right behind Buzz, who was galloping along on Bullseye!

Everyone was safe. Watching the plane take off into the sky, the toys cheered.

When Andy arrived home from Cowboy Camp, he was surprised by what he found. "New toys!" he cried. "Thanks, Mum!"

Jessie and Bullseye had joined all his favourites, welcoming him home. Andy couldn't wait to play with everyone... right after he sewed up Woody's shoulder.

Someday Andy would grow up, and maybe he wouldn't always play with toys. But Woody and Buzz knew there was no place they'd rather be. Besides, they'd always have each other – for infinity and beyond!

Funny Faces

Hugo, Victor and Laverne were gargoyles at the great Cathedral of Notre Dame. Most of the time they were stone, but they came to life in the presence of Quasimodo, the bell ringer at Notre Dame. Although they were all good friends, Hugo and Victor were always finding something to bicker over, and today was no exception.

"That's ridiculous!" Hugo snapped at Victor.

"No, *you're* ridiculous!" Victor shot back.

Victor had suggested that Quasimodo tell Frollo, the Minister of Justice and Quasi's master, that he wanted to take some time off. Hugo had pointed out that Frollo would sooner become a gypsy than give Quasimodo a holiday. Then the argument had really taken off.

"Well, you started it," Hugo told him.

"I started it?" Victor asked.

"That's right, stone face!" Hugo shouted.

"Who are you calling stone face? Blockhead!" Victor fought back.

Suddenly, a loud whistle interrupted them.

"May I have your attention, please?" Laverne said. "I would like to propose a way for you to settle this dispute like gentlemen."

"What is it?" Quasi asked.

"A face-making contest," Laverne said. "Here are the rules. You two take turns making faces at each other, and the first to make the other laugh, wins!"

"I'm going first!" declared Hugo, sticking his tongue out at Victor.

"Child's play," said Victor scornfully. He crossed his eyes at Hugo.

"Ha!" said Hugo. "Try resisting *this*!" Hugo crossed his eyes, flared his nostrils, and stuck his lower jaw out, baring a crooked row of teeth in a hideous grimace.

Victor managed to keep a straight face at this, but Quasimodo couldn't help but laugh out loud.

"Shh!" Laverne said. "Frollo's coming!"

"Frollo?" Hugo and Victor grew pale and quickly turned back to stone.

Just then, Frollo marched in. "What's going on up here?" he asked Quasimodo.

"Nothing, sir," Quasi said, trying not to laugh. He was having a hard time keeping a straight face because, behind Frollo, Victor and Hugo were still busy making faces at each other, each trying to make the other laugh.

"Hmm," said Frollo suspiciously. As he turned to go, Victor and Hugo stopped making faces at each other, and began making funny faces at Frollo's back. When he was out of sight, all four friends collapsed with laughter.

"You know what," Quasi told them. "I have so much fun with you guys, it beats going on vacation!"

Disney
Robin hood

Easy Come, Easy Go

One day, Robin Hood was boasting to his friends in Sherwood Forest about his skills with a bow and arrow.

"I can take from the rich and give to the poor using only a single arrow," said Robin. "And I'll defeat the greedy Sheriff with that same arrow too."

"With one arrow?" asked Little John. He knew his friend was talented, but that seemed impossible.

"One arrow is all I need," said Robin. "And it won't even *touch* the Sheriff."

"Now, that really *is* impossible!" Little John laughed. He was sure Robin was teasing.

But Robin wasn't joking. "Look," he said, "here comes the Sheriff to collect taxes from the poor villagers. I'll show you how easy it is."

Little John and Robin followed the Sheriff to the village. They watched him knock on the door of the first house.

"I am here to collect the King's taxes!" the Sheriff roared. "Give me the money or you'll be thrown in jail!"

The frightened man opened his door and gave the Sheriff a handful of coins. "It's all we have," said the man.

The Sheriff wrote the man's name in a book. "You still owe more," he said. "I'll be back next month for the rest!"

The Sheriff stuffed the coins into a leather bag hanging on his belt. Then he went to all the other houses and collected more taxes. Soon, the Sheriff's leather bag was bulging with the poor villagers' savings.

As the Sheriff prepared to leave, Little John whispered, "Robin, the Sheriff is taking everything they have. We can't let him get away with this."

"No, we can't," agreed Robin.

Drawing back his bow, Robin took aim.

"You're going to shoot him?" asked Little John.

"No need," said Robin.

Instead, Robin shot the arrow at the bag of coins, putting a hole in it. The Sheriff didn't even notice.

"Why did you do that?" asked Little John.

"Just watch," Robin said with a smile.

As the Sheriff mounted his horse, the coins began to drop out of the hole in the bag. By the time he'd trotted out of the village, all the tax money he'd collected had spilled back out. Robin and Little John collected the money and returned it to the delighted villagers. Little John slapped Robin on the back. "You did it, Robin! You robbed from the rich and gave to the poor – and with only one arrow, just like you said."

"Sure," Robin grinned. "And, as the Sheriff is about to learn, easy come, easy go!"

Donald Takes Flight

"Daisy, I have a surprise for you," said Donald Duck one clear spring day. "I've been taking flying lessons."

"That *is* a surprise," said Daisy Duck.

Donald took Daisy to a nearby airport. On the runway sat an old-fashioned plane with open-air seats. Together they climbed into the small plane. Then Donald started the engine.

"Up, up and away!" he cried as they took off.

"Can you do any tricks?" shouted Daisy.

"Sure!" called Donald. He steered the plane into a loop-the-loop.

"You're a very good pilot, Donald!" Daisy cried, clapping her hands.

Donald was so proud of himself, he told Daisy he would fly wherever she wanted to go.

Daisy thought it over. "Let's go to Paris, France!" she said. Donald was so eager to impress Daisy that he didn't think twice. "Paris, here we come!" he cried. Before long, however, the plane's engine began to cough and choke.

"Uh-oh," Donald said to himself as the plane began to drift towards the water.

"Is anything wrong?" asked Daisy.

Donald knew they were running out of fuel. But he didn't want Daisy to find out.

"Everything is fine, Daisy," Donald said nervously.

Just then, he saw something floating below them. It looked like an airport runway. But what would a runway be doing in the middle of the ocean?

As the plane drifted closer to the water, Donald realized he had no choice. He'd have to land his plane on the floating runway.

Just before he landed, Donald's eyes nearly popped out of his head. It wasn't a runway at all. It was the top deck of a huge ocean liner!

"Duck!" yelled one of the ship's passengers, and a dozen people scattered.

Donald zoomed over their heads and carefully landed the plane on the long, wide deck.

"Hey, it really *is* a duck!" cried one of the passengers.

Just then an announcement came over the ship's speakers. "Good evening, ladies and gentleman. Dinner is served!"

Donald helped Daisy out of the plane. He was sure she would be upset. But she wasn't. "Dinner on a cruise ship!" she cried. "Donald, you're just full of surprises, aren't you!"

"Yes, indeed," said Donald with a huge sigh of relief. "And here's one more surprise: I think this ship's on its way to France!"

"Oh, Donald, you're the best," said Daisy.

No, I'm not, thought Donald, as Daisy hugged him. What I really am is one lucky duck!

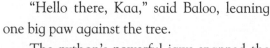

Snake Eyes

"I'm ssstarved," hissed Kaa the python as he slithered across the jungle treetops. "I need a sssnack...."

Suddenly, Kaa noticed a small figure relaxing on the ground below. It was Mowgli. Kaa slithered over to him.

"Are you feeling ssssleeeepy?" hissed Kaa. "You look sssleeepy; jussst look into my eyesss..."

Mowgli tried not to look into the snake's eyes, but it wasn't easy. When he turned one way, Kaa was there. When he turned another, Kaa was there too!

"Sssslip into ssssilent ssslumber," Kaa hissed. "And ssssleep... sssleeep... ssssleep..."

Before Mowgli knew it, his body went completely limp. Kaa had hypnotized him!

Thank goodness Mowgli's friends walked by at that very moment.

"Look!" cried Bagheera the panther. "Kaa's after Mowgli again."

"Get over there and do something," Baloo told Bagheera.

"The last time I interfered with Kaa, he hypnotized *me*," said Bagheera. "*You* do something."

Kaa's fangs watered as he coiled his long body around Mowgli. Then Kaa opened his giant python mouth above Mowgli's head and – hey! Someone had jammed a stick into his jaws, propping them wide open!

"Hello there, Kaa," said Baloo, leaning one big paw against the tree.

The python's powerful jaws snapped the stick. "You sssshould not insssert yoursssself between a sssnake and his sssnack," he hissed.

"Oh! Sorry!" said Baloo. "I was just admiring how very talented you are."

"Talented?" Kaa said. "Me?"

"Sure!" said Baloo. "I'm very impressed how you hypnotized Mowgli there. I bet you could hypnotize almost anything in the jungle. Almost..."

"What do you mean *almost*?" said Kaa.

Baloo coolly polished his claws against his fur. "Well, let's see," he said. "I bet you can't hypnotize... a fish." Baloo pointed to the pond.

"Jusssst you watch me," Kaa told Baloo as he slithered towards the pond.

Hanging his head over the water, Kaa hissed, "Jussst look into my eyesss. You feel ssssleeepy... ssssleeepy... sssssleeepy...."

Suddenly, Kaa stopped hissing. Or moving. He just stared into the water.

Bagheera stepped up to Baloo and whispered, "What's the matter with him?"

Baloo just laughed. "Kaa was so determined to prove me wrong, he didn't even notice the water was reflecting back his image. That crazy snake hypnotized himself!"

Winnie the Pooh

Pooh's Neighbourhood

"I say, it's a splendid day in the neighbourhood!" cried Owl.

"Which neighbour wood are we talking about?" asked Pooh.

"Neighbour*hood*," said Owl. "The place where we live and where all our neighbours live and are neighbourly."

"Oh," said Pooh, "it is a splendid day in it, isn't it?"

"Now I'm off for an owl's-eye view!" said Owl. He flew up and circled once around Pooh's house. "I can see the Hundred-Acre Wood spread out below me, and it's a fine place indeed."

As Owl flew off, Pooh began to think about what it means to live in a neighbourhood, and he thought perhaps he would bring a neighbourly present to his closest neighbour, Piglet. Pooh went inside his house and took a honeypot out of his cupboard. He tied a nice blue ribbon round it.

When he reached his Thoughtful Spot, Pooh suddenly had a thought: I could take the path straight to Piglet's house. Or – I could go up the path and around the whole neighbourhood. And sooner or later the path would take me to Piglet's house, anyway. So that's what he did.

As he walked the long way to Piglet's house, Pooh came across each of his neighbours in turn. He joined Kanga and Roo for a snack at the picnic spot, and collected some carrots from Rabbit. After lunch and a longish snooze at Christopher Robin's house, he soon reached Eeyore's Gloomy Place, which was where Eeyore lived.

Eeyore was feeling sad, so Pooh offered him a nice lick of honey. Pooh put the jar down, and Eeyore peered in. The honey pot was empty! Pooh walked away glumly and, before long, Owl flew over.

"I've seen our whole neighbourhood today," Pooh told him. "But now I have no neighbourly present left for Piglet."

"The bees have been quite busy at the old bee tree lately," said Owl. "Perhaps you can get a fill-up there."

So they walked together until they came to the old bee tree. Up, up, up Pooh climbed. Owl had a thought, and told Pooh to go to the very top of the tree and look around.

"Our neighbourhood!" cried Pooh. "Our beautiful home!" The Hundred-Acre Wood was spread out below him.

"That's the owl's-eye view," said Owl grandly.

Then, Pooh filled the honeypot once more, and he and Owl went to Piglet's house for supper.

Look Sharp, Jiminy!

"Gosh." Jiminy Cricket scratched his head between his antennae and yawned a big yawn. Climbing into his tiny matchbox bed, he gazed again at the wooden boy, who was fast asleep.

Jiminy still could not believe his eyes – or his luck. It had been a miraculous night. Not every cricket got to witness a wish granted by the Blue Fairy and see a puppet come to life. And not every cricket was chosen to be somebody's conscience!

Jiminy hopped out of bed. It was pointless to try to sleep. He already felt like he was dreaming. Being a conscience was a big job, but he was just the bug to do it. "Right and wrong." Jiminy looked from one of his hands to the other. "Sure, I know the difference. All I have to do is tell Pinoke. It'll be a snap." Jiminy snapped his fingers. "And I'll even look good doing it."

Jiminy ran his hands down the new jacket hanging by his bed. He picked up the hat and twirled it. "My, my," he said, shaking his head. Then he could not resist any longer. He put on his new shirt, coat, hat and shoes. Then he hopped over to Cleo's fishbowl to see his reflection.

Jiminy whistled low. "Don't you look smart," he told his reflection. "Smart enough to help that wooden boy. Except for that smudge." Jiminy leaned down to inspect a dull spot on his shoe.

He breathed on it and rubbed it with his sleeve. Soon it was shining like new. He looked like a million dollars!

Suddenly Geppetto snored loudly. Jiminy jumped and looked up. Outside the sky was starting to lighten.

"Would you look at that?" Jiminy knew he had to get to bed. A conscience needed to be alert! He hurried out of his new clothes, hung them up carefully, and tucked himself back in bed. "Big day tomorrow." He yawned. "Very big day." A moment later the little cricket was chirping in his sleep.

Jiminy woke to the sound of hundreds of cuckoo clocks. He sat up and rubbed his eyes. He barely remembered where he was. Then the events of the evening before flooded back. Why, he had work to do!

"Get up, Pinoke!" Jiminy called towards the big bed. But Pinocchio was already gone. The bed was made and Geppetto and Figaro were gone too!

Cleo swished nervously in her bowl and pointed towards the door.

"I must have overslept!" Jiminy pulled his new clothes on quickly. "I can't let Pinoke start school without me. You don't have to be a conscience to know that's wrong!" And, quick as a flash, Jiminy hopped out of the door.

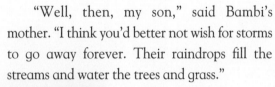

Bambi

Rain, Rain, Go Away

*R*rrrumble, rrrrumble, *BOOM*! The loud clap of thunder startled Bambi and his friends.

"I don't like thunderstorms!" cried Thumper, looking a little scared.

"I don't like them either!" exclaimed Flower.

"Bambi!" called his mother as the clouds grew dark and the rain began to fall. Bambi followed his mother out of the open meadow and into the woods. From their warm, dry thicket, Bambi watched sheets of rain pour down.

"I don't like thunderstorms," he told his mother, echoing Thumper's words. "I wish the storm would go away and never come back again."

"Oh, my," said his mother. "Do you mean you never again want to drink the cool, fresh water from the forest stream?"

"Well, no," said Bambi.

"Then, do you want the big trees to go thirsty? Their leaves to wither and branches to become brittle?" asked his mother.

"No! Of course not!" cried Bambi. "The trees give us shelter, and their branches give the birds a place to make their nests."

"Then, do you want the sweet grass to turn brown?" asked his mother.

"No," said Bambi. "We eat the grass. We'd go hungry if that happened!"

"Well, then, my son," said Bambi's mother. "I think you'd better not wish for storms to go away forever. Their raindrops fill the streams and water the trees and grass."

"But storms are so scary," Bambi said.

Just then, the rain began to let up, and Bambi's friends scampered through the underbrush and into Bambi's thicket.

"Look at the pond!" cried Flower.

Bambi peered through the thicket. The pond was alive with activity. The frogs were leaping and playing. And a family of ducks was shaking their feathers and waddling into the water.

"Uh-oh," said Thumper. "That old bullfrog's gonna get a surprise."

Bambi watched the lily pad with the big bullfrog drift closer and closer to the line of ducklings. The last duckling wasn't paying attention. The sudden collision sent the frog toppling off its lily pad with a startled *croak!* and surprised the duckling so much it did an underwater somersault!

Bambi, Thumper and Flower laughed.

"I guess I like thunderstorms after all," Bambi told his mother.

"You didn't like thunderstorms?" said Thumper. "That's silly! Why would you ever say a thing like that?"

The Shadow Game

Andy loved nothing more than going to Cowboy Camp. He looked forward to it all year. So did his favourite toy, Woody. One summer Andy decided to take all his *Woody's Roundup* toys with him.

Woody, Jessie and Bullseye had done nothing but talk about the camp for weeks. And now here they were in the great outdoors with Andy.

The first night, while the campers were fast asleep, the gang decided to sleep under the stars.

But Jessie didn't want to go to sleep. "Let's play a shadow game," she said excitedly. She jumped up. "Whoever makes the scariest shadow wins!"

Woody and Bullseye thought the game sounded like fun.

"Who wants to start?" Jessie asked.

"Ladies first," Woody replied.

"Yeeeeehah!" Jessie exclaimed loudly. She flapped her arms up and down. "Look, I'm a bat. Nah, that's too easy. I'll come up with something better."

A few minutes later, Jessie motioned Bullseye towards the fire. She put her hands in a fist and curled up her index fingers.

"Why, it's a longhorn steer!" Woody exclaimed, pointing to Bullseye's face.

"That's right, pardner," Jessie answered.

Next, it was Bullseye's turn. The horse thought for a moment. Then he leapt up and yanked the hat off Woody's head.

"Hey!" the cowboy cried. "Why would you do that?"

Then Jessie figured it out. Bullseye wasn't being rude, he was making a shadow! "It's a mountain lion, Woody," she explained pointing at the shadow shape Bullseye had made.

"Good one, Bullseye!" the cowboy said.

"Now it's my turn," Woody said. "Hold on."

He got up and ran off. A minute later, he returned with a stick. He took his hat back from Bullseye and walked towards a large rock.

"Sssss," he hissed.

"Oooh, a serpent," Jessie said. "That's more frightening than the mountain lion. But I bet I can do one that's even scarier." She tied a couple of sticks to her boot and made a shadow of a monster. "Rrrrrrrrr," she roared.

The shadow looked so real and Bullseye got so frightened, he whinnied loudly and hid behind a rock.

"It's okay Bullseye!" Jessie said. "It was just part of our shadow game."

Bullseye stopped being scared.

"Well Jessie," Woody said. "I think you made the best one!"

RATATOUILLE
(rat·a·too·ee)

Discovering the Truth

In the kitchen of Gusteau's restaurant in Paris, Remy the rat was hiding in a human chef's shirt. Remy was trying to help Linguini with his cooking. Remy tried to guide Linguini by biting and tickling him, but it wasn't working.

Suddenly, a mean chef called Skinner burst in and caught a glimpse of Remy. "The rat! I saw it!" shouted the nasty man. Linguini quickly hid Remy in his chef's hat and ducked out – almost colliding with a waiter! But Remy tugged Linguini's hair at the last minute and Linguini jerked backwards like a puppet. Could this be their new system? They went home to practise cooking. Remy guided Linguini by tugging his hair and before long, Linguini could even cook blindfolded!

In the meantime, Skinner was reading a letter that Linguini's mother had left for him when she passed away. The letter said that the late great chef, Auguste Gusteau, was Linguini's father! That meant the restaurant rightfully belonged to Linguini. Skinner was horrified. He had always thought the restaurant would be his! He had to do something to make sure Linguini never found out.

The following night, Remy the rat was relaxing in the alley behind the restaurant, enjoying his cooking success, when his brother, Emile, appeared. They hadn't seen each other since the family escaped the human house they used to live in.

Emile led his long-lost brother to the rat colony's new home. There, in honour of Remy, a hopping party filled the sewer with music. But soon, Remy said he had to leave. He tried to explain that he had new friends, a job, even a new place to live. In fact… he was living with a human.

Remy's father scowled and tried to convince his son that humans were dangerous. But Remy was sure Linguini was different. Against his father's wishes, Remy headed back to the restaurant.

On his return, Remy found the letter in Skinner's office saying that Linguini was the rightful owner of the restaurant! Remy grabbed the papers and ran. Skinner chased him. Skinner did not want those papers to get into the wrong hands!

Remy escaped, and by the time the soaking-wet Skinner got back to Gusteau's, Linguini was in his office. Linguini had discovered the truth – that the restaurant was rightfully his! Linguini fired Skinner on the spot. Remy smiled. He was excited, and happy he had chosen to stick with his new friend, Linguini.

Sarge's Boot Camp

"First gear!" Sarge shouted. Guido and Luigi started moving slowly. "Second gear! Third gear! Fourth gear!"

Luigi raced down Main Street with Guido speeding behind. Sarge had decided to start a training camp for all the 4x4s that would soon be arriving in Radiator Springs, with the opening of Lightning's headquarters.

"Hey!" yelled Sheriff, turning on his lights and siren. "Slow down, fellas!"

Sarge hurried over to explain his plan. Sheriff looked doubtfully at the two little cars, then sighed and turned off his siren and lights. "Just take them off the main road if you're going to be speeding."

Just then a big, brand-new 4x4 rolled into town. "Hi," said the 4x4. "I'm T.J."

"Welcome to Radiator Springs, T.J.!" Sarge yelled out to the newcomer. "You've reached the home of my boot camp!"

"Car camp!" Luigi shouted happily. "It will be tough! But don't worry. Guido and I are fully prepared to change your tyres at any time."

"You mean I might get a flat?" T.J. said.

"You will if you don't change that attitude!" exclaimed Sarge. "Now, let's get going!" Sarge led the group out of town to a rocky dirt road.

"Oh, no!" T.J. complained. "I've already got dirt in my grille!"

"No talking!" shouted Sarge. "Now... first gear! Second gear! Third gear!"

"Ooooo!" cried the 4x4. "This is so bumpy that my spark plugs are shaking loose."

"Come on, T.J.," said Luigi. "If Guido can do it, so can you!"

"Okay, team!" said Sarge. "We're going down that slope and across that big, muddy puddle."

T.J. gasped. He could lose control going too fast down the hill! But down, down, down they went. "I'm gonna flip over!" T.J. cried.

"Hit the brakes!" Sarge called out. "Show a bit of courage, soldier!"

Soon they were at the bottom of the hill, crossing the mud puddle. T.J. hesitated.

"Come on!" Luigi called to T.J. "You're a 4x4! This should be no problem."

T.J. thought about it, then he laughed. "I'm dirty, my paint is scratched, and I'm tired. But I can do it! Thanks, Guido. Thanks, Luigi."

"Now hit the showers!" Sarge shouted. "We've got a big day tomorrow!"

"Sir! Yes, sir!" T.J. yelled. Luigi and Guido looked up the steep hill in front of them.

"Come on, guys! Hop onto my roof rack! I'll give you a ride," offered T.J. Together the cars raced up the hill and back to town – excited about the next day of Sarge's boot camp!

A Tight Squeeze

"Calling all toys, calling all toys," Woody the cowboy announced. "The coast is clear."

It was early one morning and Andy had left for school. The toys were ready to have some fun, so Woody told them all about a game they could play.

"It's called 'sardines,'" he explained. "It's like hide-and-seek, except when you find the hider, you hide with them and wait for someone else to find you both. Then, the next toy to find you hides with you too, and so on and so on. Get it?"

"So, by the end of the game, everyone is hiding together in one spot?" Jessie the cowgirl asked. Woody nodded. "Right," he said, "except for the last toy, who is still looking for the hiders. In the next game, that toy is the one who hides!"

Now all of the toys understood the rules and were ready to play!

The toys decided that Hamm the piggy bank would be the one to hide, and Woody asked all the other toys to close their eyes and count to twenty-five. Meanwhile, Hamm hurried off to find a good hiding place.

"Eighteen... nineteen... twenty..." the toys counted. Hamm was running out of time! With only seconds to spare, he spotted one of Andy's old lunch boxes, hopped inside and closed the lid.

The next toy to open the lunch box lid was Woody, whose eyes lit up when he saw Hamm inside. He made sure he wasn't being watched before he hopped in. But soon the lid opened and Jessie had found them. There wasn't much space left, so she got wedged between Hamm and Woody.

Woody started to feel a little cramped. Buzz soon located the hiding place too, but as hard as he tried, he couldn't get the lid to close. By the time Rex found the hiders, the lunch box was completely full. He couldn't fit inside! Soon the rest of the toys were hurrying towards the overstuffed lunch box.

"Oh, well," said Woody with a laugh. "They've found us, so this game is over. Everybody out!" One by one, the toys tumbled out of the lunch box and gathered around Hamm.

"Gosh, Hamm, couldn't you have picked a bigger hiding place?" Rex asked.

Hamm replied, "Well, yeah, but isn't the point of the game to get squished? Like sardines in a can?"

The toys thought that over and had to agree. From then on, every time the toys played 'sardines', the hider made sure to pick a small hiding place – just to keep things interesting!

Flik Wings It

Flik knew that Hopper and his gang of hungry grasshoppers would soon come to steal all the food from the peaceful ants of Ant Island. So Flik headed off to the big city to find warrior bugs to help fight the grasshoppers.

On his way, Flik saw a shiny dragonfly flutter across the sky.

"Wow, I wish I could fly like that!" he exclaimed.

Suddenly, Flik had an idea. "I built a harvester that harvests pretty well. I wonder if I could invent a flying machine?"

Flik got to work. He gathered sticks and vines and leaves. He found a mushroom cap to use for a seat, and a long red feather for a tail.

When he had gathered all the parts, Flik began to strap the pieces together.

After lots of hard work, Flik took a step back and studied his invention.

"Well, it certainly *looks* like it could fly," Flik said finally. "It has wings that flap and a long red tail."

The frame of Flik's flier was made of twigs, and the wings were made of leaves. The whole machine was tied together with strong vines.

"Time for a test flight," Flik decided.

He climbed onto the mushroom cap seat and used a vine as a safety belt. Then he put his feet on the little pedals and started to pump.

Faster and faster, the green wings began to flap. Soon, Flik's flier began to rock; then it leaped into the sky!

"It's working!" Flik cried. He was flying!

With the air racing between his antennae, Flik watched the world flash under his feet. He saw frogs and turtles and other creatures that ate ants.

"Flying is so much safer than walking," said Flik.

But he spoke too soon, for high in the sky above Flik a mother bird was teaching her three little hatchlings how to fly. She spied Flik's strange-looking contraption and thought one thing – dinner!

Flik looked up and saw the mother bird and her babies coming down on him like dive bombers!

"Test flight over!" Flik cried.

Pedalling faster, Flik steered his flier through the limbs of a tall tree. The mother bird and two of her babies were blocked by the branches. But the third baby bird raced between the leaves and caught up with Flik.

Pecking wildly, the little bird ripped a wing from Flik's flier. Spinning out of control, the machine crashed to the ground.

Luckily for Flik, he had also invented a parachute out of a spider's web, and he made a soft landing in the middle of a daisy.

"Another failed invention," Flik said with a sigh. "Maybe someday I'll have a chance to make a flying machine that really works!"

101 DALMATIANS

Patch and the Panther

One dark night, 15 Dalmatian puppies sat huddled around a black-and-white television set. They watched as Thunderbolt, the canine hero, crept through a deep, dark jungle.

Suddenly Thunderbolt pricked up his ears. The puppies held their breath. Two yellow eyes peered out of the bushes. It was a panther!

"Thunderbolt, look out behind you!" Penny barked at the television.

"How will Thunderbolt escape the hungry panther?" the TV announcer asked. "Don't miss next week's exciting episode!"

"Aww!" the puppies groaned, disappointed that their favourite show was over.

"I'll bet Thunderbolt tears that ol' panther to pieces," said Patch.

"I'd be scared to fight a panther," said his brother Lucky.

"Not me!" cried Patch.

"All right, kids. Time for bed," Pongo said, shutting off the television with his nose. He watched as the puppies padded upstairs and settled down in their baskets.

"Good night, pups," Pongo said.

"Good night, Dad," the puppies replied.

Pongo switched off the light. Moments later, the sound of soft snores filled the room. The puppies were fast asleep.

All except for one. Patch was wide awake.

He was still thinking about Thunderbolt and the panther.

"I wish some ol' panther would come around here," Patch said to himself. "I'd teach him a thing or two."

Just then a floorboard creaked. Patch pricked up his ears. Then he crawled out of his basket to investigate.

The floorboard creaked again. What if it's a panther? Patch thought with a shiver. But I'm not scared of any ol' panther, he reminded himself.

Suddenly Patch saw a shadow flicker across the doorway. The shadow had a long tail. Panthers have long tails, Patch remembered. Just then two yellow eyes peered out of the darkness.

"Aroooo!" Patch yelped. He turned to run, but he tripped on the rug. In a flash, the panther was on top of him. Patch could feel its hot breath on his neck. He shut his eyes . . . .

"Patch, what are you doing out of bed?" the panther asked.

Patch opened his eyes. It was Pongo!

"I – I was just keeping an eye out for panthers," Patch explained.

Pongo smiled. "Why don't you get some sleep now," he suggested. "I can keep an eye out for panthers for a while."

"Okay, Dad," Patch said with a yawn.

Pongo carried Patch back to his basket. And in no time at all, the puppy was fast asleep.

Moon Mater

Mater and Lightning McQueen were looking up at a large full moon.

"Yep," said Mater, "I've been up there."

"Pffft! You have not," Lightning said. But Mater insisted. He began to tell a story about the time he went to the moon. Mater described driving past NASCA, the National Auto-Spacecraft Administration. Inside, a monitor showed the surface of the moon. On-screen, a moon buggy named Impala Thirteen was stuck on the edge of a crater!

"He needs a tow!" cried one of the forklifts who worked at NASCA. Then Roger the space shuttle saw Mater driving by.

Mater agreed to help. On the day of his flight, he made his way to the shuttle launchpad. He was wearing a space suit and rocket jets. He rolled onto the space shuttle and strapped in. At the base of the launchpad, smoke spilled out of the booster rockets. Then fire, followed by even more smoke. Finally, blast off! The shuttle launched into the sky.

"We have lift-off!" Mission Control announced. As Roger rocketed up into space, he whooped with joy. "Wooooooo-hooooooo!"

Inside the shuttle, Mater looked out of the window. "See ya later, Earth."

Soon Roger's rockets had carried them deep into space. They were nearly at the moon!

"Operation Tow Mater is a go!" Mission Control said over the radio. It was time for Mater's moon landing. He floated out of the shuttle and into space.

"Good luck," Roger said. "See you on Earth." The shuttle began the trip home. The rescue mission was up to Mater now. Using his jets, he steered to the surface of the moon. He bounced over to the Impala Thirteen.

"Connect your rescue apparatus to the frontal structural component of the linear axle assembly," Impala Thirteen instructed.

"Uhh," Mater replied. "How 'bout I just give you a tow?" He fastened his tow hook, blasted his jets and pulled the moon buggy free!

"Mission accomplished!" Impala Thirteen said. "Now take us home!" Mater fired his jets and rocketed towards Earth with Impala Thirteen on his towline.

In Radiator Springs, Mater had just finished his story. "Oh, come on," Lightning said. "That did not happen."

Suddenly, Roger the shuttle set down next to them. "Suit yourself," Mater said, and then he drove up a ramp into the shuttle.

Peter Pan

Peter Pan to the Rescue

One day, John and Michael disguised themselves as pirates and took a small boat towards Captain Hook's ship.

John and Michael had just climbed over the side of the ship when they found a telescope.

Suddenly Smee walked by. "Do you see anything mateys?" he asked, mistaking them for members of the crew.

"Uh, a storm!" John blurted out.

"I should go and tell the captain," Smee said.

John and Michael followed Smee and saw him enter a cabin. John peered through the porthole and saw Captain Hook. Unfortunately, the Captain also saw him!

"Spies!" thundered Hook. Smee led the boys inside. "What's the meaning of this?" Captain Hook demanded. Smee explained that they weren't spies.

"Yes," Hook agreed. "My mistake, but our attack on Peter Pan's hideout is only days away, security's very important."

When the boys were outside, John whispered, "We have to warn Peter!" Quickly, they climbed overboard and began rowing towards shore. Captain Hook laughed as he watched through his telescope. "They'll lead us straight to Pan!" he said.

When John and Michael reached the shore they realized they'd been followed and scrambled up a hill, with John leading the way. At the top, he called, "This way, Michael!" But there was no answer.

Captain Hook stood at the bottom of the hill holding Michael. "Keep going, John!" cried Michael.

A few minutes later, John burst into Peter's hideout and told them what had happened. Peter shook his head. "It was a trick."

John groaned. "I've made a terrible mess of things. Will you help?"

"Sure," Peter replied.

On the pirate ship, Smee tied Michael to a chair. Just then, they heard a girl's voice say, "Captain Hook?" It was Wendy, standing on the plank. Hook had captured her too!

"Watch the boy, Smee," Hook said. "I'll be right back!" As soon as Hook was gone, John looked into the porthole.

"Not you again!" Smee exclaimed and chased after John. The Lost Boys hurried inside to untie Michael, then climbed into a boat waiting below. Then John opened his umbrella, leapt over the side of the ship and floated down to join them. Meanwhile, on the ship's plank, Captain Hook reached out to grab Wendy. Suddenly, a green blur scooped her up. It was Peter Pan!

"Blast you, Pan!" Hook cried.

The Late Shift

The shift on the Scare Floor at Monsters, Inc., had just ended when Sulley pulled Mike aside.

"Mike, our paperwork is always late," he said. "I'm worried about us getting a bad reputation."

"You're right, Sulley," Mike said earnestly. "From now on, I'm a new monster. In fact, I'm going to start getting caught up tonight. I'm going to stay at work late, just you see. Why, Celia will be so proud of me – uh-oh . . ."

"What is it, Mike?" Sulley asked.

"Oh, nothing!" Mike grinned. "Sulley, I'll see you later. I've got lots of catching up to do. Paperwork, here I come!"

Sulley gave Mike a suspicious look but allowed himself to be pushed out the door.

But, as soon as Sulley was gone, Mike's smile faded. "What do I do?" he cried. "I have a date with Celia, and I'm already late!" Finally, Mike came to a decision. "I'll catch up tomorrow," he said to himself. "That paperwork is so late that one more day won't make a difference."

With that, Mike headed for the locker room, whistling a jaunty tune. He had just entered the quiet, empty room when he heard a noise.

"Daaaa," said a tiny voice. Mike jumped straight up in the air and gave a yelp.

"Who's there?" he asked nervously.

"Gagoooo," said the voice. That was

definitely a child! Mike turned to run – but he tripped over a can of odorant someone had left on the floor and went flying across the room.

Footsteps sounded behind him. Mike looked up, expecting to see a human child. But he saw Sulley instead! "What gives?" he asked Sulley grouchily. Sulley was laughing so hard he couldn't even talk. Finally, the big blue monster calmed down enough to explain.

"I just couldn't resist!" Sulley said, helping Mike up. "After you shooed me out I ran into Celia, who told me about your date. I knew you would rather skip the paperwork than disappoint Celia."

Mike nodded, embarrassed.

"But I told her that you were really behind on your work," Sulley continued, "and I asked if it would be okay for you two to have your date tomorrow night instead."

Mike looked up, surprised. That hadn't even occurred to him. "Did she say yes?" he asked.

"She sure did," Sulley said. "And she also said that since I'm your partner and all, I should really stay here to help you catch up. So, here I am! Now, let's grab some sludgesicles and get to work."

"Okay, Sulley," said Mike. And the two monsters went off to show that paperwork what they were made of.

A Visit in the Night

It's not easy to read with a broken arm! Alone in his room, young Carl was trying to turn a page without letting go of his flashlight.

Suddenly, he heard a gentle rubbing noise. Then a blue balloon forced its way through his bedroom curtains!

"Ouch!" cried Carl, as he knocked his plaster cast against the bedside table.

A merry little face, framed by a mop of red hair, appeared at the window and Carl let out a second cry.

"It's me! I thought you might need a little cheering up!" whispered Ellie, his new friend, before she leapt down onto the floor.

She slipped quickly under the cover that Carl had made into a tent.

"Look!" she said, showing him a small notebook. "I'm going to show you something I've never shown to anyone else. Swear you won't tell anyone; cross your heart!"

Carl promised and Ellie opened up the book. A photo of the explorer Charles Muntz had been stuck on the first page.

"It's my adventure book! When I grow up I'm going to be an explorer too. And I'll go to South America, to Paradise Falls!"

Carl looked admiringly at the beautiful waterfalls, next to which Ellie had drawn

the little house where they'd met each other that same afternoon.

"Obviously it'll be tricky to move the clubhouse all that way!" said Ellie, who had noticed Carl's look of astonishment.

The boy didn't say a word, but couldn't stop his eyes from looking up to the shelf where his collection of miniature airships stood lined up, including a model of Muntz's Spirit of Adventure.

Ellie followed his gaze and immediately understood.

"But of course!" she cried out. "You can take us there in an airship! Promise me you'll do it! Promise!"

Carl promised. He could see no reason not to. Ellie was a true adventuress!

"See you tomorrow, right?" she said, getting up. "You're one hell of a chatterbox, you know?" she added, laughing, before straddling the window and disappearing into the night.

"Wow!" murmured Carl, totally bowled over by his new friend. Just ten minutes in Ellie's company was one of the biggest adventures of his life!

That night, as he slept, he dreamt of a colourful little house perched at the top of Paradise Falls.

Disney · PIXAR

TOY STORY

Rocket Launchers

"All clear!" Woody the cowboy doll announced. "Andy's off to school."

The toys gathered in the middle of the room, surrounding a long cardboard box. Andy had brought it home yesterday.

"Now," Woody said, "let's get a look at whatever this is."

Woody opened the box flaps and looked inside. He pulled a piece of paper out of the box. After a couple of minutes, he smiled. "It's a rocket launcher!" he said.

Woody helped Buzz put the rocket together. There was a pump attached to the launch pad that sent the rocket up into the air. All of the toys lined up to have a go.

"Look at that," said Rex. "The harder you stomp, the farther it goes."

Buzz and Woody helped set up the rocket for each toy and then measured the distance the rocket flew.

"Looks like we have a tie," said Buzz after all the toys had taken a turn.

"Yep," Woody agreed. "Hamm and Slink both made it all the way to Andy's door."

"We need a tiebreaker!" Jessie said.

Hamm and Slinky would each have one final stomp. First, Slinky Dog walked over to the rocket and loosened up. The other toys fell silent. Slinky pushed down on the pump as hard as he could, but the rocket didn't move! It was decided that Hamm should have a try. He stomped his foot on the pump, but the rocket still didn't move. The toys now knew something must be wrong.

"I think we have some space invaders," Buzz said with a smile. A small door on the rocket opened up and three Little Green Aliens peered out! Once they were out, Slinky Dog stomped on the pump as hard as he could. It flew across the room. "Ooooh!" the Aliens said as they watched.

Hamm stomped on the pump and his rocket shot into the air. Then it landed... in the same place Slinky Dog's had!

The toys decided they should call it a tie, and give the Aliens a ride instead. For the rest of the morning, the Aliens rode one at a time in the rocket.

When the other toys got tired of playing, Buzz and the Aliens sat beside the globe. Woody walked over. "Slinky and Hamm were just saying that they think if they work together they could launch all three of you in one go."

"Ooooh," the Aliens said.

Buzz stood up. "There's a plan," he said. "Teamwork will get us out of the galaxy, to the moon –"

"To infinity and beyond!" Woody finished.

Disney · PIXAR

WALL•E

A Robot Kiss

When WALL•E met EVE, he had fallen in love. He had latched onto the spaceship that came to take her away from Earth. Now, the spaceship was docking inside an enormous ship called the Axiom. This was where all the humans from Earth now lived.

The Captain's robot assistant, Gopher, wrapped EVE in energy bands and drove her away. WALL•E raced after her. And M-O, a cleaner-bot, chased WALL•E. (M-O was programmed to clean, clean, clean. WALL•E, the little trash-compacting robot from Earth, was his biggest challenge ever.)

As WALL•E chased EVE, he accidentally disabled a human passenger's electronic system. The human blinked and looked around. She saw the world around her, instead of viewing it digitally over her holo-screen. She liked it!

Meanwhile, EVE was finally ready to give the plant she had found among WALL•E's treasures to the Captain. By doing so, she would prove that Earth was clean enough that a plant could now grow there. That meant everyone could return to the planet.

But EVE's compartment was empty. The plant had disappeared!

Disappointed, the Captain sent EVE to the repair ward, along with WALL•E. When they got there, WALL•E thought some orderlies were hurting EVE. So he helped her escape, along with all the reject-bots from the repair ward.

But there was a problem. Once they ran, they looked like convicts. A warning broadcast their escape throughout the Axiom. The ship's stewards tried to catch them.

To avoid being captured, EVE took WALL•E to an escape pod. She would send him to Earth where he would be safe, and then she could find the plant. Instead, Gopher appeared. He had the plant! He put it in the escape pod, and WALL•E and the plant were launched into space – not towards Earth, but far into outer space! WALL•E panicked and pushed a lot of buttons.

WALL•E pushed the wrong button. The pod exploded! WALL•E managed to escape, and EVE went to try to help him. *Whoosh!* WALL•E zoomed up to EVE and showed her that he had saved the plant. Delighted, she leaned in towards him, and an arc of electricity passed between their foreheads – a robot kiss.

Soon they were floating in space, dancing and giggling, excited about taking the Earth plant back to the Captain.

MICKEY MOUSE
An Ice Skating Game

Mickey woke up and looked outside. It had snowed last night! "It's a perfect day for ice skating!" he cried. "I'll invite all my friends to come."

On the way, Mickey picked up Goofy, Donald, Daisy, Huey, Dewey, Louie and Minnie. When they got to the pond, everyone laced up their skates and made their way to the ice. It was as smooth as glass. The friends began skating around and around.

"Hey, I have an idea!" shouted Mickey. "Let's play crack the whip!"

Nobody else knew how to play, so Mickey explained the game. "I'll start out as the leader," he said. "We all join hands and form a line. Then we all skate around and around in a big circle. Once we get going, the skater at the end of the line lets go!"

"That sounds like fun!" said Goofy.

"Cool!" cried Huey, Dewey and Louie.

They all joined hands and began skating in a circle. Around and around and around they went. Donald was at the end of the line.

"Okay, Donald, let go!" shouted Mickey. Donald let go and went sailing away.

Around and around and around the rest of the gang went.

"Now, you go, Daisy!" cried Mickey. Daisy let go and went flying away across the ice.

Next went Huey, then Dewey, and finally Louie. Goofy followed them.

Now just Mickey and Minnie were left. Around and around they skated. Then Mickey shouted, "Let go, Minnie!"

Minnie let go and zoomed off with a squeal.

Mickey was having a fine time. Now all alone, he began to spin around and around and around. When he finally came to a stop, it took quite some time for his head to stop spinning. "Wasn't that fun, guys?" he said. "Want to do it again? Guys? Where is everyone?"

Mickey looked around. Where had everyone gone? And then he saw them. Seven pairs of ice skates at the ends of seven pairs of legs were sticking out of seven different snowbanks, kicking away.

"Uh-oh," said Mickey. He dashed over to the side of the pond and, one by one, he pulled all of his friends out of the snow.

"Gee, sorry about that," said Mickey.

Goofy shook his head, and snow flew everywhere. "That was fun!" he said cheerfully. "But I sure could use a cup of . . ."

"Yoo-hoo!" came a cheerful cry. It was Grandma Duck, standing at the edge of the pond. She was carrying a flask filled with hot chocolate!

"Hooray!" cried all the friends.

Disney
Lady and the TRAMP

In the Doghouse

"Good morning, Tramp," said Lady, with a yawn and a stretch. She rolled over on her silk cushion. "Wasn't that just the most wonderful night's sleep?"

But Tramp's night's sleep had been far from wonderful. In fact, he hadn't had much sleep at all. The past night had been Tramp's first sleeping in Lady's house . . . or in any house, come to think of it.

"How do you do it?" he grumbled. "That bed is so soft, I feel like I'm sinking in a feather pool. And between Jim Dear's snoring and the baby's crying, I could barely hear the crickets chirping."

"Oh, dear," Lady said, feeling truly sorry for her mate. "I know!" she exclaimed. "Jim Dear and Darling love you so – I'm sure they'd let you sleep up on their bed tonight. There's nothing in the world better than that!"

But Tramp shook his head. "I'm afraid it's the outdoors I need," he explained. "I mean, I know you grew up this way and all . . . but it's just so much fun to sleep under the stars. And the moon too. There's nothing to howl at in this bedroom."

"You can see the moon out the window," Lady told him.

But Tramp shook his head. "It's not the same. You know," he went on, "we've still got that fine doghouse in the yard. What do you

say we go back out there tonight? It'll be like a honeymoon!"

"Well . . ." Lady looked at Tramp's tired eyes. "Okay."

And so that night, as soon as the sun set and the moon began to rise, Lady and Tramp went out to the garden.

Happy at last, Tramp turned three times and then plopped down. "Oh, how I love the feel of cool dirt on my belly!" he said with a dreamy smile . . . while Lady gingerly peeked into the dark and slightly damp kennel. The stars were not even out, and already she missed the comforts of Jim Dear's and Darling's room.

Tramp watched as Lady stretched out on the kennel floor, then got up and moved outside, then back in once again. It was plain to see: try as she might, Lady just could not relax on the cold, hard ground.

"Don't worry," Tramp announced, "I have an idea."

And with that, he ran into the house . . . and in seconds reappeared with Lady's cushion in his teeth. Carefully, he swept the kennel with his tail, and laid the cushion down just the way Lady liked it.

Lady smiled and lay down. And, do you know what? That night, they both had the sweetest dreams either one had ever had.

THE INCREDIBLES

I'm Syndrome!

Bob and Helen Parr were Supers, but they had to stop using their powers when people started complaining about them – some people didn't want to be saved! But Bob had missed his life as a Super and had started Super work again. A woman called Mirage had seen him doing this, and brought him to the island of Nomanisan and given him a mission to defeat an evil robot called an Omnidroid. He had succeeded.

Bob's wife, Helen, didn't know about any of this – Bob knew she'd be upset, so didn't tell her.

Bob was feeling good. He started exercising more and even had a new Super suit made by fashion designer Edna Mode. The new suit arrived just in time. Mirage had a new assignment for Bob.

Bob told Helen it was a business conference and flew back to the island. But Helen had discovered a blonde hair on his jacket. She wondered where he was really going....

Mr Incredible got quite a shock when he arrived for his briefing. A new and improved Omnidroid attacked him! This time the robot was unbeatable. As it defeated the hero, a stranger in a black costume appeared.

"It's too much for Mr Incredible," the stranger gloated. "I went through quite a few Supers to make it worthy to fight you. But you're worth it. After all, I'm your biggest fan."

"Buddy?" Mr Incredible said. Buddy was once Mr Incredible's number-one fan. As a boy, Buddy had asked to be the Super's sidekick. But Mr Incredible had explained to him that Supers were born, not made.

"My name's not Buddy, I'm Syndrome!" Buddy cried. "And now I have a weapon that only I can defeat!"

As Mr Incredible tried to escape, Syndrome froze him in his immobi-ray. "Who's Super now?" he yelled. But then he lost control and accidentally flung Mr Incredible off a waterfall.

Syndrome threw a bomb after him but Mr Incredible found safety in an underwater cave. Syndrome sent a probe to find him. But the hero hid behind the remains of Gazerbeam – a Super who had died battling the Omnidroid.

Just before he died, Gazerbeam had used his laser vision to etch the word KRONOS on the cave wall. What could it mean? Bob wondered.

Meanwhile, Helen had found Bob's newly mended suit. She knew that Edna must have fixed it, so she went straight to her to find out what Bob was up to – and where he was! It was up to Helen to help her husband now.

Robin Lends a Hand

It was a hot day in Sherwood Forest – a very hot day! So hot that the Sheriff of Nottingham had decided not to collect taxes, for fear the coins would burn his greedy hands!

As for himself, Robin Hood was trying to keep cool in the shade of Sherwood's oaks. Taking off his hat, he stretched out under the tallest, broadest tree, closed his eyes, and waited for a breeze.

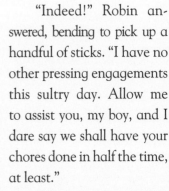

"Halt! Who goes there?" he shouted suddenly. "Oh!" His eyes rested on a startled little bunny with a load of twigs scattered about his feet. "Skippy, my good man. Forgive me. I didn't mean to scare you."

Quickly, Robin helped to load up Skippy's arms once again. "Now, then," he said, patting the bunny on the shoulder. "That's better." But Skippy didn't seem to agree. Robin didn't think he had ever seen him look so unhappy.

"Why so glum, old chum?" Robin couldn't help but ask.

"Oh, Robin," Skippy sighed. "It's so very hot, and all the other children have gone to the swimming hole. But Mother has so many chores for me to do, I don't think I'll ever be able to join them."

"I see," said Robin, nodding. "That could get a fellow down, now, couldn't it?"

"I'll say," said Skippy.

"Unless . . ." Robin went on with a big grin, ". . . a fellow had a friend to help him out!"

Skippy's sorrowful face grew brighter. "Do you mean . . . ?"

"Indeed!" Robin answered, bending to pick up a handful of sticks. "I have no other pressing engagements this sultry day. Allow me to assist you, my boy, and I dare say we shall have your chores done in half the time, at least."

"Hooray for Robin Hood!" Skippy cheered, nearly dropping his sticks once again. "Hip, hip, hooray!"

And so, working together, Robin Hood and Skippy gathered firewood. They wrung out the laundry and hung it out to dry. They picked some juicy plums and a basketful of lettuce, weeded the garden and built a scarecrow. By lunchtime, in fact, not only was every one of Skippy's chores done, but he and Robin had washed all the windows and swept Skippy's cottage floor.

"Robin Hood, how can I ever thank you? I'd still be hard at work if it wasn't for you!" Skippy asked when they were through.

Robin scratched his head and thought for a moment. "I have it!" he declared at last. "Take me swimming with you!"

"You betcha!" Skippy said happily. "C'mon, let's go! Last one in is a rotten sheriff!"

The Search for Hamm

Woody the cowboy doll opened his eyes. The sun was up and Andy had left for school. The house was quiet, so Woody walked around the room. But he soon realised that something was wrong.

Hamm the piggy bank was nowhere in sight. No one had seen him since last night! The toys decided to form a search party, and the Aliens found the first sign of Hamm on Andy's desk – a pile of coins.

Has Hamm lost his coins? Woody thought. Or maybe Andy has decided he doesn't need a piggy bank any more! Woody exchanged a worried glance with Buzz.

The toys set off to search the house. Suddenly, Rex wailed from the hallway. Buzz and Woody went rushing out. There was another pile of coins, and they were wet!

"Do you think it's dog slobber?" Buzz asked.

"What?" Rex cried. "You mean Buster took Hamm? Oh, no! I always knew that dog was out to get one of us. And now he has! Oh, poor Hamm!"

Woody, Buzz and Rex walked into the living room. Sarge was on the sofa.

"The troops have found a trace of the missing-in-action toy up here," Sarge said. On the cushions was a cluster of coins.

Just then, one of the Green Army Men sounded the alarm. Andy and his mum had arrived in the driveway outside! All of the toys raced back to Andy's room.

Seconds later, Andy dashed into the room. He threw his backpack on the floor, then ran to his toy box. "Here it is!" he said, pulling out his baseball and glove. He ran back out of the room again. Then, the toys heard a noise – clink, clink, clank, clink.

"What was that?" Rex asked. The noise was coming from Andy's backpack. It sounded like... coins! Woody rushed over and unzipped the backpack. Out tumbled Hamm!

"Hamm you big pink pig!" Woody said. "What were you doing in there?"

"Andy took me to school to collect money for a soccer fundraiser," Hamm said.

"But we thought you were in trouble," Buzz said. "There were piles of coins all over the house."

"Oh, that was just Andy playing," Hamm replied. "He was tossing me in the air like a baseball when we left this morning. And Buster was following us, drooling everywhere. That dog needs some toys."

"Well, it's sure good to have you back," Woody said, as he gave Hamm a big hug!

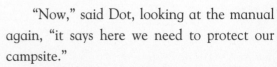

Survival of the Smallest

It was the first day of summer, and Dot and the other Blueberries were getting ready for a big adventure. They were heading out for the First Annual Blueberry Wilderness Expedition. Their journey would take them to the thicket of tall grasses next to the ant colony. It was only a few yards from home – but, to a little ant, it seemed like an awfully long way.

As the group prepared to leave, some boy ants arrived to tease them.

"How do you expect to go on an expedition without supplies?" asked Jordy.

Dot put her hands on her hips. "For your information," she said in a superior tone, "the whole point is to survive using our smarts. Whatever we need, we'll make when we get there."

The Blueberries hiked a few yards from the ant colony, then Dot consulted her survival manual. "Okay," she said, "the first thing we need to do is build a shelter from the sun."

"I know!" Daisy volunteered. "We could make a hut. All we have to do is stick twigs into the dirt side by side to make the walls, then lay leaves over the top for the roof."

The rest of the Blueberries decided this was a great idea. With a lot of teamwork and determination, they completed a shelter to comfortably hold the troop.

"Now," said Dot, looking at the manual again, "it says here we need to protect our campsite."

So the girls dug a narrow trench in front of the hut, just as the manual instructed.

The girls gathered some seeds and went into their homemade hut to have some lunch. A short while later, they heard a scream. When they went to investigate, they discovered Reed, Grub and Jordy at the bottom of the trench.

It was clear to the Blueberries that the boys had been up to no good.

"Girls," said Dot, pointing to the boys, "observe one of the Blueberries' most common natural enemies – though certainly not one of the smartest."

When it was time for the Blueberries to pack up and hike home, the boys were still stuck in the trench. "Say the magic words and I'll get you out of there," said Dot.

"Okay, okay!" Reed, Grub and Jordy agreed.

"Well?" demanded Dot.

"Blueberries rock," the boys admitted.

Dot lowered down a ladder she had expertly made of sticks. "You bet we do!" she said. "'Cause if we can survive you, we can survive anything!"

Monster Truck Mater

One day outside Flo's V8 Café, Lightning McQueen pointed out a monster truck that was driving by.

"I used to wrestle trucks bigger than that," Mater said. He began to tell Lightning about the time he was a wrestler called the Tormentor. His first match was in an arena filled with cheering fans. Mater wore a blue-and-red mask.

An ice-cream truck with monster wheels rolled into the ring. The Tormentor wasn't sure how to wrestle such a big truck. So he put on a cap, hoping to trick his opponent instead. "Can I have one double-dip sundae, please?"

"Huh?" said the I-Screamer. "Oh, sure." When the ice-cream truck reached for a sundae, the Tormentor grabbed his bumper with his tow hook and flipped him. The referee announced that the Tormentor had won.

After his first win, the Tormentor just couldn't stop winning, and soon he made it all the way to the world championship match! He was feeling confident until he saw... Dr Frankenwagon's Monster! Just one of the Monster's tyres was bigger than the Tormentor. He had a giant scoop on one side and a claw on the other. The wrecking ball on his back could crush a truck with one direct hit.

Back in Radiator Springs, Lightning interrupted the story. "Whoa!" he cried. "What did you do?"

Mater looked over at his friend. "Don't you remember nothin'? We was a tag team."

Mater continued his story, except this time, Lightning was also in the ring, wearing his own wrestling outfit.

"Tag, you're it!" said Mater, touching Lightning with his tyre. The Monster lunged for the race car, ignoring the tow truck.

Lightning saw their opponent coming straight at him. Lightning raced around the ring to avoid the Monster's wrecking ball. When the Tormentor heard Lightning call for help he ducked back into the ring. Luckily, the Tormentor had a plan.

While the Monster's wrecking ball was on the ground, the Tormentor quickly snagged it with his tow hook. Then he zipped under one side of the ring and out the other. With a wink at his fans, the Tormentor yanked his towline. He flipped the entire ring – trapping the Monster underneath!

"The winners!" the referee announced. "The Tormentor and..." He turned to Lightning. "What's your name?"

"Lightning McQueen," he replied.

"And Frightening McMean!"

Finding Ne-who?

"The coral reef is falling down, falling down, falling down."

Nemo was home, brushing up against the anemone, when the most awful singing he ever heard in his life made him cringe. He swam deeper into the anemone, but it didn't help. The song went on.

"My fair octopus."

And there was something familiar about it . . . . Still cringing, Nemo poked his head out of the golden tentacles to see who was making the awful racket.

"Dory!" Nemo should have known. How could he have forgotten that voice? Nemo swam as fast as he could toward the regal blue tang fish. "Dory! Where have you been?" It seemed like a whale's age since Nemo had seen the fish that helped his dad rescue him from the dentist's fish tank. And he couldn't wait to give her a big hug!

When Nemo got closer Dory stopped singing. That was good. But when she looked at him her face was blank. That wasn't so good.

"Did you say something, kid?" she asked.

"Dory, it's me. Nemo," he replied.

"Ne-*who*?" She looked at Nemo blankly. "Sorry, kid, don't know you. I was just swimming by, minding my own business, singing a song. Hey, why was I singing? Am I famous? Maybe that's how you know me."

"Dory! We're friends, remember?" Nemo had been missing Dory a lot. She just *had* to remember who he was.

"Friends? I just made friends with a hermit crab . . . I think." Dory swam in a circle looking for the crab, but got distracted and started chasing her tail.

"Please try to remember, Dory," Nemo asked again. "You helped save me. You helped me find my dad. You know my dad. Big orange guy? Three white stripes? Looks kind of like me?"

"My dad? Looks like you? Sorry, kid, you don't look anything like my dad." Dory looked at Nemo like he was crazy and began to swim away.

Nemo swam after her. "Just think about it for a second," he pleaded. She *had* to remember something. "I'm Nemo!"

Dory did not turn around but she slowed down. Swimming in a wide circle, she came back. She looked at Nemo sideways, and then started laughing so hard bubbles came out of her nose.

"Had you going, huh?" Dory gave Nemo a big hug and smiled at him slyly. "That was just my little joke. You know I could never forget you!"

Nemo giggled and swam circles around his friend. "Good one, Dory!" He grinned.

Dory smiled back. "Good one, *who*?"

Nemo groaned. That Dory!

Bambi

Sweeter than Clover

"Hi, Bambi," said a soft voice.

Bambi looked up from the grass he was eating, and his friend Flower stopped searching for berries. Standing there was the pretty young fawn Bambi had met that spring.

"Hi, Faline," Bambi said. "It's nice to see you!"

"It's nice to see you too," Faline said shyly.

"Faline!" a young male deer called across the meadow. "Come over and play with me!"

Bambi's eyes narrowed. He didn't like the idea of Faline going off to play with someone else.

Faline blinked in confusion. "Do you want me to go?" she asked Bambi.

"No, don't go," said Bambi. But what could he say to make her stay? he wondered. Suddenly, Bambi had an idea.

"I want to show you something special," he told her.

"Something special?" asked Faline.

"I know where to find the sweetest clover you'll ever taste," Bambi bragged. Thumper had shown him exactly where to find it.

"Where?" asked Faline.

"Just follow me!" exclaimed Bambi.

He led Faline across the meadow to the babbling brook. Then he followed the brook all the way up a steep grassy hill. Finally they came to a big waterfall.

"The sweet clover is right here by this weeping willow tree," said Bambi.

Bambi couldn't wait to share it with Faline. But, when he got to the tree, there wasn't one single clover blossom left.

"Oh, that Thumper!" complained Bambi.

"What's the matter?" asked Faline.

Bambi shook his head. He felt very silly. He'd brought Faline all this way, and now he had nothing special to share with her!

But, just then, Bambi looked up.

"Look," he whispered. "Up in the sky."

Faline looked up and gasped.

Shimmering bands of colour had formed an arc over the waterfall.

"It's so beautiful," whispered Faline. "I've never seen anything like it."

"Neither have I," said Bambi. "But I remember hearing my mother talk about it. I think it's called a rain . . . bow."

"It's wonderful!" cried Faline.

"I'm glad you think so," said Bambi, a little relieved. "But I'm sorry you came all this way for no clover."

"Oh, Bambi," said Faline. "I came because I wanted to be with you. And, besides, a rainbow is a much sweeter surprise than some silly old clover, anyway!"

A Roaring Field Trip

Andy was feeling very excited. The next day he was going on a field trip to the science museum! His mother was even going to give him some money to spend at the gift shop.

Andy's toys were worried that Andy might find some new toys at the gift shop, so Woody, Buzz and Rex decided they should go along.

The next morning, the toys climbed inside Andy's backpack for their big trip.

When Andy's class arrived at the museum, they excitedly followed their teacher inside. Much to the toys' dismay, Andy left his backpack in the cloakroom! The toys looked at each other in alarm.

"I didn't come all this way to sit in a coatroom," Buzz said.

So, the three toys decided to explore the museum on their own. They found a map and covered themselves with it as they made their way across the museum floor. Rex led them to the dinosaur exhibit and had fun mimicking the other dinosaurs. Then, Buzz spotted an outer space exhibit!

"Buzz, we don't have time for this!" scolded Woody.

"Sure we do," said Buzz. The three friends raced inside just in time. Suddenly, the ceiling lit up. Planets, moons and stars moved in the sky above them.

"That, my friends, is our solar system," said Buzz. "The planet closest to the sun is Mercury. Then comes Venus, Earth, Mars, Jupiter, Saturn, Uranus and Neptune."

"All this is extremely informative," said Woody. "But isn't anyone the slightest bit worried that Andy might get back to the coatroom before we do?"

When the show was over, a voice said: "Your attention, please. The museum will be closing in five minutes."

"We'll never make it back there in time!" cried Woody. "Andy's going to leave!"

"No, he's not," replied Buzz. "Not when we've got a spaceship." He pointed to a model suspended from the ceiling. The toys made a mad dash for the escalator, then jumped into the model spaceship.

"Everybody, lean forward!" Buzz commanded. The spaceship picked up speed, zipping along the cable that attached it to the ceiling. Once it was directly above Andy's bag, the toys jumped. They landed softly inside! Woody found a bag from the gift shop, and a roll of stickers that Andy had bought.

"Now that's what I call a good choice!" Rex said.

"It's out of this world!" Buzz replied.

Disney's
chicken little

A Day to Remember

Chicken Little started to cross the street. But he wasn't watching where he was going. *Squish!* He stepped on a piece of chewing gum.

Chicken Little tried to move, but he was stuck. Suddenly, the light turned green. Cars were headed straight for him! Quickly, he pulled a lollipop from his pocket and licked it. Then he slapped the lollipop onto a car's bumper and held on tight. The car pulled him out of the gum, but his pants had stuck to the ground!

When he got to school, Chicken Little used a bottle of fizzy drink to shoot into the air like a rocket. A little while later, Chicken Little hurried into sports class wearing a pair of origami pants he'd cleverly made out of his maths homework. The class was playing dodgeball. Suddenly, Foxy's sidekick, Goosey, grabbed Chicken Little and threw him across the room. Splat! He hit the window. As he started to fall, he grabbed a handle on the wall.

Riiiiiiiiinnngg! He'd pulled the fire alarm. Sprinklers went off! Chicken Little's origami pants filled with water until – *rrrriipp!* – they tore and slid off. When the principal found out, he called Chicken Little's father, Buck Cluck.

On the drive home, Chicken Little told his dad that he wanted to join the baseball team.

His friends helped him train but it was no use. The coach wouldn't let him play. Game after game, Chicken Little sat on the bench.

Finally, it was the last game of the season. The game was on the line, and there were only two batters left: Chicken Little and Foxy Loxy. The announcer looked at the lineup card. "Up next, Chicken Little," he said.

No one expected Chicken Little to even hit the ball. The pitcher threw the first pitch. Chicken Little swung at the ball. "Strike one!" called the umpire. The pitcher threw the second pitch. Chicken Little missed again. The pitcher wound up for the third pitch. If Chicken Little missed this ball, the Acorns would lose the game.

"Today is a new day," Chicken Little told himself. As the ball came towards him, he closed his eyes and swung his bat hard. Craaack! Chicken Little's eyes flew open. He'd hit the ball! He began to run – the wrong way! Finally, Chicken Little figured out which way to run. He slid into home just as the throw came from the outfield. After the umpire dusted off the plate, he saw Chicken Little's foot and made the call. "The runner is safe!" Chicken Little had won the game!

Chicken Little was thrilled. Maybe, he thought, things were changing after all.

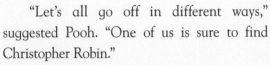

A Misunderstanding

One fine autumn morning, Winnie the Pooh found a lovely pot of honey outside his door with a note. "Whoever could have given it to me?" he wondered.

Pooh, Piglet, Rabbit, Eeyore and Tigger decided to ask Owl to read the note.

"This letter has been written by Christopher Robin," declared Owl. "He's gone far away to s-c-h-o-o-l. Skull! You must rescue him!"

To help them find the little boy, Owl came up with a plan. The friends set off with a map and came to a strange forest with scary plants and an enormous boulder towered up in front of them!

The travellers found an opening in the boulder, they looked inside and saw it was filled with a tangle of thorny branches. Then they all thought they heard a growling Skullasaurus and Piglet ran as fast as he could out of the forest – leaving his friends behind.

Piglet found himself in a valley full of butterflies. As his friends arrived, the butterflies lifted Piglet off the ground! "Are you doing parachuting, Piglet?" asked Pooh.

Pooh jumped up to rescue him. Once Piglet was back on the ground, the hikers went off in search of Christopher Robin once more, and soon arrived at a cave. Inside, there were lots of crossing paths.

"Let's all go off in different ways," suggested Pooh. "One of us is sure to find Christopher Robin."

While the others were having their own adventures, Pooh found some ice crystals that made him look big and scary. He cast a scary shadow over his friends, and they heard more growling noises that grew louder and louder.

Tigger yelled, "It's the terriblest Skullasaurus ever!"

They all ran away – including Pooh, who slipped and fell into a deep hole with an icy floor!

"Hey! Hey! Can anybody hear me?" Pooh called.

Luckily, the other friends were found by Christopher Robin and they lowered a big honey pot down to Pooh to rescue him!

"You misunderstood my message!" Christopher Robin said. "It said I was going to school."

"But what about the Skullasaurus?" squeaked Piglet. "We heard him growling!"

"That's no Skullasaurus," Christopher Robin said with a chuckle. "That's the sound of the rumbly tummy of a hungry-for-honey bear."

Christopher Robin gave Pooh the pot of honey. "Now we're all together, let's enjoy the afternoon!"

Alien Invasion

Chicken Little was tired of everyone laughing at him and calling him "that crazy little chicken".

Life was just getting back to normal when part of the sky fell – right into Chicken Little's bedroom. He thought it looked like some sort of panel.

Chicken Little called his friends Abby, Runt and Fish and they came over. "I'm sure there's a simple explanation," Abby said.

While the others tried to figure out a plan, Fish climbed on top of the panel. To everyone's surprise, it floated off the floor and zoomed out of the window!

"Come on!" cried Chicken Little. He and his pals chased after Fish. The panel came to a stop over the baseball stadium. Suddenly, a spaceship appeared! Chicken Little, Runt and Abby ran for shelter in the dugout. While the friends watched, two spidery-looking aliens dropped out of the hatch and scuttled off.

Chicken Little, Abby and Runt climbed aboard the spaceship to rescue Fish. It was dark inside. The only friendly sight was a cute orange creature floating in a beam of light. Chicken Little stopped and winked at it, and it winked back. Then it hopped down and followed Chicken Little. Suddenly, Fish jumped out from behind a screen. He was just fine.

"All right, let's get out of here," Abby ordered. But now Runt was missing! Fish pointed to a room down the hall. Runt was staring up at the ceiling with a terrified look on his face. A giant picture of the entire solar system was on the wall. Several planets were crossed out, but Earth was circled. It looked like the aliens were going to destroy the planet!

"We're running back to your house and you're going to tell your dad," Abby said.

Meanwhile, the aliens had returned to the ship and discovered that the fuzzy orange creature was missing. The aliens saw Chicken Little and his pals and assumed they'd taken it! Chicken Little, Abby, Runt and Fish left the ship and ran into the forest. The aliens were right behind them!

"We've got to ring the school bell to warn everyone!" Abby cried. They raced to the school and rang the bell. *Ding-dong! Ding-dong!*

The aliens fled back to their ship just as the alarmed townspeople gathered at the school. Everyone thought Chicken Little had imagined the whole thing – just like he had imagined that the sky was falling.

Chicken Little just knew that he had to find a way to make everyone believe him. After all, it was a new day.

Disney
MICKEY MOUSE
CLUBHOUSE

Farmer Donald's Pumpkin Patch

"Look at this!" said Daisy as she came into the Clubhouse one day. "This pumpkin won the grand prize at the County Fair!"

"Hot dog!" said Mickey. "That is one big pumpkin!"

"Aw, phooey!" Donald said. "I could grow a garden filled with the biggest pumpkins you've ever seen!"

The next day, Donald got pumpkin seeds and threw them on the dirt.

"I think it takes more than that to grow a garden," said Minnie.

Mickey nodded. "First you need to make holes in the dirt, put a seed in each hole and then cover them up."

"That's a lot of work," said Donald.

"Maybe Toodles can help," said Mickey.

Toodles showed them a pogo stick, a mirror and an elephant.

Minnie picked the pogo stick to help them make holes for the seeds. Then Donald dropped a seed into each hole and covered them all with dirt.

"See, I told you this would be easy," said Donald as he sat back down.

"I think it takes more than that to grow a garden," said Daisy.

"A garden needs water," Mickey said. "Water helps seeds grow."

The friends called Toodles again, and this time they chose the elephant. The elephant took a big drink from the pond, then using her trunk she sprinkled water over the entire garden.

"I told you this would be easy," said Donald.

"I think it takes more than that to grow a garden," said Mickey.

Donald was puzzled. "What else is there to do?"

"Plants need sun," said Minnie. "But your garden is in the shade."

Toodles had just one tool left – a mirror. "A mirror?" asked Donald. "How can that help my garden grow?"

Mickey and Minnie placed the mirror so that it reflected the sunlight onto the garden.

"Oh, boy!" shouted Donald. "Now we'll just watch the seeds grow."

Daisy giggled. "Now we have to make sure the garden keeps getting plenty of water and sunlight and care, Farmer Donald!"

Donald discovered that growing a garden wasn't as easy as he thought. But over the next few months, he worked hard.

When it was time for the pumpkin contest, Donald picked the biggest, most beautiful pumpkin from his garden, and the whole gang headed to the fair.

Judge Goofy announced, "The prize for the biggest pumpkin goes to Farmer Donald!"

Lady and the TRAMP

Lost and Found

Lady stretched and rolled over. It was so cosy up on the window seat. Sunlight shone through the glass and glinted on her diamond-shaped name tag. Lady sighed contentedly. The tag was her most prized possession. Besides her owners, of course. Jim Dear and Darling were very good to her. Just last night, they had given her and Tramp steak bones to munch on. There were so many, they had not been able to eat them all.

The bones! Lady had almost forgotten them. Leaping off the window seat, she hurried to the kitchen. Luckily, they were still right next to her food bowl.

Lady began to carry the bones into the garden. It took three trips, but soon the bones were lying in a heap on the grass. Then she got to work.

Dig, dig, dig. The soil piled up behind her as Lady dug yet another hole. She carefully nosed the last bone into the hole and covered it with soil. After prancing delicately on top to pat down the soil, she collapsed in an exhausted heap. Burying bones was hard work!

Rolling over, Lady let the sun warm her belly. The garden was the perfect place for a late-afternoon nap. She was just dozing off when, suddenly, her neck itched. Sitting up, Lady gave it a scratch. But something was missing.

Lady stopped scratching and gingerly felt her neck. Her collar! It was gone!

Panicked, Lady searched the garden for the collar. It was nowhere to be found.

I must have buried it with one of my bones! Lady realized with a jolt. She looked at all the freshly dug holes. It would take her all night to dig up the bones. But she just had to find her collar!

Tramp will help, Lady thought. She ran inside to get him. He was playing with the puppies, but ran outside as soon as he heard what was wrong. Soon the two dogs were busy undoing all of Lady's hard work.

"I see something shiny!" Tramp called. Lady was by his side in an instant, but it wasn't the collar. It was just an old bottle cap. Lady dropped her head sadly.

Lady and Tramp got right back to digging. And, just as dusk was falling, Tramp unearthed a thick blue band with a golden, diamond-shaped tag. Lady's collar!

Lady let out a happy bark. Then she carried the collar into the house and sat down at Jim Dear's feet.

"Your collar came off, Lady?" Jim asked as he fastened the collar around Lady's neck. "It's a good thing you didn't accidentally bury it with your bones!"

The Flying Blueberries

Everyone in the ant colony was in a good mood. The grasshoppers had been driven off once and for all, and none of the ants had even been hurt. But Flik's amazing fake bird had taken quite a beating, and the Blueberries were determined to mend it.

"Fixing that bird is a big job," said Mr Soil, Dot's teacher, "but I know the Blueberries can do it."

The Blueberries stared at the fake bird. It was a big mess!

"I'll be back in a little while to see how you're doing," said Mr Soil before he left.

"How can we ever fix this thing?" one of the Blueberries cried.

"We can do it!" said Dot. "I bet we can make it even better this time!"

With a cheer, the Blueberries went to work. Some picked new leaves to cover the frame. Others glued those leaves into place with sticky honey.

After hours of hard work, the bird was mended.

"Let's sit in it!" Dot said.

But, just as the Blueberries crawled inside the bird, the wind began to blow. Suddenly, the breeze caught the wings. The bird took off!

It was up to Dot to save the day. She hopped into the pilot seat and took control. The Blueberries flew around Ant Island once, then twice. Soon they weren't afraid any more.

"Look!" screamed Rose. "Real birds are attacking the worker ants!" Dot jiggled the controls. The fake bird dived out of the sky and frightened the real birds away.

"Hooray!" yelled the Blueberries.

"Don't cheer yet!" Dot cried. "This contraption is out of control!"

With a bump and a crash, the bird hit the ground and skidded to a halt.

"Everybody get out!" Princess Dot commanded. One by one, the Blueberries escaped.

"It's wrecked again!" said Rose. "And here comes Mr Soil! He's going to be so mad!"

But, surprisingly, Mr Soil was smiling.

"You're heroes!" he told them. "You saved the worker ants."

"But the bird is wrecked again," said Rose.

"And you can fix it again too," Mr Soil replied.

"Yeah," said Dot, "and when it's fixed again we'll go up for another flight."

"Hooray!" the Blueberries cried.

"And here is a merit badge for you, Princess, in honour of your first flight," said Mr Soil.

Dot was confused. "I've already made my first flight," she said, fluttering her tiny wings.

"Ah, but this is a special badge," Mr Soil replied. "It is for making your first flight not using your wings, but using your head!"

Disney·PIXAR
MONSTERS, INC.

A Child in Monstropolis

Late at night, a little boy awoke to see... a monster! He screamed! Then, the monster screamed, too! With a sigh, the teacher turned off the mechanical boy. Then she repeated the rules: "Never scream. And NEVER leave a child's closet door open. Why?"

"It could let in a child!" bellowed Mr Waternoose, the CEO of Monsters, Incorporated.

The Scarers-in-Training gasped. They knew that Monstropolis was powered by children's screams. But letting a child into the world of monsters would be deadly!

Meanwhile, across town, James P. Sullivan was exercising. His assistant (and best friend), Mike Wazowski, was coaching him. Sulley was a professional Scarer.

At Monsters, Inc., Sulley was famous for collecting more screams than anyone else. That was important because the city was having an energy shortage. Human kids were getting harder to scare, and Monstropolis needed all the screams it could get.

It was time for the workday to begin. As other workers watched in awe, Sulley led all the Scarers of Monsters, Inc. onto the Scare Floor. Together, these were the best scream collectors in the business.

One of them was Randall – a creepy and mean monster who was very jealous of Sulley.

As the Scarers prepared for work, a conveyor belt dropped a door at each station. When the red signal flashed, each Scarer would walk through his door – and into the room of a sleeping child. Hopefully, the child would let out a good scream!

Suddenly, an alarm rang out. A Scarer named George had returned from the human world with a child's sock on his back! A squad from the CDA (Child Detection Agency) arrived to decontaminate him. Poor George!

When work was finished, Mike rushed to meet his girlfriend Celia. They had planned a special date. But the company's cranky file clerk blocked Mike's way.

"I'm sure you filed your paperwork," Roz rasped. Mike had forgotten! Luckily, Sulley offered to help.

Back at the Scare Floor, Sulley noticed that someone had left a door behind, its red light still on. Puzzled, Sulley peeked through the door but saw no one. So he closed the door. Then he saw... A CHILD!

"AAAAH!" he screamed.

Human children were the scariest things in the world to the monsters in Monstropolis. What was Sulley going to do now...?

A Rave Review

A young chef named Linguini had just discovered that the great chef Auguste Gusteau had been his father. Gusteau's restaurant now belonged to him and was getting very popular. Remy the rat was helping Linguini by hiding in his hat and controlling the cooking – Remy was the one with the true talent.

But Linguini was enjoying his success a bit too much. He had stopped paying attention to food, and Remy didn't like it.

Suddenly, the famous critic Ego – the very same critic who had once ruined Gusteau's – arrived and gave his warning: "I will return tomorrow night with high expectations."

After Ego's announcement, Remy was furious that Linguini wasn't more worried about cooking, and he yanked Linguini's hair, hard. Linguini got angry. He took Remy out to the back and said, "You take a break, Little Chef. I'm not your puppet."

Remy was cross with Linguini and, later that night, Remy told the entire rat colony to take whatever they wanted from the restaurant's refrigerator. That's when Linguini returned to apologise.

"You're stealing from me?" Linguini furiously asked. "I thought you were my friend. I trusted you! Get out and don't ever come back!"

But Remy did come back. He felt horrible. Plus, Ego had come to review the restaurant. Remy knew his friend Linguini needed help. Boldly, Remy walked alone through the doors, into the bustling kitchen.

"Rat!" shrieked the chefs.

"Don't touch him!" shouted Linguini. "The truth is, I have no talent at all. But this rat – he's the cook."

From the shadows, Remy's father watched the human defend Remy!

Still, the cooks walked out. Only Remy and Linguini were left.

"I was wrong about you. About him," Remy's father told him. He had never trusted humans before. "I'm proud of you."

Django whistled, and rats instantly filled the kitchen. After going through the dishwasher to clean themselves, the rats began to cook. Even Colette came back.

Linguini, acting as waiter, served a delicious dish of ratatouille to Ego. The taste brought back a warm, comforting memory from Ego's childhood. When Ego asked to meet the chef, Linguini and Colette waited until all the other customers left the restaurant, then they brought out Remy. The next morning Ego gave the restaurant a rave review!

Carl and Ellie's House

After their first meeting, Carl and Ellie became best friends. Every day they would meet at Ellie's clubhouse to play and dream together about exploring the world.

One sunny morning, they decided there was no two ways about it – one day, they would go to South America and live next to Paradise Falls.

The years passed and Ellie grew up to be a cheerful and rather talkative young woman. Carl grew into a dependable and quiet young man.

Their friendship grew into love, and they got married when they were both aged 19. They bought the little empty house they had played in as children and set up home there.

Of course, the old house needed doing up! Ellie busied herself filling in the holes in the roof and Carl fixed a new weather vane.

They also patched up the walls, the windows and the floors. Finally, they painted the whole house in bright colours, exactly as it looked in Ellie's adventure book.

One morning, the only thing left was the letterbox. Ellie decided to take care of it. But she had hardly given the metal its first lick of paint when Carl leant carelessly against it!

Ellie burst out laughing at the big mark left by his hand. She then pressed her own hand to the side of the box. When she lifted it off, the two prints seemed to be joining as if to hold hands....

To earn enough money for their journey to South America, the couple found jobs at the town zoo. Ellie looked after the animals and Carl sold balloons to the children.

When they returned home in the evening, they were pleased to get back to their pretty house.

Ellie painted a superb picture of Paradise Falls, which she stuck above the fireplace. In front of it she placed a fragment of pottery and a small statue of a tropical bird.

Carl added a pair of binoculars and his Spirit of Adventure model. Then he put a jar on a table in which, every month, they put aside some money for their trip.

Unfortunately, whatever they managed to save steadily disappeared! They had to buy new tyres for the car, pay for a plaster cast for Carl and then replace the roof of the house.

But over the years they continued to dream, enjoy themselves and, in the evenings, dance together in their lounge.

Neither of them was worried. They knew that one day they'd leave and live out their big adventure.

UFM: Unidentified Flying Mater

In Radiator Springs, a hubcap flew past Mater and Lightning McQueen. "Hey, look, a UFO!" Mater shouted. "And I know, 'cause I seen one once."

Mater began to tell his friend a tale about the time he saw a spaceship. He had pulled up to a railroad crossing in the desert when suddenly he saw a UFO floating right in front of him! "Well, hey there," he said. "My name is Mater."

"My name is Mator," the UFO replied.

That sounded a lot like his own name, the tow truck thought. "Should I take you to my litre?"

"Your leader," the UFO echoed. Mater led the UFO to the spot where he kept his oil cans. "Here are all my litres," he said.

The UFO looked excited. Mater grabbed a can and drank the oil through a straw. When he glanced over, the UFO was slurping from a large oil drum. Later, Mater showed his new friend around. They did all Mater's favourite things, including tractor tipping. Then his new friend taught Mater how to fly! "We're going to be best friends forever!" Mater exclaimed.

Suddenly, a giant magnet dropped from the sky. ZINGGGG! It grabbed the UFO and pulled him upwards. Three military helicopters were hovering overhead.

"Mator! I'll save you!" Mater yelled.

He secretly followed the helicopters through the desert to a military base and sneaked inside. Several military and science vehicles were examining the UFO. "Dadgum!" the UFO exclaimed.

"He's trying to communicate!" one of the scientists said. "Where's Dr Abschleppwagen?"

Mater quickly put on a scientist disguise. "Here I am!" he announced.

"What does 'dadgum' mean?" asked one scientist.

"It means..." Mater began. Then he flicked a switch, turning off the magnet! Mater and Mator flew away at top speed. Everyone from the military base chased after them....

In Radiator Springs, Lightning interrupted. "Do you expect me to believe that?"

"You should," Mater said. "You was there, too!" Then he continued his story. Except this time, Mater described how Lightning was zooming across the desert too. Suddenly, an enormous mother ship appeared. It pulled Mater, Mator and Lightning aboard in a beam of light. Then the ship blasted into space. After a quick ride through space, it was time for Mater and Lightning to get back.

"Thank you!" Mater called when they were safely home. He would miss his new friend, Mator, but he was glad the little UFO was safe.

Disney
Lady and the TRAMP

A Tramp Tale

It was a warm, spring evening, just about the time the first star comes out to shine, and *long* past the time for Lady's and Tramp's puppies to go to sleep.

"Just one more story, Dad," begged Scamp.

Tramp rolled his eyes.

"Well . . ." he said, "okay, but just one."

Happily, the puppies snuggled down onto their cushion. Tramp stretched out beside them.

"Did I ever tell you kids about the time I stole my very first sausage?" he asked.

"*Tramp!*" Lady warned him from her seat across the parlour. "That hardly sounds like a proper story for the children."

"Oh, tell it, Dad!" Scamp urged him.

"Well, maybe 'stole' isn't exactly the right word," Tramp reassured his wife. "And besides, it's got a great moral!" And with that, he began his tale:

"Now this all happened way back when I was just a little pup, already living on my own in the big city. I hope you puppies know just how good you have it living here in this nice house, with Junior and Jim Dear and Darling. Your old dad, though, was not so lucky. Oh, I had a lot of friends. And I had a lot of fun. But I'd be lying if I said I wasn't hungry – just a little – nearly every day.

"Well, one day I was especially hungry, and my nose was picking up all sorts of savoury scents. If there was bacon frying a mile away, I could have told you how many strips. So you can imagine the interest I developed in a certain, spicy smell coming from the butcher shop. Well, I followed my trusty nose, which has still never let me down and, sure enough, there was a heaping tray of steaming sausages. Can you believe it?"

"So you jumped up and gobbled them all up! Right?" Scamp broke in.

"That's my boy!" Tramp laughed. "But no. Don't forget, I was just a little guy. Couldn't reach the tray. All I could do was think about how to get that sausage . . . when up walked a lady with a kid in a carriage. Well, at first I was irate. Competition! But then I noticed the crumbs all over the carriage. Hey! I thought to myself. This might be the ticket – this kid obviously can't hang on to anything. Sure enough, when the lady handed the kid a piece of sausage, the kid dropped it, and down it fell into my waiting mouth! Delicious!

"See, Lady," Tramp added with a grin, "no stealing!"

"And what exactly is the moral of that story?" Lady asked.

Tramp laughed. "Why, good things come to those who wait, of course!"

WET CEMENT

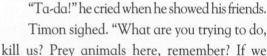

THE LION KING
Simba's Thank-you Present

Simba lounged in the jungle, feeling happier than he'd felt in ages. After the terrible stampede near Pride Rock, he didn't think he'd ever be happy again. But his new friends Timon and Pumbaa had helped him feel better.

"I should do something to thank them," Simba told himself as he watched his friends splash in the river nearby. "Something really special!"

He decided to make them a present. When he saw a large piece of bark lying on the ground, he had an idea.

"Ta-da!" he exclaimed a while later, leading his friends to the gift.

Pumbaa blinked. "Thanks," he said. "Er, what is it?"

"A scratching spot," Simba said, flexing his claws. He'd used vines to attach it to a thick tree trunk at shoulder height.

"Gee," Timon said. "Nice thought and all, Simba. But it's a little high for me." He stretched to his full height but could barely reach it.

Pumbaa nodded. "And I don't scratch." He held up one foot. "Hooves, you know."

"Oh." Simba hadn't thought of that.

"Thanks anyway, kid," Pumbaa said.

Simba decided to try again by building them a nice, soft bed to sleep in. He dug a cosy hole in the ground, then filled it with soft things – feathers, sand and bits of fur.

"Ta-da!" he cried when he showed his friends.

Timon sighed. "What are you trying to do, kill us? Prey animals here, remember? If we sleep on the ground, we become somebody's midnight snack!"

Simba sighed as they left again. Why couldn't he come up with a present they would like?

"I would've loved that scratching spot," he mumbled. "The bed, too."

Suddenly he sat up straight, realizing what he'd just said. All this time he'd been thinking of presents HE would like – but the presents weren't for him.

"I've got to think like they think," he whispered. Slowly, a smile spread across his face . . . .

A little while later he called them over. "I've got something for you." He pointed to a pile of palm fronds. "I think you're really going to like it. Ta-da!"

He pulled back the leaves. Underneath was a mass of wriggling, squirming, creeping, crawling creatures – bugs and grubs and worms of every shape and size . . . and flavour.

Timon and Pumbaa gasped with delight. "Simba!" Timon cried. "You're a prince! It's just what we always wanted!"

"Yeah, thanks," Pumbaa mumbled through a mouthful of grubs. "You're a real pal!"

Simba smiled. "No," he said. "Thank *you*. Both of you. *Hakuna matata!*"

The Lost Boys Get Lost

The Lost Boys were walking single file through the woods of Never Land, on their way home after an afternoon of adventure-seeking, when Slightly, who led the way, stopped in his tracks on the bank of Mermaid Lagoon.

The others – Rabbit, the Raccoon Twins, Cubby and Tootles – came to an abrupt halt behind him.

"Wait a minute," said Slightly. "We already passed Mermaid Lagoon. What are we doing here again?"

Behind a bush, Tinker Bell giggled as she watched the Lost Boys looking around in confusion.

Tink had spotted them on their march and had not been able to resist playing a joke. So, she had flown ahead of them and used her fairy magic to enchant various landmarks on their route home. She had made Bald Rock look like Spiky Rock, causing the Lost Boys to make a right turn where they should have turned left. Then she had enlisted the help of the sparrows, convincing them to move from their usual perch in the Sparrow Bird Grove to another group of trees, thus tricking the Lost Boys into making another right turn too soon. And finally, she had enchanted the Towering Elm Tree to look exactly like the Weeping Willow, and the Lost Boys had made yet another wrong turn, thinking they were nearly home.

But now, here they were, walking past Mermaid Lagoon, when Slightly remembered passing the same spot a good while back.

"I think we're walking in circles!" Slightly proclaimed. "Lost Boys, I think we're . . . lost!"

Tinker Bell overheard and tried desperately to stifle her laughter. But, before she could contain it, one giggle exploded into a full-fledged laugh and –

"Hey!" said Cubby. "Did you hear that?"

He darted over to a bush growing alongside the path and moved a branch to one side. There was Tinker Bell, hovering in mid-air, holding her stomach and shaking with laughter.

"Tinker Bell!" cried Tootles.

It didn't take them long to work out that Tinker Bell was laughing at *them* – and that she was the cause of their confusion.

Still laughing, Tinker Bell flitted away, taking her normal route home to the fairy glade: left at the Weeping Willow Tree, right just before Sparrow Bird Grove, right again at Spiky Rock, and on towards the Sparkling Stream, which led to Moon Falls and the fairy glade entrance.

But – wait a minute! After turning right at Spiky Rock, Tinker Bell saw no sign of the Sparkling Stream anywhere. Where was she? She had got completely lost.

Do you know how?

A Fine Feathered Friend

One afternoon, Woody was watching his favourite TV programme. In Woody's Roundup, Sheriff Woody was repainting the old jailhouse. His horse, Bullseye, whinnied and stomped the ground.

"Not today, partner," said Woody. "I've got to finish painting and then I'm helping Miss Tilley with her errands."

Bullseye snorted. Most mornings, he and Woody worked together, but lately it seemed like Woody was too busy. Bullseye wandered off to find Jessie. She was feeding peanuts to a squirrel. Bullseye bent his front legs so she could climb on his back.

"Oh, sorry, Bullseye," she said. "I promised to help this little guy gather some nuts for his friends. Some other time, fella."

Bullseye sadly lowered his head to munch some grass. He felt very lonely. Suddenly, he saw something sitting among the weeds. It was a brown speckled egg. Bullseye looked around for a mother hen, but there wasn't anyone in sight. He found an old basket nearby and used it to carry the egg back to town. When he arrived, he happily trotted into the barn. Jessie was there.

"It's hard work to help an egg hatch," Jessie said. "You'll have to keep it warm. Then, when the chick hatches, you'll have to care for it like its real mum. Do you think you can do it?"

Bullseye cared for the egg just like a mother hen. He tucked hay around it to keep it warm. Finally, one afternoon, Bullseye heard a tapping sound. *Tap-tap-tap.* It was the egg! He watched it closely. A little beak poked through, then the egg broke open! A tiny yellow chick with spots on its back appeared, and Bullseye named him Horsefeathers.

One day, Bullseye and Horsefeathers met Woody and Jessie at the corral. Horsefeathers trotted around the ring and even said "Neigh!"

Jessie looked worried. "Horsefeathers should be learning how to be a chicken, not a horse," she said quietly.

"You've done a fine job, partner," Woody told his horse. "But Horsefeathers needs to be with his real family."

Just then, a mother hen and her chicks passed by. Then Woody heard the strangest sound. "Peep! Peep! Peep!" It was Horsefeathers, chirping like a chicken for the first time!

Horsefeathers ran over to his real mother and she tucked him under her wing.

"He is one unique bird," Woody said, shaking his head.

"And Bullseye is one unique horse," Jessie added. She gave Bullseye a hug. "Good job, partner!"

ROBIN HOOD

School Days

Robin Hood was looking forward to a jolly day of giving to the poor (and possibly stealing from the rich), when whom should he run into but a troop of happy children.

"Cheerio, kids!" he called.

"Come play with us!" shouted the children.

"Ah, I wish I could," said Robin. "But, alas, my work is never done. Enjoy yourselves, though. That's what childhood is all . . . hey now! Just a minute. Shouldn't you scallywags be in school?"

"School!" exclaimed Skippy. "We haven't been to school in ages!"

"And why not?" asked Robin.

"No teacher will come to Sherwood Forest. They fear Prince John will jail them for not paying taxes!" said Sis.

"Well!" huffed Robin. "We'll just see about that. The children of Sherwood Forest shall have a teacher, or my name isn't Robin Hood!"

"Will *you* teach us?" asked Skippy.

"Ah . . . well . . . I think not," said Robin. For while Robin Hood knew his sums and spellings backwards and forwards, his science and history had grown a little rusty.

"Then, who?" asked Sis.

"Never fear," said Robin. "A teacher I will find." But where? he silently wondered . . . .

First, Robin went to the village. "I'm looking for a teacher," he announced.

"You know any one of us would if we could," said the miller. "But we already work day and night just to pay Prince John's taxes."

So Robin Hood went back to the forest to seek out his Merry Men.

"Little John!" he called. "The children need a teacher, and I think you're just the man!"

"Why, thank you, Robin," said Little John. "But I don't think I can do it. I've already promised my help to the baker and the blacksmith."

In fact, not one of his Merry Men could help Robin Hood. They were all too busy.

"Is there no one with time to help the children?" Robin sighed, when suddenly he spied Friar Tuck dozing, as usual, in a mossy glade.

"Wake up, Friar!" said Robin, giving him a shake. "Do I have a job for you!"

Robin explained, and Friar Tuck accepted happily. Then Robin headed off the other way. There was one more thing he had to do.

Later that day, just as Friar Tuck was finishing his alphabet lesson, Robin Hood appeared, carrying a heavy sack.

"What's that?" enquired the children.

"Books!" Robin replied. "Courtesy of Prince John's library! Although," he said with a wink, "he doesn't know it yet."

A Yummy Dream

Winnie the Pooh stepped into his house and sat down with a sigh. He and Piglet had been out on a long walk through the woods. Now Pooh was tired. And, more importantly, he was hungry.

"My tummy feels very rumbly," Pooh said aloud.

Pooh got to his feet and went over to his honey cupboard. There was only one pot of honey inside.

"Oh dear," Pooh said. One pot of honey was not very much. He sat down and began to eat. He ate every last sticky drop. But, when he was finished, his tummy was still feeling a tiny bit rumbly.

"Well, I suppose there's nothing left to do but go to bed," Pooh said sadly. He put on his nightshirt and his nightcap and climbed into his cosy bed. A minute later Pooh's snores filled the air. And dreams began to fill his head – dreams of honey, of course.

Pooh stood before the honey tree. It was so full of honey, it was oozing out of the trunk!

"Yummy, yummy," Pooh said. He began to fill his honeypots.

Then, suddenly, a purple heffalump appeared behind him.

"Mmmm," the heffalump said, licking his lips. The creature stuck his long trunk into one of the honeypots and gobbled up all the honey.

"Those are my honeypots!" Pooh cried.

He tried to sound brave, even though he was just a little bit scared. The heffalump looked very big and very hungry.

The heffalump just stared at Pooh.

Pooh looked at the honeypots. There were a lot of them. Some were full, but most were still empty. Pooh looked at the honey tree. It was still overflowing with honey.

"I have an idea," Pooh said. "Let's fill the honeypots together, then share a nice snack."

The heffalump nodded excitedly. He picked up a honeypot with his trunk and carried it over to the tree. Pooh did the same, and the sweet, sticky honey dripped into the pots.

When all of the pots had been filled, Pooh and the heffalump sat down together. They ate and ate until all the pots were empty and their tummies were full.

"Thank you, Pooh," the heffalump said us he got to his feet. "That was fun. We should do this again soon."

Pooh nodded in agreement and watched the heffalump walk away. Getting to his feet, he patted his tummy.

When Pooh awoke the next morning, to his surprise, his tummy wasn't the slightest bit rumbly. Then he remembered his strange dream. It had been a dream, hadn't it?

Laughter is the Best Medicine

"I hope Quasi is okay out there!" Laverne said fretfully.

The other two gargoyles in the bell tower, Hugo and Victor, nodded in agreement. Their friend Quasimodo had just left Notre Dame to help the young soldier Phoebus search for the Court of Miracles. It was certain to be a dangerous mission.

"The only thing we can do is stay strong, and be hopeful," Victor said solemnly.

Hugo smirked. "How can we *not* be strong?" he said. "We're made of stone, remember?"

"Good one!" Laverne giggled. "Rock solid."

"You know that's not what I meant." Victor frowned at Hugo. "And both of you — don't you have any sense of the seriousness of this situation? Our dear compatriot is out there somewhere, facing grave peril . . . ."

"*Grave* peril?" Laverne said. "Way to be optimistic, Victor — you've already got poor Quasi in his grave!"

"Hoo-hoo!" Hugo whooped. "You slay me! If I were alive, I'd be dying right now!"

As the two of them rolled around on the tower floor, chortling loudly, Victor glared at them.

"I see," he said sternly. "So you two would rather mock me and crack bad jokes than join me in my concern for poor young Quasimodo."

Laverne stood up and brushed herself off. "Why does it have to be an either-or thing, Victor?" she asked. "Just because we're laughing, it doesn't mean we're not worried too."

"But our friend could be in real danger!" Victor exclaimed.

"That's right," Laverne said. "And standing around here all stone-faced isn't going to help him any."

Hugo nodded. "If we spend all our time thinking about how terrible everything is, we'll go nuts."

Waving his arms to help make his point, he accidentally hit a bird's nest that was tucked into one of the eaves. The occupant of the nest squawked and flew upward. Laverne ducked just in time to avoid having the bird fly straight into her face, but then she tripped and fell and landed on the ground. The bird banked upwards, still squawking as it flew over Hugo.

Hugo leaped backwards — and landed on Laverne's hand. She yelled and yanked her hand out from under him. Hugo lost his footing, and landed in a heap on top of Laverne.

Victor stared at his friends, who were trying to untangle themselves.

Then he started to laugh. He laughed harder and harder, until he could hardly speak.

"You know," he said finally, "I think you just might be right. I feel much better already!"

Disney Bambi

A Manner of Speaking

Bambi and his mother were out for a summer's walk. As always, they stopped by the rabbit den where Thumper lived.

"And how are you today, Thumper?" asked Bambi's mother.

"I'd be better if my mum didn't just give me a dumb old bath," he said.

"Thumper! Mind your manners!" his mother scolded.

"I'm sorry, Mama," Thumper said. He looked back at the doe. "I'm fine, thank you," he replied.

Bambi and Thumper were given permission to play, and they headed off into the woods. "So, what do you want to play?" the fawn asked his friend.

"How about hide-and-seek?" Thumper suggested. "I'll hide first, okay?"

Bambi turned his back to Thumper, closed his eyes, and started to count, "One . . . two . . . three . . . four . . . five . . ."

"Save me! Help! Bambi, save me!" Thumper cried. Bambi whirled around to see Thumper hopping towards him with a terrified look on his face. A moment later, a mother bear emerged from a nearby cave with three small cubs toddling behind her.

Though he was terrified, Thumper *still* managed to make a rude comment. "That's the ugliest, meanest-looking creature I ever saw!"

"I beg your pardon?" the mother bear said.

"First, you come into my home and disturb my children while they're sleeping. And then you have the nerve to call me ugly and mean? I think you owe me an apology!"

"Do it!" whispered Bambi. "Apologize."

"I'm s-s-sorry you're ugly and mean," Thumper stammered.

"Thumper!" Bambi cried. "That isn't funny."

Thumper looked confused. "I wasn't trying to be funny," he said.

"Try again!" the bear boomed.

"Um, ma'am," Thumper tried again. "I'm, um, sorry I disturbed your cubs . . . and, um, you look just like a bear mum should look . . . which is big. And nice. Yup, you sure look nice."

Before the mother bear let Thumper and Bambi go, she said, "Like I always tell my children: manners are important. Today, young man, they saved your life!"

Bambi and Thumper ran home as quickly as they could. When they arrived at Thumper's, his mother said, "Just in time for a nice lunch of greens." Thumper was about to tell his mum how awful he thought the greens tasted, then changed his mind. "Thank you, Mama. That sounds wonderful," he said.

Thumper's mother beamed. "What lovely manners! I guess you have been listening to me, after all!" she said, pleased as could be.

Aladdin

Market Day

"What's wrong, Abu?" asked Aladdin. The normally lively little monkey hadn't been himself lately. Abu sat at the window gazing longingly towards the village. "You're right," Aladdin said. "A trip to the marketplace is exactly what we need. Let's go right now!"

The pair had a wonderful afternoon visiting old friends. Abu played with Salim the goat, joked with Kahlil the ox and teased Gamal the camel. He and Aladdin stopped at each vendor's stall to say "hello." Aladdin saw how happy Abu was in the hustle and bustle of the marketplace.

"You know, Abu," said Aladdin that night, "you can invite your friends from the marketplace to the palace anytime you'd like." The monkey jumped up and down, hugging Aladdin and knocking off his hat. "Okay! Okay! You're welcome!" Aladdin laughed.

The next day, Abu disappeared first thing in the morning. When he returned, Salim and Kahlil were with him. "Welcome," said Jasmine. "Please make yourselves at home." But they already had. The goat was chewing on the curtains, and the ox was wandering in the garden, eating the tops off the flowers.

"We can always buy new curtains or plant new flowers. The important thing is that Abu is happy again," Aladdin said to Jasmine, who sighed and agreed reluctantly.

The following day, Gamal and several other camels arrived. Jasmine was not pleased when they spat on the new carpet. "Think of Abu," Aladdin told her.

The day after that, the fruit seller rolled through the palace with his cart. Another vendor came with a pile of smelly fish. Next came the lady who sold dates, and the man who sold pottery.

"Isn't it wonderful that Abu has so many friends?" said Aladdin.

"It is," Jasmine agreed. "But have you noticed that we only see his friends coming and not going?"

"Now that you mention it, I have," Aladdin replied. "Let's find out what's going on." The couple followed Abu as he led his guests out to the garden. What they saw made them gasp. There was the entire marketplace! Aladdin burst out laughing. "I guess the next time Abu is feeling homesick, he doesn't need to go any farther than his own backyard!"

Jasmine sighed. "Aladdin, these people can't stay here." But, when Jasmine saw the sad look on Aladdin's face, she added, ". . . Well, maybe they could come back next month."

And so began a new tradition – "Palace Market Day," which happened once a month. And *that* made little Abu *very* happy!

165

Rabbit's Frightful Garden

Rabbit woke up bright and early. He had a lot of work to do in his garden. There were weeds to be pulled up. There were vines to be trimmed. And there were lots of delicious, ripe vegetables just waiting to be picked. The only problem was that Rabbit had lent all his tools to his friends – and they hadn't returned them.

In the meantime, Pooh and Piglet were enjoying breakfast at Kanga's and Roo's house when Roo bounced in with a bunch of wildflowers for his mother.

"Thank you, Roo!" Kanga exclaimed, giving him a kiss. "Let me just trim these and put them in some water." She rummaged around in a kitchen drawer, where she came across Rabbit's gardening shears. "Oh, no," Kanga said. "I never returned these to Rabbit after I borrowed them."

"That reminds me," said Piglet. "I still have Rabbit's rake. And, Pooh, I'll bet you still have Rabbit's shovel."

The friends decided the neighbourly thing to do would be to return Rabbit's tools right away. When they arrived at Rabbit's house, though, their friend was not at home. He was on his way to *their* houses to get his tools back.

"Rabbit's garden could use some work," Kanga said. "Why don't we take care of it for him as a way of saying that we're sorry for keeping his tools for so long?"

Everyone agreed that this was a splendid plan. Pooh set about weeding while Piglet raked. Kanga snipped ripe tomatoes, peppers and cucumbers off the vines. Roo gathered them into big baskets.

When they had finished, they spotted some birds hungrily eyeing the harvest.

"This garden needs a scarecrow!" cried Roo.

The work crew sprang into action, and soon a towering scarecrow was planted right in the middle of the garden. They propped the tools against the scarecrow, placed the baskets of food in front of it, and started for home. "Won't Rabbit be surprised!" Piglet said proudly.

When Rabbit returned home a few minutes later, he couldn't quite believe his eyes. First he looked at the vegetables, all neatly picked. Then he looked at his garden tools, which had mysteriously reappeared. Finally, he looked at the strange scarecrow, which seemed to be looking right back at him! "D-d-d-did you do this?" he stammered to the straw man. Just then, a gust of wind knocked over the rake resting on the scarecrow's arm.

Convinced his garden was haunted, Rabbit turned and ran for his life. "Ahhhhhhhhh!" screamed as he rushed past his friends.

"I *told* you he'd be surprised," said Piglet.

The Chase

"Whoopee!" Tod cried as he tumbled head over tail towards the water. He hit the surface with a splash. A second later, his friend Copper landed right next to him.

"It certainly is a beautiful day," Copper said.

"Yeah, it sure is," Tod agreed. The two friends swam to the edge and climbed up on the bank. As they sat in the warm sun, a great big blue butterfly landed on Copper's tail.

"Looks like you've made a friend," said Tod.

But the butterfly was frightened away by a booming voice.

"Copper!" the voice rumbled. It was Amos, Copper's master. Amos was usually grumpy, and right now he sounded angry too. "Where are you, mutt?" he shouted.

Tod silently climbed out of the water. He could tell that Amos was nearby, and that his other dog, Chief, was with him.

Copper crept up beside Tod. "I'd better go," he said. "Amos sounds awfully mad."

"Why don't you sneak back to your barrel so you're there when he gets back," Tod suggested. "He can't be mad if you're already home when he finds you."

Copper scratched behind his ear. "But he's right in my path, and Chief is with him. Chief will hear me or smell me for sure."

Tod grinned. "You just leave that to me."

He winked at his friend and dashed up the hill, right past Amos and Chief.

"There's that varmint fox!" Amos cried as Chief took off after Tod, barking like mad. Amos gave chase, running as fast as he could on his long, skinny legs.

Tod leaped over branches and darted around trees. More than once, Chief got close, his hot breath on Tod's tail. But Tod was smart. He led Chief towards a rocky outcrop and dashed into a small cave. Chief stuck his snout into the opening, growling away. But he was too big to fit.

"Never mind, Chief," Amos said when he finally caught up. "We'll get him later."

Chief gave a final growl into the cave, but Tod had already escaped at the other end and was dashing home.

Exhausted, Amos and Chief started home, too. And, by the time they got there, Tod was napping next door in front of the Widow Tweed's fireplace, and Copper was sitting in his barrel. Next to him, his supper bowl was empty.

"There you are," Amos grumbled. He shook his head. "And I suppose you've been sitting here almost the whole time. We could have used your help catching that dang fox – it's almost as if you're trying to avoid hunting him!"

THE INCREDIBLES

Elastigirl Returns

Mr Incredible and Elastigirl – now known as Bob and Helen Parr – had to give up using their powers when people started suing them. It turned out some people didn't want to be saved by the heroes. They had been trying to live a normal life and had three children. But Bob was bored of the day-to-day grind of an ordinary life.

A woman called Mirage had brought him to an island, where he'd been asked to fight an Omnidroid robot. The robot had defeated him, and the owner of the island turned out to be Buddy – a man who was once Mr Incredible's biggest fan. When Buddy was a boy, he'd wanted to be Mr Incredible's sidekick. Mr Incredible had told him Supers were born, not made – but Buddy hadn't listened. He now called himself Syndrome and he had built a weapon that only he could defeat.

Bob's wife, Helen, was trying to find out where her husband was. She had found Bob's newly mended suit and knew that fashion designer Edna Mode must have fixed it. She went straight to Edna to find out what Bob was up to.

Edna was thrilled to see Helen. She'd so enjoyed making and testing Bob's new suit that she'd made one for Helen too – and one each for their children, Violet, Dash and Jack-Jack! Each new suit came with a homing device for handy tracking.

But Helen was very upset. "You helped my husband resume secret hero work behind my back?"

"I assumed you knew, darling," Edna protested.

Helen phoned Bob's work – and learned he'd been fired almost two months ago. Where was he? Edna passed Helen the homing device that would locate him.

Meanwhile, back on the island, Bob sneaked into Syndrome's base. Using the password KRONOS he hacked into the computer and discovered Syndrome's plan.

Syndrome had killed many Supers perfecting his Omnidroid. Now, he planned to set the robot loose in the city. No one would be able to stop it. Suddenly – *BLEEP, BLEEP* – Mr Incredible's homing device went off!

Now Helen knew where he was – but so did the island's security. They shot out great sticky globules to catch him. Mr Incredible was trapped!

Back on the mainland Helen knew she must find her husband. She realized she would only be able to do it if she became Elastigirl!

It was time for the Parrs to become super heroes once more....

Little Lost Sheep

Woody was relaxing on Andy's bed when Bo Peep came running over. "Oh, Woody! It's my sheep!" Bo cried. "I can't find them anywhere!"

"Are you sure?" asked Woody. "Where did you see them last?"

Bo explained that they were with her earlier that day, but now she couldn't find them. Woody put his hand on Bo's shoulder. "We won't rest until those sheep are safe with you! Right, everyone?" All the toys in Andy's room shouted their agreement.

Woody asked Hamm to check the toy box, and he sent Sarge and the Green Army Men to Molly's room. Wheezy and RC were in charge of checking the halls. The three little green Aliens headed off to check the bathroom, while Woody and Buzz ran out the door towards the kitchen.

"Please, find them!" called Bo Peep. Then she sat down. She looked like she was about to cry. Then, the baby monitor crackled on the dresser. Andy's mother had left it in his room when she picked up the laundry that morning. The sound of Sarge's voice came from the speaker.

"This is Sarge reporting from the baby's room. There are not any sheep in here. Over and out."

"Oh, dear," said Bo. "Where could they be?"

Just then, Woody and Buzz came into Andy's room with RC and Wheezy behind them. "Kitchen is clear," Buzz said. "No sheep were found."

At that moment, the toys heard the sound of bleating sheep. Baa! Baa! Bo Peep gasped. But then she looked closer at the sheep . . .

"These aren't my sheep," she said.

Woody lifted a cotton ball off a little green head. It was the aliens! They had wanted to help. Bo Peep thanked them, but she was upset because her sheep were still missing.

Suddenly, Hamm called out, "Andy's mother is coming!"

All the toys went limp as Andy's mum walked into the room. She placed a basket on the bed and started folding Andy's clothes. After a while, she looked in the basket and laughed. She'd found Bo Peep's sheep!

"Hey there, little guys!" she said. "I hope you enjoyed your bath."

She spotted Bo Peep on the shelf. "I bet you missed these," she said, laughing. "Little Bo Peep has lost her sheep," she sang.

When the toys knew it was safe to move, they burst out laughing!

Rescue Squad Mater

Red the fire truck was watering some flowers in front of the fire station. "I used to be a fire truck," Mater said, out of the blue. Then he began to tell the story of Rescue Squad Mater...

Rescue Squad Mater was at the fire station when an emergency call came in. "Fire in progress at 120 Car Michael Way."

Rescue Squad Mater recognized that address. "That's the old gasoline and match factory!" he exclaimed. He zoomed out of the station and roared down the street. Moments later, Rescue Squad Mater sped up to the burning building. Rescue Squad Mater aimed a water hose and started spraying. He bravely battled the flames, ignoring the danger.

"Mater," Lightning said, stopping the story. "I can't believe you were a fire truck."

"You remember," Mater replied. "You were there, too!" Then he went on telling his tale. The fire had spread through the entire factory, but Rescue Squad Mater still continued to battle it. Suddenly, a frightened voice called out. "AAAh! Help! Help!" Lightning was stuck on the top floor of the burning building!

The rescue truck began to raise his ladder towards the top floor. Soon the ladder was right beneath Lightning. Would there be enough time for Rescue Squad Mater to get him to the ground – before the factory exploded? The crowd watched, waiting on the edges of their tyre treads.

KA-BLAM! The factory blew up in a huge explosion! Luckily, Lightning was out of the building by then. Mater used his ladder to lift him into an ambulance. Finally, Mater turned towards the crowd and smiled.

When Lightning arrived at the hospital, a medic rushed him to the operating room. A whole team of nurses was there, too. Lightning looked around. Where was the doctor? Then he heard a nurse's voice over the loudspeaker. "Paging Dr Mater."

Lightning blinked. Had he heard that right? Seconds later, the doctor rolled in. Lightning could hardly believe his eyes. It was Mater! "Mater, you're a doctor, too?!"

"That's right, buddy," Dr Mater replied.

Lightning spotted Dr Mater's diplomas on the wall. "Clear!" Dr Mater called out as he swung the arm of a scary-looking medical instrument towards Lightning. Then Mater stopped telling his story.

"What happened?" Lightning asked.

"I saved your life," Mater said.

"Whaaa...?" Lightning was pretty sure he would remember something like that.

Bambi
The Secret Adventure

Early one morning, Thumper hopped over to a thicket and woke Bambi up.

"Let's go. Where we're going is a secret," he said.

On the way, Bambi and Thumper spotted their skunk friend, Flower.

"We're going on a secret adventure," Bambi said. "Do you want to come?"

"Oh, gosh! I do," Flower said shyly.

Thumper then said proudly, "I want to show you what the beavers build on water!"

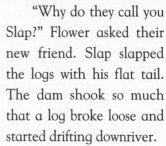

Bambi and Flower smiled. It sounded exciting. Above them, a red bird sat unnoticed. *They are heading out all by themselves,* the bird thought. *I'd better tell their mothers.*

Meanwhile, Bambi, Thumper and Flower reached a meadow.

"Shhh!" Thumper whispered. "We are close to where all the bunnies graze – including my mama."

But Thumper's sisters had seen everything. They wanted to know what their big brother was up to, so they followed him. So did Red, the bird.

Soon the three friends came to a stream. A beaver walked up to them. "My name is Slap," the beaver said. "Where are you going?"

"I wanted to show my friends what you build on the river," Thumper explained.

"We call it a dam," said Slap. Carefully the three friends stepped out onto the logs.

"Why do they call you Slap?" Flower asked their new friend. Slap slapped the logs with his flat tail. The dam shook so much that a log broke loose and started drifting downriver.

"Help, Thumper!" four little voices cried. It was Thumper's younger sisters! The log they were sitting on was floating away!

"Oh, no! My sisters!" Thumper cried. "We have to rescue them!"

All the beavers jumped into the water and quickly swam towards the log. High above, Red saw the whole thing and went to get help.

Thumper's sisters held on but they were getting close to a waterfall! The beavers eventually reached the log. They slapped their tails with all their might and got the log to the riverbank. Thumper pulled his sisters to safety and thanked the beavers.

After a while, it began to get dark. Just then, Bambi and Thumper's mothers arrived!

"Oh, I'm so glad you are safe!" cried Bambi's mother. "Luckily, Red was keeping an eye on you."

"I'm very happy to see you too mother," Bambi said, glad that the adventure was over.

Fast Friends

"Here, kitty, kitty," called Penny, peering underneath her bed. "Come on, I won't hurt you." She reached her hand out towards the old orange cat she had seen race into the girls' dormitory room at the Morningside Orphanage and dart under the bed. Now the cat was hiding under there, looking too afraid to move.

Penny had lived at the orphanage for a long time. But, in all her years there, she had never known that a cat lived there too.

"Whatcha doin' under there?" Penny asked.

Surprisingly, the cat answered her. "I'm hiding from the headmistress," he whispered. "Is she coming this way?"

Penny looked up and over towards the door of the dormitory. She saw the headmistress poke her head into the girls' room, glance around hurriedly, then head off down the hallway.

Penny hung down over the side of the bed again. "Nope, she's gone," she said to the cat. "The coast is clear."

Breathing a sigh of relief, the cat ambled towards Penny, came out from under the bed and jumped up onto the windowsill, looking at her. Now Penny could get a better look at him. The cat was wearing a red woollen scarf around his neck and a pair of glasses on his nose, and his long white whiskers looked just like a moustache. He had a very kind face.

"Thanks," the cat said to Penny. "That was a close one."

"Why was the headmistress after you?" Penny asked him.

"Oh," the cat said with a chuckle, "she got me a while back to keep mice out of the basement." He stretched, yawned and jumped down to lie in a patch of sunlight on the floor. "But I don't mouse too well any more. I'm getting too slow to chase anything. I'm not as young and spry as I used to be. Say, my name's Rufus. What's yours?"

"Penny," she replied with a smile. She reached under her pillow and pulled out her teddy bear. "And this is Teddy."

"Well, hello, Penny," said Rufus. "And hello, Teddy."

Teddy just stared back at Rufus blankly.

"Quiet little guy, huh?" Rufus said to Penny. "What's the matter? Cat got his tongue?"

Penny giggled. "Teddy's very good at keeping secrets. And so am I. You can come hide under our bed whenever you need to. We won't tell."

"You won't?" Rufus replied. "Aw, that's mighty good of you." And so, feeling safe and secure by the side of his new friends, Rufus closed his eyes and settled down for a catnap.

Dory's Surprise Party

One day, Nemo was telling his dad Marlin that Dory's birthday was coming up. Nemo wanted to throw a surprise birthday party for her!

Nemo asked his friends, Pearl the octopus, Tad the butterfly fish and Sheldon the sea horse to help plan the party.

"What kind of food should we have?" asked Nemo.

"Kelp cake and algae ice cream," Sheldon replied.

"What about sea-plant pizza?" asked Tad.

"I'm getting hungry already," said Nemo. "What about music?"

"We could be the band," said Pearl. "I'm great on the mussel tambourines."

"Yeah, and I play the clamshell drums," said Sheldon.

"Great!" cried Nemo. "Let's meet here tomorrow after school to practise."

The next day, Nemo and his friends were carrying their musical instruments when they bumped into Dory.

"Hi Mimo! Hi kids!" Dory exclaimed. She had trouble remembering Nemo's name. "What are you up to?"

"Music-class homework," Tad piped up.

The friends smiled and began to practise.

Soon, it was the day of the party! Nemo and his friends got up early and started decorating.

Then Nemo suggested they practise singing "Happy Birthday." Just as they finished the line "Happy Birthday, dear Dory," Dory appeared! "How did you know it was my birthday?" she exclaimed.

"You told me," said Nemo.

"Really, Pluto?" asked Dory, "I don't remember."

"Now the surprise is ruined," said Nemo, sadly.

"What surprise?" said Dory. It sure was helpful that Dory's memory wasn't very good!

"Another close call," said Nemo to his friends.

A few hours later, the guests arrived. They all hid and waited. When Dory and Nemo swam in, everyone shouted, "Surprise!"

"Look, Pluto, it's a party for you!" Dory cried.

"No, Dory, it's for you," Nemo said. "It's your birthday."

"Oh, yeah. Cool, a party for me!"

Later, she swam over to Marlin and Nemo. "I sure am glad your dad and I found you, Nemo. This is the best birthday I've ever had."

"Hey, Dory," said Nemo. "You remembered my name."

"What's that, Flipper?" asked Dory.

"Oh, nothing," Nemo said with a sigh. "Happy birthday!"

Tuned In

Andy's toys were gathered around the TV in Andy's room. "This again!" Bo Peep said as a superhero show came on. "We watch this every day."

"So?" said Hamm. "He's the defender of the universe! What could be better? I love this show."

Woody the cowboy doll wasn't impressed. "They just don't make TV shows like they used to," he said.

"Oh, no!" The toys groaned. They knew Woody was going to start talking about Woody's Roundup – and never stop! It was an old show. Woody was the star, along with Jessie the cowgirl and Bullseye the horse.

Rex picked up the remote control and pressed a button. Suddenly, the channel changed to a real dinosaur show.

"Agghl" cried Rex, diving under the covers. "Save me!" he called.

The Green Army Men sprang into action. "Eliminate the enemy!" Sarge ordered. "Go! Go! Go!" The soldiers jumped on the remote, and the channels began to change.

"Oooooh!" cried one of the Aliens as the channels flew by in a blur. "Perhaps this machine can help us return to our planet," they all said together. Bo Peep chuckled.

Buzz walked over. "Sheriff, I think we need to put an end to this channel surfing,"

he said. Woody agreed.

Sarge called off his troops, and Buzz marched over to the remote control. He told the Aliens the television couldn't take them back to their home planet. "However, the TV can take you to plenty of new places," Buzz said.

This started the toys thinking about their favourite shows. They couldn't decide what to watch! So, Bo Peep suggested they watch a little of each channel.

They watched super-heroes for Hamm. They watched the Animal Channel for Slinky Dog. Then they turned to the Military Channel for Sarge and the Green Army Men. They watched the Cooking Channel for Rex. Then, finally, they turned to the Cowboy Channel for Jessie.

"Howdy, partner!" the toys suddenly heard.

"Could ya keep it down, Woody," said Hamm. "We're trying to watch TV."

"Huh?" said Woody. "I didn't say anything."

"Well, would you look at that!" said Jessie, "Woody and I are on TV!" The TV was showing an episode of Woody's Roundup!

"Now there's a show!" said Woody. And everyone else had to agree!

HERCULES

A Not-so-relaxing Holiday

No doubt about it: Hercules badly needed a holiday!

"But what about your training!" argued Phil. "You can't stop now! If you're ever gonna be a god, you've got to train like one!"

"If I don't take a break," said Hercules, "I'm never going to become a god, because I'll be so burned out. Sorry, Phil, but I've got to go."

And, with that, he put away his dumbbells and his javelins, cancelled his Herculaid Sports Drink infomercial, and rounded up Pegasus.

"We're off to the Greek Islands, my friend," he told the winged horse. "Sand castles, beach blankets, umbrella drinks . . . here we come!"

And, before you can say 'Mount Vesuvius', there they were, at the finest resort in the ancient world, soaking up the sun and doing absolutely nothing.

"A hero could get used to this," said Hercules as he bobbed in the water, sipping a smoothie and adjusting his sunglasses.

Suddenly, a cry rang out from the beach. "Shark! Shark!"

"Shark?" said Hercules. "In the Aegean Sea?"

But sure enough, a big, grey dorsal fin was speeding towards the crowded shore!

"Help!" cried the people in the water.

"Help!" cried Hercules . . . until he realized he was the one who could save them.

He swam up to the shark, grabbed it by the tail and tossed it up into the sky, all the way to the Atlantic.

"Whew," said Hercules, as the people clapped and cheered.

But not five minutes later, another frightened scream rang out – this time from the hills.

"Volcano!"

From the island's mountain centre rose a plume of thick, black smoke and fiery bursts of molten lava.

"Help!" cried the people.

Hercules knew what he had to do. He raced around the island until he found the biggest boulder. He rolled it all the way to the mountain top, then with one great push, he tipped it over the edge and into the bubbling mouth of the volcano. A perfect fit. The volcano was stopped.

"Hooray!" cheered the people.

Before any more natural disasters could occur, Hercules decided it was time to pack up and head back home.

"Back so soon, Herc?" asked Phil, pleasantly surprised.

Hercules shrugged. "Let's just say that for a hero, work can sometimes be easier than vacation!"

Disney·PIXAR
MONSTERS, INC.
Boo!

James P. Sullivan – aka Sulley – was a professional Scarer and worked at Monsters, Incorporated in Monstropolis. His best friend, Mike Wazowski, trained him. The screams of human children powered Monstropolis, so it was important they collected lots of them!

Although their job was to scare children, the monsters were actually very scared of humans! There was a rule that no child's door should ever be left open, because a child could enter Monstropolis. But one night, Sulley found a door that had been left open on the Scare Floor – and a child had come through!

At a restaurant, Mike and his date, Celia, were enjoying dinner. Mike was just telling Celia what a beautiful monster she was... when suddenly, he spotted Sulley waving frantically outside the window. Sulley looked terrified.

Quickly, Sulley explained about the child. Mike was horrified... especially when Sulley showed him the kid! Then it began running around the restaurant! When the CDA arrived, Mike and Sulley hid the kid in a take-away box and ran. They were in big trouble!

Back in their apartment, Sulley and Mike tried not to touch the child. Then Mike accidentally fell and the little girl started to giggle. Strangely, her laughter made the lights burn brighter – until they burned out!

Finally, Sulley put the child to bed. But she was afraid. Sulley realized she was terrified that a monster was in the wardrobe. So Sulley stayed with her until she fell asleep.

"This might sound crazy," Sulley told Mike. "But I don't think that kid is dangerous. What if we just put her back in her door?"

Mike didn't like the idea, but what else could they do? The next morning, they disguised her and took her to work. In the locker room, Sulley and the child played hide-and-seek. "Boo!" she said playfully. Sulley was starting to really like her. But then they overheard Randall – a mean monster that was jealous of Sulley – tell his assistant that he planned to "take care of the kid". Sulley needed to get the child home quickly! But Mike made a mistake. "This isn't Boo's door," Sulley exclaimed.

"Boo?!?" Mike couldn't believe Sulley had named the child.

Oops – they suddenly realized everyone on the Scare Floor could hear them talking! When they stopped, they saw that Boo had slipped away. Would they ever be able to find her and take her home...?

Disney
MICKEY MOUSE
CLUBHOUSE

Goofy Goes to the Doctor

Mickey woke up early and checked the date. Today Goofy was supposed to go to the doctor for a check-up. Then someone rang the Mousekedoorbell. It was Goofy the Great! Mickey yawned and said, "Goof, you're early!"

"Early for what?" replied Goofy.

"Did you forget that your checkup with the doctor is this afternoon?"

"Garwsh. I did forget," said Goofy. "I came to show you some new magic tricks. But now that you reminded me about the doctor, I'm gonna show you one of my greatest tricks ever. Hokeypokey!" Goofy the Great disappeared! That was a good trick.

Mickey finally found Goofy and they went back to the Clubhouse. Daisy stopped by, and Mickey told her why Goofy looked so glum. Daisy decided this would be a good time for her to play Dr Daisy. She explained to Goofy that the doctor would examine parts of his body.

Goofy asked, "Does that hurt?"

"Nope. Not a bit," said Mickey.

Next Daisy said that the doctor uses a stethoscope to listen to heartbeats. Daisy listened to Mickey's heart. Goofy asked what it sounded like.

Daisy said, "It goes lub-dub, lub-dub."

Then Willie the giant arrived – the friendly giant wanted to help, too.

"When I go to the doctor," said Willie, "my favourite part is getting to stick out my tongue and say AHH so the doctor can examine my throat." Willie showed them how he does it. "AHHHH!"

"Oh boy," said Mickey. "Thanks, Willie. We get the idea!"

Goofy was starting to feel better. "So that's it?"

Daisy explained that was most of it, but that he might need to get an injection too. Daisy explained that sometimes the doctor gives you an injection of medicine to keep you from getting sick.

"I have a thinking trick that I use when I get an injection," said Mickey. "I close my eyes and think about things that I like; then I count them. Can you guess what I think about?"

"Hot dogs!" said Goofy.

"You betcha," said Mickey. "By the time I count three of them, it's all over."

"Say, that is a neat trick," said Goofy. "I think I'll count hot-fudge sundaes!"

It was time for Goofy and Mickey to go. Daisy explained they might have to sit in the doctor's waiting room for a little while, so it was a good idea to take a book or a toy.

Goofy felt a lot less worried, and finally he did go to the doctor. Hot diggety dog!

Trusting Trusty

"Tramp!" cried Lady one morning. "One of our puppies is missing!"

"Don't worry," said Tramp with a yawn. "Scamp is always getting into mischief."

"Its not Scamp," said Lady. "It's little Fluffy! She never gets into trouble. Tramp, what should we do?"

"You look inside. I'll look outside," said Tramp worriedly.

Tramp searched their back garden. Then he went to the next garden, and the next.

From a neighbour's porch, Trusty the bloodhound called, "Howdy! Whatcha looking for?"

"My daughter, Fluffy! She's missing," said Tramp.

Trusty's long floppy ears pricked up. "A missing puppy – now that's serious! And I should know. I used to help my grandpa track down missing persons through the swamps!"

"I know," said Tramp. He'd heard Trusty tell that story 100 times.

"Have you found a trail yet?" asked Trusty.

Tramp shook his head.

"Well, let me at it!" Trusty loped back to Tramp's garden. He put his big nose to the ground. *Sniff, sniff, sniff . . . .*

"Tramp, have you found Fluffy?" Lady called from the dog door.

Tramp ran over. "No," he replied. "But Trusty offered his . . . uh . . . services."

"He can't smell any more," Lady whispered. "I know he tracked that dogcatcher's wagon and saved you – but he hasn't tracked anything since."

"He helped us once," said Tramp. "I think we should trust him again."

Just then, Trusty shouted, "Look at this!"

He had spotted a bluebird's feather below a window. "That's the window the puppies look out," said Lady.

"Look! A bit of puppy fur," said Trusty. "And footprints!" Trusty followed the trail of footprints to the back of a shed.

And that's where Trusty found the missing puppy! Fluffy was fast asleep under a big tree.

"Fluffy! What happened?" Lady cried.

"I woke up and saw a bluebird," said Fluffy with a yawn. "And I didn't want Scamp to bark and scare it away, like he always does. So I didn't wake anyone. I followed the bird all the way to this tree. Then I guess I got sleepy."

Lady walked over and gave Trusty a kiss.

"Thank you," she told the bloodhound.

"Aw, shucks," said Trusty, blushing. "It weren't nothin'."

As the bloodhound trotted home, Tramp turned to Lady. "See that," he said with a grin, "I told you we should trust Trusty!"

THE JUNGLE BOOK

Baloo's Secret Weapon

Mowgli and his pal Baloo were taking a lazy afternoon stroll through the jungle. Suddenly, Mowgli stopped in his tracks. "Did you hear that?" he asked.

"Hear what, little buddy?" Baloo asked.

"It sounded like twigs snapping," Mowgli said. "I think somebody might be following us!"

"That was just your old Papa Bear's stomach growling," Baloo told him. "It's time for some lunch."

"And I know just where to get it," announced Mowgli. He shimmied up a tree, plucked a bunch of bananas, and tossed them down to the bear.

"That's my boy!" Baloo cried proudly.

But, as he was scrambling back down, Mowgli spotted a flash of orange and black.

"Shere Khan!" Mowgli whispered to Baloo. "We've got to get out of here!" The tiger had been after Mowgli ever since the boy had first set foot in the jungle.

The two friends didn't know which way to turn. Now that Shere Khan had their scent, it would be almost impossible to lose him. Then they both heard a lively beat drumming its way through the jungle.

"Oh, no," said Mowgli. "King Louie and his crazy band of monkeys. That's all we need!"

Baloo's eyes suddenly lit up. "That's *exactly* what we need, Little Britches!"

Still clutching the bananas, Baloo and Mowgli ran towards King Louie's compound. When they arrived, Baloo disguised himself as a monkey. The orang-utans were so busy dancing and singing they didn't notice his disguise. Then the bear quickly found a huge empty barrel, and filled it with the bananas.

"Look!" cried Baloo, peering into the barrel. "Lunch!" The monkeys ran over and jumped right into the barrel! They greedily ate the feast, tossing peels out as they made their way through the bunch.

Baloo signalled to Mowgli, who came out of hiding. "Come and get me, Shere Khan!" the Man-cub taunted.

Within seconds, the tiger appeared in the clearing, a fierce gleam in his eye. "Hello, Stripes," Baloo greeted him cheerfully. Then the bear picked up the barrel, heaved it, and sent King Louie's troop flying at Shere Khan. The orang-utans landed on the tiger's back, where they frantically jumped up and down, pulling on his tail and ears. Mowgli and Baloo watched as Shere Khan raced back into the jungle, trying to free himself from his shrieking passengers.

"Like I always say," Baloo declared as he grinned at Mowgli, "there's nothing more fun than a barrel of monkeys!"

Disney

MICKEY MOUSE

How to Unpack for a Vacation

One morning, Donald Duck heard a knock at the door. When he opened it, he found his friend Mickey Mouse standing there.

"Today is the day!" exclaimed Mickey.

"Today is *what* day?" asked Donald with a yawn.

"Don't you remember?" said Mickey. "You're driving me, Minnie and Daisy to the beach for a week's vacation." Mickey held up his suitcase. "I packed last night. Aren't you packed too?"

"No," said Donald. "I thought we were leaving next week!"

"No," said Mickey. "We're leaving today. And Minnie and Daisy will be here in an hour."

"Oh, no!" cried Donald.

"Calm down," said Mickey. "You have time to get ready. Just pack your things now."

While Mickey relaxed on the porch in a rocking chair, Donald went back inside.

"What do I pack?" Donald muttered to himself as he raced through his house. "I'll need my toys, of course, in case I get bored." Donald ran to his playroom and placed all his toys in boxes.

"What else should I pack?" Donald asked himself. "Clothes!" He ran to his bedroom and took out every suitcase he owned. Then he emptied all his drawers and filled his suitcases.

Finally, Donald calmed down. "That should do it," he said with a sigh of relief.

Mickey couldn't believe his eyes when Donald began packing up his car. Just then, Minnie Mouse and Daisy Duck arrived. They each had one small suitcase.

Minnie and Daisy took one look at Donald's car and gasped. Boxes and baskets were crammed into the back and front seats. Daisy opened the boot and found it overflowing with Donald's suitcases.

"There's no room left for *our* suitcases!" cried Daisy.

"Forget our *suitcases*!" exclaimed Minnie. "There's no room for us!"

Mickey put his arm around Donald.

"It's okay, Donald," he said. "It's hard packing for a vacation. You have to leave some things behind – even some of your favourite things. But they will all be here when we get back. I guarantee it!"

"And besides," added Daisy, "don't you want to leave room in your car to bring back souvenirs, like seashells and T-shirts and salt-water taffy?"

Donald brightened. "Seashells and T-shirts and saltwater taffy!" he cried excitedly. "Oh, you bet!"

"Good," said Mickey. Then he pointed to Donald's overflowing car. "Now let's all help Donald *un*pack for this vacation!"

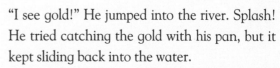

Catching Gold

One cold winter day, Woody the cowboy sat in front of the TV with his horse, Bullseye. They were watching his favourite show, Woody's Roundup. In the TV show, the Roundup gang was going fishing. The Prospector was hoping to find gold while Woody and Jessie the cowgirl fished for their lunch.

The Prospector grabbed his gold-mining pan and went down to the water's edge. "I've got a hunch there's some gold in this riverbed!" he exclaimed.

Jessie went for a walk to look for some wildflowers, while Woody stayed in his favourite fishing spot. He hadn't had a single bite yet, but he was still hopeful.

The Prospector walked along the river's edge in search of gold. Soon he came to a shallow pool. He held out his gold-mining pan as he leaned over the water. He began to sift through the sand from the riverbed. When the water had all sloshed out, he looked at the empty pan. There was no gold. He headed back up the river to where Woody was fishing.

"Any fish yet?" the Prospector asked.

"Nope," replied Woody. "What about you? Any gold?"

Just as the Prospector was about to answer, he saw something shiny in the water. He stepped closer to take another look. "Eureka!" he cried.

"I see gold!" He jumped into the river. Splash! He tried catching the gold with his pan, but it kept sliding back into the water.

"Come help me, Sheriff," the Prospector shouted. "This is the slip-slidin'est gold I ever saw!"

Woody set down his pole and leaped into the water. Together they dove after the gold. But each time, they came up empty-handed. Then, Woody had an idea. "We can use our hats!"

"Good thinking," said the Prospector.

They both used their hats to try to scoop up the swirling bits of gold. Just then, Jessie came over to the river's edge.

"What are you two doing?" she asked.

"Catching gold!" said Woody.

Jessie took a closer look inside their hats, and then she began to laugh.

"What's so funny?" asked the Prospector.

Jessie smiled. "Take a look at your catch!"

Woody and the Prospector looked at their hats. They were surprised to see goldfish swimming around!

"I can't believe it!" Woody laughed. "The Prospector was looking for gold, and I was looking for fish."

Jessie giggled. "I guess you both found what you were looking for!"

El Materdor

Mater and Lightning were out for a drive. Lightning stopped to look at some grazing bulldozers. "I was a famous bulldozer fighter in Spain," he began. "They called me 'El Materdor...'"

El Materdor stood in the centre of a packed arena. With a nod of his head, he signalled that he was ready. A door at the side of the ring opened, and an angry-looking bulldozer rolled out. El Materdor raised his tow hook. One glimpse of the red cape dangling from it and the bulldozer charged towards the cape. El Materdor stood his ground.

Again and again, the bulldozer charged. Each time, El Materdor dodged him with a last-second move. Until the bulldozer finally surprised him. He came up behind El Materdor and pushed him across the ring, driving him right into the ground! The crowd watched in silence. Then the tow truck's hook poked out from a pile of dirt. At the end of it was El Materdor's red cape. The battle would go on!

El Materdor dusted himself off and bravely faced the huge bulldozer again. Through narrowed eyes, they studied each other. Suddenly, the bulldozer smacked his front blade on the ground. Two doors at the side of the ring opened and two more bulldozers drove out. Now it was three against one!

The bulldozers charged! For a time, El Materdor fought off all of them. But then the three bulldozers circled him and began to close in. There was nowhere for El Materdor to go. Nowhere but up, that is. El Materdor waited until the last moment. Then, with a mighty leap, he jumped out of the path of the charging bulldozers, who collided and collapsed in a heap.

"Olé!" El Materdor cried, landing on top of the wrecked bulldozers. But the celebration was short-lived. Soon more bulldozers rolled into the ring. It turned out that the wrecked ones had some friends.

"There I was, surrounded," Mater told Lightning. "Bulldozers all around me."

"What did you do?" Lightning asked.

"Don't you remember? You was there, too!" Mater said. In the arena, Lightning gasped. His paint job was red – just like El Materdor's cape! The bulldozers revved their engines and began their chase.

Back in Radiator Springs, Lightning interrupted the story. "Mater," he said, "that didn't happen."

"Well, try telling that to them bulldozers," Mater replied, pointing behind Lightning. The bulldozers that had been grazing were now surrounding Mater and Lightning!

TOY STORY

Woody's Hat

It was Saturday morning, and the toys in Andy's room were waking up. Jessie yawned and stretched. "It's time for Woody's Roundup!" She hurried over to the TV and switched it on.

As the show began, Woody rushed over to watch. Just then, his hat flew off and Bullseye trampled it! Jessie told Woody she thought the hat looked pretty ragged, and Woody had to agree.

"I have lots of hats," Jessie offered. "You can take your pick." She brought Woody all the hats she could carry. They were all shapes and colours. They tumbled out of her arms. Woody picked up one of the hats and put it on his head.

"What do you think?" he asked Jessie.

Jessie smiled. "It looks mighty fine."

"I don't know," Woody said. "Do you think it's too brown?"

"How about that one?" Jessie said, gesturing towards a hat with buttons on the band. "It's a lighter brown."

"That one is not brown enough," Woody said.

"Hmm," Jessie sighed. She piled more and more hats onto Woody's lap. "There must be a hat here that you like. Keep trying. How about this one?"

"That one is pink!" Woody said.

Jessie put three hats on her own head. "What about a brown one with a gold band?"

"No, no, no," Woody said. "I'm sorry, Jessie, but none of those are right for me."

Jessie couldn't believe that Woody couldn't find one hat he liked in the huge pile she had brought.

"What we really need is a plan," she told Woody. "Why don't you tell me just what kind of hat you're looking for, then we can try to find it in the pile."

Woody leaned against the fence and thought. "I'd definitely like a brown hat," Woody said. "Not too dark or too light, but brown is best."

Bullseye began to dig his nose into the pile of hats.

"It would be nice if it had a wide brim," Woody continued. "And it should have stitching around the edge, but I don't think we'll find anything like that."

Sheriff Woody looked hopeless. Then Bullseye pulled Woody's old hat from the pile! Jessie laughed when Bullseye held up the hat.

"Woody, I think Bullseye found just the right hat!" Jessie called out.

Woody grinned. "This is exactly the kind of hat I wanted! How does it look?" he asked.

"It's the best hat in the West!" Jessie replied.

Bambi

Flower's Power

It was a warm summer afternoon in the forest, and a shy little skunk named Flower was playing a game of hide-and-seek, searching for his friend Thumper. He had been looking for quite a while.

"Come out, come out, wherever you are!" Flower called. "I give up."

"*Surprise!*" shouted Thumper, bursting out of a thicket. "Here I am! *Ugh!*" Thumper wrinkled his nose. "What's that *smell?*"

Flower blushed bright pink. "Sorry," he said miserably. "I sprayed. It happens when I get scared."

"*Whew!*" Thumper waved his paw in front of his face. "You should warn us before you let out that kind of stink!"

"Well *you* should warn *me* before you jump out like that," Flower said. "Anyway, it'll go away... in a day or two."

But a day or two was too long for his friends to wait. The smell was just too strong!

"Sorry," Bambi told Flower. "I, uh, think my mother's calling me," he said.

"Me, uh, too," Faline gasped. "See you later, Flower... in a day or two."

"Or three!" Thumper added, giggling.

And the next thing he knew, Flower was all alone.

Poor Flower. If only he weren't a skunk, he thought. If only he didn't *stink* so much whenever he got scared. What was the point? It only drove his friends away. But now it seemed he couldn't even play hide-and-seek! No matter what his mother and father said, as far as Flower was concerned, being a skunk stunk!

And that's why Flower wouldn't have been very surprised if, two days later, his friends had still stayed away. But, to his bashful pleasure, there, bright and early, were Bambi and Faline – with Thumper hopping close behind.

"Want to play?" Bambi asked Flower cheerfully.

"Anything but hide-and-seek!" said Flower.

"How about tag?" said Thumper. "Ready or not, you're It!"

But before the game could begin, a soft *crunch, crunch* of leaves made the friends turn.

"Wha-wha-what's that?" Bambi said, staring straight into a hungry-looking, red face.

"That's a fox!" said Thumper.

"A fox?" shrieked Flower. "Oh no!" He span around and lifted his tail and buried his head in fear... and the next thing the friends knew, the hungry fox was running away, whimpering and rubbing his nose.

"Sorry," Flower sighed, blushing.

"Don't be!" said Bambi and Thumper.

And do you know what? Flower wasn't!

The Sword in the Stone

In the depths of the woods, somewhere in England, Merlin the Magician was waiting for a very special visitor. His name was Wart, a clever but reckless young boy...

"Watch out, Wart! You're climbing too high." And sure enough – *CRASH!* Wart tumbled and landed on a chair in front of Merlin, just in time for tea!

"A great destiny awaits you my boy," Merlin said to Wart. "But first you need to learn a few things....

"There's no great destiny without a great teacher – and I will be that person! Just let me pack my case and then we'll be off."

First lesson: the world of water. Merlin touched his wand to Wart's head and the boy transformed into a fish! Merlin transformed himself too, and they swam in deep water. Wart waved his fins and made bubbles.

Then suddenly, they saw a monstrous fish coming straight for them! Quickly, Merlin changed back into human form and saved Wart from the jaws of the pike.

Second lesson: exploring the forest in the form of a squirrel! Wart immediately made a friend – a charming female squirrel who really liked him.

But, just when a wolf was about to attack him, Wart changed back into a child.

"I'm sorry Miss, I'm a boy, not a squirrel," Wart said to the disappointed girl squirrel.

"What's the third lesson?" Wart then asked his teacher.

"Flying through the air!" answered Merlin, transforming him into a baby bird.

In the company of Archimedes, a grumpy old owl, Wart launched himself into the air. What fun it was to fly!

But in the air, too, danger lurked: suddenly an eagle appeared and threatened the two friends!

Panic-stricken, Wart dove into a chimney. But he fell into the clutches of Madam Mim – a wicked sorceress who lived in the forest!

Luckily, Merlin appeared in the cottage. To overpower the sorceress, he changed himself into a germ and gave her the measles! Well done Merlin!

Later on, Wart came across a mysterious sword thrust into an anvil. Engraved on the sword were the words:

"Who so pulleth me out will be King of England."

To everyone's astonishment, the boy effortlessly pulled the stone out!

Wart, or rather Arthur, was to be King of England. Long Live King Arthur!

Happy Campers

It was a warm, sunny day on Ant Island – the perfect day for Princess Dot and her fellow Blueberries to go on a camping expedition! Flik volunteered to be their leader.

"Single file! Forward march!" called Flik. "Follow me, Blueberries. Watch out for those twigs!"

"This is gonna be so much fun, Flik!" said Dot, marching behind him. "Pitching our tents! Making a campfire! Telling ghost stories all night long!"

"Well, we've got to get to our campsite first," Flik reminded her. "The perfect campsite for the perfect campout!"

"Where's that?" asked Dot.

"I'm not exactly sure," said Flik. "But don't worry! I'll know it when I see it."

So on they hiked, until they came to some soft moss beside a quiet stream.

"Is this it?" asked Daisy excitedly.

Flik shook his head. "Definitely not," he said. "Too out in the open."

"We're getting tired," Dot said.

"Chins up, Blueberries," said Flik. "We'll find the perfect campsite soon. I'll bet it's just across that stream."

Flik guided the Blueberries onto a broad leaf. Together they rowed across the water. But the other side of the stream was not quite perfect enough for Flik either.

"No worries," Flik said. "See that hill over there? I'll betcha the perfect campsite is just beyond it."

The Blueberries followed him up the grassy hill and down the other side.

"We made it!" the Blueberries cheered.

"Not so fast," said Flik, frowning. "The ground is too damp here. We'll have to keep looking."

"But Flik! We can't go any further," they complained.

"Nonsense!" said Flik, tightening his backpack. "You're Blueberries! C'mon!"

And so, with the Blueberries dragging their poor, tired feet, Flik hiked on. He looked behind a big rock, but it was too dusty. He looked near a hollow log, but a troop of boy beetles was already there. He even looked inside an old, discarded shoe, which might have actually worked . . . if it hadn't been so stinky.

Just when the Blueberries thought they couldn't walk another inch, Flik suddenly froze in his tracks. "The perfect campsite! We've found it! Let's pitch those tents, Blueberries, and get a fire started!"

But instead of cheers, Flik heard only silence. He turned around and saw that those poor Blueberries, still wearing their backpacks, were already fast asleep!

THE INCREDIBLES

Supers to the Rescue

Bob Parr – aka Mr Incredible – had become bored of pretending to be normal, and had secretly taken up super hero work again. He'd kept this secret from his wife, Helen, and had ended up as a prisoner on the island of Nomanisan – owned by Syndrome, who was Mr Incredible's ex-number-one fan, Buddy.

Buddy had turned himself into a Super by building machines and an Omnidroid robot, which only he could defeat. Helen had discovered where her husband was, and she knew the only way to help him was to become Elastigirl once more.

Elastigirl followed the homing signal on Mr Incredible's suit in a borrowed jet. She soon found that her Super children, Violet and Dash, had left Jack-Jack at home with a babysitter and stowed away on the jet! They had found the Super suits that Edna Mode had made for them!

As they approached the island, missiles attacked the jet. Elastigirl told Violet to create a force field around the plane. But Violet didn't think she could make one that big.

In his prison cell, Mr Incredible listened to the attack on his family with horror. "Target destroyed," came a voice from a speaker.

"You'll get over it." Syndrome sneered.

A desperate Mr Incredible grabbed Mirage. "Release me now, or I'll crush her!" he said.

"Go ahead," said Syndrome. He knew that Mr Incredible could never do such a thing. Defeated, the hero let Mirage go.

But Mr Incredible's family was still alive. Elastigirl had stretched herself around Violet and Dash to protect them, just as the missile blew the jet out of the sky. Then she had made herself into a parachute and floated, with her children, down to the water below.

Elastigirl stretched into the shape of a boat, while Dash pushed her and Violet to shore by kicking his speedy legs. They soon found safety in a cave.

"I'm going to look for your father," Elastigirl told her children. "If anything goes wrong, use your powers... when the time comes, you'll know what to do."

After Helen left, the cave suddenly filled with a huge ball of fire. Dash and Violet fled; they only just escaped! The fire was the rocket exhaust from Syndrome's base. He had launched the Omnidroid towards the city!

The Parr family were going to have to use all their Super strength to save the city, and each other, from Syndrome.

Toys in Paradise

Andy ran around his room, throwing clothes into a bag. His best friend's family was going to Florida on holiday and had invited him along.

Andy was going to have so much fun! He would go to the beach and to amusement parks. After Andy left the room, Andy's toys came to life.

"I'd give anything to go on a tropical vacation," said Bo Peep. "Just think of it. The sandy beaches, the warm sunshine . . ."

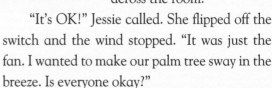

Hey, I've got an idea," said Jessie. "Why don't we make our own tropical paradise, right here in Andy's room?"

"I could use some down time," Slinky Dog admitted. "I've been feeling stretched to my limit lately."

The toys began searching the house for the things they needed. Sarge and the Green Army Men went in search of a potted plant. Hamm and Rex raided the kitchen for Buster's water dish and some sponges. Bo found a doll's parasol in Molly's room. Soon all of the supplies were gathered in the centre of the room.

"Next stop: Paradise!" Jessie exclaimed.

The toys got to work. In no time at all, they had created their own tropical paradise. Woody and Buzz stretched out on the lounge chairs they had made out of the shoebox tops and sponges.

"Wait a minute," Jessie said. "We forgot the sun."

Buzz jumped up. He dragged the desk lamp to the edge of the desk and turned it on.

Then, Jessie realised that something else was missing – an ocean breeze! She climbed up onto Andy's dresser and flipped a switch. Within seconds, the wind picked up, blowing Andy's things everywhere. The toys scurried for cover as the beach chairs skittered across the room.

"It's OK!" Jessie called. She flipped off the switch and the wind stopped. "It was just the fan. I wanted to make our palm tree sway in the breeze. Is everyone okay?"

"Almost everyone," Woody said. He pointed towards the bed where Rex's tail poked out from under the bedspread. It took a while for the toys to convince Rex to come out of his hiding place. He was still trembling with fear!

"Don't worry, Rex," Woody said. "There won't be any more storms here today."

The toys put the parasol back in its place, shading the lounge chairs from the sun.

Rex walked back over to the beach. "I hope Andy has a great trip," he said. "Because paradise can be fun... as long as you're with good friends!"

DISNEY·PIXAR

MONSTERS, INC.

Banished!

In Monstropolis there was a company called Monsters, Inc., where monsters collected human children's screams to power the city. Sulley was the top Scarer and Mike Wazowski was his best friend.

Mike and Sulley were in big trouble – they'd discovered a human girl in Monstropolis! Monsters were very scared of human kids. They thought letting a child into the world of monsters would be deadly! But Sulley had grown to rather like the human child, and had named her 'Boo'.

Mike and Sulley had brought Boo to the Scare Floor to send her home – but she had gone missing! Mike and Sulley split up to find her, but a mean, creepy monster called Randall cornered Mike. The nasty monster knew all about Boo. He ordered Mike to bring her to the Scare Floor. He said he'd have her door ready.

After Sulley finally found Boo, Mike told him about Randall's plan. Together, they went to the Scare Floor, but Sulley was still worried. "We can't trust Randall!"

Mike disagreed. To prove the open door was safe, he went right through – and was captured by Randall! Sulley and Boo secretly followed Randall. They learned he had invented a cruel new way to capture screams from kids with a scary machine. And he was about to try it out on Mike!

Sulley rescued Mike and raced to the training room. He needed to warn the boss about Randall. But then Boo saw Sulley looking ferocious, and she was terrified! Sulley felt awful. For the first time, he realized how mean it was to scare a child.

The boss, Mr Waternoose, promised he would fix everything – but he was really working with Randall! He shoved Sulley and Mike through a door into the human world. They were banished to the mountains! Sulley knew Boo was in trouble. He had to get back. Racing to the local village, he found a door that led home. He rushed to Randall's secret lab and destroyed the machine.

As Sulley raced away with Boo, Mike arrived to help. But Celia, Mike's girlfriend, couldn't understand what was going on. Quickly, Mike explained Randall's plan. She knew Mike was telling the truth.

Mike and Sulley climbed onto the machine that carried doors to the Scare Floor. The power wasn't on, so Mike made a funny face. Boo laughed, and the power surged! It seemed that human children's laughs were just as powerful as their screams!

Carl's Promise

Carl and Ellie had been best friends since they first met as children. They grew up, got married and dreamed of becoming explorers.

But Carl and Ellie didn't become explorers. They both worked at the zoo. However, they still dreamed of travelling to Paradise Falls in South America. They saved all their spare change in a jar to pay for the trip. But they could never quite collect enough.

The years went by, and Carl and Ellie grew older. After Ellie passed away, Carl kept all her things just as they had been. But it wasn't the same. He missed Ellie. To make matters worse, the neighbourhood around their beloved home was being torn down to make room for tall, modern buildings.

One day, Carl heard a knock at his door. A boy in a uniform was standing on his porch.

"Good afternoon," said the boy. "My name is Russell, and I am a Junior Wilderness Explorer. Are you in need of assistance today, sir?"

"No," replied Carl. He didn't want help. He just wanted to be left alone.

But Russell wouldn't leave. He wanted to help Carl so that he could earn his Assisting the Elderly badge.

"If I get it, I will become a Senior Wilderness Explorer," Russell explained.

To get rid of Russell, Carl gave him a task. He asked him to find a bird called a Snipe. "I think its burrow is two blocks down," Carl said.

Russell eagerly set off to find the bird, not knowing that it didn't really exist. Carl had made the whole thing up!

Not long after that, Carl received some bad news. He was being forced out of his house and sent to live in a retirement home. Carl didn't want to leave his house. All his memories of Ellie were there.

That night, Carl sat in his living room, looking through Ellie's adventure book. He remembered Ellie's dream of going to South America. He had promised her he'd take her there in an airship.

The next morning, two nurses arrived to drive Carl to the retirement home. "I'll meet you at the van," he told them. "I want to say one last goodbye to the old place."

As the nurses walked back to their van, a huge shadow fell over them. They turned to see thousands of balloons tied to Carl's house! A moment later, the whole house rose into the air! "So long, boys!" Carl yelled out of the window. He was going to South America!

Paradise Falls

Carl had wanted to be an explorer ever since he was a child. So had his friend and wife, Ellie. He had promised Ellie that he'd take her to see Paradise Falls in South America one day.

But they were never able to save enough money to go. When they grew older, Ellie sadly passed away, and Carl was told he had to move out of his house.

But Carl decided he had to keep his promise to Ellie. He tied thousands of balloons to their little house and slowly it lifted into the sky.

Carl steered the flying house using ropes attached to the weather vane. He checked his compass and map, and set a course to Paradise Falls in South America.

"We're on our way, Ellie," he said happily.

Suddenly, there was a knock at the door. Carl was shocked. He was thousands of feet up in the air! Who could be at his door?

It was Russell! A Junior Wilderness Explorer who had knocked on his door a few days before. Carl had told him to find a Snipe – a bird that didn't really exist – just to get rid of him. Russell had been under Carl's porch, looking for the snipe, when the house lifted off.

"Please let me in!" Russell begged.

What choice did Carl have? He let Russell come inside.

Carl hated to stop, but he knew he had to land and send Russell home. He started to cut some of the balloons free.

Meanwhile, Russell was watching the clouds out of the window. "There's a big storm coming," he said. But Carl didn't hear him.

A flash of lightning lit up the room. Carl desperately tried to steer the house away from the storm, but it was too late. The little house tossed in the wind. Carl ran this way and that, trying to save Ellie's belongings. Finally, exhausted, he fell asleep.

When Carl woke up, the storm was over. "I steered us down," Russell told him proudly. "We're in South America."

As Carl and Russell stepped out onto the porch, the house crash-landed and sent them both flying. "My house!" Carl cried as it started to drift away from them. Grabbing hold of the garden hose, he and Russell managed to pull the house back down. Just then, the fog cleared. There, a short distance ahead, was Paradise Falls! It looked just like Ellie's picture!

"We made it!" Carl shouted. "We could float right over there!"

Carl was amazed. He had finally made the trip he and Ellie had always dreamt about.

Disney
Lady and the *TRAMP*

A Rainy Night Out

"Yip!" Scamp barked at the squirrel nibbling on an acorn in the grass. His brother and sisters were taking a nap under the big oak tree, and there was nobody else around to have fun with.

"Yip!" Scamp barked again, and the squirrel darted across the lawn. Scamp gave chase. The squirrel zipped up a lamppost and leaped onto a nearby tree branch. With a whimper, Scamp sat down and thumped his tail on the sidewalk. That was the problem with squirrels. They always got away too easily.

Disappointed, Scamp trotted along the pavement, stopping when he got to an open space. The grass here was tall, and butterflies flitted from wildflower to wildflower.

"Yip! Yip!" Scamp raced through the tall grass. He chased the butterflies to the end of the open space and back again.

It was getting dark. Scamp decided it was time to head home. He hadn't caught a single butterfly, but he'd had fun trying. He couldn't wait to get home and tell his brother and sisters about the new game he'd invented. They'd be so impressed!

Scamp trotted up to the front porch and tried to get through the doggie door. *Thunk*! His nose hit the wood, but it didn't move. The door was locked!

"Yip! Yip! I'm home!" he barked. "Let me in!"

Scamp sat there for several minutes, barking. Nobody came to the door. Suddenly – *boom*! – thunder echoed overhead. Lightning flashed and rain began to fall.

Scamp bolted over to the big oak tree, sat down and covered his eyes with his paws. Thunderstorms were scary!

"I'm not going to cry," he told himself as his eyes started to mist over. He shivered in the dark. He'd probably catch a cold by morning!

Scamp let out a little whimper and moved even closer to the tree trunk. He buried his wet nose in his wet paws and closed his eyes.

Scamp was just falling asleep when a sound made him start. Somebody was coming up the drive!

By the time Jim Dear and Darling were out of the taxi, Scamp was dashing across the lawn as fast as he could go. He bolted through the door just as it opened.

"Scamp, you're soaking wet!" Darling declared as the puppy found his brother and sisters napping in front of the fire. And, as he lay down among them, Jim Dear came over with a warm towel to dry him off.

Home, sweet home, Scamp thought happily, as he drifted off to sleep.

Heavy Metal Mater

Everyone was gathered at Flo's V8 Café for karaoke. Lightning McQueen looked over at Mater. "Why don't you get up there and sing?" he asked.

"I don't want to steal the show," Mater replied. "I was a big rock star."

"What?" Lightning couldn't believe it.

"I started out in a garage band..." Mater described how his rock band, Mater and the Gas-Caps, rehearsed in a garage. Soon Mater and the Gas-Caps had a gig at the Top-Down Truck Stop. When the band finished, the trucks cheered.

"That so rocked!" exclaimed a waitress named Mia. "Do you guys have a record?"

The guitar player shook his head, but Mater smiled. He had an idea. Soon, Mater and the Gas-Caps were in a recording studio. Mater sang so loudly that everyone in the recording studio heard him. Doors began to open. Cars peeked out. "What's that sound?" someone asked. A music agent named Dex knew the answer. "Sounds like angels printing money to me!" He liked the song.

Dex rolled into Mater's recording booth. "Say, you boys are good," Dex told the band. Then he noticed their name on the drums. "All you need is a new name."

"'A new name?" repeated Mater. He tried

to think of one, but nothing came to mind.

At that moment, a delivery car entered the studio. "Where do you want this heavy metal, Mater?" he asked.

"That's it!"

Heavy Metal Mater was an overnight success. They packed stadiums and had thousands of fans. Their concerts instantly sold out. Word had spread quickly about their amazing performances. A giant Mater balloon with wings lifted up from behind the stage and floated over the audience.

In Radiator Springs, Lightning interrupted the story. "You were Heavy Metal Mater?"

"No," the tow truck replied. "We was Heavy Metal Mater!" Then he continued his tale. Except this time Lightning was in the band, too. Mater described how he was onstage at the concert. Then a platform rose up. Lightning was on it, wearing sunglasses. "Are you ready to rock?!" Lightning yelled. Then he jumped down and joined Mater.

At Flo's V8 Café, Lightning interrupted again. "I'm sorry," he said with a laugh, "that did not happen."

"Well, suit yourself," Mater replied, motioning to the sky. Lightning looked up. The balloon from the concert was flying overhead! Had Mater been telling the truth...?

Disney · PIXAR
TOY STORY

Toys That Go Bump In The Night

Andy was at a friend's house for a sleepover, and the toys had the whole night to themselves. Rain was pelting the windows and streaks of lightning were lighting up the sky. The toys decided it was the perfect night for telling scary stories!

Buzz, Rex and Woody took it turns to tell a story. Woody's in particular made the toys shake with fear.

"All right, gang," Woody said when he saw that the toys were afraid. "I think we've had enough stories for tonight. Let's get some sleep. Andy will be home bright and early tomorrow morning."

Woody had just fallen asleep when he felt a nudge. It was Rex. "I heard something! It's coming from under Andy's bed."

"You're going to make me get up, aren't you?" asked Woody.

"If it wouldn't be too much trouble," Rex answered.

So Woody got up and went with Rex to check under Andy's bed. *GRRRRRR!* A noise came from underneath the bed. Woody was starting to feel a little nervous, too. Then, something went *BUMP* underneath the bed. He decided they should go and get Buzz.

"I think we have an intruder here in Andy's room," Woody whispered to Buzz.

Just then, a rumbling came from under the bed. Rex wailed and then fainted in fright. The other toys gathered in the centre of the room. Buzz strode up to the bed and ordered the intruder out, but the only response was a high-pitched whine.

"Very well, then," Buzz replied. "You leave me no choice but to take you captive."

Buzz tried to crawl under the bed, but his space wings shot out and he got stuck. Sarge and his men pulled Buzz back out.

"There's something under there," Buzz said. "And it was definitely moving."

"We'll take over from here," Sarge announced. "Men, we're going to execute a sneak attack and surround the enemy. Now go, go, go!" The soldiers stormed under the bed.

"Halt!" boomed Sarge's voice. "It's one of our own! Switch to rescue-mission protocol!

The other toys looked at each other, confused. Suddenly, RC shot out into the room! "What was he doing under there?" asked Woody.

"His batteries are nearly out of juice," Sarge reported. "He just sat there revving his engine, spinning his wheels and going nowhere."

"I knew there had to be a reasonable explanation," said Rex. Woody smiled.

Island Adventure

Mickey, Minnie, Donald and Daisy were on their way to their seaside holiday. As soon as they arrived, they put on their bathing costumes and ran down to the beach.

They came to a lovely cove. "I'm going to relax right here!" Minnie declared as she spread out her blanket.

"Me, too," said Daisy, opening her umbrella.

"Those waves are just perfect for surfing," said Donald.

"You boys run along," Minnie said.

"We're happy right here," said Daisy.

Mickey and Donald surfed and swam until the sun went down.

The next day was sunny too. On their way to the beach, Mickey and Donald spied a boat for rent. "Let's go fishing!" cried Donald.

But Daisy and Minnie shook their heads. "We want to relax," they said.

So Donald and Mickey went fishing alone.

On the third day, Mickey and Donald wanted to go for a long swim.

"No, thanks," said Minnie. "I want to take it easy."

"Me, too," said Daisy. "We're going to the cove to relax."

The boys went off to swim. Daisy and Minnie headed for the cove.

While she and Minnie were lounging under the palm trees, Daisy spied a bottle floating in the water. There was a map rolled up inside. She waded into the water to get it.

"It's a treasure map!" she exclaimed.

"The treasure is on an island!" cried Minnie, pointing to a big X on the map.

Minnie and Daisy decided to follow the map. They went up one hill and then down another. They crossed a stream and reached a dock with a boat tied to it.

"That's the island," said Daisy, pointing out to sea. They hopped into the boat and started to row.

They rowed and they rowed until they reached the island. Minnie and Daisy were very tired and very hungry.

"Look!" Minnie cried. "I see a fire!"

"Pirates!" exclaimed Daisy.

But there were no pirates. Just Donald and Mickey, waiting for Daisy and Minnie to arrive. A campfire was roaring, and fish sizzled on the grill.

"Looks like they found our map!" Donald exclaimed.

"*Your* map?" cried Minnie.

"It was the only way to get you two to have an adventure with us!" Mickey replied.

"Now, sit down by the fire," said Donald. "Lunch is served!"

July
12

The New Kid

It was a beautiful morning in Sheet Rock Hills, and Manny and the tools were getting ready for their first big job of the day. "We're going to help out our new neighbours, Mr and Mrs Ayala," said Manny. "They just moved to Sheet Rock Hills and need our help setting up their son Marcelo's seesaw."

"What's a seesaw?" asked Rusty.

"It's a playground ride," Manny said. "It's a long board with a spring underneath that helps it move up and down!"

When Manny and the tools arrived at the Ayalas' house, their son, Marcelo, looked very sad. Mr Ayala explained that Marcelo missed his friends back in Argentina. Marcelo was worried about meeting new people.

"You'll make lots of new friends, Marcelo!" cheered Squeeze. "The first time I came to Manny's Repair Shop, I was worried that nobody would like me. But then I met Rusty. He's a lot like me, 'cause we both turn things with our teeth."

"That's true, and Turner and I both twist in screws," offered Felipe. "We're alike, too!"

"Marcelo, I think you will be surprised to learn just how much you have in common with the kids in Sheet Rock Hills," Manny said. "I bet you'll discover that you're not so different from them after all."

"Well… maybe you're right," said Marcelo.

With Marcelo's help, Manny and the tools put the seesaw together. Then, Manny saw Nelson playing in the yard next door. It gave him an idea.

"Marcelo, I have a bit of a problem. I want to make sure the seesaw is the right height for you," Manny began, "but I can't do it without someone sitting on the other end."

The tools called Nelson over.

"Hola, Nelson," said Manny happily. "This is your new neighbour, Marcelo."

Nelson smiled. "Hi, welcome to the neighbourhood! Hey, that's a neat seesaw."

Marcelo grinned. "Thanks! Um, would you like to try it out with me?"

"Sure!" exclaimed Nelson, climbing onto the seesaw. "Wow, you're so lucky – moving to a different place, getting introduced to new people."

Marcelo was surprised. "Lucky?"

"Yeah, I bet everyone can't wait to meet you," Nelson explained. "Being the new kid in town must be really exciting!"

Marcelo gave Manny and the tools a wink as he rode on the seesaw. "Well, it certainly has its ups and downs!"

A Bear-y Tale

It was time for Mowgli, Bagheera and Baloo to go to bed.

"Good night, Man-cub," purred Bagheera.

"But I'm not sleepy yet," protested Mowgli. "I need a bedtime story."

"Bedtime story?" said Bagheera. "At this hour?"

Mowgli turned to the big bear. "Please, Baloo?"

"A bedtime story, huh ..." said Baloo. "Now, how do those things begin?"

"Once upon a time ..." purred Bagheera.

"Oh, right . . . Once upon a time . . . in a house not far from this very jungle, there lived a clan of men," Baloo began.

"Real men?" asked Mowgli.

"Yep," said Baloo. "A father and a mother, and a little cub, just like you. Well, now, this clan, they cooked their food, and one day, don't you know, they made a mighty tasty stew . . . only thing was, when they sat down to eat, it was just too hot. So the mother got an idea. They'd go for a walk in the jungle and, by the time they got back, their stew would be nice and cool. But do you know what happened next?"

"No," Mowgli said.

"Well, that family had barely been gone a minute, when an old bear came wandering up, and stuck his nose into the Man-house."

"He did?" gasped Mowgli.

"Well, now, can you blame him? That stew just smelled so awfully good. And the next thing you know, he was tastin' it – startin' with the biggest bowl, but that was still too hot. So next he tried the middle bowl, but that was too cold. So – he tried the littlest bowl, and, don't you know, it was just right! That old bear didn't mean to, but he ate the whole thing right up!"

"What happened next?" said Mowgli.

"Oh, well, after that, this bear, he started to get tired. Real tired. And, don't you know, Little Britches, that right there in that house, looking so soft and comfortable, were three cushy-lookin' pads . . . I think men call them 'beds.' Anyway, that bear, he had to try them, too. Naturally, he laid down on the biggest one first. But it was too hard. So he tried the middle one, but that was much, much too soft. So, he tried the littlest one, and, son, let me tell you, that thing was so comfortable, he fell asleep right then and there! And he would have slept clear through the next full moon . . . if only that family hadn't returned and . . ."

"And what?" Mowgli asked breathlessly.

"And startled that bear so much, he ran back into the jungle . . . full belly and all."

Mowgli smiled and tried to cover a big yawn. "Is that a true story, Baloo?"

The bear grinned. "Would I ever tell you a tall tale, Little Britches?"

Nani and David's Stitched-up Date

Lilo sat at the kitchen table, a frown on her face. "It's not fair that we have to spend the night at old lady Kingsley's house just because Nani and David want to go to a movie," she said.

Stitch nodded.

"How is she going to watch us, anyway, when she can barely see?" Lilo asked. "And," she continued, "do you know what movie Nani and David went to see? *Invasion of the Bug-Eyed Aliens, Part VI: The Sliming* – without us!"

Stitch made a noise of outraged agreement. Lilo stood and said, "Come on, Stitch. Let's go see the movie ourselves."

Lilo and Stitch sneaked past the snoring Mrs Kingsley. Lilo opened and shut the front door as loudly as she could. Then, doing her best impression of Nani, she shouted, "We're back, Mrs Kingsley! Thanks!"

Mrs Kingsley woke up, tottered to the door and peered blindly at Lilo. "Is that you, Nani? Well, I hope you had a lovely time." And with that, the two made a break for the cinema. But, once they got there, they had two problems – money and . . .

"Sorry, kid, no dogs allowed in the cinema," the ticket taker said.

Lilo had to think quickly. "He isn't a dog. He's my teddy bear."

"He sure doesn't *look* like a stuffed animal," the ticket taker said.

"They make them very lifelike these days," Lilo fibbed. "Now, can we go inside? My mother is looking for us and, if we don't find her soon, I think I may start to cry."

"Okay, okay," the ticket taker said.

By the time the two had got into the cinema, the bug-eyed aliens had begun the 'sliming,' and everyone in the cinema was screaming. Lilo and Stitch immediately joined in – perhaps a little too enthusiastically, since Nani and David noticed them right away.

"Excuse me, excuse me," Nani said as she made her way out of her row and down the aisle, cola spilling and popcorn flying.

Nani grabbed hold of Lilo's arm and dragged her out of the cinema. David and Stitch were right behind them.

"I'm so angry with you I'm going to . . . I'm going to–" Nani stuttered.

"–take you out for ice cream," David finished her sentence.

"Out for ice cream?" Nani said.

"It's a beautiful night, and I can't think of anything more wonderful than two sisters having ice cream together." David turned to Lilo and Stitch. "Don't you think?"

A Day Without Pumbaa

"Mmm!" said Timon. "Breakfast time!" Timon was showing Simba how to catch some very sneaky bugs in the jungle.

"Too bad Pumbaa has to miss out," Timon said. "I haven't seen him. Have you? Ooh! There's a good one!"

Timon crouched behind a log and was about to pounce, when – "AAAHHH!" Without any warning, Pumbaa swooped out of the trees, swinging wildly on a vine. He crashed straight into Timon. "Oops! Sorry, Timon," Pumbaa said.

"Sorry?" shouted Timon.

"But it wasn't on purpose," Pumbaa said.

"You never do anything on purpose," Timon replied. "You're a disaster! You couldn't catch a bug if it flew into your mouth."

"That's not true!" Pumbaa protested. "I'll prove it." The clumsy warthog lunged for a grub, only to fall headfirst into a puddle. Mud splattered Simba and Timon from head to toe.

"That's it!" cried Timon. "I've had it!"

Pumbaa hung his head. "It would be better if I just left," he said.

With that, Pumbaa plodded into the jungle. Just then, the clouds thickened, and a bolt of lightning shot through the sky. Simba looked up at the threatening clouds. "Timon, we can't let him go!"

But Timon wouldn't even watch his friend leave. The storm came and went. And then so did lunchtime – but still, no Pumbaa.

"We shouldn't have been so hard on him," Simba said. "I wonder if he's okay."

"He's fine," snapped Timon. "Besides, he walked out on us, remember?"

By the time Simba and Timon finished dinner, they were both grumpy. Their friend still hadn't returned.

"There's got to be something fun to do," said Simba.

Timon had no ideas. But then they heard a rustling sound coming from along the riverbank. *Wham!* Pumbaa tumbled out of the jungle, knocking into Timon and Simba. All three of them crashed into a large tree trunk. Pumbaa had brought bugs for his friends, but they went flying into the air.

"I'm back," Pumbaa said.

"So we see," mumbled Timon, trapped under the warthog.

Embarrassed, Pumbaa stood up. "I came back to say I missed you," he said. "But now look what I've done! I'm the worst friend ever."

"Now, wait one minute!" cried Timon. "That's just not true!"

"You're a wonderful friend, and we missed you!" Simba said. "We even missed your disasters," he added. Pumbaa smiled.

199

Disney Pinocchio

Imagine That!

The carnival was in town. Pinocchio grabbed his friend Jiminy Cricket and off they went. Pinocchio was amazed at the marvellous sights. There were jugglers to see and games to play. He even saw an elephant doing tricks!

"That elephant is amazing!" Pinocchio cried.

"I suppose," said Jiminy politely.

Next they came to a lion's cage. The big cat opened his mouth and roared.

"Look at those teeth!" Pinocchio marvelled.

Jiminy Cricket nodded. "They're pretty big, it's true."

Then they saw a giraffe.

"What a long neck!" Pinocchio exclaimed.

"Giraffes are all right, I guess," said Jiminy with a shrug. Pinocchio was confused.

"If you don't like elephants, lions or giraffes, what kind of carnival animals do you like?" Pinocchio asked.

"Fleas," said Jiminy.

"Fleas?" Pinocchio said, even more confused.

"Come on! I'll show you," said Jiminy.

Jiminy led Pinocchio to a tent with a sign that read FLEA CIRCUS.

Inside Pinocchio saw a tiny merry-go-round and little swings. There were small animal cages and a little trapeze. There was even a tiny Big Top with three miniature rings. But no matter how hard he looked, Pinocchio could not see any fleas.

"That's because there *aren't* any fleas," Jiminy explained.

"What's the point, then?" Pinocchio asked.

"The point is imagination," said Jiminy. "Why, you can do anything with your imagination," he continued. "You can even see the fleas at the flea circus."

"But I don't see them," said Pinocchio, confused.

"You have to pretend to see the fleas, and pretty soon you can," said Jiminy. "Like that juggling flea over there. Oops, he dropped his juggling pins."

Pinocchio laughed and joined in the game.

"That flea is going to jump through a ring of fire," Pinocchio said. "I hope he makes it!"

"Now the fleas are doing acrobatics," Jiminy declared.

"They've made a flea pyramid," said Pinocchio. "And the flea on top is standing on his hands."

Finally, it was time to go home.

"What did you think of the Flea Circus?" asked Jiminy Cricket.

"It was the most amazing circus I ever saw, and I didn't really see it at all," Pinocchio replied.

"Yes, indeed. You imagined it," said Jiminy Cricket. "Imagine that!"

Mater the Greater

Lightning McQueen and his friends were enjoying a few oil cans at Flo's V8 Café when... "Whoa!" Mater sped backwards over a ramp. He crashed into a pile of cans. "I used to be a daredevil," he explained.

Mater began to tell the story of his days as a daredevil. One of the events was at a sports arena. The announcer called: "Ladies and gentlecars, Mater the Greater!"

In the stands, fans waved signs and cheered. It was nearly time for Mater's big stunt. He would try to jump over a very long line of cars!

"And he's off!" the announcer called out. Mater's wheels burned rubber as he drove towards the ramp.

THUD! Mater the Greater landed on the first two cars past the ramp. Each car in the line-up groaned as Mater the Greater tiptoed all the way down the row.

"'Scuse me!" he said. "Pardon me! Comin' through!" At last, Mater the Greater rolled over the last car.

"He did it!" the announcer cried. The crowd went wild! Mater the Greater had made his way over all the cars. It didn't matter to them how he had done it.

"I did all kinds of stunts," Mater told Lightning as he continued. He described being shot from a cannon through a ring of flames. In another stunt, Mater the Greater dove from a high platform into a tiny pool of water. "The biggest stunt Mater the Greater ever did was jumping Carburetor Canyon," Mater said. He said even with a rocket strapped to his hood, the jump seemed impossible.

Lightning was starting to doubt the story. "Jumping Carburetor Canyon? No way."

"Yes, way," Mater replied. "You remember. You was there, too."

Mater continued his story, except now Lightning was with him. Lightning had a fancy new paint job, and three huge rockets were strapped to his roof. He even had on Mater the Greater souvenir teeth!

"Ready, buddy?" Mater the Greater asked. But Lightning didn't really have a chance to answer. Someone lit his rockets and pushed him down the ramp! Lightning shot down the ramp and launched into the air. Lightning was about halfway across the canyon when his rockets sputtered... and went out. By this time, everyone at Flo's V8 Café was listening. They were all waiting to hear the end of Mater's story. "Well, what happened?" Lightning asked.

"You didn't make it," Mater replied. "Well, see ya later!"

Flik's Big Date

Flik loved Queen Atta very, very much. So, he decided to plan the most romantic evening for the two of them an ant could possibly imagine.

"I'll pick you up at eight tonight," Flik told Atta when he met her in the anthill early in the morning. Then off he hurried to get ready for their big date.

First, there was the dinner to prepare: sprouted wheat with sunflower seeds and wild truffles; free-range millet on a bed of dandelion greens; and Queen Atta's favourite dessert: gooseberry mousse.

The perfect menu! Flik thought. It was sure to impress Atta.

Then Flik went down to the stream to find the perfect leaf for a romantic moonlit cruise. "This elm leaf should do," Flik said as he tied the leaf to a root near the shore. "And I'll use this twig for my oar. Yes, Atta's going to love this."

But that wasn't all that Flik had planned.

"How's it coming?" he asked the circus bugs, who were back for a visit and busy practising their instruments just up the hill from the stream.

"Brilliant!" Slim replied. "Just brilliant. Don't worry about a thing. It's all under control. We'll have Atta's favourite song

memorized by tomorrow night, no problem!"

"But our date is tonight," said Flik.

"Oh," said Slim sheepishly.

"Told you so," said Francis.

"Don't worry," said Slim. "Remember, we're professional entertainers. You want an orchestra to dance to, and you'll have an orchestra to dance to."

"Are you sure you wouldn't like some magic instead?" Manny the Magician asked. "I have found that nothing inspires romance in a lady quite like cutting her in half."

"Um, I think I'll stick with the dancing," said Flik. But, speaking of inspiring romance, he'd almost forgotten all about the fireflies!

"Come on, guys!" he called to the dozen or so he'd hired for that evening. "I want some of you in the trees, some of you along the water, and the rest of you over there by the picnic blanket . . . perfect!" he said as their thoraxes lit up the quickly falling night. "Dinner is ready. Boat is ready. Music is . . . almost ready. Everything is set to go!"

Suddenly, Flik looked down at his watch, and his heart skipped a beat. "Oh, no! It's eight o'clock!" he yelled. "I've really got to go!"

Can you believe it? Flik was so busy getting everything ready, he'd almost forgotten to pick Atta up for their date!

Showdown

One afternoon, Jessie was watching Woody's Roundup on TV. In the old Wild West, Sheriff Woody and Jessie were talking about who was the best cowpoke.

"I can out-cowpoke you any day," Jessie said with a grin.

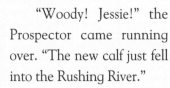

Woody smiled. "Who cares? We're both good cowpokes. Let's forget it."

Woody knew Jessie was a great cowpoke. But he didn't think she was better than him. Just then, the Prospector walked over with Woody's horse, Bullseye. Jessie told the Prospector what they were talking about.

Woody sighed. "Well, Jessie, should I just say you're as good a cowpoke as I am?"

Jessie grinned. That was all she wanted to hear. She knew Woody was a fine cowpoke.

"Whoa, hold on a rootin' tootin' minute," the Prospector said. "A true cowpoke never backs down from a challenge, Sheriff. How will you prove you're the roughest, toughest cowpoke in the West?"

Jessie suggested they each try to teach Bullseye a trick, but Bullseye wouldn't budge. Next, the Prospector suggested a dance contest, and ran off to do some work while they practiced. Jessie started swinging and swaying around, while Woody did a cowboy jig.

"Wow, you're a good dancer," Woody said, stopping to stare.

"Thanks," Jessie said. "You, too."

Woody smiled. "This contest stuff is dumb. What if…"

"Woody! Jessie!" the Prospector came running over. "The new calf just fell into the Rushing River."

The two cowpokes quickly climbed onto Bullseye's back and raced to the river. They soon spotted the calf wedged against a rock, struggling and mooing. Jessie grabbed her lasso and threw it neatly around the calf's neck. Then, Woody carefully climbed down, hopping from one slippery rock to the next. He patted the calf and lead it all the way back across the river. Meanwhile on the riverbank, Jessie and Bullseye held the rope so the calf wouldn't be swept downstream.

"Woody saved the day!" Jessie exclaimed, once the calf was safely on shore. "He's the bravest cowpoke ever."

"Jessie's the real hero," said Woody. "She lassoed the calf like a great cowpoke."

"Seems we still don't know who is the roughest, toughest cowpoke in the West," said the Prospector.

"Yes, we do," said Woody, grinning at Jessie.

"We're both great cowpokes!" they cried.

ATLANTIS
THE LOST EMPIRE

The Power of Reading

Princess Kida and Milo were helping the fishermen pull their nets to shore after a long day of fishing for tuyeb.

"This is hard work," Milo declared.

"But worth the effort," Kida replied. "Tuyeb is an Atlantean delicacy."

Milo's net was filled with strange-looking creatures with long, slimy tentacles and a tail like a lobster.

"You actually eat these ugly things?" asked Milo.

"They are very delicious!" the princess insisted. "The meat is sweet, and the tentacles are excellent when fried. We will have some for dinner tonight."

"I think I'll stick to tuna!" said Milo.

Milo and the princess went back to work. It took a long time to drag in the nets to shore – so long that most of the tuyeb slipped through the nets and swam away.

"There has to be a better way." Milo sighed, wiping the sweat from his brow.

"If there is, we have not found it," Kida said.

When they reached the shore, Milo yawned. "I'm tired. Let's take a break."

They sat down next to a great big statue of a tuyeb with long, metal tentacles.

"What's this thing for?" Milo asked.

"I do not know," Kida replied. "There are many of these statues along the shore, but no one knows why they are here because no one can read the words written on the statues."

"I'll bet I can," Milo declared.

He adjusted his glasses and began to read the ancient words.

"This is amazing!" Milo cried. "This thing is a machine."

"But what does it do?" Kida asked.

"You'll see!" said Milo. "But first you have to power it up with your crystal."

Kida plugged her crystal into a slot in the statue's head.

"Now, watch!" said Milo. He pressed a few buttons and the statue began to hum.

"It's moving!" Kida cried.

"Look out!" Milo warned.

Fishermen on the beach scattered as the mechanical tentacles shot out over their heads, grabbed nets full of squirming tuyeb, and dragged them to the beach.

"It is incredible!" Kida cried, clapping her hands. "This machine will make catching tuyeb much easier!"

To Milo's surprise, the princess gave him a big hug. "You have given us a wonderful gift. Thank you," she said.

"It was nothing," Milo replied, blushing. "All I did was read the instructions. That's the power of reading – if you can read, you can learn anything!"

Disney
MICKEY MOUSE
CLUBHOUSE

Space Adventure Part 1

Mickey and the gang had a treasure map from Professor Von Drake, and they were going to outer space to find treasure! "Let's go, space adventurers!" said Space Captain Mickey.

"Not so fast!" said the Professor. He explained that Mickey and the gang must find ten Treasure Stars. These stars would lead them to a mystery planet, and to the treasure! Everyone was on board.

But the gang didn't know that Space Pirate Pete was spying on them!

"Arrgh!" Pete said. "That space treasure will be mine!" Pete had a new helper named Quoodles, who looked a lot like Toodles. Pete asked Quoodles for a tool to stop Mickey's ship – he brought milk cartons. All the milk cartons blocked the rocket.

Space Pirate Pete said, "You're surrounded by milk. Give up the treasure map!"

"No way!" said Mickey. "We need a Mouseketool. Oh, Toodles!"

But Toodles didn't show up. Where was he? Toodles had seen Quoodles outside the ship. Toodles had never seen anyone else who looked like him! They smiled at each other.

"Oh, TOODLES!" called Mickey.

Toodles heard Mickey. He waved goodbye to Quoodles. Toodles brought a Mouseketool – a giant cookie! The cookie floated away, and the milk cartons followed it! Minnie giggled. "Everyone knows milk goes with cookies."

On the Moon, Mickey met Moon-Man Chip and Moon-Man Dale. Mickey asked if they had seen any Treasure Stars. Moon-Men Chip and Dale led them to their locker. Goofy opened it. There were Treasure Stars one, two and three! The Stars stuck to the spaceship like magic!

On Mars, Mickey met Martian Mickey and Pluto from Pluto! Mickey asked Martian Mickey if he knew where to find any Treasure Stars. Martian Mickey said, "They may be in the Star Tree Forest!"

Meanwhile, back at the ship, Toodles saw Quoodles again. He gave her some flowers. But Pirate Pete stopped by. "Quoodles," he said, "we gotta get that treasure map!"

Martian Mickey took the gang to the Star Tree Forest. Stars four, five and six were on the tree! But Space Pirate Pete had another trick up his sleeve. He pretended to be a little old lady who was lost in space. The little old lady asked Goofy for a map.

"Goofy, nooooo!" cried Donald.

But it was too late. Goofy gave Pete the treasure map! How would they get it back...?

Space Adventure Part 2

Goofy sure goofed. The gang had to get the map back! Mickey, Goofy and Donald chased Pete around the rings of Saturn, but they couldn't catch that tricky space pirate. Then Mickey fell off the rings and floated into space! Mickey bumped into space rocks until Pluto rescued him. "Thanks, Pluto," said Mickey.

Pluto and Mickey flew back to Saturn and the ship. On the way, they found the last Treasure Stars: seven, eight, nine and ten!

Back on Saturn, Toodles brought a Mouseketool – a big birdcage – to trap Pete. Donald grabbed the map back. But then, Quoodles brought a Space Chicken to help Pete get away!

Now Mickey and his crew had the map and all ten Treasure Stars, the stars lit the way to the mystery planet. "Let's call it Planet Mickey!" said Goofy. The stars shone on the X that marked the spot. And it was off to Planet Mickey to find the treasure!

Uh-oh – Space Pirate Pete got to Planet Mickey first and found the X that marked the treasure spot. Pete had one last trick. He threw out a sticky web. "Now when those little space adventurers try to pass through here and get the treasure, they'll get stuck!" said Pete.

But it was Quoodles who got stuck! "Poor Quoodles," said Pete. "I gotta rescue you!"

"Help!" yelled Pete. "Somebody HELP!" Mickey heard him and came right away. But now Toodles got stuck in the sticky web, too!

"I'm going to use a Mouseketool!" Mickey said.

"That's a great idea," said Pete. "And I'll use a Quoodles tool!"

Toodles sent Mickey a Mouseketool. It was... Space Pirate Pete! And Quoodles' tool was Mickey the Space Captain Mouse!

"It means we can save Toodles and Quoodles if we work together as friends!" said Mickey. So, Mickey and Pete jumped up and down on the arch holding the web. The arch broke. Toodles and Quoodles were free! Wheeee!

Everyone was happy to meet Quoodles – and to see that Pete had given up his "piratey" ways. Pluto pointed to the X. He knew where to dig. Pluto dug up the treasure chest. Inside was Professor Von Drake's remote control. Mickey pushed the button. The ground shook and up came... the Mickey Mouse Space House! What a terrific treasure!

"Now when you visit us, you'll have a fun place to play," said Martian Mickey.

"Hot dog!" said Mickey, and everyone did an out-of-this-world Hot-Dog Dance!

Buzz to the Rescue

"**T**here you go, pardners," Andy said as he packed Woody, Jessie and Bullseye the horse into his backpack. He was taking them to Cowboy Camp and Jessie couldn't wait. Andy's mum poked her head into his room. "You know the rules. You can only take one toy to camp with you."

Andy sighed. He lifted Jessie and Bullseye out of the bag and placed them on the windowsill. The two toys were disappointed. Jessie climbed down from the window and flopped into a box full of books. Andy's mum had just put the box in his room that morning and Jessie thought it would make a nice place to sit by herself.

Suddenly, a Green Army Man yelled, "Red alert!" Someone was coming. All of the toys fell lifelessly to the floor. Jessie was still inside the box. The babysitter for Andy's little sister walked in. She picked up the box Jessie was in and took it to the attic. It was full of old books! The rest of the toys looked at each other in shock.

"We've got to do something!" Buzz cried.

In the attic, Jessie looked for a way back to Andy's bedroom. The door would not budge. Suddenly, she had an idea. She found a jump rope, made a lasso and threw the loop over the window lock. She opened the window a few inches and crawled outside.

"Don't look down," she told herself as she stepped onto the ledge. Just then, she heard someone fiddling with the attic doorknob. Oh, no, she thought. The babysitter! She grabbed the rope and jumped.

But the noise wasn't the babysitter at all. It was the other toys opening the attic door to rescue Jessie. Buzz ran into the attic, but Jessie was nowhere to be found! He gasped when he spotted the open window. He saw Jessie hanging onto a jump rope.

"Don't let go, Jessie!" Buzz shouted. "I'm coming for you!"

Buzz deployed his wings. Then, taking a deep breath, he dove out the window. Jess looked up and saw her friend falling towards her. Thinking fast, Jessie swung her legs out and caught Buzz. He was heavy and the rope jerked under his weight. They swung forwards – right through Andy's open window! The rest of the toys raced down the stairs to Andy's room.

"We saved Jessie!" Buzz announced.

Jessie laughed. "Saved me?" She paused. I was the one who rescued Buzz, she thought. What does it matter, though?

"Well, thanks, everybody!" Jessie grinned as she looked around at her friends. "Even though I didn't get to go to Cowboy Camp, this has been the best adventure ever! Yee-hah!"

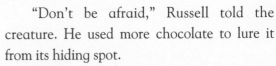

Strange Animals

Carl Fredricksen and a Junior Wilderness Explorer named Russell had just arrived in South America! Carl had dreamed of seeing Paradise Falls his whole life. He had promised his wife, Ellie, that he'd take her there one day. Sadly, Ellie had died before they could take the trip.

When Carl was told he had to move out of their home, he decided it was time to keep his promise to Ellie. He tied thousands of balloons to their house, and it lifted into the air!

But Carl hadn't planned on taking a companion along – Russell had been on Carl's porch when the house took off. They hit a storm and crash landed near Paradise Falls.

There was just one problem: the crash had sent them flying, and they couldn't get back into the house! It was hovering too high off the ground.

Russell had an idea: they could walk the house to the falls. They made harnesses out of the garden hose so they could pull the house.

"This is fun already, isn't it?" Russell said as they trudged along. "Don't you worry. I'm gonna assist you every step of the way."

After a while, they stopped to take a break. As Russell nibbled a chocolate bar, a beak poked out of the bushes and began to nibble it too!

"Don't be afraid," Russell told the creature. He used more chocolate to lure it from its hiding spot.

When the creature emerged, Russell gasped. It was the biggest bird he had ever seen! The bird liked chocolate. It liked Russell, too. Russell named the bird Kevin. He couldn't wait to show his new friend to Carl! But Carl yelled with fright when he saw the bird.

"Can we keep him?" Russell asked.

"No," said Carl.

Carl and Russell set off again. But Russell didn't want to leave Kevin behind, so he dropped a trail of chocolate for the bird to follow.

They hadn't gone far when they met a dog. "Hi there," said the dog. "My name is Dug." A talking dog? Carl and Russell were stunned! "My master made me this collar so that I may talk," Dug explained. "My pack sent me on a special mission. Have you seen a bird? I want to find one. I have been on the scent."

Suddenly, Kevin flew out of the bushes and tackled Dug. "Hey, that is the bird! May I take your bird back to camp as my prisoner?" Dug asked Carl.

"Yes! Yes! Take it!" Carl told him. He didn't want to deal with all these strange animals – he just wanted to reach Paradise Falls. But would he ever get there?

Disney·PIXAR
MONSTERS, INC.
The Chase

At Monsters, Inc., things had become a bit scarier than usual! Best friends Sulley and Mike had discovered a human child in their world. Monsters were scared of human children because they were told they were deadly to monsters – but Sulley had realized they weren't so bad after all.

Sulley was the top Scarer at Monsters, Inc. He was the best of the best at collecting children's screams to power the city. But, thanks to Boo – the child they'd found – he'd discovered that laughs were just as powerful as screams.

Unfortunately, the boss of Monsters, Inc., Mr Waternoose, was working with a mean monster called Randall. They had invented a machine to suck screams out of human kids!

Sulley had torn the machine apart and raced away with Boo, but Randall was chasing them. They made it to the Scare Floor. But to send Boo home, they still needed to find her door. They jumped in and out of closets, until Randall grabbed Boo! But Boo fought back.

"She's not scared of you anymore," Sulley told Randall. Working together, they beat Randall once and for all.

But Sulley, Mike and Boo weren't safe yet. Now Waternoose and the CDA (Child Detection Agency) were controlling the doors. While Mike distracted the CDA, Sulley escaped with Boo. Unfortunately, Waternoose saw everything. "Give me the child!" he yelled, running after Sulley.

But luckily, Mike recorded Waternoose yelling, "I'll kidnap a thousand children before I let this company die!"

Now everyone knew that Waternoose planned to take children, and he was arrested!

It was time for Boo to go home. Sulley followed her into her room. Gently, he tucked her into bed. Sadly, Sulley returned to Monstropolis. The CDA shredded Boo's door – it couldn't be used for scaring anymore.

After that, Sulley became president of Monsters, Inc., and the Scare Floor became a Laugh Floor! It was all because Sulley had discovered that laughter produced more power than screams. Sulley still missed Boo, though. He had one tiny sliver of her door, but the rest had been destroyed by the CDA.

But before long, Mike surprised his pal. He'd put Boo's door back together! It was missing just one little piece. Sulley inserted the piece, opened the door, and saw...

"Boo?" Sulley whispered.

"Kitty!" an excited voice replied.

The two friends were reunited at last.

Like Father, Like Son

Tramp had a whole new life. He had gone from being a stray to becoming a member of the Dear household. And now, he and Lady were proud parents.

But Tramp was finding it difficult to change some of his old ways.

"Tramp," Lady said gently, "you need to set an example for the puppies – especially Scamp."

Scamp had an adventurous side just like his dad. So, it wasn't surprising that father and son often got carried away when they played together. They couldn't resist the urge to roll in a puddle of mud – and then chase each other across the clean kitchen floor.

Soon, Aunt Sarah and her two troublesome cats, Si and Am, were going to be visiting. Lady was worried.

"Don't worry, I promise to keep Scamp away from those troublemakers," Tramp said.

"And?" replied Lady.

"And I promise to stay away from them, too," Tramp added.

When the big day came, Lady and Tramp herded their pups into a bedroom and told them to stay put. But Scamp was curious. He slipped out of the room and hid behind the living room settee. Then he sneaked up behind the cats and swiped at their tails as they flicked back and forth. The cats turned and chased Scamp up and over the settee, under a table and into a cupboard.

Well, Tramp thought, I suppose I'm going to have to chase those nasty old cats whether I want to or not!

He enthusiastically dived into the cupboard. Seconds later, Tramp and Scamp emerged. Much to Aunt Sarah's horror, Si and Am were later found inside tied together with a scarf. When no one was looking, Tramp and Scamp shared a victory wink.

Tramp and Scamp were banished to the garden for their antics. When Lady came out that evening, she found that they had dug up the entire garden looking for bones. Father and son saw the look on Lady's face and knew that they were about to get a lecture.

Tramp looked at Lady innocently. "You want him to get exercise, don't you?" he asked.

"Try it, Mum!" Scamp cried. "It's fun."

"What am I going to do with you two?" Lady said, laughing.

Tramp and Scamp dragged a huge bone out from behind the kennel.

"Join us for dinner?" Tramp replied.

"Well, all right," Lady said. "But, as soon as we're done, we're cleaning up this yard."

"Yes, ma'am!" chorused Tramp and Scamp, looking very pleased with themselves.

Oscar's House of Smoothies

Handy Manny and the tools were at Oscar's House of 18 Smoothies. Oscar had accidentally dropped a blender that morning, and cracked his counter. "Thanks for coming to help so quickly," he said.

"De nada, Oscar. You're welcome," Manny said as he inspected the damaged counter.

"Let me show you the very first smoothie I made today," Oscar said. "It's my favourite – banana."

Oscar explained to Manny and the tools that smoothies are like milkshakes, but healthier. He showed them how they're made with fruit, a little juice, honey and ice cubes, all mixed up in the blender.

"Delicious and healthy!" said Manny.

Oscar smiled, pointing to the sign above his counter. "And I have 18 different fruit smoothies customers can choose from!"

Stretch looked, and realized Oscar actually only had 17 flavours on his menu!

"What am I going to do?" cried Oscar. "I came up with all the smoothie flavours I could possibly think of!"

Dusty chimed in. "We can help you come up with another flavour!"

"I have a plan," said Manny. "I'll go to Kelly's to buy the supplies we need to fix the counter. While I'm gone, you guys can help Oscar come up with another flavour."

The tools were excited. Turner had an idea. "Guys, it would be smart to check out Oscar's kitchen. Let's look around and see if there's an ingredient he hasn't used yet."

So the toys and Oscar looked at the 17 smoothies already on the menu, and realized the only ingredient Oscar hadn't used was peanut butter! But just then, Mr Lopart – who owned the sweet shop – burst into Oscar's kitchen. He was zooming around on his new office chair with wheels!

Manny returned to find Mr Lopart on the floor of Oscar's kitchen, covered in food. "Are you okay?" Manny asked.

Mr Lopart wiped some of the food from his face, and licked his fingers. "Hmm, it's quite tasty! Is that peanut butter and banana mixed together?" Mr Lopart said.

Stretch jumped up and down, excited. "Peanut butter and banana could be a new smoothie flavour!" Stretch said.

Oscar grinned. "That is a wonderful idea!"

While Oscar cleaned his kitchen and made his brand-new smoothie, Manny and the tools fixed the counter. When they were done, everyone tried the Peanut-Butter-Banana Smoothie. It was delicious!

Tokyo Mater

One afternoon at Flo's V8 Café, three flashy modified cars roared past. "I used to be an import," Mater said. Mater described how he was driving through Carburetor County and saw an older car....

Mater pulled up. "Looks like you could use a tow somewhere," he said.

"It is very far," replied the older car. His name was Ito-san.

"Well, no tow is too far for Tow Mater!" exclaimed Mater. Mater towed Ito-san all the way to Tokyo! Mater had never seen so many tall buildings. Then Mater accidentally bumped into Kabuto, the leader of a gang of ninja cars.

"You scratched my paint," Kabuto snarled. He circled around Mater. "Dorifuto de shoubu da!" he said in Japanese.

"He challenges you to a drift race." Ito-san said that in a drift race, a car drives fast and steers hard into turns. That type of driving makes the car slide on the road. "We will race at midnight," Kabuto said, then sped away.

"You need modification," Ito-san said. With help from some other cars, Mater soon got a slick blue paint job and a large rear spoiler. At midnight, he pulled up to the starting line.

"Race to the top of Tokyo Tower. First one to seize the flag will become King of All Drifters," Ito-san explained.

Kabuto and Mater zipped through the streets. Mater was driving so fast that he missed a turn. "You can't drift! Ha!" Kabuto laughed. But then Mater went the wrong direction on a one-way street, and sped down an alley. He saw Kabuto up ahead, and drove up next to him.

"Good," said Kabuto. "But not good enough. Ninjas, attack!" A group of ninjas suddenly appeared. Mater was forced to slow down while Kabuto sped off.

Back in Radiator Springs, Lightning asked, "What did you do?"

"Well, shoot. You oughta know," Mater replied. "You was there, too!"

Mater described how he was surrounded by ninjas. Suddenly, Dragon Lightning McQueen was there. "I'll take care of this – dragonstyle!" he said. With a kick of his rear tyre, Lightning sent each ninja flying.

Meanwhile, Kabuto was nearly to Tokyo Tower. But just then, Mater landed in front of him. "Well, hey!" Mater shouted. He took off down the highway, driving backwards. Kabuto chased after him. Then Kabuto pushed Mater over the railing. Mater quickly threw his tow hook onto the tower and pulled himself up to the top. He had finished the race first! "I win!" Mater said proudly.

Disney
Winnie the Pooh

Piglet's Night-Lights

Winnie the Pooh knocked on Piglet's door. "Ready for our camp-out, Piglet?" Pooh called.

Piglet opened the door and looked around anxiously. "It's getting awfully dark out there."

As Pooh and Piglet walked, Piglet got more frightened.

"What's that?" he asked suddenly, pointing to a scary-looking shape in the trees.

"Hello!" called a voice from above. Pooh and Piglet both jumped, startled.

"Who's there?" Pooh asked.

"Why, it's me – Owl," the voice answered. "I thought you two might need a little help finding the others. We owls can see quite well at night."

By the time the friends reached the campsite, it was completely dark.

"Have no fear, Tigger's here – with illuminagination!" Tigger said, holding up a lantern.

The friends set up the tent and Piglet climbed inside and began to unpack. A few minutes later, he poked his head back out. "Oh, no!" he wailed. "I forgot my night-light!"

"Don't worry, Buddy Boy," Tigger said.

"You can use my lantern!" But just then, the lantern flickered out.

Pooh pointed to Eeyore, who was standing next to Rabbit and Owl. "Can't have a camp-out without a campfire," Eeyore said. They went to gather some sticks, and minutes later a fire was burning.

"Campfires certainly are pleasant," Piglet said. "They make a very good sort of light."

The friends played shadow puppets until bedtime. Piglet wouldn't leave the light of the fire, though, so Pooh kept him company. Soon, the fire began to fade. "Maybe we should go to sleep now, Piglet," Pooh said, yawning.

"I can't sleep without a night-light, Pooh," Piglet replied.

Looking up at the night sky, Pooh thought of something. "The stars are night-lights, Piglet," he said, pointing up at the sparkling stars.

Piglet looked around. "You're right, Pooh!" he cried. Piglet pointed to the moon. "Look how bright the moon is tonight. I feel much better."

"Do you think you might be able to sleep now, Piglet?" Pooh asked with a huge yawn. "Piglet?"

But Piglet was already fast asleep.

Pinocchio
Fish Food

Figaro the cat was scared. He was also hungry. But he knew there wouldn't be any dinner. Figaro, Geppetto and Cleo the goldfish had just been swallowed by a whale!

"Don't worry, Figaro," Geppetto said, seeing the cat's worried look. "We'll get out of here somehow – and when we do, we'll keep searching for Pinocchio. We won't stop until we find him."

That Pinocchio! Figaro growled. After all that Geppetto and the Blue Fairy had done for Pinocchio, he had run away from home without a care in the world. That was how they ended up inside the whale! Now what would become of them?

Figaro decided then and there that if they ever found Pinocchio, he was going to use both of the wooden boy's legs as scratching posts. It would serve him right.

Meanwhile, Geppetto was peering into the puddle of water at the bottom of the whale's stomach. Figaro watched curiously.

"Let's see," Geppetto murmured, bending over and poking at the water. "There must be something in here . . . .

"Aha!" Geppetto cried happily. He was clutching a small, soggy clump of seaweed.

Figaro blinked. Seaweed?

A moment later, Geppetto bent down again. "Aha!" he cried once more.

The little cat began to purr, imagining that Geppetto had caught a wonderful snack. But when he peered into Geppetto's hand, all Figaro saw was – more seaweed.

Seaweed was *fish* food, Figaro thought with a scowl. Surely Geppetto didn't expect *him* to eat that for dinner.

But, as he watched, Geppetto carefully divided the seaweed into three portions. He placed one portion in Cleo's bowl. He set one portion in front of Figaro. The third he kept for himself.

"Let's eat!" Geppetto said, smiling bravely.

Figaro sniffed his seaweed. He stirred it around with his paw. But he just couldn't eat the seaweed. With a twitch of his tail, Figaro turned away.

Geppetto watched the little cat with sad eyes. Figaro sighed. He couldn't help but feel ungrateful.

Reluctantly, Figaro turned back to his dinner. He nibbled at the seaweed. It was cold. It was slimy. But it tasted like – *fish*!

Figaro gobbled down the rest of his meal. With his belly full, the little cat felt better. He decided that if they found Pinocchio, he would only use *one* of the puppet-boy's legs to sharpen his claws on.

Probably.

Lucky's Last Laugh

It was getting quite late at Pongo's and Perdita's house, but their darling little puppies were still not asleep. Not that they didn't want to go to sleep. At least most of them. No, the problem was that one of them wouldn't let them go to sleep – Lucky!

"And then, don't you remember, you guys, the part at the very beginning, when Thunderbolt jumped across that canyon? Whoosh! Like a rocket! Clear to the other side!" Lucky said.

"Yes, Lucky, we remember," his sister Penny said with a groan. "How could we forget? You've reminded us 101 times!"

"Yeah! It was so great! And then there was that part when – "

"Lucky!" wailed Rolly. "We all watched the same episode of Thunderbolt tonight. You don't have to tell us about it."

"Yeah, I know, but I just wanted to tell you about the part when Thunderbolt found the little girl, then ran back to tell the sheriff – "

"Lucky! It's late! We want to go to sleep!" barked Patch.

Lucky laid his head on his paws. "Okay," he said. "I'll be quiet."

All the puppies closed their eyes.

"Oh! But what about the part when the sheriff told Thunderbolt to climb up that cliff, and he got to the top, and he grabbed that rope with his teeth, and he pulled up the little girl – "

"Lucky!" yelped Pepper. "We don't care about Thunderbolt. We want to go to bed!"

"Right." Lucky sighed, lying down once again. "Wait a sec!" He sat up. "Don't care about Thunderbolt? How could you not care that he carried that little girl across that broken bridge and through those raging rapids?"

"We mean," said Freckles, "we want you to be quiet so we can go to sleep!"

"You mean," said Lucky, "you don't want me to tell you about the last part where Thunderbolt ran back to the mountains and into that cave, and found that amazing thing?"

"Yes!" Lucky's brothers and sisters shouted together.

"Why didn't you say so?" said Lucky. "Good night."

And with that, Lucky closed his eyes. For a minute, everyone enjoyed the silence. Then Penny sat up.

"Hey, wait a minute," she said. "What thing did he find?"

"Yeah," said Patch. "I missed that part."

"Me, too," said Rolly. "What was it exactly that he found, Lucky? Tell us."

But there was no answer. Lucky was fast asleep. And now the *other* Dalmatian puppies were wide awake!

Time to Come Clean

Just as Manny opened his repair shop, the phone rang. "Hola! You break it, we fix it! This is Manny."

"Hello, Manny. This is Mrs Ayala. Remember you helped put together my son Marcelo's seesaw? We have a problem with our tub. It seems to be clogged. Do you think you can help us?"

"Absolutamente, Mrs Ayala. We'll be right over!"

Mrs Ayala was relieved to see Manny and the tools. "Thanks for coming so quickly," she said.

"No problem," said Manny. "Now, when did you first notice a problem?"

"This morning, when I started the shower – the water just filled up the tub instead of going down the drain. That's when I knew there was a clog."

"Who was the last person to use the tub?" Dusty asked.

Mrs Ayala thought. "Let's see... Marcelo took a bath right before bed at seven."

"Okay, tools," said Manny, "let's get to the bottom of this clog. First we need to unscrew the drain top!"

Felipe unscrewed the drain top, then Manny lowered the snake into the drain. "I think I feel something," said Manny. "Yes, got something!"

"Hey, I know that toy – it's Diver Davy, the scuba-diving action hero!" exclaimed Squeeze.

"Well, I don't want to jump to conclusions," Dusty said, "but there's only one person in the house who has action figures."

Just then Marcelo came into the room. "Is there something you want to tell us, Marcelo?" asked Manny.

Marcelo looked at the floor. "I'm sorry, Manny. I tried to make Diver Davy dive down the drain for a special mission after my bath last night, but then I couldn't get him back out!"

"But why didn't you just tell your mum and dad?" asked Pat.

"I was afraid they'd be mad at me," Marcelo explained.

"You have to tell your mum. Honesty is the best policy!" insisted Manny.

Manny and the tools followed Marcelo into the kitchen. He confessed about what had caused the clog. "I'm sorry, Mama."

"Telling the truth is always the right thing to do," said Mrs Ayala. "You've learned a very important lesson today."

"That's right," said Dusty in her most serious voice. "It's always important to come clean –"

"Especially after a bath!" joked Felipe.

HERCULES

Family Reunion

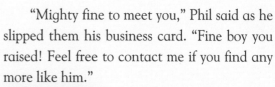

Meg paced up and down the room. "What's wrong?" Hercules asked his girlfriend.

"We're going to visit your parents," Meg told him. "I want to make a good first impression."

"You're smart and kind and intelligent," Hercules said, smiling. "How could you make anything other than a great impression?"

"All right, all right!" Phil cried. "Enough with the sweet talk. I have a cavity already. Can we get out of here?"

"Absolutely!" Hercules exclaimed. Pegasus galloped over and whisked them away.

Meanwhile, Hercules' parents, Amphitryon and Alcmene, were getting ready for their son's visit. Amphitryon was pacing too.

"Is everything all right?" Alcmene asked.

"Yes, of course," Amphitryon answered. "Why wouldn't it be?"

"Maybe you're nervous because your son is coming home and you haven't seen him in quite a while," Alcmene said.

Before Amphitryon could answer, they heard a sound.

"Look!" Amphitryon cried. "It's Hercules!"

And, sure enough, Hercules came charging up to the door. He leaped off Pegasus and gave a hearty hug to each of his parents. Then he introduced Phil.

"Mighty fine to meet you," Phil said as he slipped them his business card. "Fine boy you raised! Feel free to contact me if you find any more like him."

"And who's this?" Amphitryon asked.

"This is my friend Meg," Hercules said, blushing.

Just then, Pegasus snorted. "Oh, and how could I forget my pal Pegasus?" Hercules cried.

"All right, all right, enough with the niceties," Phil interrupted. "It's been a long trip. I'm hungry. Where's the grub?"

"Wait!" Hercules said. "I know you have prepared a wonderful meal, but first, I want to tell you what has happened since I left." He took a deep breath. "I've learned that I'm the son of Zeus and Hera. That's where I've got all my physical strength. But, without everything I learned from you, my adoptive parents," Hercules continued, "all that would mean nothing."

Amphitryon and Alcmene beamed with pride.

Then they all sat down for a feast worthy of the gods. Amphitryon and Alcmene were glad to have Hercules home; Hercules was happy to be home; Meg was honoured to be their guest; and Phil was thrilled to finally get to eat some home-cooked food!

THE EMPEROR'S
NEW GROOVE

Leaping Llamas!

"So Yzma and Kronk were out to get me the whole time! Some friends *they* were," Kuzco muttered as he trotted through the forest. Things had not been going very well for the Emperor-turned-llama. First, well, he had been turned into a llama. Then, while trying to get back to his palace, he had learned that his trusted adviser, Yzma, had actually been trying to kill him!

No, Yzma was no friend of his. Kuzco paused to scratch his ear with a hind hoof. And now he was all alone, without a friend in the world – not even that grubby peasant, Pacha. Actually, Pacha had probably been the closest thing Kuzco *had* to a friend. But now he was gone too.

Kuzco sighed. His best bet was still to get back to the palace. The problem was, Kuzco had spent his whole life having things done for him. Now that it was time to actually do things for himself, he wasn't sure if he could.

"Why me?" the llama whined to himself, as he wove in and out of vines and bushes. He was pretty sure he was headed in the right direction, but the forest was so dense and dark. Why, there could be *anything* hiding in that tree . . . under that fern . . . behind that rock . . . .

Behind that rock! Kuzco quickly leaped back as a panther lunged at him from behind a large rock. The panther's hungry jaws clicked shut just inches from Kuzco's snout.

"Heeeelp!" the llama bleated. Kuzco ran as fast as he could, but the panther was still gaining on him. This is it, thought Kuzco. I'm doomed!

Up ahead of him, Kuzco spotted a deep ravine. It was only about ten feet wide. "Okay," Kuzco said to himself. "Here's your chance. Llamas are nimble. Llamas are quick. Llamas can jump . . . really . . .

"Faaaaaar!"

Thump.

Kuzco shook his head and looked around him. He had leaped across the ravine! And, back on the other side, snarling and pacing back and forth, was the angry panther.

Kuzco stuck his tongue out at the panther and trotted on his way. He had done it! He had escaped a panther, all by himself! "But I know," he said thoughtfully, "that I could do even better with a friend at my side. I wonder where Pacha went, anyway."

Just then, the forest opened up into a broad, sunny field. Kuzco heard a faint bleat. Llamas! There were llamas here, and Pacha was a llama herder. A broad smile appeared on Kuzco's furry face. He headed towards the herd, and, sure enough, there was Pacha. For the first time since the day he had woken up as a llama, far from home, Kuzco began to feel like he might really stand a chance. It was good to have friends.

a bug's life

A Silo Scare

Flik took a step back and gazed up at the giant silo he and a troop of ants had just finished building. Now that the colony was using his harvester, they had a surplus of wheat. The silo would store the wheat safely.

"Nice job, Flik," Queen Atta said.

Flik blushed. A compliment from Atta always made his face feel warm. Atta was the smartest and prettiest ant in the colony. She was also its new Queen.

"Thanks, Atta," Flik said, trying to sound casual. "It should keep our wheat dry all winter."

Suddenly, a voice called down from the top of the silo. "Hellooooo," it said.

Flik and Atta looked up. It was Dot, Atta's little sister. She and her Blueberry friends were sitting on top of the silo.

"The view up here is amazing!" Dot called.

"Dot! Be careful!" Atta said worriedly.

Dot grinned down at her sister. "We will!"

"Don't worry," said Flik. "I built in several safety – "

Atta interrupted him. "I have a meeting," she told Flik. "Stay out of trouble," she added in a louder voice. For a second Flik thought Atta was talking to him. Then he realized that she was talking to the Blueberries.

"I'll keep an eye on them," Flik said.

"Come on up, Flik," Dot called as Atta hurried away. "You just have to see the view!"

"Coming!" Flik replied. He did want to see the view, and he also wanted to keep a close eye on the Blueberries.

But, just as Flik got to the top, one of the Blueberries leaped into the silo.

"Wheeeeee!" she cried as she zoomed down towards the pile of wheat.

"The silo is not a playground," Flik told the other girls. "It's for storing wheat, and I built in all these extra safety devices – "

"Come on, Flik," Dot interrupted. "We don't need any safety devices!"

Grinning, she jumped into the silo and slid to the pile of wheat at the bottom. Two other Blueberries followed. But then – whoops! – another Blueberry accidentally pushed down a lever. A big pile of wheat tumbled into the silo, heading straight for the Blueberries below!

Panicked, Flik hit a switch. The falling wheat was caught halfway down by a handy-dandy wheat stopper – one of the safety devices he'd built into the silo.

The Blueberries stared at Flik. Just then, Atta walked by. "Dot, what are you doing?" she asked.

"Uh, Flik was just showing us his great safety devices," Dot said sheepishly.

"And they really work," said Flik, sighing with relief.

The Longest Day

"Could I have everyone's attention, please?" called Woody. The toys quickly gathered around him.

"It's good news!" Woody said. "Today is Andy's last day of school. Starting tomorrow, it's summer vacation! And you know what that means..."

All the toys knew that meant they would get to play with Andy all day, every day. They wanted the fun to start straight away, but they had to wait until Andy came home. One by one, the toys suggested ways of passing the time. They played a game of Roundup, which was Jessie's idea, and then Buzz Lightyear made up a game of laser tag.

"But it's still only morning," Rex protested when tag was over. "This is the longest day of my life!"

"Don't despair, Rex," Buzz said. "There are plenty of other things we can do."

The toys decided to play knights-and-dragon in the castle Andy had built the night before. Rex played the dragon and pretended to attack the castle, letting out a roar. Then suddenly, Andy's puppy, Buster, came skidding into the room and attacked it for real!

"Bad Buster!" Woody said as the dog ran out of the room. He hurried over to the mess. "We're going to have to rebuild the castle so it looks exactly like it did before."

The toys worked together restacking the blocks. When they were done, the castle looked as good as when Andy built it! Woody looked over at the clock. "We've still got a little time before Andy gets home," he said. "What else can we do?"

The toys decided to take a rest. By three o'clock, they were all waiting anxiously for Andy.

"I'm positive this is the last day of school," said Woody, as he climbed up onto Andy's desk. Then, he spotted a note. "Oh, I'm sorry guys," he said. "It appears there's a party after school."

"So what time will Andy get here?" asked Rex. Woody didn't know the answer.

Suddenly, the toys heard the happy shouts of children playing. Woody looked out the window and saw lots of kids in Andy's backyard. Andy's entire class was here for the end-of-school party! No wonder it took him longer to get home, Woody thought. Footsteps thundered up the stairs, and Andy and his classmates burst into the room.

"Wow! Great toys!" a boy shouted as he picked up Buzz and Rex. The other kids grabbed more toys until Woody and all his friends were part of the celebration. This is going to be the best summer ever! Woody thought happily.

Disney
MICKEY MOUSE CLUBHOUSE

The Bake Sale

Minnie looked around the Clubhouse and smiled at her friends. "Let's start baking my cranberry-oatmeal biscuits! We promised to make a lot of them for today's bake sale."

"Yes!" said Daisy. "The bake sale is for a really good cause. All the money raised will go to the local animal shelter!"

"You betcha, this is important!" said Mickey. "Let's get some Mouseketools to help us!" Toodles brought the Mouseketools: A red wagon, a blue pen, five cans of paint and the Mystery Mouseketool.

Minnie was so happy to be baking her favourite biscuits, she called for ingredients very quickly. "Flour! Sugar! Eggs!" she called out. "Baking biscuits involves a lot of counting and measuring. We are going to make double batches to speed things up. So, Daisy, you need to break four eggs into that bowl. Goofy, you can help me measure out the oatmeal, flour and other dry ingredients," said Minnie. Then Minnie had Goofy carefully measured sugar, salt, baking powder and flour. A tiny speck of flour landed on Goofy's nose.

"ACHOO!" Goofy sneezed. The flour went everywhere!

"Gawrsh," said Goofy, "I guess flowers and flour make me sneeze. I'm sorry, Minnie."

"That's okay, Goofy," said Minnie. "But we have to start again." She tied a towel over Goofy's nose so he wouldn't sneeze. They quickly mixed the dough.

"We need to bake the biscuits for a little more than twelve minutes," said Minnie. "But I don't see a timer. I exercise for twelve minutes every morning. We can all do that while the biscuits bake!"

"That's a great idea, Minnie," said Mickey.

"I usually use weights. Is there something we can use?"

"Hmm. This sounds like a good time for a Mouseketool! Five cans of paint will do the trick!" said Mickey. "If we do Minnie's twelve-minute workout, the biscuits will be done when we're done!"

Minnie popped the trays in the oven, and everyone grabbed a can of paint. For the next twelve minutes, Minnie led everyone in lifting paint cans, doing sit-ups and jogging in place.

"This is fun!" said Daisy.

"Yeah," said Donald, "and it's probably a good idea to get some exercise if we're going to a bake sale!" When they finished Minnie's workout, everyone went back to the kitchen. The smell of freshly baked biscuits filled the air.

"Let's each have one," said Minnie.

Mickey bit into his biscuit. "These are the best cookies ever!" he said.

Mater Private Eye

Lightning McQueen drove up to the air pump. "My tyres are going flat."

Just then, Mater popped out of nowhere. "Flat tyres, ya say? I thought I solved that crime. I was a private eye," Mater explained. Then he told his friend about his detective days. "It was seven fifteen on a Friday night..." he began.

Mater sat behind the desk in his office reading an article about accidents caused by tyres blowing out. "I was on to something big," Mater explained. "There was a counterfeit-tyre ring."

A car named Tia drove in. "I need you to find my sister, Mia," cried Tia. "She's been carnapped! She was last seen working at Big D's club, The Carbacabana."

Big D was a sedan who had recently opened a nightclub. That night, Mater went to the club. A singer was performing. After her song, she came to Mater's table. "I'm looking for Mia. Have you seen her?" Mater asked.

"I saw her a couple of days ago with Big D. She smelled salty, like the ocean." Then Mater was thrown out of the club.

Luckily, a friendly rubbish truck gave Mater a clue that led him to the docks. There, he saw Mia on the deck of a huge cargo boat! Mater tried to sneak onto the boat to rescue her but he was spotted! Then Big D rolled out.

A crane grabbed Mater and hoisted him up.

Just then, Tia rushed forwards. She had told Big D Mater would be coming to the docks. Tia explained it was the only way to save her sister. The crane held Mater over the water.

Back in Radiator Springs, Lightning was on the edge of his bumper. "WHAT DID YOU DO?"

Mater laughed aloud. "Like you don't know, Lieutenant McQueen!"

Mater continued telling his tale. Police Lieutenant Lightning McQueen drove onto the docks with a group of squad cars. "Looks like we finally caught you, Big D," he said. But workers pushed barrels down the boat ramp to keep the police away. Meanwhile, Tia hit a switch on the crane, and it lowered Mater to the ground. Mater threw his tow hook at another crane, which dropped its crate – right on Big D! The crate split open, and tyres spilled all over Big D.

"Aha! Just what I thought – counterfeit tyres," Mater said. Big D had been swapping good tyres for fake ones. It was his fault there had been so many car accidents lately. Now that Mater had uncovered Big D's scam, the police stepped in.

"You led us right to him, Mater," Lightning announced gratefully. "Take him away, boys!"

Celia's Bad-hair Day

"Some encrusted evening," Mike sang to himself as he danced around the bathroom getting ready for his date. He could not wait to see his girlfriend, Celia. The round green monster was in the mood for love.

Pulling his car into the restaurant car park, Mike hopped out and hurried inside. "Here I come, my little Schmoopsie-Poo," he murmured.

When Mike caught sight of his snake-haired sweetie, his heart skipped a beat. The stunning cyclops was sitting alone at a table for two. Her green scales glowed in the candlelight. She was monstrously beautiful.

But, as Celia turned towards Mike, he noticed something. Rather than rustling happily, her hair-snakes were writhing angrily!

"How's my little Schmoopsie Woopsie?" Mike decided to ignore the grumpy-looking snakes. He leaned in to kiss Celia on the cheek, but the closest snake lashed out at him.

"Yowch," Mike exclaimed, jumping back. "Bad-hair day, snookums?"

"Oh, Googly Bear." Celia sighed, running her hand through her serpentine tresses. "It's just awful. I'm out of conditioner, my shower went cold on me, and I've been in an awful tangle ever since. Are they terrible?"

Choosing a seat far enough away from his sweetie to avoid being bitten, Mike looked closer. Celia's snakes glared at him, their fangs bared. Mike tried not to flinch when they hissed at him. But, he had to admit, they were a little knotted, and they did not have their usual body or lustre.

"They're not so bad," Mike fibbed. He blew Celia a kiss from across the table and tried to smile. This was not the romantic evening he'd been looking forward to.

At the next table a pair of many-armed monsters held hands and hands and hands. They rubbed their warty noses together and whispered sweet nothings into each other's many ears. Mike sighed. They looked so cosy. Then he had an idea.

"Excuse me, my sweet." Mike stood up and approached the couple. When he came back to the table, he was holding a large purple hat. "Amelia, Ophelia, Octelia, Bobelia and Madge," Mike addressed Celia's snakes. "How would you like to cosy up in this until we can get you untangled?" Celia's snakes cooed in delight.

"Oh, Googly Bear!" Celia cried. She wound her hair-snakes and stuffed them into the hat. "You even know how to fix a bad-hair day!"

With her hair contained, Celia gave Mike a big hug and a well-deserved smooch.

FINDING NEMO

A Real Sleeper!

"Time for bed, Nemo," said Marlin. "It's a school day tomorrow," he added. "You need to get your rest."

"Okay, Dad," said Nemo. "But can you tell me a story? How about one when you were younger?"

"Well, just one then," said Marlin, swimming back over to his only child. He thought for a moment, then smiled broadly. "Did you know that when I was younger – much younger, actually – did you know that I wanted to be a comedian?"

Nemo's eyes widened with surprise. "*You*? A comedian? Aren't comedians supposed to be . . . funny?"

"Well, you see, son," said Marlin, "life is not easy for a clownfish. You may as well realize that right now. See, when you're a clownfish, everyone you meet assumes that you are funny. It's a common mistake. Anyway, years ago, I figured that as long as everyone expected me to be funny, I would try being funny for a living."

"But, Dad," said Nemo, "you aren't funny at all."

"Hey, now! Wait just a minute!" Marlin said, a bit huffily. "In my day, I was known as quite the crack-up! Let me see. I'm sure I can remember some of my old routine, if I just think about it for a minute." He thought for a moment. "All right, it's all coming back!" He cleared his throat. "Good evening, ladies and jellyfish! The ocean sure is looking *swell* tonight. Would you like me to give you a coral report about the latest happenings on the reef? Get it?" he said, looking down at Nemo. "You see, there's something called an oral report, and the words coral and oral sound quite a bit alike."

Nemo gave his father a pained look.

"So, the other day my appendix nearly burst," Marlin went on. "So I decided I'd better go to a sturgeon!"

Nemo blinked. "Dad, these really aren't that funny," he said with a yawn.

"A *sturgeon*. Get it? Rather than a surgeon?" Marlin sighed and continued his routine. "A funny thing happened on the way to the show tonight. I met a guy, nice fish and all, but he seemed to be a bit down on his luck. He told me he was living on squid row."

Nemo's eyes were starting to droop sleepily.

"Do you know why the whale crossed the ocean?" Marlin continued. "Now, don't try to guess. I'll tell you: the whale crossed the ocean to get to the other tide. The other *tide*."

Nemo's eyes were now completely closed, and a tiny snore escaped from him. Marlin smiled at his sleeping son.

"Works every time," he said with a chuckle.

Andy's All Grown Up

There was a train robbery underway, and Sheriff Woody had to work quickly! Standing atop the moving train, Woody confronted One-Eyed Bart. But Bart threw Woody off the train, then escaped in a getaway car driven by Aliens! Luckily, Woody was caught by the brave cowgirl Jessie, galloping nearby on Bullseye. Still, the train plunged over a cliff – until Buzz Lightyear lifted it to safey! The battle continued, good guys vs. bad, until the evil Dr Porkchop finally cornered Woody and his crew.

"Buzz, shoot your laser at my badge!" Sheriff Woody ordered. Buzz's laser ricocheted off the badge and up at Dr Porkchop's spaceship. ZAPPPP!!! The bad guys were no more. It was another thrilling adventure for the toys in Andy's room.

With Andy, the toys felt as if anything was possible. Maybe they'd be villains trying to take over the world – or maybe they'd be the heroes who would save it. For years, the toys could do anything Andy's imagination dreamed up. They loved every single day with Andy, and they all agreed: being loved and played with by a kid – by their kid – was the best feeling in the world.

But lately, the toys had been spending more time in the toy box. Andy hardly ever took them out. The toys decided to take action.

"All right, guys, we got one shot at this," said Woody, gathering everyone together. Sarge and two of his men appeared in Andy's room, dragging a mobile phone behind them. "Mission accomplished!" Sarge reported.

"Make the call," Woody ordered.

Jessie dialled some numbers on a cordless phone. The other toys were very nervous. The mobile phone began to ring. "Just like we rehearsed it, guys," instructed Woody.

Hearing the cell phone, Andy entered the room and looked around. He went to the toy box, lifted the lid and stuck his hand inside, rummaging around. Finally, he found the mobile phone wedged between Rex's arms.

"Hello?" Andy said into the phone. "Hello... anyone there?" But no one answered.

"Molly, stay out of my room!" he yelled, clicking the phone off.

"I wasn't in your room!" his sister shouted.

Andy just rolled his eyes. He glanced at Rex for a moment, then dropped the dinosaur back into the toy chest and closed the lid.

The toys were disappointed. They knew the truth: Andy was a teenager now, and he didn't want to play with toys anymore.

Meeting a Hero

Carl and a young boy called Russell were in South America. They had flown there in Carl's house with thousands of balloons tied to it! Carl had been married to a woman called Ellie for many years. They had always dreamed of becoming explorers and visiting Paradise Falls in South America. Sadly, they were never able to save enough money to take their trip, and Ellie had passed away. But Carl still wanted to make their dream come true.

Since arriving in South America, Carl and Russell had met a strange, huge bird – Russell named him Kevin – and a talking dog called Dug! Dug was on a mission to find Kevin and wanted to take the bird prisoner.

They were walking to Paradise Falls, holding on to the house with the garden hose. That night, they stopped to rest. "Dug says he wants to take Kevin prisoner. We have to protect him!" Russell told Carl while the others slept. Carl agreed that Kevin could come with them to the falls.

"Promise you won't leave Kevin? Cross your heart?" Russell asked Carl.

Carl thought for a moment. The last time he'd crossed his heart was when he'd promised Ellie he would take her to Paradise Falls.

"Cross my heart," he finally told Russell.

The next morning, they found Kevin perched on the roof of the house. The bird was calling towards the distant rocks. "The bird is calling to her babies," Dug explained.

"Kevin's a girl?" Russell asked in surprise.

Soon Kevin set off for her home. Russell wanted to go with her. But Carl was in a hurry to get to the falls. "She can take care of herself," he told Russell.

Suddenly, three fierce dogs burst from the bushes. They surrounded Carl, Russell and Dug, and demanded the bird. The dogs were part of Dug's pack. When they realized that Dug had lost the bird, they wanted to take the travellers to their master.

The dogs led Carl and Russell to a huge cave. An old man stood in the entrance, surrounded by more dogs. When the man saw Carl's house, he laughed. He had thought that Carl and Russell were explorers – but real explorers wouldn't come in a floating house! "My dogs made a mistake," he told Carl.

Carl thought the man looked familiar. "Wait," he said. "Are you... Charles Muntz?"

Carl couldn't believe it – Muntz was his and Ellie's childhood hero! "My wife and I, we're your biggest fans!" he said, shaking Muntz's hand. Carl wished that Ellie was there – he knew she would have been thrilled.

A Major Mess

High in the bell tower of Notre Dame cathedral, the gargoyles, Victor, Hugo and Laverne, began their 45th game of hide-and-seek that day.

"Ready or not, here I come!" called Victor. "And no one better be hiding in Quasimodo's underwear drawer! It's neither funny nor proper." And with that, he leaped over a pile of rumpled clothes and began searching among stacks of books and games and other scattered objects.

The tower, you see, was a mess! Quasimodo had only been away for a few days and still the tower looked like a hurricane had hit it. And why was that? Simply because the gargoyles were slobs!

Quasi had asked them to look after his things – particularly his carvings and precious bells – while he was away. "And of course," Quasi told them, "feel free to make yourselves at home." And, well, they had!

They had tried on his clothes and left them scattered all over the floor. They had leafed through his books and played all his games, without ever putting a single thing back. And they had even used his pillows for pillow fights!

And so it was with some shock and horror that Victor suddenly stopped their game and shrieked, "Do you know what day it is?"

"Excuse me?" said Hugo, peeking out from behind a pillar.

"It's Friday!" said Victor. "The day that Quasi returns home!"

"Oh!" Hugo gulped, gazing at the mess. "He's not going to be happy with us, is he?"

"Oh, but he is," said Victor, "because we're going to clean all this up. If we don't, he'll never trust us again."

"Maybe he shouldn't," muttered Hugo.

"Where is Laverne? Laverne!" Victor called. "Come out, come out, wherever you are. We have work to do!"

And work they did. They folded the clothes. They made the bed. They put the books back on the shelf. They washed the dishes and scrubbed the floor. They dusted Quasi's hand-carved models and carefully put them back. And they polished every one of Quasi's bells.

"You missed a spot on Big Marie!" Victor called to Hugo . . . just as Quasimodo arrived.

"Guys! I'm home!" he shouted.

"Quasi! We missed you! How was your vacation?" the gargoyles asked.

"Great!" said Quasimodo. "You should try it sometime!"

And, after all the work the gargoyles had just done, a holiday is exactly what they needed!

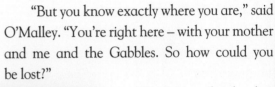
Wherever You Go, There You Are!

"Oh, dear! Oh, dear!" said Amelia Gabble. The goose and her twin sister, Abigail, had been waddling along the road to Paris, when Amelia suddenly stopped.

"What's wrong?" asked Abigail, bumping into her.

"Just look and you'll see," said Amelia. Stretching out one big white wing, she pointed to the road ahead. Abigail looked, and then the two geese put their heads together and began to argue in low voices.

Behind the geese, Thomas O'Malley, Duchess and her three kittens gathered together.

"I wonder what's wrong," said Duchess.

"Guess I'd better find out," said O'Malley.

He sauntered forward. "Ladies, ladies, what's going on?" he asked the twin geese.

"We know this is the road to Paris," Amelia explained. "But up ahead, the road divides."

Sure enough, the single road split in two.

"I think we should go right," said Amelia.

"And I think we should go left," said Abigail.

The three kittens began to worry.

"Mr O'Malley, are we lost?" asked Marie in a small, frightened voice.

O'Malley smiled down at the little white kitten. "Lost? What's lost? I don't know the meaning of the word."

"I do," said Berlioz. "If you're lost, then you don't know where you are."

"But you know exactly where you are," said O'Malley. "You're right here – with your mother and me and the Gabbles. So how could you be lost?"

Duchess shook her head and said, "Mr O'Malley, if we want to get to Paris and we don't know the way, then I do believe that we are lost."

"But Paris is just a place," said O'Malley. "And places are easy to find."

"Look, Mama, look!" Toulouse shouted. "I see something over that hill. It's the top of the Eiffel Tower!"

"Toulouse, you're right!" said Duchess.

"Nice going, little tiger," said O'Malley. Then he turned to the Gabble sisters. "Well, ladies, looks like Paris is thataway!"

Soon they arrived in Paris, where the Gabble sisters met up with their Uncle Waldo. The geese waved goodbye.

Marie sighed with relief. "I'm glad we're not lost any more."

"Aw, honey," said O'Malley, "someday you'll understand. Places may come and places may go but, when you're a free spirit, you can never be lost."

"Never?" asked Marie.

"Never," said O'Malley. " 'Cause wherever you go, there you are!"

Marie nodded. She liked the sound of that!

Winnie the Pooh

Eeyore Beats the Heat

One day, when it seemed the sun was shining even more sunnily than ever over the Hundred-Acre Wood, Eeyore sighed and wished that autumn – if it wouldn't be too much trouble – would hurry itself up and get there.

"Something the matter, Eeyore?" asked Roo.

"Oh, it's just that it's so terribly hot," replied Eeyore. "If I weren't stuffed with sawdust, I think I would melt."

"Well, come with me!" squeaked Roo. "I'm going to the swimming hole to cool off."

But Eeyore shook his head. "Can't do, Roo," he said. "Not with my sawdust and all . . . I'd probably just sink. And that's if I'm lucky."

And so Roo, who felt sorry for Eeyore, but who was also eager to swim, continued on his way.

Soon, another friend came along. And this friend was Winnie the Pooh.

"You're looking a little warmish, Eeyore," Pooh said.

"Same to you," said Eeyore with a sigh. "Same to you."

"Ah," said Pooh, "but I am off to catch a breeze – and pay a call on some bees – with my trusty balloon here. Care to join me?"

"No, thanks, Pooh," said Eeyore. "I never did like feeling like the ground was missing. And . . . I expect that with my luck, the balloon would probably pop."

"Well, Eeyore, I understand completely. Wish me luck, then, won't you?" Pooh replied.

"Good luck, Pooh," said Eeyore. "As if anything I ever wish comes true . . ."

The next friend to come upon Eeyore was little Piglet.

"Hello, there, Eeyore," said Piglet. "Whoo! Are you as uncomfortably hot as I am?"

"Oh, no," said Eeyore. "I'm sweltering. Parched. Smouldering. Torrid. Yes – 'uncomfortably hot' would be an understatement."

"Poor Eeyore," said Piglet. "Why don't you come play in the cool mud with me?"

But once again, Eeyore shook his head. "Afraid mud is not an option, Piglet," he explained. "Once I get dirty, I'll never get clean. No. Go enjoy yourself on this hot day like everyone else. All except me. As usual. I'll just suffer."

And suffer poor Eeyore did . . . until not too terribly much later when his friends all returned with something sure to cool even Eeyore off on this sultry day.

"Guess what we've brought you, Eeyore!" Roo squealed with delight.

"It's ice cream," whispered Pooh.

"Ice cream, huh?" Eeyore sighed. "I suppose I'll have to eat it all before it melts."

And do you know what? He did!

DUMBO

'Ears a Job for You, Dumbo!

It had been a hard day for little Dumbo. It was bad enough that everyone made fun of his ears except his mother, but then they had put his mother in a cage, so Dumbo couldn't even be with the one person who loved him and treated him decently.

What made things even worse was that Dumbo didn't have anything to do. It seemed that he was the only creature in the circus who didn't have a job. Everyone had a purpose except Dumbo. All he could do was feel sad and be laughed at.

Dumbo heaved a sigh and went for a walk through the circus tents. Soon, he found himself among the refreshment stands. Everyone here had a job too. Some were squeezing lemons to make lemonade. Others were popping popcorn or roasting peanuts. Wonderful smells filled the air.

Finally, Dumbo came to a little candyfloss wagon. The puffy cloud of sugar looked tempting, and Dumbo wanted a taste, but there were so many customers he couldn't get close enough.

Suddenly Dumbo heard a loud buzzing. Then all the customers waved their hands over their heads and ran away.

The smell of sugar had attracted a swarm of nasty flies!

"Scat!" cried the candyfloss man. "Go away before you scare off my customers."

Dumbo reached out his trunk to smell the delicious candyfloss.

"Not you, Dumbo!" the candyfloss man cried. "It's bad enough chasing flies. Do I have to chase elephants too?"

Poor Dumbo was startled. With a snort, he sucked candyfloss right up his nose.

Ahhh-choo!

When he sneezed, Dumbo's ears flapped – and something amazing happened.

"Remarkable!" the candyfloss man cried. "All the flies are gone. They think your ears are giant fly swatters!"

The candyfloss man patted Dumbo's head. "How would you like a job?"

Dumbo nodded enthusiastically and set to waving his ears. Soon, the candyfloss stand was the most popular refreshment stand in the circus – and had the least flies. But, best of all, Dumbo now had something to do to take his mind off his troubles. He was still sad, but things didn't seem quite so bad. And, who knows, perhaps soon he'd have his mother back.

"I wonder what other amazing things those big ears can do?" said the candyfloss man, giving Dumbo a friendly smile. "I'll bet they carry you far . . . ."

FINDING Nemo

Hide, Dude!

"Come on, Squirt!" Nemo cried happily. "Race you to the coral shelf!"

Nemo took off, pumping his mismatched fins as hard as he could. His young sea turtle friend laughed and swam after him.

Squirt was visiting Nemo at his home on the reef. "This way, dude!" Squirt yelled, flinging himself through the water. "I'm catching some rad current over here!"

Nemo hesitated for just a second, watching as his friend tumbled along head over heels past some stinging coral. Squirt was so brave! Even after all that Nemo had been through – being captured by a scuba diver, then escaping from a tank to find his way home again – he still got scared sometimes.

With a deep breath, he threw himself into the current. He tumbled after Squirt, fins flying as the water carried him along. Finally, he came out the other end of the current, landing in the still ocean beside Squirt.

He giggled. "Hey, that was fun!" he cried. "Let's do it again! Squirt? Squirt, what's wrong?"

The sea turtle was staring into the distance, his eyes wide. "Hide, dude!" Squirt cried.

Before Nemo could respond, Squirt's head and legs popped into his shell and he landed on the sea floor with a flop.

Nemo started trembling. What had scared Squirt so much? He stared around, expecting to see a shark or something equally frightening. But all he could see nearby were a few pieces of coral with a lone Spanish dancer floating along above them.

He swam down and tapped on Squirt's shell. "Hey," he said. "What is it? There's nothing scary here."

"Whew!" Squirt's head popped out. He looked around, then gasped and hid again. When he spoke, his voice was muffled. "It's totally still there!"

Nemo blinked and looked around again. Again, all he saw were the coral and the Spanish dancer.

"Hey, wait a minute," he said, suddenly realizing something. "Haven't you ever seen a Spanish dancer before?"

"A – a Spanish wha-huh?" Squirt asked, still muffled.

Nemo knocked on his friend's shell again. "It's a kind of sea slug," he explained. "Don't worry, Spanish dancers are nice – you don't have to be scared. I promise."

Finally Squirt's head popped out again. He smiled sheepishly at Nemo.

"Sorry, dude," he said. "I never saw one of those before. It totally freaked me out."

"It's okay." Nemo smiled back. He already knew that new things could be scary – and now he knew he wasn't the only one who thought so. "Come on, let's go play."

THE GREAT MOUSE DETECTIVE

A Lesson in Confidence

"Oh dear!" Olivia, a very worried little mouse, sat with Dr Dawson next to the fireplace in Basil of Baker Street's home.

"What's the matter?" Dr Dawson asked.

"What's the matter?" Olivia repeated indignantly. "My father's been stolen by a peg-leg bat! Have you forgotten already?"

"No, no, dear," Dawson reassured her. "Of course not. I know you must be quite upset."

"Quite upset!" Olivia cried angrily. "I couldn't possibly be more upset!"

"But we're at Basil's now, and he's the best. You even said so yourself," Dawson said.

"But what if he doesn't want to help me?" Olivia asked.

"Why wouldn't he want to help you?" Dawson asked.

"You heard him," Olivia answered. "'I simply have no time for lost fathers,'" she said, quoting the detective.

"He didn't mean it," Dawson said reassuringly. "He's just in the middle of something. Perhaps we caught him at a bad time. But, whatever the circumstances, my dear, you must try not to fret."

"I know you're trying to help me, Dr Dawson," Olivia said, as politely as she could manage. "But I don't know if I can really avoid fretting. My father is out there somewhere, and I just *have* to find him!"

"You're right!" Dawson said. "You do have to find him. You have to help Basil track down your father and, in order to do that, you are going to need a clear mind. Now, can you have a clear mind while you're fretting?"

"Well, it probably doesn't help," said Olivia reluctantly.

"Can you think logically while you're upset?" Dawson asked.

". . . Probably not," Olivia said.

"Can you work side-by-side with Basil of Baker Street, the great mouse detective, to save your beloved father while you are *worried*?" Dawson asked.

"No!" Olivia paused as the truth sank in. "No, I can't. I owe it to my father to be level-headed. I can be sad and scared later – right now I have to be a detective, like Basil!" she finished triumphantly.

"That, my young lady, is the smartest thing you could have said. And, if you can hold on to that attitude, your father will be found in no time." Dawson smiled at Olivia.

Just then, Basil came swooping back into the room. "Of course he will. I never miss my mark. Your father is as good as found, because I am just that good!"

Olivia smiled secretly. She knew *she* was just that good too.

Secret Agents and the World Grand Prix

A British secret agent called Finn McMissile had received a distress call from a fellow agent. Finn travelled to the agent's location in the middle of the Pacific Ocean, to an oil derrick. Using his grappling hooks and magnetic wheel armour, Finn drove up the side of the oil derrick. He hid inside and saw a wanted criminal named Professor Z. Beside the Professor and his crew was a special TV camera. Then Finn saw his fellow agent – he had been crushed into scrap metal!

Suddenly, Professor Z spotted Finn and sent his gang after him. When they cornered Finn, he leaped off the derrick, turned into a submarine and escaped!

Meanwhile, in the town of Radiator Springs, Mater had called all his friends together to welcome home his best friend, Lightning McQueen. The racecar had just won the Hudson Hornet Memorial Piston Cup!

Lightning finally arrived home and the friends were overjoyed to see each other. Mater wanted to hang out with his best buddy, but Lightning was exhausted. He went off to spend a quiet evening with his girlfriend, Sally. Mater was disappointed.

Later that night at the Wheel Well restaurant, Mater called in to a TV show. He defended Lightning against an Italian race car, Francesco Bernoulli, who swore he was faster than Lightning. Soon, Lightning was on the phone too. He agreed to race in the World Grand Prix – a three-event race hosted by former oil tycoon, Sir Miles Axlerod.

Mater, Luigi, Guido, Fillmore and Sarge all offered to be Lightning's pit crew. Soon "Team Lightning McQueen" was on a plane heading off to the first race in Japan!

Lightning and his friends had a fantastic time sightseeing in Tokyo. There were skyscrapers and high-tech gadgets everywhere! They all went to a fancy welcome party. Finn McMissile and another British agent, Holley Shiftwell, were also there. They were looking for an American agent who had some top-secret information.

Mater embarrassed Lightning at the party by leaking oil on the floor right in front of Miles Axlerod! Lightning sent Mater to the bathroom to clean up. Outside Mater's cubicle, Professor Z's goons, Grem and Acer, had cornered the American agent, Rod "Torque" Redline. When Mater came out, the agent secretly stuck the top-secret information on Mater.

Holley thought Mater was the American agent she was supposed to meet! Little did Mater know, but this was just the beginning of his secret agent adventures.

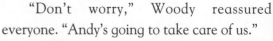

Packing for College

Woody, Buzz and the rest of Andy's toys were sad. They knew the truth: Andy was a teenager, and he didn't want to play with toys anymore.

"Andy's going to college any day now," Woody said. "We all knew this day was coming. Every toy goes through this."

Buzz noticed Sarge and his men climbing up to the windowsill. "What are you doing?" he asked.

"We've done our duty," Sarge replied.

"And," added another soldier, "when the trash bags come out, we Army guys are the first to go." They parachuted out of the window.

"We're getting thrown away?" cried Rex. Then everyone started squeaking and shouting. No one wanted to get thrown away!

"Whoa! Hold on!" shouted Woody. "Through every yard sale, every spring cleaning, Andy held on to us. He must care about us, or we wouldn't still be here. You wait – Andy's going to tuck us in the attic..."

"And we'll be together," added Buzz. "Let's get our parts together, get ready and go out on a high note."

"I'd better find my other eye," said Mrs Potato Head. She could still see images through the lost eye, remotely – and wherever it was, it was seeing a lot of dust.

"Don't worry," Woody reassured everyone. "Andy's going to take care of us."

Just then, the toys heard footsteps in the hall. They scrambled back into the toy box as Andy returned to the room. And his mum was right behind – carrying rubbish bags. "Okay, let's get to work here," she said. "Anything you're not taking to college either goes in the attic, or it's trash."

Andy's mum suggested Andy donate his old toys to the daycare centre. But Andy shook his head. "No one's going to want those," he told her. "They're junk."

Inside the toy box, the toys gasped!

"Fine," Andy's mum replied. "You have 'til Friday. Anything that's not packed for college or in the attic is getting thrown out."

Andy opened the toy box. He scooped up Rex, Hamm, Slinky and Mr and Mrs Potato Head – and dumped them into a rubbish bag!

But when Andy came to Woody and Buzz, he paused. They had always been his two favourite toys. He looked at each, then made his decision: Buzz went into the rubbish bag, and Woody went in the box bound for college.

Buzz lay on top of the other toys, feeling shocked. Had he really been dumped? What were they going to do now?

Disney

HANDY MANNY

Tools for Toys

Handy Manny and the tools were at Mr Singh's house. They were inspecting the swing set that needed to be repaired, when a little girl pushed her wobbly doll's pram towards them.

"Daddy!" she shouted.

"Hello, Leela," smiled Mr Singh. "This is Manny. He's come with his tools to fix your swings."

Leela was thrilled. "Goody! That means we can play on them right after the tea party with my dollies. Right, Daddy?"

"Well, I would love to, sweetheart," said Mr Singh. "But I have a very busy day."

Leela was very sad to hear this. While Manny and Stretch went to inspect the broken picnic bench with Mr Singh, the rest of the tools got ready to work on Leela's doll carriage.

"Hi, Mister Tool!" Leela exclaimed to Turner. "Would you like to play with me?"

"Uh, sorry. I-I-I'm a tool, n-n-not a toy..." Turner stammered.

"I think you'd make a really nice dolly!" gushed Leela. "Are you hungry?" Then Leela put a toy baby bottle in Turner's mouth!

When the other tools finally stopped laughing, they realized Leela had wheeled Turner away in her doll's pram.

"Uh, excuse me, little girl," said Rusty, who found Leela playing with her dollhouse.

"We've come to get our friend, Turner."

"Oh, you mean my dolly," said Leela.

Then Turner peeked out of the dollhouse window, wearing a pink bonnet! The tools couldn't help but laugh. Then they told Leela they had to get to work. Leela frowned. "My dad always says he's very busy, too."

The tools felt bad, so they drank make-believe tea with Leela. Before long, Manny, Stretch and Mr Singh arrived, hoping the pram had already been fixed. "We took a little tea break to play with Leela," confessed Dusty.

"Well, taking a short break is fine," Manny began, "but now it's time for my tools to get back to work, Leela."

Seeing Leela sad made Mr Singh feel awful. "Don't worry, I'll play with you, Leela."

"B-but you're too busy!" cried Leela.

"Too busy? Is that what you think, sweetie?" Mr Singh hugged his daughter. "I can't think of anything more important than spending special time with you."

So, Mr Singh and Leela went off to play while Manny and the tools finished their repairs. When it was time to leave, Leela gave Turner a little pink bow.

"You know, Turner, you look pretty good when you're all dolled up!" teased Felipe.

Lady and the TRAMP

Sledging

Lady stood on the porch as Jim Dear and Darling walked up the front path. Jim pulled a sledge and Darling held their son. They were all covered in snow, rosy cheeked and smiling from ear to ear.

"That was fun! Wasn't it, Darling?" Jim asked.

"I don't know the last time I had so much fun," Darling agreed, patting Lady on the head.

"But we should get out of these wet clothes before one of us catches a cold," Jim said, leaning the sledge against the side of the house.

"I agree," Darling said. And the three of them hurried inside.

Just then, Tramp came walking up the front path. "Hey, Pidge," he said to Lady. "What do you say we take this old thing for a spin?"

"What is it, anyway?" Lady wanted to know.

"A sledge!" Tramp told her.

"What do you do with it?" she asked.

"You ride down hills," Tramp explained.

"That sounds dangerous," Lady said hesitantly.

"Nah, it's fun!" Tramp cried. "So, what do you say?"

"It's awfully cold out here," Lady said. She wasn't convinced at all.

"Oh, come on," Tramp said. "It'll be great! You saw how much fun Jim Dear and Darling had." Tramp grabbed the rope in his teeth and pulled the sledge across the porch and down the steps.

Lady took off after him. "Wait for me!" she cried anxiously.

"Come on, Pidge!" Tramp encouraged her. "Jump on!"

Lady jumped onto the sledge, and Tramp pulled her down the snow-covered street and up to the top of a nearby hill. "What a view, huh?" he said.

"What a view indeed," Lady agreed. "What now?"

"Now, we ride," Tramp said. He pushed the sledge forward and took a running leap onto it, sending them racing down the hill.

"Oh, dear!" Lady yelped as they plummeted down the hill, the wind blowing her ears back.

"Just hold on!" Tramp instructed.

Lady squeezed her eyes shut, and Tramp barked with excitement. But suddenly they hit a patch of ice, the sledge spun, and they went flying – right into a snowbank!

Tramp jumped to his feet. "Pidge, are you okay?" he asked anxiously.

"Okay?" Lady asked. She was already pulling the sledge back up the hill. "Hurry up, Tramp! Let's do it again!"

a bug's life

Red Alert!

"Nice work with the wheat husker," Flik said. He smiled with satisfaction as he watched a troop of ants lower the contraption that lightly smashed the wheat kernels. How had the colony got along without his clever inventions? Flik wondered.

"How's it going with the berry masher?" called a voice. It was Atta, the colony's Queen.

"I was just heading over to take a look," Flik said, smiling at Queen Atta. "Care to join me?"

"Sure," Atta said as she led the way to the berry-mashing area. Mashing berries was messy, so the ants did it in a special part of the anthill.

"Cowabunga!" called a large ant. Ten dozen ants leaped off a rock onto a giant lever. The lever lowered, pressing a flat rock onto a pile of berries. Sweet red juice squirted out from the sides and dripped into carved wooden bowls.

When all the juice was squeezed out of the berries, Atta dipped her finger into a bowl for a taste.

"Delicious," she said. Red juice stained her mouth and chin.

"The berries were especially sweet this year," Flik said modestly.

"And with your new invention we should have plenty of juice for this year's feast," Atta said. "As long as Dot and the Blueberries don't drink it all first," she added.

Flik laughed. Dot and her Blueberry friends loved berry juice and were always trying to dip into it before the feast. They had been shooed away from the berry masher more than once in the last week. Three times, in fact!

"Good work, masher ants!" Flik called to the horde that was climbing back up to their jumping rock. Another group was making a pile of fresh berries.

They had nearly finished piling a huge mound of berries, when suddenly the alarm sounded.

"Alert, alert!" a guard ant called through a megaphone made from a rolled-up leaf. "Red fire ants are storming the colony!"

Flik, Atta and the masher ants fled the food area as fast as their legs could carry them. Sure enough, they soon ran into half-a-dozen red ants. Flik was about to charge when he heard a familiar voice.

"Flik, it's me!" it said. The voice sounded like . . . Dot's.

"Hold on!" Flik shouted. The ants stopped. Flik quickly wiped the first red ant's sticky face. "These aren't fire ants," Flik explained. "They're Blueberries – covered in berry juice!" He smiled at Atta. "Maybe we should call them Redberries, instead!"

Disney · PIXAR

TOY STORY 3

A Rubbish Mistake

Andy was a teenager now, and would soon be leaving for college. He had put Woody – his favourite toy – into a box he was taking with him. But Buzz and the rest of the toys had been thrown into a big rubbish bag!

Woody was shocked. The Andy he knew would never throw his toys away! So, after Andy carried the bag out of his room, the cowboy sprang to the door. Woody watched as Andy pulled down the attic ladder. What a relief! Andy had planned to put the toys in storage, after all.

Suddenly, though, Andy's sister needed help. Andy left the rubbish bag in the hall. While he was gone, the ladder started to go back up into the ceiling! When Andy's mum walked by, she noticed the rubbish bag on the floor. Assuming it was to be thrown out, she picked it up. Woody started to panic – Andy's mum was making a huge mistake! She went outside and threw the bag by the rubbish bins!

Inside the bag, the other toys knew they were in trouble.

"We're on the curb!" cried Jessie.

"Pull, everyone! Pull!" ordered Buzz, desperately trying to rip open the bag.

"Andy doesn't want us!" Mrs Potato Head wailed. "What's the point?"

But that gave Buzz an idea. He told everyone to push Rex's pointy tail into the side of the bag. The friends shoved the dinosaur against the plastic – but they were running out of time!

Meanwhile, Woody climbed out of the window and slid down the drainpipe. He pulled out a pair of scissors he had tucked into his holster. Frantic, he sliced open one bag, then another – but his friends weren't inside. When the rubbish truck arrived, Woody hid. He watched as the man hurled the bags into the back of the truck.

Seconds later, the truck rumbled off to the next house. Woody watched in horror as the truck's compactor activated, crunching its load! Then Woody noticed an upside-down recycling bin moving across Andy's drive. His friends were alive! Inside the garage, the toys came out from underneath the bin.

"Andy threw us out!" exclaimed Slinky.

All the toys had heard Andy call them 'junk'. They thought it was Andy who had dumped them! Jessie had a solution to everything. By the time Woody arrived, she had convinced everyone to climb into the car, and into the daycare donation box!

They thought the nursery could be the ideal place for them to go – but they didn't know what awaited them there...

Bambi

Night-time is for... Exploring!

As the moon rose above the forest, Bambi snuggled close to his sleeping mother. What a day it had been! Exploring new places, learning new words and meeting new friends. Bambi yawned and closed his eyes . . . .

"Bambi! Oh, Bambi!"

Bambi slowly opened his eyes. "Thumper?" he whispered. "Why aren't you asleep?"

"Asleep? Come on!" cried Thumper. "Sleep is for the birds! How can you sleep when there's so much to see and do at night?"

"But everybody knows that night-time is for sleeping," Bambi said.

"Oh, brother," Thumper said. "Do you have a lot to learn! Follow me, Bambi, and I'll show you how the night is a whole new day!"

And suddenly, at the prospect of an all-new adventure, Bambi's sleepiness disappeared. Quietly, he stood up and let Thumper lead the way.

Thumper was right – the forest was as busy at night as it was during the day, but with a whole new group of animals. Owls, opossums, raccoons and badgers – all those animals that Bambi thought spent most of their lives asleep – were now as lively as could be.

"Wh-wh-what's that?" Bambi exclaimed, as a dot of light landed on his nose.

"Don't worry, Bambi, it's just a firefly,"
Thumper said with a giggle.

"'Firefly'," Bambi said. Then suddenly, the little light disappeared. "Hey, where'd it go?"

"There it is!" cried Thumper, pointing to Bambi's tail. "No, wait. It's over there."

Happily, Thumper and Bambi chased the firefly as it flitted from one friend to the other. "I think he likes us!" Thumper cried.

But their game was soon interrupted by a flurry of sound. Thousands of leathery wings were suddenly beating overhead.

"Duck, Bambi!" hollered Thumper, just as the whole group swooped around their heads.

"Boy, that was close!" said Thumper.

"Were those fireflies too?" Bambi asked.

"Naw," Thumper laughed. "They didn't light up! Those were bats."

"'Bats'," repeated Bambi. "They're really busy at night."

"You can say that again," agreed Thumper, trying to stifle a yawn. And, since yawns are contagious, Bambi's own yawn was not far behind.

"This was fun," Bambi told his friend. "But what do you say we go home and go to bed?"

But there was no answer . . . for Thumper was already fast asleep!

The Sleepover

Oliver couldn't wait. "Are we there yet?" he wondered as he peered out of the limousine window.

"Don't worry, Oliver," Jenny told him. "We'll be there soon."

At last, Jenny's limo pulled up to the docks. Even before the chauffeur could open the door, Oliver leaped out of the window and began racing towards the barge. Then, remembering Jenny, he stopped, turned around and waved his paw in her direction.

"Goodbye, Oliver!" she called. "Have a fun sleepover!"

Don't worry! thought Oliver. I will!

This was the first time, you see, that Oliver had been back to the barge since he'd gone to live in Jenny's mansion. And, though he loved Jenny dearly, boy, did he miss his friends!

"Tito! Einstein! Francis! Rita!" Oliver called as he ran in to find his four-footed friends waiting for him.

"Hey! What about me?" barked a voice from the back of the barge.

"Dodger!" yelled Oliver. He leaped up on the shaggy dog and gave him a friendly face-rub. "It's so good to see you!"

"So how's life in the mansion?" Dodger asked.

"I can't complain," said Oliver. He told his friends about his latest cruise on Jenny's yacht.

"All those fish!" he said dreamily. Then he told them about her house in the country. "The best part is just lying out in the sun! You've got to come with us someday!"

"Hey," said Dodger, "check out what good ol' Einstein found for our viewing pleasure this evening." He pulled out a scruffy blue backpack and shook it until a video fell out.

"It's *The Aristocats*!" Oliver cried. "My favourite!"

Just then, Fagin walked in carrying a great big tray. "Oliver, my good friend! Welcome back! I do hope you're hungry!"

Oliver's eyes grew wide as he took in the piles of hot dogs, chicken drumsticks and fish fingers (his favourite!).

Oliver and the dogs tucked in and ate . . . and ate . . . until they could not eat another bite. Then it was time for games!

Fagin dealt the playing cards.

"I'm gonna stay up all night!" Oliver cried.

"Whatever you say, little buddy," Dodger said. "It's your night."

So they played a little Go Fish, then some Duck, Duck, Goose. Then Fagin told them some of Oliver's favourite spooky stories.

When he had finished, Dodger turned to Oliver. "So, what's next, little buddy?" he asked.

But Oliver didn't answer . . . he was fast asleep!

Bedtime for Duchess

"Come, my precious ones!" Duchess called to Berlioz, Toulouse and Marie. "It's time to go to sleep."

"Oh, Mother!" Toulouse complained.

"But I'm not tired!" Marie joined in.

"I'm not going to sleep," Berlioz added. "Night-time is just when things start happening for us alley cats." Berlioz crouched down low, hindquarters in the air, and pounced on an imaginary opponent.

"Who does he think he's kidding?" Toulouse whispered to Marie, who rolled her eyes in agreement.

"Now, now, it's been a long day," Duchess told them. "I don't want to hear any more protests."

"Mother!" Berlioz whined.

"We need a bedtime story!" Marie insisted.

"A story? My darlings, it's way past your bedtime, and I'm just too tired tonight," replied Duchess.

"Then why don't we tell *you* a story?" Toulouse offered.

"Yeah!" Berlioz chimed in.

"What a lovely idea," said Duchess.

"Once upon a time . . ." Marie began.

"There was a big, mean, ferocious alley cat," Berlioz continued.

"Berlioz!" Marie protested. "It's not supposed to be scary. She'll have nightmares!"

"Sorry, Mama," Berlioz said.

"That's quite all right," Duchess told him.

"Now where were we?" Toulouse asked.

"Once upon a time . . ." Marie began again.

"Yeah, once upon a time there was this amazing kitten," Toulouse said. "And he could paint like no other kitten you've ever seen."

"And that's because the model for his paintings was the most beautiful kitten you've ever laid eyes on," Marie added.

"Give me a break!" Berlioz said, grumbling under his breath. He and Toulouse snickered.

"Very funny." Marie was not amused. "Can we get back to the story?"

"This kitten was a painter by day and a smooth-talking, alley-hanging, danger-seeking hepcat by night," Berlioz continued.

Toulouse tapped Berlioz with his paw. He looked up and saw what both Toulouse and Marie were seeing. Duchess herself had fallen asleep!

Berlioz, Toulouse and Marie each gave their mother a kiss good night.

"Good night, Mama," said Marie.

"Good night, Mama," said Toulouse.

"Good night, Mama," said Berlioz.

Then all three curled up beside Duchess and promptly fell asleep too.

Stuck in the Mud

Robin hood

"**C**ome on, Rob!" Little John called as he stepped over a fallen log. The two were out for a misty morning romp in the forest, but Robin Hood was lagging behind.

"Shhhh!" Robin put a finger to his lips. "I think I hear something."

"Let's have a look-see," said Little John. A minute later, they stopped at the edge of the forest and peered out from behind a bush. There, stuck in a muddy ditch, was a fancy coach.

"I'd know that coach anywhere," Robin whispered. "It belongs to Prince John."

"That snivelling coward," Little John said. "Serves him right to get stuck."

"Get me out of the mud, now!" a voice whined from inside the coach. It certainly was Prince John.

The driver's shoulders slumped. "But sire, the coach is laden with gold. I'll never be able to push it out by myself. Perhaps Your Highness would consider stepping out of the coach so as to lighten the load? Just until the wheels are free of the mud, of course," he added quickly.

"Step out of the coach?" Prince John bellowed. "And stand in the rain? I most certainly will not. And now I order you for a second time: get me out of the mud!"

The driver wiped the rainwater from his brow and walked to the back of the coach.

"I believe I have a plan that will help Prince John and that driver," Robin said. "Not to mention the poor."

Little John nodded with a grin. He knew exactly what sort of plan his friend had in mind. Robin reached into his satchel, pulled out a few items, and put them on. Little John did the same. Now they looked like two ordinary hunters. Little John stepped onto the road.

"Need some help there?" he asked the driver loudly. "I'd be glad to lend a hand."

Meanwhile, Robin sneaked around to the side of the coach. He was just opening the door when Prince John leaned out of the window on the other side.

"Hurry up, you fools!" he hollered.

Little John sidled up to the window. "You'll be out in a jiffy," he assured the prince.

Robin saw his chance. While the prince was distracted, he opened the other door and removed several bags of gold.

"Get pushing, then," Prince John snapped.

"I said, be glad to," Little John replied. He strolled to the back of the coach and, along with the driver, gave a single push. And, while Robin slipped into the woods with the gold, Prince John and his muddy-wheeled coach rolled down the road to Nottingham, the load a little lighter than before.

Disney
HANDY MANNY

Finding Flicker

"Vamonos! Let's go!" shouted Felipe. Manny and the tools were packing for a trip to one of their favourite spots – Lake Nochanailin! Someone else was going too – Abuelito was riding his motorcycle to the lake and meeting them at the cabin.

Then Manny noticed he was out of batteries for Flicker, his torch. "I need to go to Kelly's," he said.

"Aw, that's going to make us late," said Squeeze.

"That's the trouble with tools that need batteries," said Pat. "I don't need them. I'm a hammer!"

When Manny returned from Kelly's hardware store, the tools were in a tizzy.

"What happened?"asked Manny.

"It's Flicker," said Squeeze. "He's gone!"

Turner looked at Pat and said, "I think someone hurt his feelings."

"I know you didn't mean it, Pat," said Manny. "Let's find Flicker. Pronto!"

They tried Mr Lopart's sweet shop first, but he wasn't there. Next, they headed to Mrs Portillo's bakery – Flicker wasn't there either! Manny and the tools looked in the park, but Flicker wasn't there!

Manny and the tools wondered where to look next. "Flicker loves story time at the library," said Felipe.

"Good idea," said Manny.

But Flicker wasn't at the library, either! Manny was worried. Where was Flicker? Then the phone rang.

"Manny," said Abuelito, "If you are looking for Flicker, he is safe with me!"

"Bueno!" replied Manny. "That is so good to hear. How did you find him?"

"He found me," said Abuelito. "When I got to the cabin, I found Flicker hiding in my motorcycle bag!"

Manny and the tools arrived at the lake just after sunset. "Ooh, the cabin looks very dark," said Rusty.

"Si," said Manny. "I wonder if something is wrong."

"Manny," said Abuelito. "You got here just in time. The electricity went out. My homemade Dulce con Leche ice cream will melt!"

"It's a good thing you found Flicker," said Manny. "I can't fix the electricity without him. I need your light, Flicker!"

"La luz! La luz!" shouted Flicker.

Manny and tools went outside the cabin to fix the fuses. Flicker was a big help!

Abuelito's ice cream was delicious.

"Hooray for Flicker!" the tools shouted. And Pat shouted loudest of all.

Welcome to Sunnyside Daycare

"Have you all lost your marbles?" Woody asked the toys. Andy was leaving for college, and the toys had accidentally been put out with the rubbish! Andy had meant for them to be stored in the attic, but his mum had thrown them away.

Woody knew the truth, and he tried to explain Andy's mum's mistake, but the toys didn't believe him. Jessie had convinced Buzz and the rest that they should go to Sunnyside Daycare – the nursery to which Andy's mum was donating some old toys.

They were in the boot of the car, in the box marked 'Sunnyside Daycare' when suddenly, Andy's mum shut the boot, got in and pulled the car out of the driveway. Woody instantly began planning their return to Andy's house. "We'll hide under the seats..." he began.

The others didn't think it was a good idea. "He left us on the curb!" Jessie pointed out.

Woody insisted the toys would be sorry. "Daycare is a sad, lonely place for washed-up old toys who have no owners," he said.

But when they arrived, Sunnyside Daycare didn't look sad or lonely at all. It looked cheerful and colourful! Inside, Andy's mum greeted the receptionist and the woman's young daughter, Bonnie. The receptionist took the box of toys right to the Butterfly Room.

The children were outside playing, but Andy's toys couldn't contain their excitement. They accidentally knocked over the box and spilled out onto the floor. The room looked wonderful to them. And the daycare toys were friendly! When they spotted Andy's toys, they cheered!

Friendliest of all was a big, pink bear who smelled like strawberries. "Welcome to Sunnyside!" he called warmly. "I'm Lots-o'-Huggin' Bear! But, please, call me Lotso!"

Lotso's smile was comforting. "You've been through a lot today, haven't you?" he asked. "Just you wait – you'll find being donated is the best thing that ever happened to you."

"Mr Lotso," asked Rex. "Do toys here get played with every day?"

"All day long. Five days a week," Lotso answered.

"But what happens when the kids grow up?" Jessie asked.

"When the kids get old, new ones come in," Lotso replied. "You'll never be outgrown or neglected. Never abandoned or forgotten. No owner means no heartbreak."

To Andy's toys, daycare was sounding better and better! Woody still wanted to go home to Andy, but no one would listen. Maybe the daycare centre would be okay, after all?

THE
LION KING

The Very Best Fisherman of All

Simba and his friends Timon and Pumbaa were hungry. They wandered through the forest until they came to an old, rotten tree. Timon knocked on the trunk.

"What's it sound like, Timon?" Pumbaa asked.

"Like our breakfast!" Timon replied.

He yanked at the bark and hundreds of grubs slithered out.

Timon handed Simba a grub.

"No, thanks." Simba sighed. "I'm tired of grubs."

"Well, the ants are tasty," said Timon. "They come in two flavours. Red and black."

Simba shook his head. "Don't you eat anything but bugs?"

"Fish!" Pumbaa declared.

"I love fish!" Simba exclaimed.

"Why didn't you say so?" said Timon. "There's a pond at the end of this trail." The three friends started off down the trail.

"What now?" asked Simba when they arrived at the pond.

"That's the problem!" said Timon. "We're not the best fishermen in the world."

"I'll teach you!" Simba said.

The lion climbed up a tree and crawled onto a branch that hung over the water. Then he snatched a fish out of the water.

"See!" Simba said, jumping to the ground nimbly. "Not a problem. Fishing's easy."

"Not for me!" Timon cried. He dangled from the branch, but his arms weren't long enough to reach the fish.

Simba laughed. "Better let Pumbaa try."

"What a joke!" cried Timon. "Pumbaa can't even climb this tree."

"Want to bet?" asked Pumbaa.

"Stay there," Timon warned. "I don't think this branch is strong enough for both of us."

With a hop, Pumbaa landed on the branch next to Timon. The limb started to bend.

"Yikes!" Timon cried as he leaped to another tree.

Crack! The branch broke under Pumbaa. With a squeal, he landed in the pond. The splash was enormous!

Simba, sitting on the bank, was soaked. Timon was nearly blasted from his perch. Pond water fell like rain all around them.

Simba opened his eyes and started to laugh. So did Timon.

Pumbaa was sitting in a pool of mud where the pond had been. He'd splashed so much of the water out that dozens of fish squirmed on the ground, just waiting to be gobbled up.

"Wow!" Timon cried. "I think Pumbaa is the very best fisherman of all!"

A Prize-winning Pair

Max and his dad, Goofy, were sitting at the breakfast table. Max looked at the funny pages, while Goofy leafed through the rest of the paper. "Listen to this!" said Goofy. "Channel 10 sponsors the Father & Son of the Year Contest. The father and son who can prove that they have achieved something truly incredible together will appear on national TV on Father's Day to accept their award."

"Too bad Bigfoot ruined that video we took of him last summer," said Max. "Finding him and living to tell about it – now that was incredible!"

Max paused for a moment. "Hey, I know! Why can't we go back and find him again? And this time we'll make sure we have proof."

"Okay, Maxie. Count me in!" said Goofy. "And we can even get a little fishing in too."

Goofy and Max reached the campsite that night, pitched their tent, and went to sleep. Soon they were awakened by a loud crash.

"It's him!" cried Max. "Get the camera!" But, when they poked their heads out, they saw it wasn't Bigfoot at all, but Pete and P.J.

"I'm sorry," said P.J. "I told my dad about your trip, and now he wants *us* to win that prize. We're out here looking for Bigfoot too."

The next day, Pete set up a barbecue with several juicy steaks. "This will lure him out for sure," he told P.J. The trick worked. In a matter of minutes, Bigfoot crashed through the trees and made a beeline for the meat. "Tackle him, P.J.!" yelled Pete.

Though he was scared, P.J. did as he was told. Bigfoot threw him around like a rag doll while Pete turned on the camera. "The judges are going to love this!" cried Pete.

"Help!" P.J. begged.

Goofy and Max heard P.J.'s cries and came running from the lake. Without saying a word, Goofy jabbed the monster in the backside with a fishing lure while Max threw a fishing net over the monster's head. Howling, the monster dropped P.J. to the ground.

"You were awesome," Max told Goofy.

"Right back at you, son," Goofy replied.

"Got it!" Pete said triumphantly. "Here, P.J., take some footage of me." He struck a hero's pose in front of the captive monster.

Back at home, Pete sent the video to Channel 10. But, after viewing the tape, the judges decided it was Goofy and Max who deserved the award instead.

But on Father's Day – the day they were to appear on TV – Goofy and Max decided to go to the beach together instead. They realized they didn't need anybody to tell them what an incredible father-and-son team they were. They knew it already!

The Monster of Paradise Falls

Carl Fredickson had dreamed of becoming an explorer since he was a boy. He had met a girl called Ellie who shared his dream, and they grew up and got married.

Carl had promised Ellie he'd take her to Paradise Falls one day. But they never managed to save enough money to go. When Ellie passed away, Carl missed her very much. One day, when he was being forced to move out of their home, he tied thousands of balloons to the house and flew to South America – to Paradise Falls. And he accidentally took a young boy called Russell along with him.

Carl and Russell had met a big, strange bird – Russell had named it Kevin, but then discovered it was a girl! They also met a talking dog called Dug. He had been sent by his pack to capture Kevin. More dogs had appeared and taken Carl and Russell to their leader. Much to Carl's surprise, their leader was Charles Muntz – a famous explorer who had been his and Ellie's childhood hero!

Muntz invited Carl and Russell into his giant airship – the Spirit of Adventure! When Dug tried to follow, the other dogs blocked his way. "He has lost the bird," declared Alpha, the leader of the pack. Dug was left outside.

On board the airship, the dogs served dinner while Muntz told Carl and Russell about the Monster of Paradise Falls.

"I've spent a lifetime tracking this creature," Muntz said.

"Hey, that looks like Kevin!" said Russell, noticing a bird skeleton.

"Kevin?" Muntz asked.

"That's my new giant bird pet," Russell explained. "I trained it to follow us."

Muntz became very angry. He thought Carl and Russell were trying to steal the bird from him.

At that moment, they heard a wail outside. Kevin had followed Carl and Russell into the cave! All the dogs began to bark. In the confusion, Carl and Russell slipped away.

"Get them!" Muntz roared at his dogs.

Carl and Russell untied the house and started to run. The snarling dog pack came racing after them. Kevin scooped Russell and Carl onto her back and raced for the cave opening, with the house still floating behind.

But Kevin wasn't fast enough to stay ahead of the pack. The dogs were closing in. Suddenly, an avalanche of rocks tumbled down and blocked the dog pack. "Go on, Master. I will stop the dogs!" someone cried.

It was Dug! He had come to rescue Carl and Russell. But would Carl, Russell and Kevin be able to escape…?

The GREAT MOUSE DETECTIVE

Dawson Takes the Case

"My little boy is missing!" a sobbing Mrs Mousington cried to Basil, the Great Mouse Detective. "Can you help me find him?"

"I'm terribly sorry," said Basil. He was examining a brick wall very closely, looking for clues. "But I'm working on an important case for the Queen. I don't have time."

"No, wait!" cried Dr Dawson, Basil's partner. "Madam, if the Great Mouse Detective is too busy, then perhaps I can offer you my services."

"A splendid idea!" said Basil.

Before Dawson left with Mrs Mousington, Basil stopped him. "Don't forget this," he said, handing Dawson an umbrella.

"But it's a sunny day," said Dawson, puzzled. "Why would I need an umbrella?"

"A sunny day can turn dark quicker than you think," advised Basil. "Remember that, Dawson, and you'll do fine."

Dawson shrugged and took the umbrella. Then he turned to Mrs Mousington and said, "Show me where you last saw your son."

Mrs Mousington took him to a shop with a tall tree in front of it. Dawson searched the area and found a long, white hair. But a closer look told him this was not just any hair. It was a cat's whisker!

Calling to a nearby bird, Dawson asked for a lift up. On the shop's roof, Dawson saw a cat dozing, and beneath its paw was a tiny mouse's tail.

The bird set Dawson down on the roof, and he wondered how he was going to lift the cat's heavy paw. Then he remembered the umbrella!

Using one end as a lever, he heaved. Beneath it he found Mrs Mousington's terrified son.

"The cat was saving me for dinner!" the little boy mouse cried.

Dawson pulled the little mouse free. With relief, he waved at the boy's mother, who was waiting on the sidewalk below. But before Dawson could signal another bird for a ride down, the cat woke up.

Dawson saw only one escape – he opened his umbrella and jumped with the little boy mouse in his arms.

Mrs Mousington let out a terrified scream. But the umbrella filled with air and slowed their fall until they landed gently on the sidewalk.

Mrs Mousington hugged her little boy close. "Oh, Dr Dawson, thank you!" she cried.

Back at the Great Mouse Detective's house, Basil was delighted to hear how Dawson had saved the little boy.

"It was easy," Dawson told Basil. "Thanks to your umbrella, I'd call it an open-and-shut case!"

A New Life

Woody, Buzz and the gang had just arrived at Sunnyside Daycare. Andy would soon be leaving home for college, and had meant to store the toys safely in his attic. But Andy's mum had mistaken the bag of toys for rubbish and thrown them out!

Luckily, the toys managed to escape and jump into a box going to the nursery.

On first impressions, Sunnyside seemed like a pretty great place. A pink teddy bear called Lotso welcomed the new toys.

"Now let's get you all settled in," Lotso said. "Ken! New toys!"

Ken emerged from the doorway of a dollhouse. "Folks, if you want to step right this way..." Then he spotted Barbie. To the two dolls, time seemed to stop. It was love at first sight – they were made for each other!

Lotso broke the romantic spell. "Recess doesn't last forever!" he reminded Ken. The children would soon be coming in from outside. Barbie linked her arm through Ken's, and the toys set off on the Sunnyside tour.

"You've got a lot to look forward to!" declared Lotso. "The little ones love new toys."

Lotso and a doll named Big Baby led the tour around Sunnyside. Lotso nodded towards Big Baby and whispered sadly, "Abandoned by his owner, just like the rest of us."

Finally, Lotso and Ken ushered the group to their new home: The Caterpillar Room.

"Look at this place!" cried Jessie excitedly.

It was time for Lotso, Ken and Big Baby to head back to the Butterfly Room, but Ken hesitated.

"Barbie!" he blurted out. "Come with me. Live in my Dream House!"

Barbie cast a glance at her friends. The toys smiled and nodded their approval, and Barbie joined Ken.

Most of Andy's toys stood in the Caterpillar Room, counting the seconds until the children would arrive. They hadn't been played with in a long time, and they couldn't wait! Woody felt differently.

"It's nice here," said Woody, "but we need to go home now."

"We can have a new life here, Woody," Jessie declared. "A chance to make kids happy again."

The other toys agreed.

"What's important is that we stay together," said Buzz.

"We wouldn't even be together if it weren't for Andy," Woody shot back. He walked to the door. "I'm sorry. I've got to go."

Woody just couldn't abandon Andy. He had to get back to his oldest friend.

Peter Pan

A 'Snappy' New Ship

"My ship, my beautiful ship!" Captain Hook moaned. It had not been a good day for the pirate. Peter Pan and the Darling children had stolen his ship. And now, Hook was stranded on an island with Smee and the other pirates, their rowing boat having been chomped to bits by the crocodile.

"It's a nice island, Captain," offered Smee, trying to cheer up his boss. "And you could use a vacation. Why, look at those dark circles under your eyes."

Captain Hook turned to Smee with a furious look on his face. "Pirates don't take vacations!" Hook boomed. "Pirates seek revenge! Which is precisely what we are going to do, as soon as we have a new ship to sail in."

Smee looked around. "Where are we going to find a ship around here, Sir?" he asked.

"*We* aren't going to find one," Captain Hook answered. "You and the rest of this mangy crew are going to *build* one! And I don't mean a little one either. I mean a big, menacing, fit-for-a-magnificent-pirate-like-me one!"

For weeks, the pirates chopped trees and cut them into planks for the ship. They whittled thousands of pegs to use for nails, and crushed countless berries to use for paint. "You're not moving fast enough!" Hook complained as he sat in the shade, sipping juice out of a pineapple.

Finally, an exhausted Smee fetched Hook as he awoke from his afternoon nap.

"It's ready, Captain!" he announced.

Even Hook had to admit the ship was magnificent. Shaped like a gigantic crocodile, it was painted a reptilian shade of green. "No one will dare come near this ship. Not even that pesky crocodile. He won't want to tussle with anything this terrifying," Smee assured him.

Captain Hook was delighted. "We set sail tomorrow!" he crowed.

That night, Smee couldn't resist putting one more finishing touch on the ship. He painted a row of eyelashes on the crocodile's eyelids.

The next morning, Captain Hook and the crew climbed aboard and pushed off. The ticking crocodile soon appeared.

"Smee!" yelled a terrified Captain Hook. "I thought you said he wouldn't come near us!"

"But look how calm he is," said Smee, puzzled. "He's even smiling!"

Smee leaned over the side of the railing. "You know, it might be those eyelashes I painted. Maybe the croc thinks the ship is its mother."

Hook lunged at the roly-poly pirate. "You made my ship look like a *mother* crocodile? This vessel is supposed to be terrifying!"

"Mothers *can* be terrifying, sir," said Smee. "You should have seen mine when I told her I was going to become a pirate!"

The Twilight Bark

Rolly, Patch, Lucky and the rest of the puppies were watching the end of "The Thunderbolt Adventure Hour". As the credits began to roll, Pongo turned off the TV.

"Aw, come on, Dad!" Patch complained.

"We let you stay up late to watch the whole show," Pongo said.

Lucky sat staring at the blank television screen, hoping it would magically turn itself back on.

Perdy licked his face encouragingly. "Sit down, children," she said. "Your father and I need to speak with you."

"Uh-oh," Penny said worriedly.

"Oh, it's nothing like that," Pongo assured her. "We just think it's time to tell you about the legend of the Twilight Bark."

"Sounds cool!" Pepper cheered.

"What's the Twilight Bark?" Freckles asked.

"Legend has it," Perdy began, "that there's a special way that dogs can send each other messages. It stretches from the farthest side of the city all the way to the farthest part of the countryside."

"Wow!" Penny gasped. "Why would you need to do that?"

"Sometimes," Pongo began, "you need to communicate information from one place to another quickly, and you don't have time to go

to the other place yourself."

"I don't need any Twilight Bark!" Patch said. "I can take care of myself."

"Fat chance!" Lucky said under his breath.

"What do you know?" Patch barked.

"If you ever get into any trouble," Perdy told the pups, "just go to the top of the highest hill you can find, and bark out your message, and the members of the Twilight Bark will pass it along until someone can come and help you."

"That sounds like a bunch of baloney," Patch told his parents.

"Patch!" Pongo scolded his son. "That isn't very nice."

Just then, Lucky started howling at the top of his lungs.

"What's got into you?" Perdy asked.

"I'm trying out the Twilight Bark," Lucky said. "To get us rescued from Patch."

"Lucky," Perdy scolded him, "apologize to your brother."

"That's okay," Patch said. "I don't need his apology. I was right anyway. All that howling and no word from the Twilight Bark."

Just then, the doorbell rang. All the puppies gasped and turned to look at Patch.

Perdy and Pongo smiled at each other, knowing it was actually Roger returning from the shop with milk for tomorrow's breakfast.

Disney
Lilo & Stitch

An Out-of-this-world Party

Every year, one of Lilo's classmates had a party to celebrate the last day of school. This year, Lilo begged Nani to let her have the party at their house. She wanted to show off her new friends Jumba and Pleakley to her classmates – and to prove to them that even though Stitch wasn't a very good dog, he was a great alien!

Lilo gave invitations to all her classmates – even Myrtle, but only because Nani said Lilo had to invite her. Myrtle didn't want to go to the party any more than Lilo wanted to have her there, but she didn't want to be left out either.

On the big afternoon, everyone went straight to Lilo's house after school.

Lilo ushered all the children to a stage in the garden. Then she pulled back the curtains to reveal Stitch in a funny rock-and-roll costume. Stitch crooned into a microphone while swivelling his hips and strumming his guitar. All the children thought he was cool – except Myrtle. When Stitch tried to give her a kiss on the cheek during a love song, she shrieked, "Ooooh! Yuck! Dog germs!"

"Time for crafts!" Pleakley called. "Today, you are each going to make your own intergalactic communicator. You'll need to decide which planet you would like to contact so we can program your device accordingly."

A little while later, one boy shouted, "Hey, I called Jupiter!"

Another child yelled, "I'm talking to Mars!"

Myrtle stamped her foot. "This dumb thing doesn't work," she said. "All I've got is static!"

Jumba turned to Lilo and gave her a wink. "Who wants to play Pin the Smile on the Man in the Moon?" he asked.

"I do! I do!" shouted Myrtle.

Jumba hustled Myrtle into a small spaceship with no windows. Then he handed her a large, paper smile. "When you pass by the moon in a few hours," said Jumba, "try to pin the smile in the correct position. Remember that you will be travelling at several thousand miles per hour, so act quickly!" Then he shut the cockpit door.

"But the spaceship is fake," Lilo said to Jumba. "It's not moving or anything."

"Ah, but Myrtle doesn't know that," Jumba replied. "Inside the ship, it looks like she's heading to the moon. This should keep her busy for a few hours while we enjoy ourselves." He smiled. "Now, who's up for cake?"

The kids cheered, and everyone moved over to a picnic table, leaving the spaceship behind. As she followed them, Lilo heard Myrtle grumble from inside the little ship, "This is the most boring party game ever."

Secret Agent Mater!

British secret agents Finn McMissile and Holley Shiftwell were on the trail of a wanted criminal named Professor Z. They were in Tokyo, where Lightning McQueen was racing in the first World Grand Prix event. Holley had just mistaken Mater for an American spy!

Professor Z then questioned the real American spy, and guessed he had passed a secret device to Mater. The Professor sent his goons, Grem and Acer, to find Mater and get the device.

On the day of the race, Finn and Holley watched all the cars fill up with a new alternative fuel called Allinol. Miles Axlerod, the inventor of Allinol, was hosting the World Grand Prix to introduce the fuel.

Grem and Acer aimed Professor Z's special TV camera at one of the race cars. The camera emitted a beam of radiation that made the Allinol in the car boil and explode! Then Acer headed down to the pits to grab Mater. Holley spoke to Mater through his headset and guided him to safety. Mater happily followed Holley's instructions. He thought he was going to meet her for a date!

Suddenly, Grem and Acer started to close in on Mater – but Finn jumped in to save him.

Mater thought the fight was the best karate demonstration he had ever seen!

Back at the race, Lightning lost to Francesco Bernoulli. Lightning was upset – he had listened to Mater watching the 'karate demonstration' and followed his instructions. Lightning thought Mater had given him bad racing tips.

Reporters surrounded Miles Axlerod and asked him if Allinol was to blame for the engine blowouts during the race. He insisted his fuel was absolutely safe.

Meanwhile, Mater had returned to the pit garage and was trying to explain to Lightning what had just happened. But Lightning didn't believe him. He was angry with Mater for making him lose the race. Mater felt terrible. He left a goodbye note for Lightning and went to the airport to fly home. But Finn, who was disguised as an airport security guard, was there waiting for him. Finn still thought Mater was a secret agent!

Soon Grem and Acer showed up and tried to capture Mater again. Holley saved Mater and Finn from the attack by whisking them off on a spy plane named Siddeley.

At the hotel, Lightning read Mater's note. Lightning hadn't wanted him to leave, but at least now he wouldn't have to worry about Mater getting into trouble – or would he?

THE INCREDIBLES

Mr Incredible's Greatest Adventure

Syndrome – previously named Buddy – had just launched a deadly robot towards the city. Syndrome had once been Mr Incredible's number one fan, but when Mr Incredible told him, "Supers are born, not made," the boy had decided to prove his hero wrong.

Syndrome had lured Mr Incredible to his island and held him prisoner. Mr Incredible's wife, Elastigirl, had discovered where her husband had gone and set off to save him. Their two Super children, Violet and Dash, stowed away on the jet.

At headquarters, Mirage – who was working for Syndrome – had decided to set Mr Incredible free. She was angry that Syndrome had challenged the hero to hurt her. She wanted Mr Incredible to know that his family was still alive.

Mr Incredible was so happy to hear this news that he hugged Mirage. But just then Elastigirl burst in! *THUMP!* She punched Mirage from across the room. Mr Incredible tried to explain, but Elastigirl was too angry.

"Where are the kids?" asked Mr Incredible.

"They might've triggered the alert," said Mirage. "Security's been sent into the jungle!"

Syndrome's guards had indeed found Violet and Dash. They chased the two young Supers. Vi protected herself and Dash with a force field. Then Dash began to run. They raced through the jungle. Mr Incredible and Elastigirl eventually found them.

Together, the family fought off Syndrome's guards. But suddenly Syndrome arrived and locked the Incredibles in his immobiray! "Looks like I've hit the jackpot!" Syndrome gloated."

Then he took them to his base and suspended them in an immobi-ray cell. The family was helpless as Syndrome described his evil plan. "The robot will emerge dramatically, do some damage, and just when all hope is lost..." the villain explained. "Syndrome will save the day!" He sneered at Mr Incredible. "I'll be a bigger hero than you ever were!"

"You killed off real heroes so that you could pretend to be one!" said Mr Incredible.

Syndrome cackled and took off for the mainland.

"I'm sorry," Mr Incredible told his family. "I've been a lousy father. So obsessed with being undervalued that I undervalued all of you. You are my greatest adventure."

As he spoke, Vi was creating a force field, allowing her to escape the energy beams and set her family free. Soon the Incredibles were back in action! It was up to them to stop the Omnidroid before it attacked the city.

Turner Goes to the Library

"The Little Toolbox heard a roar and turned around,'" Manny read aloud, "'then found himself staring right into the eyes of –'"

"'...a big, scary dinosaur!" Manny finished.

Just then, the phone rang. It was Marion the librarian. "Marion needs us to fix the turnstile at the biblioteca," Manny said as he hung up the phone.

When Manny and the tools entered the library, Felipe hollered, "We're here to check out the turnstile, Marion!"

"Thanks for coming!" Marion called. "I'll be right there."

Manny put some oil on the turnstile. To check the repair, Squeeze grabbed a handle and spun the turnstile around. The turnstile broke off and fell to the floor! Squeeze felt awful, but Manny told him not to worry. They looked inside the turnstile to see what kind of screwdriver they would need. When Turner realized he wasn't needed, he hopped away.

"Why aren't you helping the others, Turner?" asked Marion.

"Why bother?" Turner scowled. "They're not interested in hearing any good ideas."

"Well, there are always plenty of great ideas in a library," Marion said with a smile. "There's something for everyone here: storybooks, picture books, even repair manuals – almost anything you can think of!"

Turner perked up. "Repairs? Now that's an exciting subject!"

Marion smiled. "You know, I bet this is a book you might enjoy!"

Turner jumped up and down. "Hey, guys, come over here! I've got a book to show you – it's a real page-turner!"

Felipe was puzzled. "Turner's interested in a libro? What's he doing with a book?"

"It's a repair manual with instructions for fixing a turnstile!" said Manny. "Great find, Turner. Let's get to work!"

With the help of the manual, the team fixed the turnstile.

"Wow, you finished just in time," Marion said, looking at her watch. "Okay, the library is officially open for business! The readers of Sheet Rock Hills are waiting outside!"

Back at the shop, Manny and the tools settled into his armchair, ready for story time.

"Uh, I have a book I'd like to share with everyone," Turner said. "Would you mind reading it to us, Manny?"

"¡Naturalmente! Of course," Manny said, looking at the book. "How to Fix Broken Stuff! It's one of my favourites, Turner."

Turner smiled. "Mine, too!"

Winnie the Pooh

Playing School

Now, it just so happened that when the wind changed ever so slightly, and the leaves began to turn scarlet or golden, depending on their preference, and the days grew ever so much more eager to be over and done, this was also the time that Christopher Robin returned to school, as well as the time, not so surprisingly, when his friends in the Wood felt as if they should really do the same.

But *playing* school, as you might suspect, is not as similar to real school as perhaps it should be. First of all, there's no teacher to tell you what to do. And, after sitting at their desks for what seemed like a good three and a quarter hours (but was really just five or so minutes), Winnie the Pooh and his friends came to the conclusion that something rather important in their game of school was missing.

"Perhaps it's time we had a snack," suggested Pooh.

"I don't think that's it, Pooh," said Piglet.

"Our problem," announced Owl, "is that we do not have a teacher. No classroom is complete – and this is a well-known fact – without a teacher. Which is why I'm quite happy to offer my considerable expertise."

"Just a minute, Owl," Rabbit broke in. "And why is it, exactly, that we should let you be the teacher? Some might say – myself included – that I'm better suited to the job."

"You?" Owl scowled.

"Perhaps we should have a vote," said Piglet. "I'd like to nominate Pooh."

"Me?" Pooh said. "Why, thank you, Piglet. I gladly accept. Now . . . what's a 'teacher' again?"

"Really!" said Owl, with no small amount of scorn. "A 'teacher,' my dear Pooh, is the someone who stands before the class."

"To give out snacks?" asked Pooh hopefully.

"No," said Owl. "To give out knowledge."

"Oh," said Pooh. "I don't think I'd enjoy that nearly so much."

"Well, if it's all the same to you, and if anyone cares, I'll be the teacher," Eeyore said glumly. "I probably wouldn't have made a good student anyway."

"That will never do!" exclaimed Rabbit.

"Hi-ho!" said Christopher Robin, returning from a thoroughly enjoyable, and very well-taught, day at school. "Whatever are you up to?"

"Playing school . . . I think," said Pooh.

"Only we don't have a teacher," Piglet explained.

"I could teach you. I learned ever so many things today," said Christopher Robin.

"Hooray!" cheered Roo. "Let's start right away!"

Disney
Pinocchio
A Bright Idea

One day, Geppetto told Pinocchio, "I am off to deliver these puppets. I will be gone for a few hours. Stay out of trouble!" But Geppetto had not been gone for 15 minutes before Pinocchio became bored. "I have nothing to do," he said.

"You could clean the shop," said Jiminy Cricket.

"That's no fun," said Pinocchio. "I'll paint a picture instead."

"Where will you get paint?" Jiminy asked.

"From the workbench," said Pinocchio.

"You know you're not supposed to go near Geppetto's workbench," warned Jiminy. But the cricket's warning came too late.

"Oops!" Pinocchio cried.

He'd spilled red paint all over the workbench. Hurriedly, he grabbed a rag and tried to clean up the mess, but the paint just smeared. He'd made the mess even bigger!

Pinocchio looked around desperately. When he noticed Geppetto's kitten, Figaro, sleeping by the hearth, he had an idea.

"I'll say Figaro did it," Pinocchio said.

Jiminy shook his head. "That would be wrong," he said.

"What else can I do?" Pinocchio asked. "The workbench is ruined, and my father will be furious!"

"Why don't you paint it?" suggested Jiminy.

"That's a very good idea!" said Pinocchio.

So he set to work. First, he painted the bench top bright red. Then he painted the drawers green and yellow.

Figaro woke up and investigated, getting paint all over his whiskers.

Soon, the job was done.

"It looks wonderful," said Jiminy.

"Yes, it does," Pinocchio agreed. But he did not feel proud at all.

"It's a work of art!" Geppetto cried when he got home. "It's so colourful it makes the whole shop cheerful."

Then Geppetto saw the paint on Figaro's whiskers. "Did Figaro knock over the paint again?" he asked. "Is that why you painted the workbench?"

"No," Pinocchio said. "I spilled the paint. I couldn't clean it up, so I painted the whole workbench. I'm sorry."

Geppetto was quiet for a moment, and then he said, "I'm proud of you, Pinocchio."

"Because I painted the workbench?" Pinocchio asked.

"No," said Geppetto. "I'm proud of you because you told the truth and apologized instead of telling a lie. That takes courage. Now, every day, when I see my beautiful workbench, I'll remember you did the right thing, and that will make the colours seem even brighter!"

Disney
MICKEY MOUSE
Spring Cleaning

Mickey Mouse hummed as he straightened up his messy house. He swept up some leaves that had blown in through the front door. Then he shook the mud off his doormat.

He was picking up some old magazines when one of them caught his eye.

"'Make a Fresh Start with Spring Cleaning,'" Mickey read aloud. "Hmm. Spring cleaning, eh?"

He looked out of the window. It wasn't spring – it was autumn! What was he doing cleaning his house?

"Whew!" he exclaimed as he dropped his broom and flopped onto the sofa. "Looks like I have a whole day free now. I think I'll see if Minnie wants to come over!"

A short while later, Minnie Mouse rang the doorbell. "Hi, Mickey!" she said cheerfully. "What do you want to do to – "

She gasped. Mickey's house was a mess! There was mud on the floor, dust on the shelves, dirty dishes on the table, laundry piled here and there, books and magazines everywhere . . . .

"What's wrong?" Mickey asked.

"Mickey," Minnie said, "er, when was the last time you cleaned your house?"

Mickey laughed. "Don't be silly, Minnie!" he said. "I don't need to clean this place for months."

"M-m-months?" Minnie gasped. She couldn't believe it. In a few months, Mickey's entire house would be buried in mess!

"Sure!" Mickey shrugged. "Haven't you ever heard of spring-cleaning?"

Minnie wasn't sure what to do. She didn't want to be rude, but she had to convince Mickey to clean his house – and it couldn't wait until spring!

"You know, Mickey," she said casually, "I just read something about a fun new trend."

"Really?" Mickey smiled. "What's that, Minnie? Maybe it's something we could do today, since we have the whole day free!"

"Oh!" Minnie pretended to be surprised at the idea. "Why, I suppose we could! I hadn't thought of that."

"So, what's the trend?" Mickey asked eagerly. "Waterskiing? Rock climbing? Fondue parties?"

"No," Minnie said cheerfully. "Autumn cleaning! It's the newest rage."

"Autumn cleaning?" Mickey said doubtfully. He blinked, then smiled. "You know, that's so crazy, it sounds like fun! Come on, let's try it!"

Minnie smiled and picked up the magazine with the spring-cleaning article in it. "Good," she said. She stuffed the magazine into the dustbin. "I'll start right here!"

101 DALMATIANS

One Lucky Pup

"Where are we going?" Penny asked.

"Why do we have to get in the car? We're going to miss 'Thunderbolt'!" Pepper pouted. The puppies all hated to miss their favourite dog hero TV show. They groaned in disappointment.

"This will be even more fun," Perdy said soothingly as she coaxed the puppies into the car. "I promise."

Roger and Anita got into the front seat. It didn't take long to get out of the city. Soon the car was winding down a country lane. The puppies smelled all kinds of good things. They smelled flowers and hay. Then they smelled something sweet – peaches!

"Here we are!" Anita opened the car door.

"Where's here?" Freckles asked Lucky.

"It looks like an orchard!" Lucky yipped. He loved to eat fruit.

Roger stretched. "You dogs run and play," he said. "We'll call you when it's time for our picnic."

"Don't eat too many peaches," Pongo barked, but the puppies were already running off.

All morning, the puppies romped and played in the green grass until Pongo and Perdy came to call them. "Time for lunch!" Pongo barked.

"I'm not hungry," Rolly said, rolling over in the grass.

"I hope you didn't eat too much," Perdy said.

The big dogs herded their puppies up the hill towards the spot where Roger and Anita were laying out a picnic. Perdy scanned the group. "Wait a minute," she said to Pongo. "Where's Lucky?"

The black-and-white pack stopped in its tracks. Pongo counted them. Lucky was definitely missing!

Perdy sighed and began to whimper.

"Don't worry, Mother," Pepper said sweetly. "I have an idea." He turned to his brothers and sisters. "Hey, everyone. Let's play 'Thunderbolt'!" he barked. "We have to find Lucky!"

All of the puppies yipped excitedly and tumbled over one another to find Lucky's trail. Soon every nose was sniffing the ground.

Penny sniffed around a tree and behind a patch of tall grass. She'd caught the scent! "Here he is!" Penny barked.

The rest of the dogs gathered around to see the puppy asleep in the grass. Lucky's ears covered his eyes, but there was no mistaking the horseshoe of spots on his back, or the pile of peach stones by his nose!

"Lucky is lucky we found him," Perdita said with a relieved sigh.

"And," Pepper joked, "he'll be *really* lucky if he doesn't wake up with a tummy ache!"

Winnie the Pooh

The Ups and Downs of Babysitting

"Roo, I have to go out tomorrow evening," said Kanga. "So you'll need a babysitter. Who would you like?"

"Tigger!" shouted Roo.

Kanga was not surprised. Tigger was the only animal she knew who liked to bounce more than a baby kangaroo!

The next day, Tigger came over to Kanga's house.

"Now, Tigger, I know you and Roo like to bounce," said Kanga. "But a good babysitter must know when to put the bouncer to bed."

"Don't worry, Kanga!" said Tigger.

For hours, Tigger and Roo had a fine old time bouncing around. Then Tigger looked at the clock and said, "Time for bed!"

Roo hopped right into his room.

"That was easy," Tigger said to himself. "Now I'll just tuck you in and – hey! I said bounce *into* bed. Not *on* it!" cried Tigger. But Roo wouldn't stop. So Tigger gave up and started bouncing too.

Then Tigger remembered Kanga. "Wait a minute! I'm the babysitter!" said Tigger. "I'm supposed to be tucking you in!"

"I don't want to be tucked in!" said Roo.

"What if I read you a story?" asked Tigger.

"No," said Roo. "I'm not even sleepy. I could bounce all the way to Pooh's house!"

"But it's time for *bed*, not bouncing," said Tigger. "I'll get you some milk. That will make you sleepy."

But when Tigger came back to Roo's bedroom, Roo was gone!

"Uh-oh!" said Tigger. He rushed to Pooh's house.

"I'm sorry, Tigger," said Pooh, "but Roo isn't here."

Then Tigger rushed to Piglet's house. But Roo wasn't there either. And he wasn't at Owl's or Rabbit's.

Finally, Tigger returned to Kanga's house. Where could Roo be? Just then, Tigger passed Roo's room – and saw Roo in his bed!

"Where were you, Tigger?" asked Roo.

"Where was I?" said Tigger. "Where were *you?*"

Roo explained that when Tigger had gone to get the milk, Roo had decided he did want to hear a story. But his favourite book was under the bed.

"You were *under* the bed?" cried Tigger.

"I'm home!" called Kanga at the front door.

Tigger sighed with relief.

"How did it go?" she asked Tigger.

"Kanga," said Tigger, "the wonderful thing about Tiggers is bouncing – and from now on I'm sticking with that. Babysitting just has too many ups and downs!"

The Caterpillar Room

Andy was soon leaving for college, and he had planned to store his toys in the attic. The toys, however, thought Andy was going to throw them away! They escaped and instead got taken to the Sunnyside Daycare nursery.

Woody knew Andy would never throw them away, and that it must have been a mistake. Most of the toys decided staying at the nursery was for the best. But Woody had to get home. The cowboy doll slipped out of the door just as the caretaker was passing by with his cart. The cowboy hopped a ride into the bathroom, and then made his way up to a window and onto the roof.

From his perch, Woody saw a tall wall surrounding the playground. He wasn't sure how he would get over it... until he found an old kite on the roof. Grabbing it, he leapt off the building. The kite glided gently over the wall and down towards the ground. But then a gust of wind yanked him back into the air!

The kite soared wildly through the air, then – SNAP! – the kite broke, sending Woody hurtling down through a tree outside the day care centre. Luckily, his pull-string caught on a branch, saving him from a crash.

The nursery's receptionist's little girl, Bonnie, was playing outside, and she ran over to see the dangling toy. Just then, her mum honked the car horn. It was time to go home. The little girl grabbed Woody, shoved him into her bag and ran to the car.

"Oh, great!" Woody whispered. He just wanted to get back to Andy!

Back in the nursery, in the Caterpillar Room, playtime was about to begin! Andy's other toys waited as footsteps thundered towards them and a crowd of energetic toddlers burst into the room. Shrieking with delight, the children grabbed the new toys.

But this playtime was not what the toys expected. The toddlers tangled Slinky's coil, dipped Jessie's hair in paint and covered Hamm with glitter and glue. They hammered with Buzz's head and stuck the Potato Heads' parts in their mouths. The toys couldn't believe it! Andy had never treated them like this!

A toddler tossed Buzz into the air. Buzz flipped onto the windowsill and lay still, looking out the window... into the other daycare room, the Butterfly Room. Inside, Buzz could see a group of older children playing gently with Lotso and the other toys. Buzz wondered: Why had he and his friends been put into a room where they were handled so roughly? There must have been a mistake. Buzz knew he'd have to ask Lotso – if he survived the afternoon!

A Purr-fect Night for a Stroll

Bernard was sweeping the floor of the Rescue Aid Society when Miss Bianca appeared.

"I'm going for a stroll," she said. "Would you like to join me?"

"Gosh, I don't know," Bernard said. "It's dark out. And it's raining too!"

"Yes," Miss Bianca said, smiling. "It's the *perfect* night for a stroll!"

Outside, Miss Bianca pulled her collar tight. Bernard opened a big umbrella.

"Let's walk to Central Park," said Miss Bianca.

Bernard choked. "But that's *thirteen* blocks away. Thirteen is unlucky!"

"Don't be silly," Miss Bianca said.

As they walked, it rained harder.

Suddenly, Bernard stopped. "Listen!" he cried.

"Meow!"

"It's a kitten," said Miss Bianca. "He's in trouble."

"Stay back!" Bernard warned. "Cats are dangerous. They eat mice like us!"

"Over there!" cried Miss Bianca, pointing.

Under a mailbox, a little orange kitten cowered from the rain. His fur was wet and he looked very sad.

"We've got to help!" Miss Bianca said.

"Let me go first!" Bernard insisted. He crept up to the kitten. "Er . . . hello," he stammered. "Are you lost?"

"I'm lost and very hungry!" the cat cried.

"I was afraid of that," said Bernard, eyeing the kitten's sharp teeth and claws nervously.

"Where are your parents?" Miss Bianca asked.

"I'm an orphan," the kitten replied.

"We must help him!" said Miss Bianca.

"I have an idea," said Bernard. "Follow us!" Bernard took Miss Bianca's arm and they walked to Morningside Orphanage. They knocked, and old Rufus the cat answered.

"Nice to see you two again," Rufus said. "Who's your friend?" he asked.

"He's Young Mister Kitten, and he's an orphan," Miss Bianca replied.

"He's hungry," said Bernard nervously.

"Here's a nice bowl of milk," said Rufus. The kitten lapped it up.

"You know," Rufus said. "I could use a helper around here. Would you like to be adopted?"

The kitten threw his paws around Rufus's neck and purred with joy.

It was late, so Miss Bianca and Bernard said good night. Out on the street, Bianca took Bernard's arm.

"See," she said. "I told you it was the purr-fect night for a stroll!"

262

DISNEP·PIXAR
MONSTERS, INC.

A Mother's Touch

Work was piling up in the offices of Monsters, Inc. Celia was off with the flu, and there was no one to cover for her.

Sulley, the president of Monsters, Inc., knew he had to act fast. "Who can we get to fill in?" he asked.

"I know!" answered Mike. "I'll call my mum. She'd love to help out."

And so, later that day, in walked Mrs Wazowski. Sulley and Mike went off to discuss some new plans for the laugh factory, while Mrs W. made herself at home – *very* at home. When Sulley and Mike returned at lunchtime, they scarcely recognized the reception area. Mike's mum had hung ruffled curtains and scattered fluffy rugs everywhere. Mike gave Sulley a weak smile.

"We'll change it back when she leaves," he whispered.

Later that day, Mike rehearsed some new comedy routines. "What do monsters eat for breakfast?" asked Mike. "Anything they want!" Sulley and Mike laughed until their sides hurt.

"I couldn't help but overhear," said Mike's mum. "It might be funnier if you wore a silly hat."

Sulley shot Mike a look. "Thanks, Mum," said Mike. "That's a very helpful suggestion. Say – isn't that the phone I hear ringing?"

A little while later, Sulley and Mike summoned her over the intercom to come to the Laugh Floor. "Um, Mum, do you know anything about this?" Mike asked nervously. He pointed to the card keys, which were now filed by colour, making it impossible for anyone to know which card belonged to which door.

"I certainly do!" Mrs W. replied proudly. "I have an 'eye' for organization, if I do say so myself."

Sulley turned and spoke to Mike through gritted teeth. "She's *your* mother. Do something!"

Just before the day was over, Mike went to the front desk, sat down and took his mother's hand. He'd never fired his mother before. This wasn't going to be easy! "Mum, you know I love you. And you make a terrific receptionist, but – "

Just then, Celia walked through the front door. "Schmoopsie-Poo!" called Mike.

"Googly Bear!" Celia cried.

"What are you doing here?" Mike asked. "You're supposed to be home in bed."

"I couldn't stand being away from you one day longer," Celia gushed.

Mrs Wazowski beamed. "He *is* irresistible – isn't he? That's because he takes after my side of the family. Well, I guess my work here is done!" she said, gathering up her things.

Suddenly, Mrs W. stopped. "Oh, Mikey, what were you about to tell me?"

"Not a thing, Mum," said Mike as he gave her a kiss. "Not a thing!"

DUMBO
A Tail Tale

Dumbo and Timothy Mouse has made a new friend, called Eeny. He lived at the circus with his brothers Meeny, Miny and Mo. Like Dumbo, with his great big ears, Eeny also had something special about him: a very, very long tail!

"I wish my tail was just like every other monkey's," Eeny sighed.

"Don't be silly," said Timothy. "Your tail is terrific. Isn't it, Dumbo?"

Dumbo nodded, flapping his great big ears.

"But my brothers are always making fun of me," said Eeny.

Timothy Mouse told Eeny how Dumbo was also teased. Until they realized he could do special things – like fly!

"I bet your tail can do some spectacular things!" said Timothy Mouse.

"I doubt it," replied Eeny, gloomily.

"Well, first you've got to cheer up!" exclaimed Timothy. Dumbo nodded and tootled a happy little tune with his trunk.

Eeny brightened up. Holding his tail like a string bass, he plucked it to get a tune. Together, he and Dumbo continued their song.

Right away, Meeny, Miny and Mo ran up to investigate. "Eeny's making music with his tail!" they cried.

Miny and Mo loved Eeny's musical tail.

But Eeny's brother, Meeny, wasn't as impressed.

"What's so great about thumping a tail?" he muttered to himself.

"Hey, Dumbo," said Timothy Mouse, "grab the end of Eeny's tail."

Holding Eeny's tail in his trunk, Dumbo twirled it around like a skipping rope. Miny and Mo jumped in.

Suddenly, a yell came from inside the big top.

Eeny, Miny and Mo ran into the tent, followed by Timothy Mouse and Dumbo. Meeny was hanging by the tip of his tail from the highest trapeze. He was jealous of Eeny, and he had wanted to show what his tail could do. But it hadn't gone as planned.

"Dumbo," Timothy Mouse cried, "we've got to fly up there!" But before Dumbo's ears could even start flapping, Eeny had climbed the pole and was lowering his tail to his brother. "Just grab my tail and I'll pull you up," Eeny shouted. Meeny held on, and a few minutes later, the two monkeys were safe.

"Boy, am I lucky to have such a brave brother," Meeny said with a sigh.

That afternoon, in honour of their brother the hero, Meeny, Miny and Mo put on a tail-band concert of their own. And from that day on, they never, ever made fun of Eeny's long, long tail again.

Quincy's Dream

The Little Einsteins met in the clubhouse after school one day to talk about their upcoming mission. Everyone was excited, except Quincy. "Are you daydreaming, Quincy?" teased Annie.

"I'm really tired." Quincy said. Quincy told his friends what was bothering him.

"I had this scary dream last night, and now I'm afraid to go back to sleep," Quincy said. "I used to think I was really brave, but now I just feel silly."

"I'm sure even the bravest knight in the world has a scary dream sometimes," said Leo. "We all have them!"

"But what should I do if I have another bad dream?" he asked.

"Do what I do," offered June. "Use your imagination to change what happens in your dream. If I have a dream about a big, scary tiger, I just use my imagination to turn him into a cuddly orange kitten."

Annie spotted something she thought could help Quincy.

"A dream catcher!" she shouted. "We can use it to catch your bad dream, Quincy!"

Quincy was puzzled. "It looks like a spiderweb with feathers hanging from it."

"Some Native American tribes believe that if you hang a dream catcher over your bed, you can 'trap' your bad dreams in its web," explained June.

"I've got a plan!" exclaimed Leo. "Catch your bad dream in this dream catcher tonight, and then bring it to the clubhouse tomorrow."

The next morning, Quincy brought the dream catcher to the clubhouse. Leo, Rocket and the team were all going to jump into Quincy's bad dream and show him how to change the ending. With his friends by his side, there was nothing to be afraid of!

When the team landed in Quincy's dream, he was dreaming that a famous painting had come to life.

"Yikes!" Annie gasped. "It's a monster!"

"Hey, you can't say I didn't warn you!" Quincy said.

"Okay," June said to the team, "Everyone concentrate on the monster. Imagine, that instead of stomping his feet in anger, he's actually dancing!"

Suddenly, the angry monster changed into a graceful ballerina.

"We did it!" shouted Leo.

Quincy was proud of himself, too. "You were right, guys. When you use your imagination, anything is possible!"

Gas-Guzzling Engine

Lightning, Mater and their friends from Radiator Springs had been in Tokyo, where Lightning had taken part in the first event of the World Grand Prix – hosted by oil tycoon Mile Axlerod. During the race, some cars working for a known criminal, Professor Z, had used a special TV camera to blow up one of the cars! The press had asked Axlerod if his new alternative fuel, Allinol, was to blame – he said it wasn't.

Two British secret agents called Finn and Holley were on the trail of Professor Z. In Tokyo, an American spy had placed a secret device on Mater – then Finn and Holley thought Mater was the American spy! Professor Z had sent his goons, Grem and Acer, to find the tow truck and get back the device. Mater had then accidentally caused Lightning to lose the race, and Lightning was upset. Mater felt bad and decided to fly home, but Finn and Holley met him at the airport!

Mater didn't realize that Finn and Holley thought he was a secret agent – but he helped them anyway. Together they looked at a holographic photo that was on the device that the real American spy had given Mater. Mater said the photo was of a poorly made, gas-guzzling engine with some expensive new parts. But he didn't know who the engine belonged to.

Finn, Holley and Mater flew to Paris. Finn was hoping a parts dealer named Tomber could tell them who the mysterious engine in the photo belonged to.

Mater explained the engine must belong to a Lemon – a car that didn't work right. Gremlins and Pacers were both types of Lemons. Tomber said there was going to be a big meeting of Lemons in Porto Corsa, which was also the location of the next World Grand Prix race!

Lightning and his crew had just arrived in Italy for the next race. Their first stop was Luigi and Guido's hometown!

Lightning told Luigi's Uncle Topolino about his quarrel with Mater. The wise, old car told Lightning that even good friends fight sometimes. But it's important to make up fast. No fight is more important than friendship.

Meanwhile, Holley was disguising Mater as one of the Lemons' tow trucks so that he could sneak into the meeting. She gave Mater lots of cool spy gadgets, too!

Lightning was starting to really miss his best friend, Mater. He didn't realize that Mater was actually nearby – and had been caught up in a secret agent adventure!

A Difficult Decision

Carl Fredricksen and Russell had flown to South America in Carl's house. Carl was an old man who had dreamed of being an explorer since he was just a boy. His best childhood friend, Ellie, had had the same dream. They grew up and got married, and Carl promised Ellie he would take her to see Paradise Falls. But they never managed to save enough money to go, and sadly Ellie passed away.

Carl was being forced to move out of their home, so he decided to take the trip that he and Ellie had dreamed about. He accidentally took Russell along for the ride. Whilst walking towards Paradise Falls with the house in tow, they had met a strange bird called Kevin and a talking dog called Dug. Dug was part of a pack of dogs who wanted to capture Kevin for their leader – the great explorer, Charles Muntz!

But Charles thought Carl and Russell were trying to steal the bird from him, and he sent his pack of dogs after them. Luckily Dug was on their side and he blocked the other dogs' path with some rocks. But he couldn't stop the pack for long. One dog – Alpha – shoved him aside and jumped over the rocks. Up ahead, Carl, Russell and Kevin had come to the edge of a cliff. They were trapped!

Luckily, Carl and Russell were holding onto the house by the garden hose. Just then, the wind lifted the house into the air – taking Carl and his friends with it! Alpha grabbed Kevin's leg, but he lost his grip. The house floated to safety.

Carl and his friends had escaped, but Kevin's leg was badly injured. Russell realized that the bird needed help to get back to her babies. Out of nowhere, a spotlight appeared and shone down on the bird. Muntz had followed them in the Spirit of Adventure! Before Kevin could escape, a net shot from the airship and trapped her. Carl sawed at the net with Russell's pocketknife, trying to set her free.

"Get away from my bird!" Muntz snarled. Then he set Carl's house on fire!

Carl couldn't let his house go up in smoke – it held all his memories of Ellie. So he quickly made the decision to give up Kevin instead. The dogs dragged the wounded bird onto the airship. As Muntz lifted off with his prize bird, Carl ran to his house and beat back the flames.

"You gave away Kevin," Russell said.

Carl felt terrible, but what could he do? "I didn't ask for any of this!" he snapped. "Now, whether you assist me or not, I am going to Paradise Falls if it kills me."

Russell watched sadly as Carl walked away, pulling the house behind him.

Sleep Tight, Nemo!

It was late at night at the bottom of the sea – but little Nemo was wide awake.

"Nemo," said Marlin, poking his head into the anemone, "you should be asleep!"

"But I can't sleep," said Nemo. "I need another story."

"No more stories," said Marlin. "I told you five already."

"Then maybe another snack?" said Nemo.

But Marlin rolled his eyes. "No, Nemo. You just had a plankton snack five minutes ago. What you *should* do now, young clownfish, is go to sleep!"

"Okay, Dad," said Nemo. Then he did as his dad told him and closed his eyes. But, seconds later, they popped open again.

"Dad!" Nemo called out. "Daaaad!"

"Nemo!" Marlin groaned. "I'm beginning to lose my patience!"

"But, Dad," said Nemo, "I . . . I . . . I heard a noise."

"What kind of noise?" Marlin asked.

"Um . . . a . . . a spooky noise," answered Nemo.

"*Hmph.*" Nemo could tell Marlin did not like this reason for being awake either. But still, Marlin stopped and listened . . . and listened . . . and listened.

"I don't hear anything, Nemo," he said after a moment.

So Nemo tried his best to shut his eyes really tight and get comfortable. He wiggled this way . . . then that way . . . then this way again. But nothing worked.

"Daaaaaaaaaaad!" he called out.

"Nemo," Marlin said. "For the last time, it's time to go to sleep. If you call for me again, it had better be a good one or . . . or . . . or *else*. Good night!"

Now, Nemo knew his father well, and he knew when Marlin was just a teeny, tiny, itsy, bitsy bit angry with him. But Nemo also knew that when you can't go to sleep, you can't go to sleep. And no matter how many moonfish or angelfish or sea stars you count; no matter how tightly you close your eyes; no matter how mad your dad gets – you'll never go to sleep until you're absolutely, positively, no-doubt-about-it ready. And Nemo wasn't. But why not?

Suddenly, Nemo bolted up. "Dad!" he shouted. "Dad! Oh, *Daaaaad*!"

"All right. That's it, Nemo!" Marlin said.

"But, Dad," Nemo said. "There's one more thing I really, really, truly need. Then I promise, I'll go to sleep."

And with that, he snuggled into Marlin's fins for a great big good-night hug.

"I love you, Dad," he said. "See you in the morning."

Woody Meets Bonnie

Woody had escaped Sunnyside Daycare and tried to get home to Andy, but a little girl called Bonnie had found him dangling in a tree and taken him home!

Now at Bonnie's house, Woody was part of a lively game of pretend.

"We need a spaceship," Bonnie said, heading to the wardrobe.

"Look," Woody said once Bonnie couldn't hear, "I need to know how to get out of here."

"But why?" asked the doll. "This is the best place ever."

Bonnie returned and swept the toys up into a game of make-believe that ended with the toys being launched into the air! They landed on the bed, as Bonnie laughed happily. She hugged them all close. Woody hated to admit it, but he was having a great time.

Back at Sunnyside, Andy's toys were unhappy after being played with by some rough toddlers! The children had gone and the toys were putting themselves back together.

"Andy never played with us like that!" cried Rex as he freed his tail from a pegboard.

"We should be in the Butterfly Room with the big kids!" said Mrs Potato Head.

Buzz offered to sort everything out. "I'll go talk to Lotso about moving us to the other room," he said. But when he tried to leave, they discovered all the doors and windows were locked.

"We're trapped!" said Mrs Potato Head.

Finally, Buzz spotted an open space above the door. Working together, the toys managed to get Buzz through, and out of the room. From up high, Buzz could hear two toys named Twitch and Chunk in the hallway below. The pair stopped by the Butterfly Room to pick up Ken, then continued to the teachers' lounge. After they disappeared inside, Buzz jumped down and followed the group. He sneaked into the lounge just as they were climbing into a vending machine.

Buzz followed Ken and the others, and discovered a group of Butterfly Room toys sitting at the top of the vending machine! Buzz hung back in the shadows.

"So what do you guys think of the new recruits?" Ken asked the others. "Any keepers?"

"All of them toys are disposable," replied Twitch. "We'll be lucky if they last us a week!"

Buzz was shocked! These toys knew how dangerous the Caterpillar Room was – and they had sent Andy's toys there on purpose! He had to warn his friends!

But when he turned to go, Big Baby was waiting for him... What was going to happen to Andy's toys now?

Disney·PIXAR
MONSTERS, INC.

Monster Day Care

Mike always arrived at Monsters, Inc. at half past eight, put his lunch box in his locker and promptly reported to his station on the Laugh Floor. But one morning, as he came out of the locker room, there was Celia. "We have a little problem, Mike," she said. "The day care teacher is sick today, so we need a sub. And seeing as how you've already met your laugh quota for the month, I thought maybe you –"

"Day care!" cried Mike. "Wait just a – "

Just then Sulley stepped in. "Happy to do it, Celia," he interrupted. "Day care, here we come."

"Are you crazy?" Mike grumbled.

"What's the big deal?" Sulley shrugged. "We handled Boo, didn't we? What's a few more kids? We'll eat a few snacks. Watch a few videos. Play a little peekaboo. It's like having a paid vacation, Mike, my man!"

But the minute they opened the day care room door, they both knew Sulley was wrong. . . .

There were monster children everywhere! Swinging from the ceiling. Slithering up the walls. Bouncing from corner to corner. Mike's and Sulley's jaws dropped open. What were they going to do?

Sulley took a deep breath. "We just have to let them know who's in charge, is all," he told Mike. "Okay, kids!" he announced. "Uncles Sulley and Mike are here. It's time to settle down."

But, instead of settling down, the little monsters dived for Sulley and Mike, yelling, "Horsey rides! Yeah!" and "Play ball!"

"I think they know who's in charge," Mike said as an oversized, six-handed monster child scooped him up and tossed him to his twin. *"Help!"*

Sulley quickly intercepted Mike and set him back down on his feet.

"'Paid vacation,' my eye," muttered Mike.

"All we need to do," said Sulley calmly, "is get their attention. Let's see . . . a video?" But the TV was too covered with monster slime and finger paint for anyone to watch it.

A snack? No. Every cracker and fright roll-up had been gobbled up long before.

A story? Of course! Except a four-eyed toddler seemed to be happily tearing the pages out of each and every book.

"How about a song?" said Mike finally.

"Great idea!" said Sulley. And do you know what? It was! They sang "The Huge Gigantic Spider" and "The Wheels on the Monster Bus". Before long even Mike was having fun.

"What did I say, Sulley? I said it'd be like paid vacation, and it is! I don't understand why you were so reluctant," Mike said.

Sulley rolled his eyes. "Whatever you say, Mike."

Laugh, Cobra Bubbles!

Lilo thought she was a very lucky girl. She had a lot of good friends, who she loved to laugh with. Stitch had a funny, scratchy laugh, to go with his scratchy voice. Pleakley giggled, and Jumba shouted out big guffaws. But as for Cobra Bubbles, well, the truth was, Cobra Bubbles just didn't laugh. Ever. And Lilo was just dying to find out what his laugh sounded like.

So Lilo tried to get Cobra Bubbles to laugh. She showed him the latest episode of "The World's Funniest Lobster Videos," but he didn't crack a smile, even when a lobster ate an entire jar of pickles. She made funny faces at him until her face hurt, but he just looked at her, expressionless. She even tried (at Stitch's suggestion) a whoopee cushion. But she was too busy running away to see if he laughed or not when he sat down on it.

Clearly, something had to be done. It just wasn't healthy for a person never to laugh. She explained the problem to Nani.

"Nani, Cobra Bubbles is one of my best friends. He's practically family! But he never laughs. I think I need to help him," Lilo said.

"Well," Nani said thoughtfully. "What have you tried?"

"I tried lobsters, funny faces and a whoopee cushion," said Lilo, ticking the items off on her fingers. "But none of them worked! He didn't even blink!"

"Hmm," said Nani, "I think I see the problem. Do *you* think those things are funny?"

"Well, no," Lilo admitted. "I'm scared of lobsters, my face still hurts from making funny faces, and I think whoopee cushions are silly."

"Maybe Cobra Bubbles thinks so too," said Nani. "You know, he might laugh if he is having a good time. Why don't you start out by doing something fun?"

So, the next day, Lilo enrolled Cobra Bubbles in her hula class. The music started, and the dancers came out on stage, swinging their hips and swirling their grass skirts. And there, in the middle of them, was Cobra Bubbles. He did his best to follow the complicated steps of the dance, and Lilo did her best to keep a straight face. But it was impossible. Cobra Bubbles in a grass skirt was the funniest thing she'd ever seen. The other kids in the class thought so too. Soon they were all laughing – even the hula teacher!

Then, to Lilo's surprise, Cobra Bubbles began to smile. And then he chuckled. And, soon enough, Cobra Bubbles was actually laughing! Lilo thought that Cobra Bubbles's laugh was somehow both quiet and big, and very nice. Just like him.

Mickey and the Pet Shop

One day Mr Palmer had to go away, so he asked Mickey to look after his pet shop. All the animals seemed happy – except for a cute little puppy who wouldn't stop crying.

"Poor little fella," said Mickey. "What you need is some attention." He lifted the puppy from the kennel. The puppy wriggled out of Mickey's arms and raced over to the fishbowl for a drink of water. The puppy knocked over the bowl and the fish went flying across the shop! Mickey caught the fish and put it in a new fishbowl. Then he put the puppy back in the kennel. Just then, the door opened. It was Mickey's first customer! He was so excited, he forgot to lock the kennel door.

"Can I help you?" Mickey asked. But before the customer could answer, the puppy had got out and opened the door to a cage full of mice. Now mice were everywhere! Mickey gathered up all the pets and put them back where they belonged.

Then Mickey went upstairs for the night and tried to sleep, but the puppy howled loudly. Mickey didn't know what to do. Finally, the puppy got what he wanted – a spot under the covers, right next to Mickey!

When Mickey woke up, the puppy was gone. Mickey couldn't believe his eyes when he walked into the shop. It was a mess!

The puppy wasn't there. Mickey began to look for his little friend. He was about to give up when he remembered to check the store room. Sure enough, the puppy was there. Mickey brought the puppy back to the kennel and locked the door.

As Mickey tidied up, the puppy began to whine. Mickey felt bad, so he opened the kennel door again. The puppy followed him around, trying to be good. He helped Mickey put the books back and sweep up the mess.

Mickey and the puppy had just finished cleaning up when Mr Palmer strode in. "It looks like everything went smoothly," he said. "I hope none of the animals gave you any trouble."

"It was as easy as pie," a very tired Mickey replied.

Then Mr Palmer handed Mickey his paycheck. "Thanks for helping me out," he said. "I hope you will come back soon."

Mickey just smiled. Suddenly he had an idea – maybe he could take the pup instead of the pay! Mr Palmer agreed.

"But what should I call you?" Mickey wondered. Just then, Mickey saw some pictures of outer space in a newspaper. The headline read: NEW PICTURES OF PLUTO! "That's it! I'll call you Pluto!" he exclaimed.

Disney
HANDY MANNY

Manny Goes to Pre-School

Today was Community Helper Day at the pre-school. Manny and the tools were preparing a slide show for the kids. But then the projector's bulb burned out!

"We'd better go to Kelly's store," said Manny.

"We'd better hurry," said Stretch. "It's almost time for our show."

Manny and the tools went to Kelly's and bought a new bulb. They arrived back just in time.

"Hola, Miss Diaz," said Manny to the teacher.

"Hola!" said Miss Diaz. Miss Diaz told the children that Manny and the tools were special community helpers. She explained that Manny would show slides so the class could see how he and his tools fixed things all around Sheet Rock Hills. The children sat quietly as Manny showed the first slide. But someone was in the way.

"Get out of the way!" another child called.

"Lo siento. I'm sorry," said Carlos. Carlos was the same age as the other children, but he was very tall. As Carlos got up to move, he bumped into the screen. It fell with a crash!

"Don't worry," said Manny. "We can fix it."

But some children pointed at Carlos and called him 'Clumsy Carlos'! Carlos turned red and ran out of the room.

"It was an accident," Miss Diaz said. "No problema. Manny can fix it."

"Sí," said Manny, "but there is something I need to do first."

Manny told the tools to stay and talk to the children. Then he found Carlos outside.

"My long legs get in the way," cried Carlos. "And now I broke your screen. I am clumsy!"

"Carlos, everyone has accidents and breaks things: tall people, short people – all kinds of people," said Manny. "If people didn't break things, I wouldn't have a job. Then I would be the one crying!"

Carlos smiled at Manny. Then Manny said, "Sometimes being tall is a good thing. Like right now. I need your help."

"Really?" said Carlos.

"Sí," said Manny. "Come on."

Back in the classroom, Manny spoke to the class. "The tools and I are going to fix the screen, but we need someone tall to help us," said Manny. "We need Carlos."

Everyone watched while Carlos helped Manny and the tools fix the broken screen. Then Manny said, "Now we can watch the slides. And you get to meet Sheet Rock Hill's newest community helper – Carlos!"

Everyone cheered, "Hooray for Carlos!"

Carlos stood up tall, feeling very proud.

Stuck at Sunnyside

All of Andy's toys – except Woody, who had tried to go home but had been found by a little girl – were stuck at the Sunnyside Daycare centre. They had thought Andy wanted to throw them away, so they jumped into a box going to the nursery instead.

The trouble was, the toys were trapped in the Caterpillar Room – where young toddlers played very roughly with them! Buzz had just sneaked out of the room and overheard a meeting some of the Sunnyside toys were having – Buzz heard them say they *knew* the toddlers would play rough!

Back in the Caterpillar Room, the other toys gathered around Mrs Potato Head. She had started to see strange images, coming to her through the eye she'd lost at Andy's house.

"Andy's out in the hall," she said, holding a hand over her remaining eye. "He's looking in the attic. Why is he so upset?" She gasped. "Andy's looking for us! I think he did mean to put us in the attic!"

"Woody was telling the truth!" Slinky cried. Now that the toys realized their mistake, they knew what they had to do.

"Guys, we've got to go home!" cried Jessie.

Down the hall, Big Baby and the others had discovered Buzz. They tied him to a chair inside a cupboard. When Lotso arrived, he released Buzz and acted as if the space ranger's capture had been a mistake. Lotso even said Buzz could be moved to the Butterfly Room – as long as his friends stayed behind.

"I can't accept," said Buzz. "We're a family. We stay together."

Angrily, Lotso called for the Bookworm to bring the Buzz Lightyear Instruction Manual. The gang held Buzz down, and then, using the booklet as a guide, opened up Buzz's back panel. "Stop! Nooooo!" Buzz cried, as they flipped a switch in his back.

Then, Lotso and his henchmen went to the Caterpillar Room. Andy's toys, knowing nothing about what had happened, were relieved to see him. "There's been a mistake," Mrs Potato Head explained. "We have to go!"

But Lotso didn't care. "Here's the thing, Sweet Potato," he said, grinning nastily. "You ain't leaving Sunnyside." He wanted Andy's toys to stay with the littlest kids, so his gang wouldn't have to!

Then, suddenly, Buzz appeared. But instead of greeting his friends, he began knocking them over with kung-fu kicks!

Jessie and the others stared in shock, wondering what had happened to their friend. Why was Buzz acting so strangely?

DISNEY·PIXAR
MONSTERS, INC.
The Spooky Sleepover

It was a quiet morning at Monsters, Inc. Sulley had arrived early to catch up on paperwork when he got a phone call from dispatch. "Annual slumber party at Shannon Brown's house. Waxford is out sick. We need a replacement."

"I'll get right on it," replied Sulley. He knew there would be a lot of kids at the party, and he wanted to make sure he had a monster there to tell jokes and capture laughs. Who better for the job than his one-eyed pal, Mike?

Mike was in the locker room getting ready for work when Sulley entered and explained the situation.

"Piece of cake," Mike said as a door slid into his station on the Laugh Floor. Then Mike walked through the wardrobe in Shannon Brown's room. It was empty. "Uh... hello?" Mike called. Just as Mike started to leave, he heard the sound of laughter.

Just then, thunder cracked across the sky. Mike ran to the wardrobe door to return to the factory. He jiggled the doorknob, but it just opened into the wardrobe, not the Laugh Floor at Monsters, Inc.!

Mike soon realized that lightning must have struck the door and broken it. He took a deep breath and headed into the hallway.

Meanwhile, back at Monsters, Inc.,

Sulley was working on the Laugh Floor. The floor manager came running over. "Sulley!" he shouted. "Mike hasn't returned from the slumber party. He's never been gone this long!"

When Sulley went to check on the door, he saw it had broken and brought someone in to fix it. After a few hours, the door was working! Now it would open into a different room at Shannon's house.

Back at Shannon's, Mike heard laughing down the hall. When he found the right room and went in, it was quiet. Slowly, Mike entered the dark, silent room. All of a sudden, a light went on! Mike jumped. Shannon Brown and all her friends started roaring with laughter! They thought Mike looked funny sneaking into the room. Mike screamed in fright.

At that exact moment, the wardrobe door opened and Sulley burst into the room. Sulley was so surprised to find Mike screaming that all he could do was scream too! Then he and Mike huddled in fright. Shannon and her friends laughed even harder.

"Looks as if our work here is done," Sulley said to Mike.

"I was never scared for a second," said Mike.

"Me neither, buddy," Sulley replied, his fingers crossed behind his back. "Me neither."

Bambi
Winter Nap

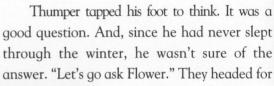

Bambi nosed under the crunchy leaves, looking for fresh grass. There was none. He looked up at the trees, but there were no green leaves there either. Food was getting scarce in the forest.

"Don't worry, Bambi," Thumper said when he saw the confused look in Bambi's eyes. "We'll get through the fall and winter. Dad says we always do. We find what we can when we can, and we always make it until spring."

Bambi sighed and nodded. Thumper's dad was smart. He knew lots of things about the forest.

"Besides, it's better to be awake than napping all winter. Yech!" Thumper hated to go to bed, even at bedtime.

"Napping?" Bambi didn't know that some animals slept through the winter months.

"Sure. You know, like Flower, and the squirrels, and the bears. They hole up for months. Haven't you noticed the chipmunks putting their acorns away the past couple of months?" Thumper pointed towards an oak tree.

Bambi nodded.

"That's their food for the winter. As soon as it gets cold enough, they'll just stay inside and sleep," Thumper explained.

"But how will they know when it's time to wake up?" Bambi couldn't imagine life in the forest without all the other animals.

Thumper tapped his foot to think. It was a good question. And, since he had never slept through the winter, he wasn't sure of the answer. "Let's go ask Flower." They headed for the young skunk's den.

"Hello," Flower said.

"Flower, you sleep all winter, right?" Thumper asked.

"It's called hibernation." Flower yawned a big yawn. "Excuse me," he said, blushing.

"So, Bambi wants to know who wakes you up in the spring," Thumper said.

"You'll be back, won't you, Flower?" Bambi asked worriedly.

The little skunk giggled. "Oh, we always come back. Just like the grass and the flowers and the leaves," Flower explained. "I never thought about what wakes us up before. It must be the sun, I guess."

Bambi smiled. He didn't know the grass and leaves would come back in the spring too! He was feeling much better about the forest's winter nap.

Suddenly, Thumper started laughing. He rolled on his back and pumped his large hind feet in the air.

"What is it?" Bambi and Flower asked together.

"You really are a flower, Flower!" Thumper giggled. "You even bloom in the spring!"

Peter Pan

A Feather in His Cap

Peter Pan and Tinker Bell were off on an adventure and the Lost Boys were bored.

"Never Land is a dull place without Peter Pan," Slightly complained.

Then Rabbit spoke up. "We can play Pirates! That's always fun."

"Can't," said Slightly. "I lost the feather off my pirate hat."

"We could find another feather," Tootles suggested.

"An extraordinary feather," Cubby said. "Like Captain Hook's."

"That it!" Slightly cried. "I'll steal Captain Hook's feather!"

A short time later, the Lost Boys were sneaking aboard Hook's pirate ship. Luckily for them, the pirates were taking a nap!

There, hanging from a peg on the mast, was Captain Hook's hat.

"There it is," whispered Tootles. "Get it!"

"M-m-m-me?" stammered Slightly.

Smee, Hook's first mate, awoke with a start. He thought someone had said his name. "Smee you say! That be me. But who be calling Smee?"

He opened his eyes and spied the Lost Boys. "Ahoy!" he cried, waking up the others. Quick as a flash, the Lost Boys were caught.

Captain Hook burst from his cabin. "Lash them to the mast!" he commanded. "We'll catch Peter Pan when he comes to save his friends."

Floating high on a cloud, Peter Pan and Tinker Bell saw their friends being captured.

They flew down to Pirates' Cove and landed on the ship's mast. Peter cupped his hands around his mouth and made a most peculiar sound.

"Tick tock," Peter went. "Tick tock!"

Down on deck, Captain Hook became very frightened. "It's that crocodile!" he cried. "The one that ate my clock and my hand! Now he's come back to eat me!"

"Tick tock … tick tock," went Peter.

"Man the cannons!" Hook cried. "Shoot that crocodile!"

The Lost Boys, tied to the mast, were forgotten. As the pirates ran in circles, Tinker Bell began to flap her wings. Fairy dust sprinkled down onto the Lost Boys. Soon they floated right out of the ropes and up into the clouds. On the way, Slightly snatched the feather from Hook's hat and stuck it in his own.

Peter Pan, Tinker Bell and the Lost Boys met on a drifting cloud.

"Thanks for saving us!" exclaimed Tootles.

"You helped me scare old Hook!" Peter Pan cried. "That's a feather in all your caps."

"But the best feather of them all is in mine," Slightly said, as he showed off Captain Hook's prized feather!

THE JUNGLE Book

Monkey Trouble

"Hey, let me go!" Mowgli cried. "Baloo!" But the big bear couldn't help him. Mowgli was being carried off through the treetops by a band of wild monkeys!

The monkeys laughed and chattered as they swung Mowgli from one tree to another. One monkey dropped him, and Mowgli yelled. But another monkey caught him by the ankles just in time. Then a third monkey pulled him away by one arm, swinging over to another tree on a large vine, where more monkeys grabbed at him.

Soon Mowgli was out of breath and confused. "Hey!" he yelled. "Quit it! I want to go back to Baloo! Let me go!"

The monkeys laughed. "Sorry, Man-cub!" one shouted. "We can't let you go. You might as well forget about that bear!"

"Yeah!" another monkey said, catching Mowgli by the arm. "You're with us monkeys now. We're better than any old bear! You'll flip for us monkeys."

He tossed Mowgli straight up. Mowgli felt himself flipping head over heels.

A second later a pair of monkeys caught him by the legs. "See, Man-cub?" one of them said. "Monkeys know how to have fun!"

Mowgli laughed, feeling dizzy. "That was kind of fun!" he cried. "Do it again!"

The monkeys howled with laughter. They tossed Mowgli up, over and over. Mowgli somersaulted through the treetops until he couldn't tell up from down any more. After that, the monkeys taught him how to swing from branch to branch and vine to vine. They even showed him how to shake the trees to make bananas fall into his hands.

"Being a monkey is fun!" Mowgli exclaimed through a mouthful of banana.

Maybe it was good that the monkeys had found him, Mowgli thought. Being a monkey might even be more fun than being a wolf or a bear. And it was definitely more fun than going to the Man-village.

Mowgli swallowed the banana and looked around at his new friends. "What are we going to do next?"

A monkey giggled. "We're going to see King Louie."

"Yeah!" another monkey said gleefully, clapping his hands. "He's the most fun of all!"

"King Louie?" Mowgli said suspiciously. He didn't like the way the monkeys were grinning at him. "Who's that?"

"You'll see, Man-cub!" the monkeys cried, swinging through the treetops.

Mowgli shrugged. How bad could this King Louie be?

Lilo's Riches

Stitch stretched his blue arms and folded them behind his head, soaking up the rays on the wide Hawaiian beach.

Flash! Lilo snapped his photo. *Flash*! Lilo turned and snapped a picture of Nani and David riding their surfboards.

Suddenly Stitch stood up. He grabbed Lilo's camera. Lilo struck a hula pose and – *Flash*! – Stitch caught it on film.

"Let's take some more!" Lilo giggled, running toward the shoreline. Stitch was right behind her, snapping picture after picture. *Flash*! He got two kids splashing. He turned quickly and – *Flash*! – he momentarily blinded a bald man holding an ice-cream cone.

The man looked at Stitch, dazed. Lilo had seen that look before. Most people didn't know what to make of Stitch. Then, as the man stared, his mint-chocolate-chip ice cream rolled off his cone and splatted in the sand.

"Sorry," Lilo muttered. She grabbed Stitch's arm and tried to lead him away, but Stitch strained against her, pulling her closer to the melting green blob.

With one swipe of his tongue, Stitch lapped the mess up. "Ptooey!" He spat it out, all over the man's feet. It was too sandy. "Ptooey! Ptooey!" Stitch continued spitting out sand as Lilo dragged him away.

As soon as he stopped spitting, Stitch pointed at the snack shack.

"Sorry, Stitch. I don't have any money for ice cream," Lilo explained. "How about if we play a few songs instead? Here, you play," Lilo tossed Stitch the ukulele. "I'll dance."

At first, Stitch just plucked a few sour notes. But soon the rhythm got him and he was playing like a real-life rock star.

Lilo was enjoying dancing so much, she didn't even notice that the tourists had begun to toss coins to them.

Stitch hammed it up, tossing his head and wiggling his hips. Lilo waved her arms and smiled her most winning smile. When the song ended, the two took a bow. Quickly, Lilo gathered the coins.

"We've got enough! Come on!" Lilo went running towards the snack shack.

"Three mint-chocolate-chip cones, please," Lilo said.

Lilo handed one cone to Stitch. She took a quick lick of the second one as she scanned the beach. Spotting the bald man, she hurried over and thrust the third cone towards him. "Here," she said. "Sorry about before."

The man smiled and he took the cone. Then Lilo handed him her camera. He snapped a picture – *Flash*! – of Lilo and Stitch eating ice cream.

Pinocchio
In a Tangle

One night, while Pinocchio was sleeping, a loud crash woke him. He jumped up and raced downstairs to Geppetto's workshop.

"Is anybody here?" Pinocchio called nervously.

"Meow!" came the reply. It was Geppetto's little kitten, Figaro.

"I hear you, but I can't see you!" called Pinocchio.

Suddenly, the puppets above Geppetto's workbench began to move.

"Yikes!" cried Pinocchio, startled.

Pinocchio looked up to see Figaro tangled in the puppets' strings. Pinocchio began to laugh.

"That's funny!" he said.

"Meow!" cried Figaro. He didn't think it was funny! The kitten struggled to get free, but he only became more tangled in the strings.

Pinocchio just laughed harder.

Jiminy Cricket hopped down from the hearth. He rubbed his tired eyes. "What's going on?" he asked.

Pinocchio pointed to the little kitten.

"Pinocchio, maybe you should help poor Figaro instead of laughing at him," Jiminy said.

"Maybe I should leave him there," replied Pinocchio. "Then Geppetto can see how naughty he's been."

"Meow!" poor Figaro wailed.

"That's not very nice," said Jiminy. "How would you feel if you were all tangled up?"

Pinocchio sighed. "I guess I wouldn't like it very much."

He was about to free the kitten, when he suddenly exclaimed, "Hey, Jiminy, look at that!"

Figaro's paws were now wrapped around the strings in such a way that when his paws moved, the puppets began to dance!

"That's a neat trick," said Pinocchio. "Figaro can work the puppets!"

The kitten moved his paws some more, and all the puppets danced on their strings.

"I have an idea," said Jiminy Cricket. "Do you want to hear it?"

Pinocchio and Figaro both nodded.

The next morning when Geppetto awoke, he got a surprise.

"Look, Father!" Pinocchio said. "Figaro can make the puppets dance!"

Pinocchio winked at Figaro, and the cat leaped onto the puppet strings again.

"Amazing!" Geppetto cried, watching the show. "We can put on a puppet show for all the children of the town!"

Pinocchio was thrilled to see Geppetto so happy.

"But when did you discover Figaro's talent?" asked Geppetto.

"Just last night," said Pinocchio, "when I found him in your workshop . . . uh, hanging around."

Peter Pan

Tiger Lily

It was a hot summer night in Never Land – so hot, in fact, that the poor Lost Boys couldn't sleep. And so it was decided that instead of trying to stay in their hideout in Hangman's Tree, Peter Pan and the Lost Boys would camp out for the night in the wild, wild wilderness.

Certainly, they thought, the woods would be cool and shady, and the tall trees would catch any breeze kind enough to blow through. But little did they know how mysterious – and downright spooky – a forest could become once the sun went down.

"It's dark out here," said Cubby.

"And awful quiet," said Tootles.

"Won't you tell us a story, please, Peter?" asked Slightly, who was shivering in his fox suit despite the sticky heat.

"Very well," agreed Peter. "If it will make you all be quiet! I will tell you the story of the very first time I ever camped out in the wilderness – which, by the way, was the first time I met Tiger Lily . . .

"I had made myself a fire, a great big one, 'cause it was fall and the nights were getting cool. I'd just laid my head down on a patch of nice, soft moss, when all of a sudden I heard a rustling in the shadows."

"Indians?" the Lost Boys gasped.

But Peter shook his head. "Not Indians,"

he told them. "That's what I thought at first too. No, this was something bigger. It was a *bear*! It jumped out of the trees, growling and snarling and waving its big, fat paws in the air like Captain Hook swattin' blue flies. I've never seen such a mean, angry beast, before or since!"

"So wha-wha-what did you do?" asked the Lost Boys.

"Told him to get lost, of course. To *scram*! Apparently, he didn't understand English, however, 'cause he just kept charging. Well, I'm not going to lie to you; I started to get nervous. And then, there she was – Tiger Lily – as quiet as a mouse. Without a 'hi' or 'how do you do', she grabbed a stick from my fire and waved it at the bear. And the next thing I knew, the bear had turned around and was running off crying! I suppose Tiger Lily saved my life that night," said Peter. "And it wasn't the last time either. The end. Good night."

"Um . . . Peter," said Cubby, peering out into the darkness, "do you know what ever happened to that bear?"

Peter thought for a moment. "Nope," he said and shrugged. "Probably still out there, wandering around, I guess." He yawned a big, mischievous yawn. "Now stop yer yammerin' and close your eyes and go to sleep!"

Undercover Mater

Lightning was in Italy, competing in the second event of the World Grand Prix. He had lost the first race after Mater had confused him over the headset. Lightning didn't realize Mater had been mistaken for an American secret agent – and was now caught up in a mission with two British agents, Finn and Holley!

Little did Lightning know, Mater was nearby. With a new disguise provided by the British agents, Mater had made it into a meeting of Lemons – bad cars that don't work properly – at a casino. Holley and Finn were positioned outside, listening in through Mater's headset.

A wanted criminal named Professor Z introduced the Lemons to their Big Boss, who appeared on a TV screen. But only his engine was visible – the same engine the real American agent had photographed! The Big Boss said that once a new alternative fuel named Allinol was proven lethal, all cars would use gasoline again. Then the Lemons, who owned the oil, would be rich and powerful!

As the Big Boss spoke, Professor Z's goons, Grem and Acer, were at the next race. They aimed a special TV camera at Carla Veloso, the race car from Brazil. Finn and Holley watched from their lookout point as Carla's engine exploded on the racetrack! Finn raced to the top of the tower to stop Grem and Acer. But a helicopter captured him with a giant magnet!

Finn was taken away and Grem and Acer continued to harm more race cars. Their next victim was Shu Todoroki, the racer from Japan. Shu's engine exploded, causing him to crash into another car. Soon, there was a pile up!

At the finish line, Lightning won. By now, everyone thought Allinol was to blame for the crashes. But Lightning insisted he would still use Allinol in the final race. The Big Boss heard Lightning's statement, and gave the order to destroy Lightning at the next race! Mater tried to leave and warn his friend, but his disguise disappeared! Luckily, he escaped using his new spy gear.

When Mater finally arrived at the race track, he saw Lightning surrounded by a crowd. Lightning thought he could hear Mater calling to him, and turned to look for his friend. But before Lightning could spot him, the Lemons pulled Mater away.

The next thing the tow truck knew, he, Finn and Holley were tied up inside a giant clock called Big Bentley! They were in London, England, the location of the final race! How would Mater save Lightning now...?

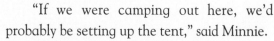

The Overnight Camp-In

I guess we won't be able to camp after all," said Minnie. "The ground is wet from rain."

"Wait a minute!" said Mickey. "Maybe we can't have a campout. But we can still have a camp-in! Let's get Mouseketools!"

The Mouseketools were: Four neckties, a torch, a windup music box and the Mystery Mouseketool. Everyone moved the furniture out of the way and made a big clearing in the middle of the room.

"Okay," said Daisy. "Let's get this camp-in started. Hmmm, what's the first thing we would do if we were outdoors?"

"I always like to smell the fresh air," said Minnie.

"That's a great idea, Minnie!" said Mickey. He put a big bouquet of flowers near the fan. Then he turned on the fan. Everyone closed their eyes. They took deep breaths.

"It smells like the outdoors," said Daisy. "But I wish it sounded more like the outdoors, too."

"Maybe a Mouseketool can help!" said Mickey. "The music box makes sounds! We've got ears! Say cheers!" Mickey wound the music box. Instead of playing music, it made noises that sounded like nature.

"If we were camping out here, we'd probably be setting up the tent," said Minnie.

"Let's do it!" said Mickey. "We can set up the tent inside!" They untied the tent.

"How can we make the tent stand up?" said Daisy. "We can't stick the spikes into the floor the way we would into the ground!"

"I guess we need another Mouseketool," said Mickey. "Four neckties! Neckties are good for tying. We can use them to tie the spikes at the ends of the tent to things around the room."

"It's time for ghost stories!" said Minnie. Everyone sat in a circle by the tent. But it didn't feel spooky enough.

"We need a campfire!" said Daisy. "You can't tell good ghost stories without a campfire."

"Let's get another Mouseketool!" said Mickey. "The torch! We've got ears! Say cheers!" said Mickey.

Minnie turned off the lights. She lit the torch and held it under her chin and told scary stories.

"I guess we should all get ready for bed," Mickey said.

So they did. But before they got into the tent, everyone lay on their backs, looking up at the ceiling and thinking about what a great day they'd had.

Woody Discovers the Truth

Buzz, Jessie and most of Andy's other toys were at the Sunnyside Daycare nursery. They now knew Andy hadn't meant to throw them away – and they just wanted to get back home to him. Woody had already escaped, and been taken home by a little girl called Bonnie, but the rest of the toys were being held prisoner by the evil pink teddy bear, Lotso!

Lotso and his helpers had found Buzz's reset button – and now the space ranger was helping to hold his own friends captive!

Lotso's gang put Andy's toys into wire crates. When Mr Potato Head fought back, Big Baby put him in 'the Box' – a covered sandbox in the playground.

Suddenly, Barbie walked in. "Ken? What are you doing to my friends?" she asked in surprise. When she realized what was happening, she insisted on staying with Andy's toys. And so, she became a prisoner, too.

"We've got a way of doing things here at Sunnyside," Lotso explained. "Life here can be a dream come true. But if you break the rules..." He threw Woody's hat, which he had found, onto the floor.

The toys gasped. "What did you do to him?" cried Jessie. Lotso simply chuckled and left, leaving the captives under Buzz's guard.

Meanwhile, Woody had discovered that Bonnie lived just blocks from Andy's house.

"If you guys ever get to Sunnyside Daycare," Woody told Bonnie's toys, "tell them Woody made it home."

"Sunnyside?" Bonnie's toys gasped. Quickly, they took Woody to Chuckles, an old clown toy who knew all about Sunnyside – and Lotso. Long ago, Chuckles explained, he, Lotso and Big Baby had belonged to a little girl named Daisy. One day, the toys were accidentally left behind during a trip. Lotso led them on a long journey home, but when they arrived, Daisy had a new pink bear. Heartbroken, Lotso turned to Big Baby and ripped off the pendant with Daisy's name. Eventually, the three ended up at Sunnyside, but Lotso had never stopped being angry. He controlled the nursery with cruelty, and Andy's toys were in danger.

Woody was worried. He wanted to get back to Andy, but he couldn't leave his friends. He had to go back to and rescue them!

The next day, Woody hitched a ride back to Sunnyside in Bonnie's bag. He sneaked into the Caterpillar Room and looked for his friends. What he saw was horrid – his friends were getting beaten up by toddlers! He had to save them.

The New Neigh-bour

Pegasus grazed peacefully outside the house where Hercules and Meg lived. Now that Hercules was a mortal and not a god, life was a little quieter than it used to be. This morning, however, there was some excitement in the village. Some new neighbours were moving in.

"Let's go over and make them feel at home," Hercules told Meg. They gathered some flowers and headed over to meet them.

A little while later, Pegasus heard a soft whinnying. He turned to discover a beautiful mare approaching him. His heart soared. But then Pegasus remembered the time that Pain and Panic had disguised themselves as a filly and captured him. He was determined not to fall for their trick a second time. He spread his wings and charged, shooing the horse down the hill.

The mare raced past Meg and Herc as they returned home. "Pegasus, what are you doing?" asked Meg. "That's no way to make our neighbours' horse feel welcome." Pegasus gulped. The beautiful horse who had tried to meet him really *was* a beautiful horse!

"If I were you, I'd get over there and try and make it up to her," suggested Hercules.

Within minutes, Pegasus pranced across the neighbours' field, stopped in front of the mare and struck a noble pose. He doubted any filly would be able to resist a stallion as handsome as himself. The lovely horse was unimpressed. She turned so that her tail swished right in Pegasus's face! Herc's horse knew he would have to do something amazing to impress this beauty. He flapped his wings and rose into the air. Then he dipped and swooped and somersaulted across the sky. When the filly started to walk away, he flew alongside her – and crashed right into a tree!

Hercules was watching from the hillside. Pegasus certainly does need some help, he thought.

Meg had an idea. "The right gift might convince that mare to forgive him," she said. She piled a basket high with apples and oats and tied a huge red ribbon around it.

But, when Pegasus went over to deliver the gift, holding the basket handle in his teeth, the female horse kicked it over. Then the mare whinnied and stomped, letting Pegasus know exactly what she thought of him.

Finally, Pegasus realized what he had to do. He sheepishly walked over to the filly with his head bowed. Then he gently nudged her with his muzzle. She neighed and nuzzled him back. All she had wanted was for Pegasus to say he was sorry. Now she understood that even though he was a bit of a birdbrain, her new friend had a good heart.

Late for Supper

Widow Tweed filled the large baking pan with meat and vegetables, then rolled out a flaky crust and set it on top. After crimping the pie's edges, she slipped the pan into the oven. "Chicken pie," she said. "Tod's favourite!"

Humming to herself, she washed the dishes in the sink and tidied up the cottage. Then, she set the table with her best tablecloth and dishes. She added a special milk saucer for Tod.

Widow Tweed looked out of the window and noticed that the sun was setting. "I wonder where that clever little devil has got to," she said.

She watched the sun sink behind the rolling forest hills, then sat down and picked up her knitting. She had a project to finish. Besides, the pie should be ready soon, and Tod was never late for supper.

"Knit one, purl two, knit one, purl two," the Widow said quietly as she put the finishing touches on a soft blanket she was knitting for Tod's bed. She knew the little fox had a fur coat of his own, but everybody liked something cosy to lie on when they curled up to go to sleep.

The smell of chicken pie drifted past her nose, and the Widow got up to take it out of the oven. The crust was golden brown, and the creamy sauce was bubbling around the edges.

She set it on the counter just as she heard a scratching at the door.

"Right on time, as usual," she said as she opened the door. "Dinner's ready, Tod."

But Tod wasn't there. The scratching had just been a small twig blown against the door by the wind. "Tod?" the Widow called, peering into the darkness. "No playing tricks now." But the little red fox did not appear.

The sky was dark now. A few clouds drifted across the moon. The Widow shivered. "Oh, Tod," she said. "Where are you?"

Stepping back into the house, she pulled on her shoes and a sweater. She'd just have to go out to look for him. After lighting an old kerosene lantern, she opened the door for a second time – and nearly tripped over the red fox on her front porch. He sat there quietly, a colourful bouquet of wildflowers at his feet.

"Oh, Tod!" she cried. She picked up the bouquet and scooped him into her arms. "You sweetie pie."

Tod nuzzled the Widow's neck as she carried him into the house and deposited him on his chair at the kitchen table. Soon, the two were sharing a delicious feast of chicken pie. And, after supper, the Widow admired her bouquet above the mantel while Tod curled up in his bed with his cosy new blanket.

The Four-legged Festival

Quasimodo was a kind young man who was always quick to offer help to anyone in need. He was especially drawn to those who were alone in the world. After spending years confined to the bell tower of the cathedral, Quasimodo knew just how terrible loneliness could feel.

It wasn't surprising, then, that Quasimodo had a growing collection of orphaned animals. First he had taken in a stray kitten, and then an abandoned puppy. Next he adopted a lamb, an old donkey, a baby bird and an ox. Esmeralda and Phoebus helped him build a pen. But they weren't sure how he could afford to continue feeding so many pets. "I'll find a way – somehow," Quasimodo told the couple. "They're counting on me!"

The Festival of Fools was coming up, and Quasimodo was a little worried about how his pets would react to all the noise and excitement. "While you're helping Clopin with his puppet show at the festival," said Esmeralda, "why don't we have Djali keep an eye on the animals?" Djali was Esmeralda's clever little goat. He was used to crowds, and often danced with Esmeralda in the village square.

"Why, thank you, Esmeralda!" replied Quasimodo. "That's a wonderful idea."

The day of the festival arrived. Esmeralda brought Djali and put him inside the pen with the other animals. The square quickly filled with people wearing costumes and masks. Delicious smells drifted through the air from the sellers' stands. The animals pushed at the sides of the pen, wanting to investigate the new smells and sounds. Djali also wanted to join the fun. He nibbled at the latch of the pen and the gate flew open.

Djali heard the tinkling of Esmeralda's tambourine on the far side of the square and ran towards the sound. The other animals followed – even as the goat crashed through a stall full of masks for sale! Everyone turned to see the animals, which were now disguised as jesters and kings, songbirds and queens. The masked animals danced right past Clopin's puppet wagon and onto Esmeralda's stage. Quasimodo watched in amazement as Djali and the others joined in the gypsy's merry dance. The crowds cheered and showered the performers with coins.

When the show ended, Esmeralda climbed down from the stage and delivered the money to Quasimodo. "This should take care of whatever food you need to buy," she said happily.

Quasimodo felt like dancing for joy – but he decided to leave that to the animals!

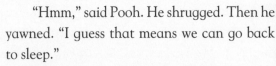

The Sleepover

"Comfortable, Piglet?" Pooh asked. The two friends were having a best-friend sleepover.

"Oh, yes," Piglet replied. "Goodnight Pooh Bear."

Piglet lay in the darkness of Pooh's room. Although, the darkness at Pooh's house was much, much darker than it was at Piglet's house. Then he noticed it was much quieter than Piglet's own room at night.

"Pooh Bear?" Piglet whispered. There was no answer. He heard a soft, low rumbling. It was curiously similar to the sound of a sleeping bear snoring. The sound grew louder and then softer, over and over again! *Was it the sound of an approaching heffalump?* Piglet wondered.

"Oh dear!" Piglet shouted, running to Pooh's bed. "Wake up! P-p-please, P-P-Pooh!"

"Hmm?" Pooh said drowsily, sitting up. Piglet was hiding under the covers in Pooh's bed.

"Why, Piglet," said Pooh. "What's the matter?"

"It's that horrible n-n-noise, Pooh," he stammered. Piglet listened for the noise, then realized he couldn't hear it.

"That's funny," said Piglet. "The noise stopped as soon as you woke up, Pooh."

"Hmm," said Pooh. He shrugged. Then he yawned. "I guess that means we can go back to sleep."

"Pooh Bear," said Piglet timidly, "I don't mean to be a bad best friend. But could we, well, have the rest of our sleepover another night? I'm just used to sleeping in my own house."

Pooh put his arm around Piglet. "I understand, Piglet," he said.

Pooh helped Piglet gather his things, then hand in hand, they walked to Piglet's house.

Piglet was happy to be at his own house. "Thank you so much for understanding," he said. "I suppose you'll need to get home to bed now?"

"That does sound like the thing to do," Pooh replied. "But first I might sit down for a little rest."

While Piglet put away his things, Pooh sat down in the chair.

By the time Piglet came back, Pooh was making a soft, low rumbling sound. But in the comfort of his own house, it did not strike Piglet as anything other than the sound of one sleeping bear snoring.

"Sweet dreams, Pooh Bear," he whispered. Piglet climbed into his own bed and drifted off to sleep. It seemed that he and Pooh were having their best-friend sleepover, after all.

An Uncle Mickey Day

Morty and Ferdie Mouse were oh-so-very excited. Today was their number one favourite kind of day. An Uncle Mickey day! That meant their Uncle Mickey was going to take them out to do all kinds of special, surprising things.

"Uncle Mickey!" the twins shouted when he came to pick them up. "What are we doing today?"

"What *aren't* we doing today, you mean," said Mickey. "I thought we'd start with bowling."

"Hooray!" cheered Morty and Ferdie.

At the bowling alley, Morty and Ferdie discovered that if they rolled the bowling ball together, they could knock at least four or five pins down every time.

Then it was off to the park for some hide-and-seek and a game of catch. Uncle Mickey didn't mind being the finder in hide-and-seek every time. And he didn't mind chasing the balls that Ferdie sometimes threw way, way over his head.

"I'm hungry," said Morty when at last they stopped to rest.

"Me, too," said Ferdie.

"How about some pizza?" suggested Mickey.

"Okay!" the twins shouted together.

At the pizza parlour, Mickey let Morty and Ferdie choose their favourite toppings. Morty picked pepperoni. Ferdie picked black olives. Mickey, meanwhile, had his usual: extra cheese!

"All finished?" asked Mickey. "We'll have to hurry if we're going to go to the carnival."

"All right!" the boys shouted.

After the carnival, where they each won a prize, the boys told Mickey what a great day it had been.

"Well, it's not over yet," Mickey told them.

"Really?" said Morty.

"What's next?" asked Ferdie.

That's when Mickey held up three tickets – and a mitt. A baseball game! Oh, wow!

There was nothing in the whole, wide world that Mickey's nephews liked better than baseball games . . . and popcorn . . . and peanuts . . . and ice cream. And to make things even better, Uncle Mickey caught a foul ball, and their favourite team won. They even watched fireworks at the end of the game.

"Wow, Uncle Mickey! Thank you so much!" said the twins when they finally returned home, tired and full and very, very happy. "This has been one of the best Uncle Mickey days ever!"

"Oh, this was nothing," said Uncle Mickey. "Just wait until next time!"

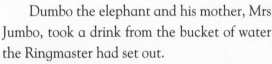

DUMBO
Lend Me Your Ears

"I think I can, I think I can, I think I can," chugged Casey Jr, the circus train. The train moved slowly around a bend. "I think I can. I think I . . . *Ah-choo!*" he sneezed. Suddenly, he came to a halt. "I know I can't," he admitted finally. The animals and the performers poked their heads out, wondering what was wrong.

"Well?" asked the Ringmaster.

"Casey Jr here has a cold," the engineer replied. "He's going to need some rest before he can take us any further."

The Ringmaster frowned. "But we're due at the fairground in a few hours. What will we do? After all, the show must go on!"

The engineer just shrugged and turned his attention back to the sneezing, coughing and spluttering little engine.

The Ringmaster went down the train, swinging open the doors to all the cages and cars. "Come on, everyone," he said. "Might as well stretch your legs."

The animals lumbered, scampered and pranced onto the wide open field. Next, the clowns and acrobats and animal trainers sauntered out. Some set up crates in the grass and played cards, others rehearsed and a few pulled out packed lunches and sprawled on the ground.

Dumbo the elephant and his mother, Mrs Jumbo, took a drink from the bucket of water the Ringmaster had set out.

Mrs Jumbo gazed around. "Looks like we're in the middle of nowhere," she said. "I do hope poor Casey Jr is feeling better soon."

"Me too," Dumbo's friend Timothy Q. Mouse said hopefully.

Just then a clap of thunder sounded. Raindrops began to fall from the sky. The animals and performers ran for the shelter of the circus wagons. Dumbo held on to his mother's tail, but just as they were about to board, the wind picked up. The gust caught Dumbo's huge ears and sent him flying backwards.

"That's it!" yelled the Ringmaster over the howling wind. "Dumbo, come with me!" He led Dumbo over to the train, climbed onto the front wagon, and motioned for the little elephant to join him.

"Now spread out those great ears of yours!" the Ringmaster said. Dumbo's ears billowed out, catching the wind like giant sails and pushing Casey Jr along the tracks. "The show will go on!" the Ringmaster shouted happily.

"I know I can. I know I can. I know I can," chanted Casey Jr. And then he added, "Thanks to Dumbo!"

Nemo's Best Shot

"Come on, Dad! We're going to be late!" cried Nemo.

Nemo and Marlin were hurrying through the busy swimming lanes of the colourful Great Barrier Reef.

"Are you sure you want to play pearl volleyball?" Marlin asked nervously. "There are lots of other things you can do. Sponge jumping, for example. Or maybe reef dancing."

"Reef dancing!" cried Nemo, horrified. "No way! That's for babies! I want to play pearl volleyball!"

After they arrived at Sea Urchin Stadium, Mr Ray gave the opening announcements. "Hello and welcome, everyone! Before we get started, let's give a big thank you to Ms Esther Clam for donating today's ball."

Everyone applauded as Esther opened her shell and spat out the pearl.

"Let's play pearl volleyball!" cried Mr Ray.

"Good luck, son," said Marlin. "Just remember what I told you – "

"I know! I know!" said Nemo, rolling his eyes. "When you give it your best shot, even if you lose, you win."

The players lined up on either side of the sea fan net. Ray's Raiders were on one side, and Nemo's team, the Fighting Planktons, were on the other.

Marlin watched anxiously. He was sure that Nemo wouldn't be able to play as well as the other fish because of his small fin.

Marlin wasn't the only one who had doubts. Turbot Trout sidled up to Nemo on the court.

"Coach may be letting you play today," Turbot snapped, "but you better not mess up the Planktons' winning streak."

Nemo narrowed his eyes. Turbot didn't know that Nemo had spent many hours smacking around pebbles in a dentist's office aquarium.

"Just watch and learn," murmured Nemo.

Suddenly, the pearl came right to Nemo. *Smack!*

Using his good left fin, Nemo sent the pearl flying right over the net. The pearl flew so fast, the other team couldn't return it. Nemo scored his first point for the Planktons!

Nemo played like a pro. He scored again with his good fin, then with his tail. And, just to show his father and Turbot Trout, he scored the winning point with his little fin.

"Go, short fin!" cried Turbot Trout. "With a player like you, we're going to go all the way to the Lobster Bowl Clam-pionship!"

"Wow, Nemo," said Marlin after the game. "That was amazing."

"Thanks, Dad," said Nemo. "I gave it my best shot, like you said. And we actually won too!"

THE
LION KING

The Hic-hic-hiccups

"What a day!" Pumbaa said as he led Simba and Timon through the forest.

"What a day, indeed," Timon agreed.

"*Hic!*" said Simba.

"What was that?" Timon cried.

"Don't be scared. It's just that I have the – *hic!* I have the hiccups," Simba explained.

"I'll tell you what to do," Timon said. "Forget about it! They'll go away – eventually."

"Forget about it? *Hic!* But I can't roar," Simba explained. And to demonstrate, he opened his mouth really wide. But, just as he was about to roar, he hiccupped! "See?" he said sadly.

"Have you tried licking tree bark?" Pumbaa asked.

"Licking tree bark?" said Simba.

"It always works for me," Pumbaa explained. "That or closing your eyes, holding your nose and jumping on one foot while saying your name five times fast – backwards."

Timon watched Simba hop around on one foot, holding his nose with his eyes closed. "Abmis, Abmis, Abmis – *hic!* It's not working!" Simba cried.

"Maybe there's something caught in his throat," Timon offered.

"There's nothing caught in his throat," Pumbaa said.

"How do you know?" Timon asked.

"I just know about these things," Pumbaa answered.

Suddenly, right on cue, Simba interrupted their argument with the biggest hiccup of all.

"*HIC!*"

And, wouldn't you know, just then the biggest fly you've ever seen came soaring out of Simba's mouth. It flew right into a tree and crashed to the ground. The fly stood up groggily and shook itself off.

"It's about time, buddy!" the fly said to Simba.

Simba was about to reply, but he was interrupted by two voices, shouting in unison –

"DINNER!"

The fly gave a frightened squeak and flew off, as Timon and Pumbaa both pounced on the spot where it had been just a moment earlier.

Peter Pan
Where's Tink?

Peter Pan was in a hurry to meet Tinker Bell. (Because you know how Tinker Bell gets if you keep her waiting.) Today they had a date for a game of tag.

"Tink!" he called as he arrived at his hideout. He took off his hat and placed it on the table. "I'm home!"

But there was no reply.

How strange, thought Peter. Tinker Bell was never late. He called her name again as loudly as he could. But still no answer. He started to worry.

"Wake up! Wake up!" he shouted to the Lost Boys, who were napping in hammocks. "Tinker Bell is missing!"

"Tinker Bell?" Cubby yawned. "I know I saw her flying around here this morning."

"Yeah," said Rabbit. "She helped me fix my slingshot."

"Well, she's not here now," said Peter.

"Where would she go?" asked Tootles.

Peter thought for a moment. He knew that Tinker Bell liked to fly around Never Land. And she especially liked paying visits to other fairies. But not when she had a game of tag to play with Peter. No, that was not like Tinker Bell at all.

"The question," Peter Pan finally declared, "is not where would she go, but who could have taken her!"

"Oooh . . ." the Lost Boys shuddered.

"Do you mean . . ." the Raccoon Twins began.

"Indians?" finished Peter. "I certainly do. I can see it right now. While you were sleeping, a whole band crept in and stole our Tinker Bell away."

Then Slightly spoke up. "Or what if it was . . ."

"Pirates!" cried Peter. "Of course! Those dirty, rotten scoundrels! It would be just like them to lure Tinker Bell outside, ambush her and kidnap her and hold her for ransom! They probably have her chained up in the deep, dark hold of their ship at this very moment!

"Men!" Peter cried. "We can't just stand here while Tinker Bell suffers in the grimy hands of bloodthirsty pirates – in mortal danger! I hereby declare that a rescue mission be formed at once. Are you with me?"

"Hoorah! Hoorah!" the boys cheered.

"Then let's go!" said Peter. And with that, he grabbed his hat and–

Ring-a-ling! Ring! Ring! Rrrring!

"Tink!" Peter exclaimed as his missing (and furious!) friend shot up into the air. "Where have you been? You had me worried sick!"

Tinker Bell just jingled angrily at Peter. She hadn't been kidnapped. She'd been trapped under Peter's hat the whole time!

Mater Saves the Day

Two British secret agents, Finn and Holley, had mistaken Mater for an American secret agent, and he was helping them track the activities of a criminal, Professor Z. The professor was blowing up racecars that used the new alternative fuel, Allinol, so that everyone would go back to using oil. This would mean the Lemons – bad cars who ran the oil reserves – would be rich and powerful!

Lightning McQueen was taking part in the World Grand Prix, and races had already taken place in Japan and Italy. Lightning and Mater had argued after the first race. Mater had left to go home, but instead he had gone with Finn and Holley – now the three of them were tied up inside a huge clock called Big Bentley in London!

Professor Z's goons, Grem and Acer, told Mater that they had planted a bomb inside Lightning's pit at the final race. Lightning was using Allinol, so they wanted to blow him up. After the pair left, Mater escaped and rushed to save his friend. Finn and Holley soon broke free, too. Then they realized the bomb was actually on Mater!

As Mater arrived at the pits, Finn radioed the tow-truck to tell him the bomb was on him. Mater tried to leave the pits to save his friend, but Lightning was so happy to see Mater, he hooked himself onto his buddy. Mater rocketed off before Professor Z could set off the bomb.

Holley flew off to help Mater, while Finn went after Professor Z. Finn captured the Professor with cables!

Back in the streets of London, Grem and Acer were about to crash into Mater and Lightning. Holley rammed into the bad cars, who went flying into the air! Finn arrived with Professor Z and ordered him to deactivate the bomb on Mater. Professor Z told Finn that only the one who activated the bomb could turn it off – and that was not the Professor.

Other Lemons arrived to get rid of Finn, Holley, Mater and Lightning for good. But the Radiator Springs crew came to the rescue!

Just then, Mater figured out who the Lemons' Big Boss must be. He flew straight to Buckingham Palace with Lightning attached to his tow hook! Mater explained that Miles Axlerod had invented Allinol and made it look dangerous so everyone would go back to using gas. Then Axlerod and all the Lemons who owned the supply of oil would get rich! Axlerod was trapped, and had no choice but to deactivate the bomb. Mater had saved the day! No one was prouder of him than Lightning.

The Great Escape

Buzz, Jessie and most of Andy's other toys were trapped at Sunnyside Daycare. Woody had escaped, but had come back after hearing an evil bear named Lotso controlled the nursery. Woody had crept inside the room where his friends were trapped and watched as they got played with roughly by toddlers. He was shocked!

RIIING!!! RIIING!!! A toy telephone sidled up to Woody. The cowboy picked up the receiver and heard, "You and your friends aren't ever getting out of here now." Lotso kept tabs on everyone, the phone said. The only time toys left was when they were thrown out. The telephone said there was a toy monkey who, whenever he spotted an escaping toy, screeched until the toy was caught.

After the kids went out to play, Woody came out of hiding. The others told him about Lotso's cruelty, and Buzz's strange behaviour – Lotso had reset Buzz, and he didn't recognize his own friends anymore. They also gave Woody back his hat that he had left behind.

"Oh, Woody," said Jessie, "we were wrong to leave Andy."

"It's my fault for leaving you guys," he replied. "From now on, we stick together."

But Jessie knew Woody needed to get home before Andy left for college.

Woody nodded. "We're busting out of here tonight." He pointed out the window. The rubbish chute would be their escape route!

That night, the toys put a complicated escape plan into action. Some of the toys distracted Buzz, which gave Woody and Slinky a chance to surprise the Monkey – and grab the nursery keys.

Barbie forced Ken to confess that Buzz had been reset to 'demo' mode. Then Mr Potato Head distracted Big Baby, which gave the toys a chance to capture Buzz. Then, Mr Potato Head's parts escaped and attached themselves to a tortilla! He kept a lookout while Jessie and the others got the keys from Slinky, allowing everyone to slip into the playground!

Barbie found Buzz's instruction manual. Then she, Woody and Slinky held Buzz down while Hamm found the instructions to reset the space ranger. Suddenly, Buzz beeped – and began speaking Spanish! There was no time to figure out what had happened. They hustled Buzz out the door and into the playground. When Buzz saw Jessie, he dropped to his knees: "Mi florecita del desierto!"

"Did you fix Buzz?" asked Jessie, confused.

"Sort of," Woody replied.

Would Buzz ever get back to normal?

Patch's Plan

"Whoa!" Patch said, "Look at all these other puppies!"

His brothers and sisters were still whimpering with fear. They had just been dognapped and, after a long, bumpy ride in a car, they had arrived at a big, draughty house. But Patch was already trying to work out a way to get back home. He looked around the large shabby room. "Hey," he asked the closest stranger. "Where are we?"

The spotted puppy smiled at him. "Oh, you must be new!" he said. "Which pet shop did you come from?"

Patch scowled at the strange new puppy. "We're not from a pet shop – we were stolen from our house."

Several other puppies heard him and moved closer. "Stolen? Really?" they exclaimed.

The first puppy shrugged. "Well, bought or stolen, we're all stuck here now."

"Maybe *you're* stuck here," Patch said boldly. "Our parents and their human pets will be here soon to rescue us, just see if they don't!"

"I hope so," Patch's sister Pepper said. "I wonder why someone would want to steal us, anyway?"

Patch didn't know. But he was sure that their parents would find them soon. In the meantime, he wanted to make sure he and his siblings stayed well away from all the pet-shop puppies, so there wasn't any confusion.

"We don't know why there are so many of us," the strange puppy told Pepper. "I guess Cruella just really likes puppies."

Patch gasped aloud. "Cruella?" he cried. "Do you mean Cruella De Vil?"

His brothers and sisters shuddered. Their parents had told them scary stories about that nasty woman. Could it be true?

"Yes, she's the one who bought us," several of the other puppies spoke up, while others nodded their heads.

This changed everything! "We have to get away," Patch declared.

Rolly sighed. "We know," he said. "Mum and Dad will be here soon. I just hope we get home in time for breakfast . . . ."

"No, you don't understand!" Patch shook his head. "Cruella is bad news – that's what Dad always says. We have to get away from her now – all of us!" He gestured to the entire group of puppies, bought and stolen. It didn't matter where they'd come from. What mattered was they were in this mess together. "We have to work as a team."

The first puppy smiled at him. "I'm with you!" he exclaimed. "When we're done with her, Cruella will be seeing spots!"

First Day of School

It was the first day of a brand-new school year for Nemo and his friends.

"Hey, Tad! Hey, Pearl!" called Nemo as he swam into the playground. "Isn't it great to be back at school?"

"Well," said Tad, "I wouldn't go *that* far."

"What do you mean?" asked Nemo. "It's gonna be awesome! I heard this year we get to learn how to subtract and speak Prawn."

"Sure," said Tad, "but did you also hear who's gonna be teaching us all that?"

"No," said Nemo. "Who?"

Just then, up swam Sheldon, Jimmy and Jib.

"Hey, Sheldon," Tad called out. "Why don't you tell Nemo here about our new teacher, Mrs Lobster?"

"Mrs Lobster?" said Nemo.

"Yeah," said Sheldon. "Ooooh, they say she's the worst!"

"Who says she's the worst?" asked Nemo.

"Well, Sandy Plankton, for one. He says his cousin, Krill, had her last year – and that she was so mean, he'll never go to school again!"

"And you know what I heard from Sandy," said Tad. "I heard she has these great big claws, and that she uses them to grab students real hard when they give the wrong answer!"

"Oh!" said Pearl. "Don't say that. You're going to make me ink!"

"Yeah," said Nemo. "That sounds awful!"

"I know," said Jimmy. "Sandy says Mrs Lobster never goes on field trips like Mr Ray did. And she sends you home with tons of homework, and makes you stay after school if you forget to bring it in the next day!"

Oh, no! Nemo shuddered. All summer long he'd been looking forward to this day. And now school hadn't even started yet and already he wished it would end!

"Don't look now," Sheldon whispered, "but I think she's coming!"

"I'm gonna ink!" whimpered Pearl.

Nemo shut his eyes and wished with all his might for his dad to come and take him back home . . . .

"Hello there," said a warm voice. "You must be my new pupils! I'm Mrs Lobster."

Huh? thought Nemo. Surely, this wasn't the Mrs Lobster the kids had been talking about. And yet, when he opened his eyes, there she was, taking the register.

"Jib, Jimmy, Nemo, Pearl, Sheldon, Tad . . . my, what a smart-looking class. I do hope you kids are ready to have fun."

Nemo sighed. That silly Sandy Plankton – they should know by now not to believe everything he said. Because now Nemo was pretty sure: this was going to be a great year, after all!

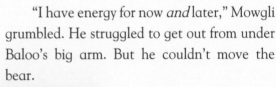

Mowgli's Nap

Mowgli leaned forward for a better look. When Baloo yawned, you could almost see his tonsils. The big bear closed his gaping mouth and blinked sleepily.

"Am I ever sleepy." Baloo stretched, leaned against a tree trunk and scratched his back as he slid to the ground. "I think it must be time for an after- noon snooze."

"Good thinking, my friend." High above them, stretched out on a branch, Bagheera the panther dan- gled a limp paw. His golden eyes were half closed in the heat of the day.

"A nap? Not for me!" Mowgli shook his mop of dark hair. "I'm not tired."

"Now, hold on a second there," Baloo said. "Don't you want to go hunting with us after it cools off? You're going to need energy."

"I have plenty of energy," Mowgli insisted. "I have energy right now!" He started to walk away from the bear, but Baloo stretched out a paw and grabbed the boy's ankle.

"Not so fast," Baloo said.

"You may have energy but, if you use it now, you will not have it to use later," Bagheera said wisely.

"Listen to the cat." Baloo yawned. "He knows what he's talking about." And with that, Baloo pulled Mowgli onto a pile of leaves and held him down with one great paw.

"I have energy for now *and* later," Mowgli grumbled. He struggled to get out from under Baloo's big arm. But he couldn't move the bear.

"Good nap, Man-cub," Bagheera purred at the scowling Mowgli.

A moment later, the panther and the bear were sleeping soundly. As soon as Mowgli heard their snores he hoisted up the arm that was pinning him down.

"Good nap, yourself," Mowgli whispered. And he tiptoed off to swing in the trees and drop sticks on the animals below.

Baloo's snores shook the jungle for an hour, perhaps two, before Mowgli returned to the shady napping spot again. He'd had a grand time in the treetops, but the sun and the swinging had tired him. The great grey bear looked so soft and peaceful lying against the tree that Mowgli could not help himself. He curled up against his friend and closed his eyes.

Not two minutes later, Bagheera awoke and stretched his inky paws. The panther flicked his tail under Baloo's nose.

"I'm up. I'm up and ready to go!" Baloo sat upright. Then, spying Mowgli, the bear gave the boy a good shake. "How about you, Man- cub? You awake?"

But the only sound that came from Mowgli's mouth was a loud snore.

Homework Helper

Stitch didn't care for weekdays much now that Lilo was back in school. To Stitch they were the longest and most boring days of the week, spent waiting . . . and waiting for Lilo to come home.

And so you can imagine Stitch's excitement when three o'clock finally rolled around and Lilo's school bus dropped her off.

"Lilo!" Stitch would shriek, racing down to meet her. "Play time! Play time! Lilo and Stitch play time!" And, usually, Lilo would toss her backpack onto the porch and they would hop on her trike.

But then, one day, Lilo didn't drop her backpack. And she didn't run after Stitch. "Sorry, Stitch," was all she said. "My teacher says if I don't start doing my homework, she's going to have a talk with Nani!" And Lilo certainly didn't want that to happen! Her sister had enough to worry about – and so did Lilo.

And so, with that, Lilo went inside her house, took out her schoolbooks, and sat down at the dining-room table to study.

Stitch didn't understand. "Homework?" he said, peeking into Lilo's backpack. "What's that?"

"Homework," said Lilo, "is maths problems and a book report and a week's worth of spelling words that I have one day to learn! Now please, Stitch, be a good alien and shoo."

But Stitch wasn't about to give up so soon.

He was back in less than a minute with a basket full of Lilo's favourite action figures.

"You've got to be kidding," said Lilo. "I am not playing superheroes. Can't you see I'm busy?!"

"Noogy Bay!" muttered Stitch. This was very frustrating! But Stitch loved a challenge. Off he ran again. And this time he came back wearing a catcher's mask and vest, carrying a baseball, a bat and Lilo's glove.

"Play ball!" Stitch shouted.

And, for a second there, Lilo almost got up. Then she shook her head. "No, Stitch," she sighed. "If I don't start these spelling words now, I'll never finish them tonight."

Stitch thought for a second, then dashed off once again. Lilo could hear all sorts of banging and slamming coming from her room. It sounded as though Stitch was turning it upside down! Oh, great, she thought to herself. But at least he's leaving me alone . . . .

Then, to Lilo's surprise, Stitch once more appeared before her, carrying a book of crossword puzzles under his arm.

"Lilo play *and* spell words!" Stitch cheerfully told her.

"Why didn't I think of that!" said Lilo. "Stitch, you can help me with my homework any time!"

My Heart Belongs to Daisy

Andy's toys were escaping from Sunnyside Daycare, and from an evil bear, Lotso. They wanted to get back home to Andy, before he left home for college.

Together, the friends crept past Big Baby and across the playground. Quickly, the group headed over to the tool shed... and the rubbish chute.

Woody climbed into the chute and slid down into the dark. When he stopped, he was outside – the sky above and a huge bin full of rubbish below. "Come on down!" he called.

Once all the toys had arrived, Slinky formed a bridge between the chute and the lid of the huge bin. But suddenly, Lotso appeared! He kicked Slinky's paws off the bin's lid.

The toy telephone wheeled into view and joined Lotso and his gang. The bear had forced him to reveal Woody's escape plan! "I'm sorry, Cowboy," the phone said. He looked bruised and battered. "They broke me!"

As the groups stood and looked at each other, a rubbish truck turned into the alley. The toys could hear it rumbling towards them.

"Why don't you come back and join our family again?" Lotso asked the toys.

"You're a liar and a bully and I'd rather rot in this dumpster than join any family of yours!" Jessie replied.

Lotso scowled. "I didn't throw you away," he replied. "Your kid did. There isn't one kid who ever loved a toy, really."

"What about Daisy?" Woody asked. "She lost you. By accident."

Woody had found out that Lotso had once belonged to a little girl called Daisy, but he'd been replaced when he'd got lost. Woody held up the old pendant a clown called Chuckles – who had also belonged to Daisy – had given him. It read: "My heart belongs to DAISY."

Lotso was stunned. "Where did you get that?" he demanded.

"She loved you Lotso," declared Woody. "As much as any kid ever loved a toy!" He threw the pendant across the huge bin, where it landed at Lotso's feet.

"She never loved me!" Lotso exploded. "She left me! Love means being together forever or it isn't love!"

Lotso's gang stared at him in disbelief. They had never seen Lotso so angry and upset. Big Baby stepped towards the pendant and picked it up. His eyes filled with tears and his lip trembled. "Mama!" he cried – Big Baby had also once belonged to Daisy. She had loved her toys as much as Andy loved Woody, Buzz and the rest of his toys. Now would Lotso let Andy's toys go home?

300

Disney Pinocchio
Boy's Best Friend

Like all little boys, Pinocchio wanted a puppy. And, like all little boys, he promised to feed it and walk it and do everything and anything required to care for it.

"Puppies are a lot of work," Geppetto told his son. "And puppies like to chew things, like slippers – and wood." The toy maker glanced over at the rows and rows of wooden toys on his workbench. "No, I don't think a dog is a good idea," he said finally.

That afternoon, when Pinocchio returned from school, Geppetto had a present waiting. The boy wasted no time in opening the box. "It's a dog," Pinocchio said, trying to hide his disappointment. "A wooden dog." Not wanting to hurt Geppetto's feelings, Pinocchio thanked his father and placed the toy on his bed.

A few days later, as Pinocchio was walking home from school, he heard a puppy whimpering in an alleyway. With a little coaxing, the puppy emerged. "Why, you look just like the wooden dog my father carved for me," Pinocchio said.

Pinocchio wondered what to do. "Well, I can't leave you here all by yourself," he decided. The boy went home and tied the dog to a tree a few doors up the street. Then he sneaked the puppy a bowl of food and went back inside.

After Geppetto had fallen asleep,

Pinocchio slipped outside and scooped up the dog. "Now, you're going to have to be very quiet," he warned.

Once inside, the puppy sprang from Pinocchio's arms and made a dash for Figaro. As the dog bounded after the fleeing cat, they upset chairs and knocked over crockery. "Look out!" cried Pinocchio. Geppetto soon appeared in his night clothes. "What's going on here?" he asked.

"Well," Pinocchio began. Suddenly, the puppy sprang onto Pinocchio's bed, knocking the wooden dog beneath it. Geppetto blinked. The puppy looked just like the toy he had made for his son!

"Could it be?" the toy maker asked. "Pinocchio! You wanted a puppy so much that the Blue Fairy must have turned your toy dog into a real one!"

Pinocchio just picked up the pup and brought it over to meet Geppetto. A day later, when Pinocchio finally found the courage to tell Geppetto the truth, the little puppy was in no danger of becoming an orphan again. "Well," Geppetto said affectionately when he found the pup carrying the wooden dog around the house, "I suppose we have room for two dogs here – especially if one of them walks the other!"

Cruella Sees Spots

Cruella looked around the living room of the old De Vil mansion and rubbed her hands together. The room was full of Dalmatian puppies. Everywhere Cruella looked she saw spots, spots, spots! At last, her dream was coming true! Cackling with glee, Cruella thought back to the day this had all started . . . .

It had begun as a perfectly miserable day. Cruella had been shopping for fur coats all morning and she hadn't found a single thing she liked.

"Too long! Too short! Too black! Too white!" she screeched, knocking an armload of coats out of the shop assistant's hands. "I want something unusual! I want a coat that has never been seen before!"

Cruella stormed out of the shop, slamming the door so hard that the glass cracked. She needed something to cheer her up. Just then she remembered that her old school friend, Anita, lived nearby.

Soon Cruella stood at the door, ringing the buzzer impatiently. She could hear cheerful piano music coming from an open window.

Just then, a pretty brown-haired woman answered the door. Her eyes opened wide when she saw the skinny woman covered in fur standing on her doorstep. "Oh, Cruella!" she cried. "What a surprise!"

"Hello, Anita, darling," Cruella said, walking into the sitting room. At that moment, a tall, thin man strolled down the stairs, smoking a pipe. But, when he caught sight of Cruella, he leaped back in fright!

"Ah, prince charming," Cruella said, smirking at Anita's new husband. Roger scowled. Suddenly something else caught Cruella's eye. Two black-and-white spotted dogs were sitting in the corner of the room.

"And what have we here?" Cruella asked.

"Oh, that's Pongo and Perdita," Anita explained. "They're wonderful pets." But Cruella wasn't looking at the dogs. She was looking at their coats. Their glossy fur wasn't too long or too short. It wasn't too black or too white. Cruella had never seen anything like it before. It was perfect.

"And soon we'll be even happier," Anita went on. "Perdita is going to have puppies!"

"Puppies!" Cruella shrieked. Suddenly she had an idea that made her smile an evil smile.

"Oh, Anita, you have positively made my day. Now, you must call me just as soon as the puppies arrive. I think they are *just* what I have been looking for."

Pongo snarled, but Cruella didn't notice.

"What a perfectly *marvellous* day," Cruella said to herself as she strode out of the door.

. . . And *that* was how it all started.

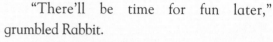

Tigger's Moving Day

After breakfast, Tigger likes to bounce. Sproing! Sproing! Sproing! He likes to bounce all day long, but he is always bumping into things. Thump!

"Tigger, you don't have enough bouncing room in this little house," said Rabbit. "We've got to find you a bigger house. That's all there is to it!"

By evening, everyone was excited about the big new house they had found.

"It IS a bouncy house," said Tigger. "The kind of house tiggers like best!" He bounced, and he didn't bump into anything. "But," he said, sighing, "I won't live next door to little Roo anymore."

"I know you'll miss being neighbours with Kanga and Roo," said Christopher Robin, "but now you'll live much closer to me. We can have fun being neighbours."

Kanga told Tigger she would bring Roo to visit. Tigger felt better and invited everyone to stay awhile. Rabbit put his paws on his hips. "We aren't finished yet. We need to move all your things from your old house to this house," he explained. Rabbit told everyone to bring all the boxes they could find to Tigger's house. Then he told Eeyore to get his donkey cart.

"Wow! Boxes are fun!" cried Roo as he and Tigger bounced in and out of the boxes everyone brought.

"There'll be time for fun later," grumbled Rabbit.

Tigger packed all his games and his stuffed animals in a box. He took his favourite lion out and hugged him. Rabbit packed Tigger's dishes. Kanga packed Tigger's hats and scarves. Pooh and Piglet packed Tigger's food. Soon Eeyore arrived with his donkey cart. Christopher Robin and Owl hoisted Tigger's bed and table and chairs onto the cart.

"Now my new home will be perfect," Tigger said, as they unloaded the cart and carried everything inside. "Thanks for your help, everyone!"

After his friends had gone, Tigger put all his things just where he wanted them. When he was finished, he sat down to rest. Hmmm. Seems like an awfully quiet house, he thought. He tried out a few bounces, but decided he wasn't in such a bouncy mood, after all. But just then, Tigger heard a little voice.

"Hallooo!"

"Roo!" cried Tigger. "Kanga! Come on in!"

"Hallooo! Hallooo!" Tigger soon heard all his friends calling outside his new door. Everyone had brought housewarming presents!

"Our work's all done," said Rabbit. "Now it's time for fun!"

Wild Life

Tod the fox had just arrived at the nature reserve, a vast, beautiful forest where wild animals were protected from hunters. Widow Tweed had brought him there to keep him safe, since her next-door neighbor, Amos Slade, had vowed to hunt him. Amos was angry with the fox because his beloved dog, Chief, had been injured while chasing after him.

At first, Tod didn't understand why his kind owner, Widow Tweed, had left him in the middle of this strange forest, alone and afraid. But she had seemed to be as sad about leaving him as he was about being abandoned.

The first night was dreadful. It had poured with rain and, although he tried to find shelter in different hollows and caves, they were always inhabited by other animals. There was no room for the poor, wet little fox. But the next morning, things began to look up. Tod met a pretty young fox named Vixey. She showed him around the forest, which had many beautiful waterfalls and streams full of fish.

"I think I'm going to like it here, Vixey," said Tod. Having lived his whole life with the Widow Tweed, he had never met another fox before, least of all one as lovely as Vixey.

But Vixey had lived the life of a wild fox, and she knew more about the world than Tod. "You must be very careful, Tod," she warned

him. "Remember, we're foxes, and we have many enemies. You must always be on the alert for danger!"

"Come on, Vixey," scoffed Tod. "We're in a game preserve! I heard the Widow Tweed say that there's no hunting allowed in this forest. What could possibly happen to us here? We don't have a care in the world!"

Suddenly, a huge shadow fell over the two foxes. A look of great fear crossed Vixey's face. Turning around slowly and cautiously, Tod saw why. A huge bear was standing up on its hind legs. And it was staring straight at them!

"Grrrr!" the bear growled.

"Run!" yelled Vixey.

Tod didn't need to be told twice. The two foxes dashed away from the bear, scampering over hills, racing through a hollow tree and jumping over a narrow stream. When they were well away from the bear, they stopped and leaned against a rock, panting hard.

"Okay," Tod said, when he had caught his breath a bit. "I see what you mean about the dangers, Vixey. From now on, I'll be a lot more careful."

"Mmm-hmm," she replied. Then she smiled. "Come on," she said to Tod. "Let's go fishing!"

The Real Adventure

Russell was a Junior Wilderness Explorer, and he had knocked on Carl Fredricksen's door to see if he needed help. Carl had been in a bad mood – he was being forced to move out of his home. He told Russell to find a bird called a Snipe.

Carl had been married to his childhood friend, Ellie. They both dreamed of being explorers and Carl had promised her they'd visit Paradise Falls in South America. But they had never managed to save enough money to go. When Ellie passed away, Carl missed her very much.

Then Carl decided he had to keep his promise and go to Paradise Falls. He tied thousands of balloons to his house and it lifted into the air. He didn't realize that Russell was still on the porch, looking for the Snipe!

Soon the pair landed in South America. They pulled the house along as they walked towards Paradise Falls. Before long, they met a strange bird called Kevin – who was actually a girl – and a talking dog called Dug. There was a whole pack of dogs who were controlled by the great explorer Charles Muntz – he wanted to capture Kevin. Russell and Carl managed to escape with Kevin, but then Charles set Carl's house on fire! Carl couldn't let all his memories of Ellie go up in flames, so he gave up Kevin.

Russell was very upset, because Carl had promised to protect Kevin. They wanted to help her to get back to her babies.

Carl told Russell he no longer needed his help, then he towed the house the rest of the way to Paradise Falls by himself. He placed the house exactly where it appeared in Ellie's drawing of Paradise Falls.

Russell was still angry with Carl. "Here," he said bitterly, throwing his Wilderness Explorer sash on the ground. "I don't want this anymore."

With a sigh, Carl picked up Russell's sash and went into his house. Carl found Ellie's adventure book. He had kept his promise. But he still felt sad. He wished Ellie were there with him.

Carl started to close the book, but something caught his eye. It was a photograph of their wedding day. Carl turned the page. He had never looked through the whole book before. To his astonishment, it was filled with photographs of the two of them over the years. On the last page, there was a message from Ellie:

Thanks for the adventure. Now go and have one of your own.

Carl smiled, realizing that Ellie had got her wish after all. Their life together had been the real adventure.

Big Baby Gets Revenge

Andy's toys were escaping from the Sunnyside Daycare nursery – they wanted to get back home to Andy, before the teenager left home for college. But an evil pink bear, Lotso, had stopped them. Lotso didn't want Andy's toys to leave.

Standing on the edge of a huge rubbish bin, Woody mentioned Daisy. He had found out about Lotso and his sidekick Big Baby's old owner, a little girl who had loved them very much, but had lost them. Big Baby was upset hearing Woody talk about his 'Mama'. Furious, Lotso shoved Big Baby. "What? You want your mummy back? She never loved you!"

The bear turned to Stretch, the octopus, who was standing behind Woody and the others. "Push them all in!" he commanded. "All of them, or you're next!"

But Big Baby was upset. Suddenly, he hoisted Lotso into the air – and threw him into the huge bin! Then Big Baby slammed the lid... and smiled. He'd had enough of Lotso's cruelty. He was ready for a better life.

"Come on! Hurry!" cried Woody, starting to run across the closed lid towards safety. A rubbish truck was on its way to collect the rubbish – including them! The toys followed, and climbed to safety on a wall.

But suddenly, Woody heard a squeak. He turned and saw an Alien caught between the bin lids!

"No one gets left behind!" Woody cried, running back to free his little friend.

Just then, Lotso's paw reached up from the bin and grabbed Woody's leg! Horrified, the toys watched as Woody was yanked down – just as the rubbish truck arrived!

Jessie, Buzz and the rest of Andy's toys fearlessly jumped onto the huge bin lid and tried to pry it open. But the rubbish truck was lifting the entire container and tilting it towards the back of the truck.

The lid swung open, with Woody desperately clinging on.

"Jess!" cried Woody.

"Woody!" Jessie shouted, grabbing the cowboy doll's hand just as Lotso went tumbling past.

But as the huge bin tilted upside down and rubbish rained down on them, Woody and Jessie couldn't hold on any longer.

First Woody, then all the rest of the toys, fell into the back of the rubbish truck, heading for the landfill site!

How were they going to get home to Andy now?

Disney·PIXAR
MONSTERS, INC.

Happy Halloween!

"Boo?" James P. Sullivan whispered, poking his head through the door. "Hey, Boo, are you here? I came to wish you a Happy Halloween. Boo?"

There was no answer. The big, furry blue monster took one step into the quiet bedroom, then another. He saw the familiar mobile dangling from the ceiling. Toys, books and games were put away neatly on the shelves, and the bed was made. But there was no sign of his little human friend.

Sulley sighed, his shoulders slumping. "Oh, well. Guess you're not here right now," he murmured.

He couldn't help feeling disappointed. He'd been looking forward all day to visiting his favourite human child that evening. There was no Halloween in Monstropolis, but Sulley knew that it was the one day of the year when human children actually *liked* being scared. It seemed like a good day for a visit from a monster – especially a friendly monster.

Sulley yawned. It had been a long day on the Laugh Floor at Monsters, Inc. – his best friend, Mike Wazowski, had broken yet another laugh record that afternoon – and Sulley was tired.

"Guess I could just sit down here and wait," he murmured, sitting on the edge of Boo's bed. His eyes drooped. He leaned back on the bed and yawned again.

"Guess I could just rest my eyes for a little . . ." Sulley mumbled as he drifted off to sleep. "*Zzzzz*."

The next thing Sulley knew, a cool breeze was tickling his fur. He felt someone poking him in the foot. "Not yet, Mike," he grunted. "It's too early to get up for work, I– AHHHHH!"

He had just opened his eyes. Instead of Mike's familiar round green body, he saw . . .

"A GHOST!" he shrieked. He leaped up and started to run out of the room to escape the horrifying, flapping white creature standing at the end of the bed. "Oh, nooooooo!"

The ghost giggled. "Kitty?" it said happily.

Sulley stopped in his tracks. "Er, what did you say?"

"Kitty!" the ghost cried again. It reached up, grabbed its ghostly white hood, and pulled it back from its face.

When Sulley saw what was under the hood, he broke into a smile. Suddenly he felt very foolish. He'd completely forgotten that every Halloween, human children dress up in costumes to try to scare each other. It had certainly worked on him!

"Boo!" he exclaimed joyfully, reaching out to hug her. "It's you! Happy Halloween, you little monster!"

THE INCREDIBLES

The Supers Work Together

Bob and Helen Parr – Mr Incredible and Elastigirl – and their children, had been trying to live normal lives. Since all Supers were banned from using their powers, Bob had been working at an insurance company. But he soon got bored of ordinary life and started doing super-hero work in secret – without telling his wife. He'd ended up being lured into a trap by Syndrome, a self-made Super who had created a robot that only he could defeat.

Syndrome had killed off real heroes so that he could be one himself!

The Incredibles were trapped on Syndrome's island. Syndrome had launched his deadly robot to the city, and had just left to 'save the day'. Luckily, Violet – Mr Incredible's daughter – had created a force field, allowing her to set her family free. The Incredibles were back in action!

The family escaped from the island in a rocket and flew towards the city where the robot was already destroying everything it could find. The people of the city were terrified.

"Someone needs to teach this hunk of metal a few manners!" Syndrome told the crowd. Sneakily he worked the robot's remote control and removed the Omnidroid's arm. The crowd cheered, and Syndrome loved it.

But the Omnidroid was a learning robot, and it realized Syndrome was controlling it. It knocked Syndrome out!

The Incredibles crash-landed in a van that Elastigirl had attached to the rocket. Then Mr Incredible announced he would fight the robot alone. When Elastigirl objected, Mr Incredible begged her, "I can't lose you again," he said. "I'm not strong enough."

Elastigirl smiled. "If we work together, you won't have to be."

The Supers fought as a team. Mr Incredible's old pal Frozone helped them too. Still, the Omnidroid proved to be quite strong – that is, until Mr Incredible remembered that the only thing that could defeat the Omnidroid was itself. He grabbed an arm that had fallen from the robot. Elastigirl, Frozone and the children pushed buttons on the remote while Mr Incredible aimed the arm so it pointed at the Omnidroid. Just then Elastigirl found the right button....

The rocket on the robot arm ripped the robot apart. The city was saved!

Syndrome recovered to find everyone cheering the Supers! No one cared about him! Furious, he crept away.... determined to get revenge on The Incredibles.

THE ARISTOCATS

Street Cats

"Oh, Mama!" said Marie dreamily. "Paris is so pretty in the morning! May we please go explore just a bit?" The kittens and their mother had spent the previous night in Mr O'Malley's swinging bachelor flat, and were now making their way through the streets of Paris back to Madame's house.

"All right, darlings," their mother replied. "But just for a few minutes. Madame must be missing us terribly. Be sure to stick together!"

They passed a doorway to a jazz hall, where the previous night's party appeared to be still in full swing. "Oh, yeah!" said Toulouse as he danced in the doorway to the swinging beat.

"Come on, Toulouse," said Berlioz crossly. "I'm hungry!"

A few steps down the block, a fishmonger was just setting out his wares in the window of his shop. The three kittens put their paws on the windowsill, licking their lips as they watched him lay out the gleaming fish. The fishmonger smiled at them through the window, then came out of his shop and tossed them each a sardine. "Here you are, my pretty cats!" he said to them.

Yum! Sardines! The three meowed back a thank you and gobbled up the tasty treat.

"The streets of Paris are the coolest place on Earth!" said Berlioz as they continued walking. "I don't want to go back to Madame's house!"

"Berlioz! You mustn't speak like that!" said Marie. "You know how much Madame needs us...." Suddenly, she broke off. Her brothers followed her gaze, which was directed at the window of a fancy pet shop. "Oh, my!" she cried out delightedly. "Look at those!" In the window of the shop were several jewelled cat collars, all in different shades of the finest leather. Marie thought they were simply beautiful – especially the pink one. "I must say, the streets of Paris are a wonderful place!" Marie said dreamily.

Just then, they heard a deep barking. A moment later, a huge dog came bounding around the corner. The kittens froze in fear for a moment. Then all three of them turned and scampered back down the street in the direction of their mother and Mr O'Malley, with the dog hot on their heels.

"Paris is a fine city," said Berlioz, panting, as he raced down an alleyway. Darting behind some dustbins, the kittens were able to lose the snarling dog.

"Yes," replied Marie. "But I'm not sure how I feel about the Parisians – particularly the canine kind!"

Disney
DUMBO
Dumbo's Parade Pals

When Dumbo's circus came to town, the animals and circus folk marched in a big parade. The crowd loved seeing all the circus animals marching down the street.

Well, it may have been fun for the crowd, but it was no fun for Dumbo. His feet hurt, and he was *hungry*.

Then Dumbo noticed a peanut on the ground. He picked up the peanut with his trunk and ate it. Then Dumbo saw another peanut, and another. Leaving the parade, Dumbo followed the trail of peanuts all the way to a playground.

"See, the peanuts worked!" exclaimed a little girl with pigtails. "Now we have our own elephant to play with."

The girl and her friends surrounded Dumbo, patting his head. They marvelled at his long trunk and big ears. "What a wonderful little elephant!" they cried.

"Let's have our own circus," said a boy.

"I'll be the ringmaster!" cried the little girl. She led Dumbo to the middle of the playground. "Ladies and gentlemen! Presenting our star attraction – The Little Elephant!"

Dumbo knew just what to do. He stood up on his two back legs. Then he juggled some balls with his trunk. The children cheered.

Suddenly, Timothy Q. Mouse appeared. "Here you are!" he said to Dumbo. "We have to get back to the circus camp and get ready for the show!"

Dumbo nodded, and waved goodbye to his new friends. The children watched him go, looking terribly disappointed.

"I wish I could go see him in the circus tonight," one of them said. "But I don't have enough money for a ticket."

"Me neither," said the other children.

Dumbo was sorry that the nice children he had met would not be able to go to the circus. That night, he felt very blue as he put on his stage makeup and warmed up his ears. Finally, he tucked Timothy into the brim of his hat, then climbed onto a tall platform.

"Ladies and gentlemen!" the ringmaster cried. "I give you *Dumbo, the Flying Elephant!*"

Dumbo leaped off the platform, and his giant ears unfurled. The crowd cheered as Dumbo flew around the tent.

Suddenly, Dumbo spotted his playground friends. They were sitting in the first row! He swept by them, patting each child on the head with his trunk. The girl with pigtails waved at Dumbo. "Your mouse friend gave us free tickets!" she cried.

Dumbo smiled and reached his trunk up to the brim of his hat, where Timothy was riding. He gave Timothy a pat on the head too. He was the luckiest elephant in the world to have such wonderful friends!

The Ghost-Light Fish

Nemo loved school. So did his friends, Tad, Pearl and Sheldon. Mr Ray made everything so much fun. He took his students all over the reef.

That day, Mr Ray was taking them exploring.

"Okay, explorers," Mr Ray said. "Let's see if each of you can find a shell."

Tad was the first to find something. "Hey, guys!" he cried. "Look at this!"

Everyone stared at the gleaming white shell Tad held in his fin.

"Cool!" said Sheldon.

"It's heart-shaped!" Nemo exclaimed.

Minutes passed when suddenly Nemo heard an odd noise. He looked up and saw his friends Tad, Pearl and Sheldon bolting out of the cave, screaming loudly.

"What's the matter?" Nemo asked.

"It's a g-g-ghost fish!" Sheldon replied fearfully.

"Yeah, right," Nemo replied. He noticed Tad's fin was empty. "Where's your shell?" he asked.

Tad looked down. "I must have dropped it in there. But I'm not going back for it!"

"Don't worry," said Nemo. "I'll find it." So Nemo swam bravely into the cave.

"See?" he said to himself. "Nothing to be afraid of."

Nemo froze. On the cave wall was a huge, fish-shaped shadow! He took a deep breath. "Uh, excuse me, Ghost Fish?" he asked.

"A ghost fish?!" a tiny voice said nervously.

Nemo followed the voice and to his surprise, the ghost fish was actually a tiny glow-in-the-dark fish!

"Don't be afraid," Nemo said. "My name's Nemo. What's yours?"

"I'm Eddy," replied the little fish. "You mean there's no ghost fish?"

Nemo explained the whole funny story.

"By the way," said Nemo. "How do you glow like that?"

Eddy shrugged. "I just do," he replied.

Nemo thought of someone who would know more about Eddy's glow – Mr Ray! So, Nemo invited Eddy to meet everyone.

Outside, Nemo rejoined his friends. "I didn't find your shell," Nemo said to Tad. "But I did find your ghost fish!"

Everyone wanted to know what made Eddy glow!

"Good question, Nemo," Mr Ray replied. "There are tiny glow-in-the-dark organisms inside these patches on either side of Eddy's jaw."

Everyone ooohed and aaahed.

Mr Ray smiled at Nemo. "I think you deserve an A in Exploring today, Nemo!"

MICKEY MOUSE
A Wonderful/Terrible Day

"What a wonderful day!" Mickey Mouse said to himself. He hummed as he strolled through the outdoor market. The air was crisp. The leaves were pretty shades of red, yellow and orange. And the perfect hunk of cheese was right in front of him.

"I'll take that cheese and a loaf of bread," he told the market seller.

"You're just in time," the seller replied. "I'm about to close up shop."

Meanwhile, Donald Duck was just leaving his house. "What a terrible day!" he said in a huff. He had overslept and woken up with a crick in his neck. He hurried to cross the street, but had to stop for a red light.

When the light turned green, he stepped into the street.

H-o-n-n-k-k! A big truck roared past, just missing Donald.

"Watch where you're going!" Donald shouted. He raced ahead to the market.

"I'll take a loaf of bread," he told the seller.

"Sorry," the seller replied. "I'm sold out."

"Sold out?" Donald's eyes bulged in his head. "Sold out?"

Down the block, Mickey Mouse was having a friendly chat with Goofy. "How have you been, Goofy?" he asked.

"Fine," Goofy said as he peeled a banana. He ate the whole thing in one bite and dropped the peel on the ground.

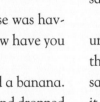

In the market, Donald sulked. He was hungry!

"This is so unfair!" he said. Slumping his shoulders, he started off towards the park at the end of the street. But a second later he slipped on a banana peel.

"*Ooof!*" Donald fell to the ground with a thud. Scowling, he got to his feet.

Not far away, Mickey was spreading out his picnic blanket in the park. All around him, children were laughing and playing.

"Hey, kids!" he called with a friendly wave. He took a big bite of his cheese sandwich and chewed happily. "What a wonderful day," he said again.

Donald kicked a pebble on the sidewalk while his tummy growled. And then, all of a sudden – *thunk*! – a ball hit him on the head.

"Watch it, kids!" Donald shouted. He rubbed his sore head. "What a terrible day."

Just then, Donald heard a familiar voice call out, "Hey, Donald! Come have a cheese sandwich with me!"

Donald saw Mickey waving to him from under a tree. Donald wanted to stay mad. But the truth is that no duck can resist a cheese sandwich. He smiled and ambled over. Maybe it wasn't such a bad day after all!

THE LION KING
Timon and Pumbaa Tell It All

It was a very hot day on the savannah, Simba, Timon and Pumbaa were lying in the shade, barely moving. It was too hot for the three friends to do anything except talk. Pumbaa had just finished telling a story about the biggest insect he had ever eaten (to hear him tell it, it was the size of an ostrich) and a silence fell over the little group.

"I know," said Simba. "Hey, Timon, why don't you tell me the story of how you and Pumbaa met each other?"

Timon looked at Pumbaa. "Do you think he's ready for it?" he asked.

"Knock him dead," said Pumbaa.

"It all started in a little meerkat village far, far away," began Timon.

"No," interrupted Pumbaa. "You've got it all wrong. It all started near a little warthog watering hole far, far away."

"If I recall correctly, Simba asked *me* to tell the story," said Timon. "And this is the story as told from *my* point of view."

"All right," said Pumbaa sulkily.

"And in that little meerkat village there was one meerkat who didn't fit in with the rest. All the others were content to dig, dig, dig all day long," said Timon. "*I* was that isolated meerkat. How I hated to dig! I knew I needed to go elsewhere, to find a home of my own, a place where I fitted in. So I left. Along the way I ran into a wise old baboon who told me what I was seeking – *hakuna matata* – and pointed me in the direction of Pride Rock. So I boldly set off towards this rock of which he spoke. And on my way there, I . . ."

"Met me!" Pumbaa interrupted.

Timon gave him a dirty look and continued. "I heard a strange rustling in the bushes. I was scared. What could it be? A hyena? A lion? And then I found myself face to face with a big, ugly warthog!"

"Hey!" said Pumbaa, looking insulted.

"We soon realized we had a lot in common – our love for bugs, our search for a home to call our own. So we set out for Pride Rock together. A lot of bad things happened along the way – hyenas, stampedes, you name it. But before long we managed to find the perfect place to live. And then we met you, Simba!"

"That's a nice story," Simba said with a yawn. "Now I think I'm going to take a nap . . . ."

Pumbaa cleared his throat. "It all started near a little warthog watering hole far, far away," he began.

"You always have to get the last word, don't you?" said Timon.

"Not always," said Pumbaa. And then he continued with *his* side of the story.

All in this Together

While escaping the Sunnyside Daycare centre, Andy's toys had been foiled by Lotso – the evil pink bear that ran the nursery. Now they were stuck inside a rubbish truck! They wanted to get home to Andy, before he left home for college.

Inside the truck, the toys found themselves in darkness. "We all here?" Woody asked as they gathered together.

The truck rumbled forwards, then lurched to a stop. Woody could hear its forklift picking up another huge bin. "Against the wall! Quick!" he yelled.

But Jessie was stuck. Buzz raced over and freed her just as the bin began emptying above them. He threw her out of the path of falling rubbish – as a TV crashed down on him!

Desperately, his friends dug him out... and were thrilled to discover that Buzz was back to his old self! He had been reset to 'demo' mode by Lotso, and had ended up speaking Spanish when the others had tried to fix him.

Soon the truck arrived at the Tri-County Landfill, and dumped its whole load out onto the ground. The dirty, frightened toys struggled out from under the debris and saw a huge rubbish heap. In the distance, they could see a huge crane. "The claaaaw!" shouted the Aliens excitedly, as they toddled off towards the crane. Woody tried to go after them, but a huge bulldozer roared in his path. The Aliens were gone. Then the bulldozer turned towards Woody and his friends. Soon, the toys were trapped in a churning tide of rubbish... heading straight towards an open pit!

The toys fell and fell until they landed on a conveyor belt. Buzz, whose head was stuck in a can, suddenly flew up and stuck to another conveyor belt, above them. It was magnetic! Slinky got pulled up, too – and saw that the lower belt led right into a shredder! The rest of the toys tried to save themselves by grabbing onto any metal they could find.

Suddenly, a pink paw reached out from underneath a bag. "Help!" begged Lotso.

Woody and Buzz dropped down and used a golf club to pry the bag off the trapped bear. The shredder was just inches away!

As Lotso scrambled free, Woody grabbed his paw. They pointed the golf club towards the magnet and all three were lifted to safety.

"We're all in this together," Woody told the grateful bear as they joined their friends.

Even though Lotso had been cruel to Woody and the other toys, the sheriff knew, in times of trouble, they should all stick together.

Kronk's Feast

"One more time!" Kronk cried. The Junior Chipmunks looked at their leader, took deep breaths and launched into "We're Not Woodchucks" for the fourth time. "We're the ch-ch-chipmunks. We're not w-w-woodchucks," the kids sang, halfheartedly puffing out their cheeks.

The tired troop sagged on their log. Next to them, Bucky the squirrel and three of his friends sang along too – in Squirrel. "Squeak sq-sq-squeak. Sq-sq-squeak squeak, squeaker, squeak." The furry animals' tails drooped.

"I'm hungry," Tipo whispered to his sister Chaca.

"Keep singing," Chaca said behind her hand. "He's got to be done soon."

While the children began another verse, Kronk stood at the fire. He mixed, flipped and seasoned in a frenzy. He had been cooking for hours, and the smells drifting towards the tired troop were delicious.

"I'm . . . almost . . . ready." Kronk struggled to balance several plates on his arm before spinning around to present them to the troop. "Voilà." The big man grinned. "Bon appétit!"

The troop leaned forward and smiled. The food looked as good as it smelled. They began to help themselves.

Kronk stood back modestly. "I do pride myself on being a bit of a gourmet," he said.

Everyone was pleased. Everyone, that is, but Bucky and the squirrels. Where was *their* food?

"Squeak! Squeaker, squeaker, squeak," Bucky mumbled behind his paw. He gave a quick nod, and all of them ran off towards Kronk's tent. This was an outrage! The squirrels were Junior Chipmunks, too!

Bucky held open the tent flap and the squirrels ducked inside. "Squeak," Bucky commanded as he pointed at Kronk's sleeping bag. The other squirrels nodded. They knew what they were supposed to do – chew holes in Kronk's bedding! Just as the squirrels were about to get to work, they were interrupted.

"Oh, squeeeaak," Kronk's deep voice crooned from outside. "Squeaker squeeaak!"

The squirrels peeked outside the tent.

There was Kronk, holding a new plate. Balanced upon it were a golden-brown acorn soufflé and a bowl of steaming wild-berry sauce.

Bucky shrugged sheepishly at the leader.

"Thought I forgot you, huh? Would Kronk do that?" The leader set the tray down. "How about a hug?"

The four squirrels grasped the large man's legs and squeezed. All was forgiven. Together all the Junior Chipmunks enjoyed their meal.

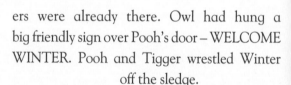
Pooh Welcomes Winter

Pooh had heard that Winter was coming soon, and he was very excited about having a visitor. Pooh and Piglet decided to throw a party to welcome Winter to Hundred-Acre Wood. The two friends set off to tell everyone.

Outside, it was snowing. They met Tigger along the way, and they walked to Kanga and Roo's house together. They all decided to go by sledge to the party. Owl landed on a branch overhead.

"Winter has arrived!" he declared. "I heard Christopher Robin say so."

Pooh told Owl about the party, then they all jumped on the sledge and slid down the hill towards Christopher Robin's house.

"There's Winter!" Tigger cried. "Tiggers always know Winter when they see him. That big white face – that carroty nose. Who else could he be?" said Tigger.

"Well," said Pooh, "he looks shy. We should be extra friendly." He walked right up to Winter. "How do you do? We are giving a party in your honour." Winter did not say anything.

"Oh d-d-dear," said Piglet. "He's frozen!"

"Quick!" cried Tigger. "We'd better get him to the party and warm him up." They hoisted Winter onto the sledge. When they slid up to Pooh's house, the oth-ers were already there. Owl had hung a big friendly sign over Pooh's door – WELCOME WINTER. Pooh and Tigger wrestled Winter off the sledge.

"Give him the comfy chair by the fire!" said Rabbit. Still, Winter did not say a word. His carrot nose drooped.

Just then, Christopher Robin tramped up to the door in his big boots. "Has anyone seen my snowman?" he asked.

"No," said Pooh glumly, "but we brought Winter here for a special party. He doesn't seem to like it."

"Silly old bear!" Christopher Robin laughed. And he explained to Pooh that Winter was not a person, it was a season. A time of year for cold snow, mistletoe, warm fires and good friends.

Pooh scratched his nose thoughtfully. "Yes, I see now," he said. "Of course, I am a bear of very little brain."

"You're the best bear in all the world," said Christopher Robin. "Come on, we'd better get the snowman back outside before he melts completely."

They undrooped the snowman's nose and stuck his hands back in. They decided to have the party anyway, to celebrate Winter. So everyone sang songs and danced around the snowman until they couldn't dance any more.

Travelling at the Speed of Stitch

Stitch was bored. Everyone seemed to have somewhere to go and something to do during the day but him. Lilo went to school. Nani went to work. And Jumba and Pleakley headed off to serve beachgoers at their new snack stand, the Galactic Burger.

So Stitch decided he needed a job. He and Lilo looked through the newspaper, searching for a job just right for a small, blue alien with a huge love of adventure. "Listen," said Lilo, pointing to an advert. "'Wanted: tour guide. Must have an outgoing personality and lots of energy.' That's you!"

So, the next morning, Stitch arrived at the tour agency, wearing his best Hawaiian shirt and a big smile. The woman doing the interview thought he was pretty scary-looking, but a group of tourists was arriving from the airport any minute and no one else had turned up to apply for the job. "You're hired!" she said.

"Aloha!" Stitch exclaimed when the holidaymakers arrived. He stacked leis on them up to their eyeballs and shook their hands enthusiastically. "Welcome onto the Hawaiian galaxy!" He showed them to a tour bus and pressed down on the accelerator as far as it would go. "Palm trees!" he yelled as the scenery passed by in a blur. "Pineapples!" he shouted as they drove through a fruit stand. Finally, the bus screeched to a stop at the beach.

"Surfing!" Stitch announced, hurling his group onto surfboards and pushing them out to sea. After being battered by the waves, the tourists were eventually tossed onto the beach.

Stitch herded them over to a barbecue. "Luau!" he explained.

"Now, that's more like it!" an elderly woman said, collapsing onto a bench.

"I'm starving," admitted a man with a lobster still hanging on to his Bermuda shorts.

But, instead of food, Stitch returned with several flaming torches. Nani's friend, David, had taught Stitch how to juggle fire. The little alien was sure the tourists would want to learn too. Thank goodness Stitch just happened to bring along a fire extinguisher!

The last stop on Stitch's tour was the 24-hour Hula Marathon. He gave his guests grass skirts and insisted they dance until they dropped as he played the ukulele.

When the holidaymakers returned to the tour agency that night, they emerged from the bus exhausted, battered, bruised and confused. The first thing they saw was the sign on the front of the tour agency: HAWAII: THE MOST RELAXING PLACE ON EARTH. Unless, of course, your tour guide happens to be from the planet Turo!

We're Going on a Picnic

"Cap'n?" Mr Smee knocked softly on Captain Hook's door. There was no answer. The chubby first mate pushed his way inside, carrying a breakfast tray. "I've got breakfast, Cap'n."

"I'm not hungry!" Captain Hook replied. "Go away!"

"But, Cap'n. You have to eat." Smee was getting worried. The Captain hadn't eaten in days. In fact, he hadn't even got out of bed! "I know you feel bad about Pe–" Smee stopped himself from saying the dreaded name just in time, "–that flying boy. And the croc – I mean – that ticking reptile, too." Captain Hook was really angry about being beaten by Peter again. Even worse, Peter had set the crocodile right back on Captain Hook's trail. "But we haven't seen hide nor scale of either of them for a week, I think the coast is clear."

There was no reply from Captain Hook.

Smee thought for a minute. "I know how to cheer you up!" he cried. "We'll have a nice old-fashioned picnic! Won't that be lovely!"

Again, silence from Captain Hook.

"Ah-ah-ah! No arguments!" Smee left the breakfast tray and hurried down to the galley. A picnic on Mermaid Island was just what the doctor ordered!

Smee whistled merrily as he made herring-and-pickle sandwiches (Captain Hook's favourite) and packed them in a wicker basket. This was Hook's day! Smee carefully folded a gingham tablecloth and placed it in the basket, along with his tin whistle. He was going to make sure that Hook had a good time, whether he wanted to or not!

Once the picnic basket was packed, Smee called down to Hook, "It's time to go, Cap'n!"

After a while, Captain Hook finally appeared on deck, blinking in the sunlight. "Fine," he said grumpily. "But I know I'm not going to have fun!"

Smee let the rowing boat down into the water and Hook began to climb down the rope ladder. Once he was safely in the boat, Smee picked up the picnic basket.

TICK TOCK TICK TOCK TICK TOCK.

"Smee!" cried Hook. "Help me!"

Smee peeked over the side of the ship. The crocodile was about to take a bite out of the boat!

In a panic, he threw the only thing he had on hand – the picnic basket. It landed right in the crocodile's open mouth. The crocodile stared at Smee in surprise. Then, without a sound, it slipped back under the water.

"My picnic!" cried Smee. "My tin whistle!"

"Next time you have any smart ideas about cheering me up," said the Captain, glaring at his first mate, "keep them to yourself!"

THE LION KING

Hot on the Trail

"Over here!" Simba said, sniffing the trail. "It's going this way!"

"Yup, this way," Nala said with a nod, sniffing a stick. "And not long ago."

"I saw that stick first," Simba said. Nala was a good tracker, but Simba had learned from an expert – his mum. She was one of the best hunters in the pride.

"Hmm," Nala said with a sniff. "So what are we following then, master tracker? Can you tell me that?"

Simba was silent. They had seen some footprints, but they weren't clear enough to read. They'd also seen some dark wiry hair on a log, but that could belong to lots of animals.

"Something that isn't very graceful," Simba said. They had seen lots of crushed grass and broken sticks.

"Mmm-hmm." Nala nodded impatiently.

"A rhino!" Simba said confidently.

"A rhino?" Nala rolled onto her back, laughing. "Simba, you crack me up!"

"What?" Simba couldn't hide the hurt in his voice. It *might* be a rhino!

"The footprints aren't big enough," Nala said. "It's Rafiki, the baboon."

Now, it was Simba's turn to laugh. "Rafiki likes the trees, he doesn't use trails like a hyena!" The giggle died in Simba's throat and he felt the fur on the back of his neck stand up.

Hyenas were clumsy and had dark wiry hair . . . .

Nala didn't say anything, but her fur was standing up a little too.

The two lions walked in silence. Ahead of them they heard noises – thrashing and grunting.

"Simba," Nala whispered, "maybe we should turn back."

"Just a little further," Simba whispered. They were almost there!

The young lions crept through the grass on their bellies as quietly as they could. The grunting and thrashing grew louder. They could see a dust cloud rising. Simba stifled a growl. Something about the smell and the sound was familiar, but Simba could not put his paw on it.

As they crept closer, two bodies came into view by the side of a termite mound. Simba pounced!

"Pumbaa! Timon!" he shouted, landing between his friends.

"Simba!" the warthog said, grinning. Termites dripped out of his muddy mouth. "Want some?"

Timon held a handful of wriggling insects towards Nala. "There are plenty to go around."

"Uh, no thanks," Nala said as she came out of the grass, giggling. She shot a look at Simba. "I think I'll wait for the master tracker to hunt me up some lunch!"

Donald Duck Goes Camping

Huey, Dewey and Louie had just found out that their uncle, Donald Duck, was taking them camping. A few hours later, they arrived in the woods and found a camping spot. Huey and Louie helped their uncle put up the tent while Dewey read from a camping guidebook.

"The guidebook says to hang the food locker from a tree," said Dewey.

"I know everything there is to know about camping," Donald said. Just then, two squirrels scampered down from a tree and snatched a bag of peanuts. "Hey!" Donald shouted. "Come back here!"

"The guidebook says it's good to share with little animals," said Louie.

"I don't care what the book says. Those are my peanuts!" replied Donald.

Huey looked up from his camping book. "Uh-oh!" he said, pointing into the woods. A large bear was charging towards them!

The bear stopped at the picnic table, and began to sniff at the food locker. The two squirrels had arrived with him. With one swipe of his paw, the bear broke open the food locker. Then he took a baked ham and ambled off.

The two squirrels ran along the tree branches and chattered at Donald again. This time, they seemed to be laughing at him. "I'll get even with you!" Donald yelled. He climbed towards the squirrels. Just as he was about to grab them, they leapt onto a thin branch.

"The book says to stay off small branches!" Dewey cried.

CRRRACK! Suddenly, the branch broke, and Donald fell into the river.

"Help!" Donald cried. "Pull me out!" He tried to swim towards land, but the current was too strong. He spotted a rock and grabbed on to it. "Do something!" he called to his nephews. "Look in the guidebook!"

Huey, Dewey and Louie started flipping through the book. They only looked up when the squirrels returned – with a brown beaver!

The beaver waddled to a tree that stood beside the river and began to gnaw at it.

"He's trying to help!" Dewey said. "If the tree falls into the river, it might be long enough to reach Uncle Donald."

A few minutes later, the tree fell over with a crash. Donald climbed along the tree trunk towards dry land. Once safely ashore, Donald ran towards his car.

"Where are you going?" his nephews called. Donald returned in an hour. His car was filled with presents for the beaver that had helped him, and the other animals. They were delighted and munched on their treats!

The Journey Begins

Bernard couldn't believe this was really happening. Even though he was a caretaker, he had been selected by the Rescue Aid Society to come to the aid of a little girl named Penny, who appeared to be in grave danger. And what's more, he, Bernard, had been selected over all the other mice to be partners with the very beautiful and clever Miss Bianca. It was Bernard's first rescue mission ever and, even though he was very nervous, he was excited to get started.

Bernard had got himself packed and ready to go in minutes, and now he had arrived to pick up Miss Bianca.

"I'll just be a few more moments, darling!" she called to him as he waited outside her door.

"Uh, okay, Miss Bianca!" he called back, glancing quickly at his watch.

Just as soon as Miss Bianca had finished packing, they'd be on their way . . . .

"Uh, Miss Bianca?" called Bernard after a while. "We really ought to be going, I think. We don't want to miss our flight!"

"All right, darling!" said Miss Bianca. "Come give me a hand with this suitcase, please!"

Bernard found Miss Bianca trying to close her overstuffed suitcase. She had already packed several boxes as well. "Are you quite sure you'll be needing all those evening gowns,

Miss Bianca?" Bernard panted as he sat on the bag and tried to zip it up. "And that tea set? And 14 pairs of shoes?"

"A lady must be prepared for anything, darling," she crooned. "Now, I'll just put on my hat and we'll be off."

Bernard gave a final bounce on the suitcase and was able to snap it closed. After what seemed like hours, Miss Bianca appeared at last in a cloud of dizzying perfume. She was wearing a beautifully cut travelling cape and a stunning little hat.

"I'll take that!" said Bernard as Miss Bianca reached for the suitcase. It felt as though it was full of bricks, but Bernard managed to manoeuvre it through the door, where he grabbed his much lighter bag in his other hand.

"Darling," Miss Bianca said sweetly as they headed to the airport, "please don't fret. Everyone knows that flights are always delayed!"

Even when the plane is an albatross? Bernard wondered to himself. Yes, Miss Bianca and Bernard certainly made an unusual team. But he was sure now that they would get the rescue job done.

Just as long as he didn't drop her suitcase on his toe!

A Circle of Friends

After escaping the Sunnyside Daycare nursery, Andy's toys had ended up at a landfill site! They were on a conveyor belt, but had managed to save themselves from being shredded to bits. Woody had even saved the evil Lotso, even though the pink bear had been horrid to Andy's toys.

All that Andy's toys wanted was to get home. Andy was soon leaving for college, and the teenager wanted to take Woody with him. The rest of the toys were meant to be stored safely in the attic.

The conveyor belt they were all now standing on was angled upwards towards a bright light. At first, they thought they were heading for daylight. But then they realized it was an incinerator! Everyone started running frantically. Lotso managed to reach an Emergency Stop Button.

"Push it!" yelled Woody and Buzz. Lotso was about to push it, to save everyone... then he stopped. He looked back at the other toys, then, with a cruel smirk, he ran off.

"NOOOOO!!!" yelled Woody.

The toys tumbled downwards towards the fiery blaze. A terrifying roar filled the air. They struggled to climb and claw their way back out, but the rubbish that poured off the belt kept pushing them closer to their doom.

Finally, each toy grabbed onto another until the circle of friends was complete. They were determined to face their fate the best way they knew how – together.

Then, suddenly, a large shadow passed over them. A giant crane was lowering down, down, down over them. Then the jaws opened, scooping up Woody and all the others, too! The toys soared up and away from the fire. As they soared through the air, the toys saw into the cab of the crane – the Aliens were controlling it!

"The clawwww!" The Aliens steered their friends over the landfill and dropped them gently to the ground. But there was no time to celebrate. "Come on, Woody," said Jessie. "We've got to get you home."

"What about you guys?" Woody asked. "Maybe the attic's not such a great idea."

"We'll be there for Andy," Buzz declared.

Still, the toys wondered if they could make it before Andy left. Luckily, they spotted their neighbourhood rubbish collector nearby, just climbing into his truck! The toys hurried forwards, ready to hitch a ride home.

Lotso found his way onto a truck, too. But he wouldn't be hopping off anytime soon! He was strapped to the front of a huge lorry.

Now Andy's toys just had to get home.

Disney
ROBIN
hOOD

For Old Times' Sake

At last, good King Richard had returned to Nottingham and sentenced greedy Prince John and his cronies, the Sheriff of Nottingham and Sir Hiss, to hard labour in the rock mines.

"Brave Robin Hood," said the King upon summoning Robin to the castle one day soon after his return. "In light of the fact that Prince John has harassed and over-taxed the good people of this kingdom, and in recognition of all you have done to defend and protect them while I was gone, I ask if you would do the honour of returning this 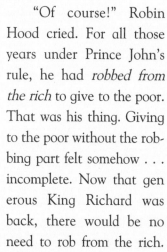 money to the citizens of Nottingham, to whom it rightfully belongs."

Robin Hood beamed. "Your Majesty," he replied, "it would be my honour."

The next day, at the appointed time, Robin Hood arrived at the castle, ready to perform his duty. He had brought Little John to assist him. They found King Richard waiting for them just inside the main gate. Next to the King was a wagon overloaded with bags of gold coins.

"Well, my boy," the King said to Robin Hood, "here is the people's money. I trust you to distribute it fairly."

Robin Hood smiled and looked at the wagon. He looked at Little John. He looked at the King. He looked back at the wagon.

Then his smile faded.

"Something doesn't feel right," Robin Hood said, turning to face Little John. "Something is . . . *missing*."

"Missing?" Little John said, surprised.

"Of course!" Robin Hood cried. For all those years under Prince John's rule, he had *robbed from the rich* to give to the poor. That was his thing. Giving to the poor without the robbing part felt somehow . . . incomplete. Now that generous King Richard was back, there would be no need to rob from the rich. Naturally, thought Robin, that was a good thing. And yet . . . it *was* the end of an era.

"Your Majesty," Robin Hood said to the king, "I don't suppose you could make this handing over of the money a bit more . . . oh, I don't know . . . *challenging?*"

King Richard wrinkled his brow. "Challenging?" he replied, puzzled.

Robin Hood turned to Little John, who also looked confused. "What do you say? One last heist . . . for old time's sake?"

Little John smiled.

King Richard also understood, which is how it happened that, later that afternoon, Robin Hood and Little John 'stole' a wagonload of gold from the castle yard.

And wouldn't you know it – King Richard did not seem to mind at all!

Knock, Knock! Who's There?

Standing in her brand-new bedroom, Lilo grinned. The walls were almost complete. In her mind, Lilo could see it all finished. Her bed would be against one wall, and Stitch's little bed would sit right beside hers. Lilo hugged herself with excitement. She wasn't quite sure that the wardrobe was in exactly the right place, but she loved everything else, so she didn't mind.

"Lilo, I want you to stay out of the workers' way," Nani said. "And keep an eye on Stitch! He keeps licking our nice new windows!"

Nani was worried. Cobra Bubbles was coming today to see how they were doing.

"We'll stay out of trouble," Lilo smiled angelically. "Right, Stitch? Stitch?" Lilo looked around.

Stitch wasn't exactly staying out of trouble. He had a tool belt around his waist, and his mouth was full of nails. With amazing force, Stitch spat the nails into the floor, accidentally fastening the end of his own belt to the ground.

"That'll keep you out of trouble." Lilo shrugged. Just then there was a knock at the door. "I'll get it!" Lilo called. She opened the new door. Cobra Bubbles filled the door frame.

"Hello," he said, without removing his sunglasses.

"Hey, come on in and see our new digs!"

Lilo cried, happy to see her friend.

Cobra Bubbles stepped over a power cord and walked around a pile of flooring. "You don't actually live here yet, do you?" he asked slowly.

"Not yet," Lilo chirped. "It's supposed to be finished next month."

"And where is . . . Stitch?" Cobra Bubbles peered around Lilo's room.

"Lilo?" Nani asked with a fake smile.

Lilo frowned. Stitch was no longer nailed to the floor. Suddenly, they heard a knock. Lilo and Nani looked at each other. It wasn't coming from the front door – in fact, it sounded as if it was coming from Lilo's room!

"Who is it?" Lilo asked quietly.

With a monumental crash, Stitch burst through one of the new walls in Lilo's bedroom. "Here he is!" Lilo shouted.

"I see." Cobra Bubbles tried to keep frowning, but couldn't.

"Yes," said Nani nervously. "Stitch sure is, uh, helping out with the construction. Why, here he's decided on a new spot for Lilo's closet. We didn't really want it there, anyway." Nani gave Cobra Bubbles a weak smile, then turned to look at Stitch's handiwork.

"Actually," Nani said with a real smile, "this is a much better spot for the closet. Thanks, Stitch!"

Bambi

First Frost

Slowly, Bambi opened his eyes. Curled next to his mother, he was toasty warm in the thicket. Bambi blinked sleepily, peering past the brambles. Something was different. The forest did not look the same. The air was crisp and cold, and everything was frosted and sparkling.

"Jack Frost has been here," Bambi's mother explained. "He's painted the whole forest with ice crystals."

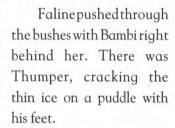

Bambi was about to ask his mother who Jack Frost was and how he painted with ice, when he heard another voice, an impatient one.

"Get up! Get up! Come look at the frost!" It was Thumper. He tapped his foot impatiently. "We haven't got all day!"

Bambi stood and looked at his mother. When she nodded approvingly, he scampered out of the thicket. Bambi looked closely at the colourful leaves on the ground. Each one was covered in an icy white pattern. He touched his nose to a big orange oak leaf. "Ooh, it's cold!" he cried.

"Of course it is!" Thumper laughed.

"I think it's beautiful," said Faline, as she stepped into the clearing.

"Me, too," Bambi agreed.

"Well, come look at this!" Thumper hopped away and the two young deer followed,

admiring the way the sun sparkled on the frost-covered trees and grass.

Thumper disappeared under a bush; then Bambi heard a new noise. *Creak, crack.*

Faline pushed through the bushes with Bambi right behind her. There was Thumper, cracking the thin ice on a puddle with his feet.

Bambi had never seen ice before. He pushed on the icy thin puddle covering with his hoof. It seemed to bend. Then it shattered!

Soon the three friends were stomping on the ice-covered puddles. When all the ice was broken, Faline had an idea. "Let's go to the meadow!"

Bambi thought that was a great idea. The grass would be sparkling! They set out at a run, bounding and racing each other through the forest. But when they got to the meadow's edge, they all stopped.

They looked, sniffed and listened quietly. They did not sense danger – no, the trouble was that in the meadow, nothing was different. There was no frost.

"What happened?" Bambi asked.

"Frost never lasts long," Thumper explained. "It melts as soon as the sun hits it. But don't worry. Winter is coming, and soon we'll have something even better than frost. We'll have snow!"

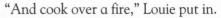

Scrooge's Nature

"Would you look at that!" Huey pointed to a picture of a Junior Woodchuck relaxing in a hammock, while another camper fished in a nearby lake.

"And that!" Dewey's eyes widened. He pointed at a picture of a star-filled sky in the same brochure.

"Camping at Faraway Lake sure looks fun," Louie agreed. "Do you think Unca Scrooge would . . . ?"

"You never know. He might pay for us to go," Huey said. The three boys looked at one another.

"Nah!" they said in unison. Uncle Scrooge may have been the richest duck in the world, but he did not part with his money easily.

"Let's show him, anyway," Huey said. "It's worth a shot."

The other boys followed Huey into their uncle's study.

Dewey nudged Huey forward. "Look at this, Unca Scrooge." Huey thrust the brochure into his uncle's lap.

"Humph." Uncle Scrooge scowled at the glossy photos. "What have we got here, lads?"

"It's a camp, Unca Scrooge. It's educational," Huey stammered.

"Looks like a waste of my hard-earned money," the old duck said.

"But . . . but we could camp out under the stars," Dewey said.

"And cook over a fire," Louie put in.

"And see nature," Huey added.

Uncle Scrooge's eyes narrowed. He looked from the brochure to his nephews' hopeful faces and back to the brochure. So, they wanted to learn about nature, did they?

"Here you are, boys," said Uncle Scrooge a short time later. He smiled from the safety of the screened-in back porch. "You have tents . . ." He indicated the three small leaky tents set up in the garden. "You can see the stars . . ." In fact, only one or two stars were visible through the branches of the tree the tents were under. "And you're cooking over a fire," Scrooge finished, pointing at the tiny, smoky little flame.

Huey slapped at a mosquito on his arm. Dewey shook his head to chase away a cloud of gnats. Louie yelped as he was dive-bombed by a bat. Who knew the garden had so much nature in it!

"This is much better than that Junior Woodchuck nonsense, isn't it, boys?" Uncle Scrooge asked, with the smile of a duck who has saved himself a penny.

"Yes, Unca Scrooge," Huey, Dewey, and Louie said. Then they turned back to the fire.

"I think . . ." said Huey.

". . . next time," continued Dewey.

". . . we ask Unca Donald!" finished Louie.

A Helping Paw

The dairy barn was warm and cosy, and 99 exhausted, hungry pups were taking turns to drink warm milk from the motherly cows.

"We'd nearly given up hope that you would get here," the kindly collie said to Pongo and Perdita, who had just arrived with the puppies.

"We're so very grateful to you for your hospitality," Perdita murmured wearily.

"Just look at the little dears," said one of the cows. "I've never seen so many puppies in one place before!"

Pongo, Perdita and the puppies had just come in from a long and weary march in the cold. It was very late, and the pups waiting for a drink of milk could barely keep their eyes open. The puppies had recently managed to escape from the dreadful old house owned by Cruella De Vil. They had been held prisoner there, guarded by two villains named Horace and Jasper. Cruella was planning to make a fur coat out of their lovely spotted fur. Luckily Pongo and Perdita had rescued them all just in the nick of time.

The pups had their dinners and gathered around the collie, thanking him for his hospitality.

"Not at all, not at all," the collie replied. "Do you have warm milk for supper every night out here in the country?" asked Rolly.

The collie chuckled. "No, but we do eat very simple country fare. I'm sure it's plainer than the food you eat in the city, but we eat big meals because of all the chores we do."

"And is it always this cold in the country?" asked Patch.

"Well, now," replied the collie. "I suppose most of you come from the city. No, it isn't always this cold, but there are plenty of differences between living in the country and living in the city. Take leashes, for instance. We don't keep our pets on leashes here, the way you do in the city, since our pets have a lot of wide-open space to roam around in. There aren't as many dogs nearby, but there are certainly other sorts of animals that one doesn't see in the city. Take cows, for instance. And then there are sheep and horses and geese, and . . . ."

Suddenly, the collie stopped talking. A tiny snore escaped one of the pups he had just been talking to. He looked around and realized that every one of the pups, as well as Pongo and Perdita, had fallen into a deep sleep.

"Poor little things," he said quietly, as he trotted outside to stand guard. "They've been through so much. I do hope they get home safely soon."

The Firebird

Once there lived the most magical bird – the Firebird! The Firebird sprinkled music from her feathers, filling the land with song and dance. But there was one person who didn't like music – the mean ogre, Katschai. He trapped the Firebird and locked her in a birdcage in his secret palace. But there was a single magical feather that a gust of wind carried far away...

Rocket saw the Firebird's feather, and caught it in his Mini Grab Nabber. He knew that his friend was in trouble and needed help.

"To save the Firebird, we'll need to get past Katschai," June said. "And he'll use plenty of magic spells to try and stop us."

"Stupendous!" exclaimed June. "We've got the magical feather which means we have the musical power to get past Katschai!"

Thanks to the Look-and-Listen Scope, the team made their way to the Instrument Forest. When they arrived, not a single instrument was playing its music! Rocket waved the Firebird's magical feather over the forest. When Katschai heard the music, he became angry. He created spooky animals to scare away the Little Einsteins.

"I've got a plan," Quincy said. "Leo, play the flute to make the bats disappear. I'll play the violin to get rid of the mosquitoes. June, play the xylophone to make the spiders leave. Annie, make the bear go away with a trumpet." It worked! The spooky animals disappeared.

Rocket continued his search for Katschai's secret palace. They saw a sad-looking seal who couldn't sing. Rocket had an idea. He sprinkled the little seal with the magical feather's musical power and helped him sing again.

But Katschai created a snow storm to stop Rocket from going any further.

"Rocket is stuck under that huge pile of snow – he can't fly!" cried Quincy.

"Don't worry, Rocket," Annie said. "I know a special song that can make the sun come out and melt the snow." And it did.

The team finally reached the secret palace. Rocket found the special rainbow key and unlocked the birdcage. The Firebird was free! She soared through the sky, sprinkling her musical power everywhere.

"The Firebird's even sprinkling her musical power on Katschai." Leo giggled.

Quincy laughed. "It's time for Katschai to finally face the music – he can't escape it now!"

"It's true," June said. "Never underestimate the power of music."

Tough Audience

The sticker on the door read: ENTER AT YOUR OWN RISK. But Mike wasn't scared. He always collected the most laughs on the floor and he had never met a child he couldn't crack . . . up. Tossing his microphone from one hand to the other, Mike sauntered through the wardrobe door to face his audience.

"Hey, how ya doin' tonight?" Mike greeted the child. The boy in the racing-car pyjamas just glared. "Did you hear the one about the monster who made it in show business? He really clawed his way to the top." Mike paused for a laugh, but the boy was silent. "Talk about making a killing!" Mike added. Still he got nothing.

"All right. I can see you're a tough audience. Enough of the B material." Mike pulled out the stops. He told his best jokes. He worked the room. He was on the stool, off the stool, hanging on the curtains, standing on the bedstead. But the child didn't even crack a smile.

Mike prepared to let the one about the seven-legged sea monster fly, when he heard tapping on the wardrobe door.

"You know you really ought to get that checked." Mike pointed at the wardrobe. "You could have skeletons in there." The child didn't blink.

Mike pulled the door open a crack. "I'm working here," he whispered.

Sulley poked his head in. "Mikey, you're dying. You've been on for 20 minutes and you're getting nothing. There are plenty of other kids to make laugh tonight. You can come back to this one later."

"No way," Mike hissed. "He loves me. When he laughs he's going to laugh big. I can feel it." A teddy bear sailed through the air and hit Mike in the eye. "See? He's throwing me presents."

"Cut your losses, Mikey. Let this one go." Sulley put a large hairy paw on Mike's head and urged him back through the door.

"I'm telling you, I've almost got him," Mike spoke through clenched teeth, and barely flinched when the unamused boy tossed a banana peel at him.

"And I'm telling you to give . . . it . . . up." Sulley pulled harder on Mike. Mike grabbed the door frame and braced himself. Suddenly Sulley lost his grip, and Mike flew backwards, skidding on the banana peel and falling flat out.

"Why, I oughta . . ." Mike leaped to his feet ready to charge Sulley but was interrupted by the sound of laughing. In fact, the child was laughing so hard tears streamed down his face. Mike high-fived Sulley. "You know, some kids just go for the physical comedy," he said with a shrug.

Eeyore's New Old House

One blustery, cold November day in the Hundred-Acre Wood, the blustery, cold November wind blew so strongly that it knocked Eeyore's house right over!

So Eeyore went to Pooh's house. "Well, Pooh," Eeyore said, "it seems that November just doesn't like me. Or my house. So I'm afraid I will have to stay here with you. If you don't mind, that is."

Pooh assured Eeyore that he didn't mind and offered him some honey.

"I'd prefer thistles, if you have any, which you probably don't," Eeyore said. "Oh, well. Perhaps Rabbit has some."

Well, Rabbit did have some thistles, so Eeyore settled down to stay with Rabbit. But Rabbit's house was so full of vegetables and gardening tools – rakes and shovels and baskets and twine – that there was scarcely room in the burrow for Eeyore. "I suppose Piglet might have more room, though I doubt it," said Eeyore.

Piglet told Eeyore he was welcome to stay with him, and even made Eeyore a little bed next to the pantry, which was full of haycorns. But Eeyore was allergic to haycorns, and soon his sneezing almost knocked Piglet's own house down.

"One house knocked down today is more than – *ah-choo!* – plenty," said Eeyore. "I'll just have to try Kanga and Roo."

Kanga and Roo were happy to put Eeyore up in their house. Roo was so excited to have a guest that he couldn't stop bouncing. Soon Eeyore was feeling dizzy just from watching him. But, just as Eeyore was about to try Owl's house, Piglet, Rabbit and Pooh arrived.

"Eeyore, we've found you the perfect house to live in!" Piglet cried.

"I doubt that," Eeyore said as they led him through the Wood. "The perfect house would have thistles, and enough room, and no haycorns, and, above all, no bouncing. But where am I going to find a house like that?"

Soon, they arrived at a snug little house made of sticks, with a pile of thistles in it. "Here it is, Eeyore," said Piglet.

"That's *my* house," said Eeyore, hardly able to believe his eyes. "But my house got knocked down."

"Piglet and I put it back together again," Pooh said, "and Rabbit donated his thistles, so now you have a house with thistles, and enough room, and no haycorns, and, above all, no bouncing."

Eeyore looked at his house, and then at his friends. "It looks like November doesn't dislike me so much after all," he said. "Maybe, that is."

DUMBO
Dumbo's Daring Rescue

Dumbo stood on his platform high above the floor of the circus Big Top. Below him, the clowns looked the same size as peanuts. He could hear them calling for him to jump.

"All right, kid. You're on," Timothy said from the brim of Dumbo's hat.

Dumbo was ready. He knew what he had to do because he did the same thing every night. When the firefighter clowns called, Dumbo would leap from the platform and plummet towards the ground. Then, at the last possible moment, Dumbo would spread his tremendous ears and fly. The audience would cheer. And the show would be over.

"Hey, kid, that's your cue!" Timothy squeaked in Dumbo's ear.

Taking a step forward, Dumbo began to fall. He sped faster and faster towards the floor of the tent. The audience swam into view. They were screaming and laughing. Then, all of a sudden, Dumbo saw something else.

There, in the first row, was a little girl sitting all by herself. She was crying and holding on to a stick of candyfloss.

In an instant, the little elephant forgot all about the act. Spreading his ears, he swooped away from the shouting clowns. He scanned the seats intently. Why was the girl all alone? Where were her parents?

"Dumbo! What are you doing?" Timothy clung to Dumbo's hat as he soared towards the peanut and popcorn sellers. "We don't have time for a snack now!"

Dumbo ignored his friend. The little girl needed help!

At last, Dumbo saw what he was looking for. There, next to the candyfloss stand, were two very worried-looking parents.

"Clara, where are you?" the father called. His voice was lost in the hollering crowd. His daughter would never hear him calling to her!

Dumbo circled the tent again, turning back towards the bench where the little girl sat sobbing. How could he tell her that her parents were looking for her? He had to bring them together. Swooping low, Dumbo stretched out his trunk and scooped up the little girl.

"Dumbo, what are you doing!" Timothy cried again.

Dumbo sailed back and placed the girl gently beside her parents.

Immediately, the little girl's tears were dried. She was safe in her parents' arms!

The crowd went wild as Dumbo soared high over the arena. Even the clowns were smiling.

"Nice work, kid," Timothy said. "Good show."

Disney · PIXAR
FINDING
NEMO

Who's in Charge?

"Now, Dory," said Marlin, "you have to promise you'll keep a close eye on Nemo while I'm gone. Can you do that?"

"I can do that!" Dory said confidently.

But Marlin was a little worried. Everyone knew that Dory forgot things.

"Now remember," Marlin instructed. "Nemo needs to do his –"

"Science homework, practise playing the conch shell and clean the anemone," interrupted Nemo. "I got it, Dad."

Finally, Marlin waved goodbye and swam off to do his errands. As soon as he was gone, Dory began swimming in circles around the anemone. "Nemo, betcha can't catch me!"

Nemo chased Dory around the anemone a few times. It was fun, and Nemo wished they could play all afternoon. But he knew they couldn't.

"Dory, come on," Nemo called to her. "That was fun, but now I have to do my science homework."

Nemo explained his assignment to Dory: he had to find a sand dollar to bring into class the next day. So Nemo and Dory swam around the reef. Before long, Nemo spotted one.

"That's great!" replied Dory. "Now we can play!"

"No, Dory," he said. "Now I need to practise playing my conch shell."

They swam back to the anemone, where Nemo put his sand dollar away and got out his conch shell. Dory kept time while he played the songs that he needed to memorize for band practice.

"Thanks, Dory!" he said at last. "We're done."

"Yippee!" Dory cried, swimming around Nemo. "Now it's playtime!"

But Nemo remembered their work wasn't done yet. "Not quite, Dory," he said. "I have to clean the anemone before I can play."

"Clean?" Dory said with a frustrated sigh.

Nemo shrugged. "Dad said I should do it before he got home," he replied.

Together, Dory and Nemo cleaned up the zooplankton crumbs. When they were finished, the place was spotless.

"Thanks for helping me, Dory," said Nemo. "That went fast with the two of us working together."

"You're welcome," Dory replied. "So, what do you want to do now?"

Nemo laughed. "What do I want to do now?" he echoed. "I want to play!"

"Play, huh?" Dory said, weighing the idea. "Now, that's a crazy idea. I like it!"

THE LION KING

One Part Hakuna, One Part Matata

"Why are you so sad?" Pumbaa asked Nala.

"I'm not sad," Nala said. "I'm just a little more on the serious side than the two of you."

"I think you could use a little *hakuna matata*," Pumbaa said.

"A whona mawhatta?" Nala asked.

"You really think she can handle it?" Timon whispered to Pumbaa out of the side of his mouth.

"Of course I can handle it!" Nala said, raising her voice. "I just need to know what it is first."

"Ahhhh, *hakuna matata*," Pumbaa said dreamily. "It's the problem-free way of dealing with all of life's inconveniences."

"It means, 'No worries'," Timon explained.

"Oh, I get it," Nala said. "Instead of dealing with your problems, you pretend they don't exist."

"*Hakuna matata* helps you relax," Pumbaa offered.

"It sounds like your *hakuna matata* is just another way of saying 'uninspired and lazy'," Nala continued.

"I think she might have just insulted us," Timon whispered to Pumbaa.

"There you are." Simba came walking towards them. "What are the three of you up to?"

"I was just learning about a strange little notion called *hakuna matata*," Nala explained.

"Isn't it great!" Simba said with a grin.

"Well, sure," Nala said. "If you don't ever want to get anything done."

Simba frowned. "It's not like that. *Hakuna matata* helps you get through things."

"Sure," Nala continued. "*Hakuna matata* – I don't have to worry. I don't have to try."

"I guess you could look at it that way ," Simba said. "But, for me, it means, 'Don't worry about it right now. It's okay.' It gives me the strength to get through the bad times."

"Wow, I hadn't thought about it like that," Nala said.

"So, are you ready to join us now?" Timon asked.

"Absolutely!" Nala smiled.

"Bring on the crunchy beetles!" shouted Pumbaa.

"Let's go tease some elephants!" cried Timon.

"Everyone to the mudhole for a mud fight!" Simba yelled, and the three of them started off.

"Oh, dear," murmured Nala, "this isn't exactly what I had in mind." But she smiled, and ran after her carefree friends. "Last one to the mudhole is a rotten egg!" she cried.

Peter Pan

Tink Learns a Lesson - Or Does She?

Tinker Bell was cross. She and Peter Pan had made plans to explore Skull Cave, but he was still playing "Pirate Treasure" with the Lost Boys. When she jingled impatiently by his ear to let him know it was time to go, he said, "Just a minute, Tink." So, she decided to teach him a lesson. She flew inside a hollow tree.

"Help, help me!" she jingled as loudly as she could. "I'm stuck!"

A moment later Peter appeared. He was out of breath from flying at top speed.

"What is it, Tink?" he gasped. "Are you in trouble?"

Tinker Bell couldn't help laughing at the worried expression on his face. She laughed so hard that she fell right out of the tree.

Peter Pan frowned. "That's not funny, Tink," he said. "I really thought you were in danger! And you interrupted my game!"

He flew away. Tinker Bell stopped laughing. Obviously Peter hadn't learned his lesson yet. He was still leaving her behind to play with his other friends!

She flew to the lagoon and hid among the reeds at the edge.

"Help!" she jingled. "I've got wet!"

Peter rushed over to the lagoon as quickly as he could. He knew how dangerous it was for Tink to get her wings wet.

"Where are you, Tink?" he cried.

Tink couldn't help herself. He sounded so worried. She laughed and laughed, until she rolled right out of the reeds.

Peter looked very, very stern. "Tink, this isn't funny!" he cried. "You're scaring me! I know you want me to finish my game, but the more you interrupt me, the longer it's going to take!"

He flew off. Tinker Bell stopped laughing. (Peter was really testing her patience!)

Tink sat down under a mushroom and thought about how to get even with Peter. One last scare would make him sit up and take notice.

But, as she thought, she became sleepier and sleepier. She leaned back against the mushroom stem and closed her eyes . . .

The next thing Tink knew, she was suddenly snatched up by a hungry hawk! Tink jingled and jingled – but Peter didn't come!

"I'm not fibbing this time, Peter!" she jingled. "I'm about to become lunch! I'm sorry I ever tried to fool you. This time it's real!"

Then she woke up. Tink was very relieved to discover that she was safe and sound under the shady brim of the mushroom.

Tink took a deep breath. That was very scary, she thought. I think perhaps I learned my lesson. . . .

Then she thought about it again. Nah!

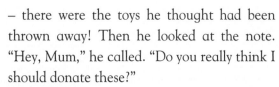

A New Home

Andy's toys were on a rubbish truck, heading for Andy's house. They had had an adventurous few days – after being mistakenly thrown away by Andy's mum, they had ended up at a nursery, held prisoner by an evil bear called Lotso. They escaped, only to nearly be destroyed at a landfill site! The Aliens saved them.

Andy would soon be leaving for college, and he wanted to take Woody with him. The rest of the toys would be stored in the attic. The toys arrived home just as Andy was loading up the car. They snuck into Andy's room and into the box labelled 'Attic' – Woody headed for the box marked 'College'.

"This isn't goodbye," said Woody.

"You know where to find us, Cowboy," Buzz said, then climbed into the box.

Woody waited in the box as Andy and his mum entered the bedroom. "I wish I could always be with you," Andy's mum said sadly.

"You will be, Mum," Andy reassured her.

Woody looked over at a photo of Andy surrounded by his toys. He knew they would remember their special time together, forever. Suddenly, he knew what to do. He sneaked across the room, wrote a note and stuck it on the attic box. When Andy returned, he opened the box and got a wonderful surprise – there were the toys he thought had been thrown away! Then he looked at the note. "Hey, Mum," he called. "Do you really think I should donate these?"

"It's up to you, honey," she called back.

A little later, Andy pulled up in front of a house. A little girl was playing on the front lawn. The note had directed Andy to a girl called Bonnie's house!

"Someone told me you're really good with toys," Andy told Bonnie. "These are mine, but I'm going away now, so I need someone really special to look after them."

Andy took each toy from the box, introducing it to Bonnie. When he got to the bottom, there was Woody. Andy was surprised – Woody didn't belong there! But Bonnie recognized Woody because she'd played with him before. Though it was hard for him, Andy decided to let Woody stay with Bonnie, too. He could see that she already loved him.

Back in the car, Andy took one last look back at his toys. "Bye, guys," he said before pulling away. Bonnie went inside, and the toys watched Andy disappear down the street.

"So long, partner," said Woody.

The others gathered around him. Their life with Andy was ending, but their adventures with Bonnie had just begun.

Disney · PIXAR

WALL·E
Finally Home

On the *Axiom*, the ship where all the humans now lived, little robot EVE delivered a special plant from Earth to the Captain. EVE had found it among the treasures of a robot called WALL•E.

The Captain was excited, because this plant meant he and all the humans could return to Earth. But the Captain's robot wouldn't let them. Quickly Auto snatched the plant and dumped it down the rubbish chute.

It hit WALL•E. The little bot was climbing up to get to EVE! Happily he delivered the plant right back to her. But Auto electrocuted WALL•E and sent him back down the chute with EVE.

WALL•E and EVE ended up in the ship's garbage bay. EVE rescued the injured little bot while WALL•E tried to give her the plant. He still thought she wanted it more than anything else. But WALL•E was wrong. EVE just wanted to help WALL•E now.

Soon EVE flew them up and out of the garbage bay, with the plant in hand. She wanted to get WALL•E home to Earth so she could find the right parts to fix him.

The Captain was fighting Auto for control of the ship by now. He sent a message to EVE, telling her to take the plant to a large machine called the holo-detector. It would ready the ship to head towards Earth.

The Captain finally managed to turn off the bad robot's power. EVE fought to reach the holo-detector. At last she put the plant inside the machine. Finally they could return to Earth.

But all was not well. WALL•E had been crushed by the giant machine! Heartbroken and more determined than before, EVE wanted to take WALL•E home to his truck, where she could find the right parts to bring him back to life.

As soon as the Axiom landed on Earth, EVE headed straight for WALL•E's home and repaired him. At last, he powered up... and began cubing trash. Something was wrong. He was just another trash-cubing robot. All the love was gone. He didn't even recognize EVE!

Sadly, EVE held WALL•E's hand and leaned towards him. An electric arc passed between their heads – the robot kiss. She was saying good-bye. Then... WALL•E's hand began to move. EVE looked into his eyes. He was coming back to life! He recognised her!

"Ee-vah?" he said. After following EVE across the universe, WALL•E had ended up right where he had started: home. But this time, he had the one thing he had always wanted – EVE's hand clasped in his own.

Disney
Pinocchio
A Nose for Trouble

School was out for the day, and Pinocchio was ready to have some fun.

"Wait for me!" Jiminy Cricket called. Jiminy caught up with Pinocchio in front of the small shop where he lived with Geppetto, his father.

"Father, I'm home!" Pinocchio called. "What are you making?"

"A cuckoo clock," Geppetto replied. "I even brought home a live bird for a model." He pointed to a birdcage.

"May I take the bird out and play with him?" Pinocchio asked.

"I'm afraid not," said Geppetto. "You aren't the only one who's been watching him."

Geppetto nodded towards Figaro the cat who was following the cuckoo's every move. At the end of the day, Geppetto went out to the market. As soon as he left, Pinocchio hurried over to the birdcage.

"Pinocchio?" Jiminy said. "What are you doing?"

"Taking the bird out," the puppet replied. As Pinocchio opened the cage door, Figaro jumped onto the table.

"Watch out!" Jiminy cried as the cat leapt towards the birdcage. The bird zipped out of the cage, spotted an open window and flew out. Just then, Geppetto walked in. He glanced at the empty birdcage. "Pinocchio!" he yelled. "I told you not to open the cage!"

Panicked, Pinocchio lied. "I didn't do it! It was Figaro! He opened the birdcage!"

"Figaro!" cried Geppetto. He picked up the cat to scold him.

At that moment, the puppet's nose began to grow. Pinocchio didn't want his father to know that he had lied. "Father," Pinocchio said, "I'm going to bed. I'm not well."

The next morning, Pinocchio got up early and spent the day looking for the cuckoo. Pinocchio told lie after lie. At the end of the day, Pinocchio's nose was longer than ever before – and he still hadn't found the cuckoo. Pinocchio headed home, determined to tell the truth.

"Figaro didn't open the cage," Pinocchio told his father. "I opened it and the cuckoo flew away. I'm sorry I disobeyed you, but most of all, I'm sorry I lied."

As Pinocchio spoke, his nose became shorter and shorter.

"I'm glad you finally told the truth," said Geppetto. "And the cuckoo came back. I was working on the clock today and he flew in through the window. I think he likes it here!"

"He should," Pinocchio said. "It's the best home anyone could ever want."

101 DALMATIANS

Puppy Trouble

Pongo and Perdita were joining Roger and Anita for a picnic with friends.

"I'm not sure we should leave the puppies," Perdita said. "Will Nanny be able to handle all fifteen of them by herself?"

Pongo reassured Perdita as she followed him out of the door.

Soon after, Lucky wanted something to do. "Let's get Nanny to take us for a walk!" he urged the other puppies. Nanny turned and saw fifteen puppies holding their leashes in their mouths.

When they reached the playground, Nanny unhooked their leashes and breathed a sigh of relief as the puppies scampered off to play.

They were so busy playing, that they didn't see Lucky chasing a butterfly and jump from the top of the wall and disappear. Lucky landed in the back of a fire engine, as it started speeding down the road!

"Woof! Woof!" Lucky barked. "I'm a fire dog!" Lucky enjoyed his ride, but he was glad when the fire engine stopped. He knew thathe had to get back to the playground, so he jumped off the fire engine.

"A puppy!" someone squealed.

Lucky looked up and saw a little girl pushing a doll pram. She stroked him.

"You can be my new dolly," the little girl said as she put him in the pram.

Suddenly, the little girl spotted something on the ground. "A button!" she cried. As she bent down to pick it up, Lucky jumped out and ran away as fast as he could.

Lucky raced across the street. He heard a honk as a car swerved to avoid him. Then dirty water splashed all over him, but he kept running until he reached the playground.

Nanny looked up. "Why, hello, little pup," she said to Lucky. "Too bad you can't come with us – you're not a dalmatian."

Lucky was confused, but then he spotted his reflection in a puddle. He was covered with dirt. He looked like a labrador puppy – Nanny didn't recognize him!

Lucky ran over to some children who were playing in a fountain. The children giggled as the little dalmatian splashed about in the fountain.

Lucky ran towards home. He grinned as he spotted Nanny in front of the house, unhooking his brothers' and sisters' leashes.

Later, when Pongo and Perdita came home, they found Lucky sleeping in his basket.

"You see?" Pongo whispered to Perdita. "I told you nothing would go wrong."

DUMBO
Happy to Help

"Whee!" cried Timothy Mouse as he flew through the air, seated inside Dumbo's hat. The young elephant used his big ears to fly around the circus tent. "Way to go!" Timothy said.

Dumbo smiled as he landed softly on the ground. "We had a great rehearsal," Timothy told Dumbo.

Just then some of Timothy's fans spotted him. "You can have the rest of the morning off, Dumbo. Take a nap, we'll practise later."

Dumbo was looking forward to a long nap, when suddenly he heard someone shout: "Oh, no! My beautiful balloons!"

Dumbo looked up. A bunch of colourful balloons were drifting away from a balloon seller. The elephant quickly sprang into action. He flew after the balloons, grabbed the strings with his trunk and flew back to the ground.

"You're the best!" the balloon seller said.

Happy to have helped, Dumbo made his way towards his train car to take his overdue nap. As he walked, he saw a crowd gathering. Using his trunk, he politely nudged his way in to see what was going on. A little girl stood in the middle of the crowd crying.

"I think the poor kid is lost," said a magician. "We must help her. But how?"

Dumbo walked over and tapped the girl on the shoulder with his trunk.

"Great idea, Dumbo!" said the juggler. "You could spot the little girl's mum from above!" He picked up the girl and put her on the elephant's back.

Dumbo and the little girl flew up above the circus tents. They looked down at the crowds of people.

"Mummy! There's my mummy!" the girl shouted.

Dumbo landed gently. The girl climbed off his back and ran into her mother's arms.

"Thank you, Dumbo! Thank you!" said the girl's mother. Dumbo was glad to have been able to help.

Suddenly a pie went whizzing by! Dumbo turned to see some circus clowns throwing pink cream pies at each other. They were covered from head to toe!

"What a mess!" said one of the clowns. "I think it's time for a shower," said another.

Dumbo had an idea! He flew over to the water tank and filled his trunk. Then he sprayed water all over the clowns! The clowns laughed as Dumbo rinsed away the gooey pink pie. Then Dumbo nodded and went off to finally take his long-awaited nap!

Disney
MICKEY MOUSE CLUBHOUSE

Up, Up and Away!

Donald and his friends were standing outside the Clubhouse on a bright day.

"Oh, Donald," Daisy said, "look at the sky! It's lovely!"

"Shhh!" Donald whispered. "Don't make a move! Something is following me!"

Daisy giggled. "Oh, my!" said Daisy. "There is something following you! It's wearing a sailor's cap – just like yours. And when you move, it moves, too."

"Aw, phooey," Donald quacked as he turned around and saw his shadow. "That is a fine-looking shape, but I still don't trust it!"

"Cheer up, buddy," Mickey said. "Why don't we all leave our shadows on the ground and fly our hot-air balloon?"

Soon, the friends were floating high above the Clubhouse.

"Look, everyone!" yelled Minnie. "There are so many shapes below us. I see a triangle and a rectangle. What do you see?"

"What's a triangle?" asked Goofy.

"A triangle is a shape with three sides that all have points at the ends," Minnie explained.

"Like that?" Goofy questioned, pointing to a huge triangle. It was the top of a mountain and they were headed straight for it!

"We need help," cried Mickey. "Oh,

Toodles!"

Toodles appeared with a ladder. Mickey dropped it over the side of the balloon and the friends headed down one by one. Everyone was happy to be standing on firm ground again. But they had to hike back home! The friends trudged along, growing more and more tired.

"I think we've been walking in circles," Mickey finally said. "I'm sure I've seen this tree before. Oh, Toodles!" And Toodles appeared, showing three pictures of Mickey. Mickey shared them with his friends.

"I'm standing in front of the Clubhouse and my shadow is different in each picture. In the morning, my shadow falls in front of me. At noon, I have no shadow. In the evening, my shadow falls behind me. Do any of you know what this could mean?"

"I've got it!" Donald shouted. "Right now, it's late and the sun is setting behind us. Toodles shows that in the evening, our shadows point towards the Clubhouse. If we follow them, they'll lead us back home."

Donald was correct. The shadows helped the friends head in the right direction. Soon, they arrived back at the Clubhouse.

"Well, Donald," Daisy said, "do you trust your shadow now?"

HANDY MANNY

The Un-Fun House

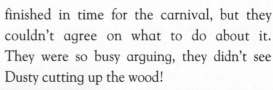

"Oh, hi, Manny," said Rusty. "We're excited about the carnival this weekend."

"I just finished the blueprints for the fun house," said Manny. He explained it would be their guide for cutting and putting together all the pieces of wood they needed.

"It doesn't look like much fun," said Turner.

Manny smiled. "Well, Turner, blueprints give you a basic idea of how the building will be made. They don't show all the colours and decorations we'll be adding."

"Gosh, it looks as though we have a lot of work to do before the weekend," Rusty worried. "Do you think we can get it all done before the carnival opens?"

"Sure we can. I'll just start sawing as soon as the wood arrives at the school," Dusty said.

The phone rang. "Hola, this is Manny. Hi, Principal Chu. The supplies have arrived at the school? Excelente! We'll be right there!"

Manny and the tools arrived at the school and unloaded the truck. Stretch took an inventory. "I think we're ready to get started," Squeeze said.

Manny's smile faded. "Wait a minute, guys. We can't start work yet. I forgot to bring the blueprints. I'll be right back, tools."

The tools started quarrelling. They were all nervous that the job wouldn't be finished in time for the carnival, but they couldn't agree on what to do about it. They were so busy arguing, they didn't see Dusty cutting up the wood!

"Dusty, what did you do?" shrieked Felipe. "This isn't the way the blueprints said to cut the wood."

"Gosh, I just wanted to help, but I've ruined everything!" cried Dusty.

Just then, Manny's truck and Kelly's car pulled up. Manny called, "Hey, tools, I brought some friends along! They've all offered to help build the fun house."

"Uh," Turner groaned. "I think we can officially rename this project the un-fun house!"

"Oh, Manny, I'm so sorry!" Dusty said with a sob. "I should have waited for the blueprints – now the kids won't have a fun house to play in, and it's all my fault!"

"Dusty, now do you see why you can't start any job without being fully prepared?" Manny asked.

"Why don't we pick up each piece and think about how we can use it in a new design?" suggested Kelly. "For example, this big triangle looks like the roof of a tower."

Everyone worked together, and made a fun-castle! "Ta-da!" shouted Felipe, admiring the castle. "It's a fun house fit for a king!"

Doggone It, Stitch

Stitch was sitting waiting for Lilo to come home from school. Just then, Lilo burst in carrying a puppy. "Hi, Stitch!" Lilo said excitedly. "My neighbour Leilani asked me to take care of her puppy, Rover, while she visits her grandmother."

"Stitch wants to listen to music," Stitch said.

"Not now," Lilo said. "I have to take care of Rover." Stitch watched Lilo make a bed for Rover. He was bored. He wanted Lilo to play. "Can we listen to music now?" Stitch asked.

"I want to teach Rover some new tricks," Lilo said. Lilo taught Rover tricks all afternoon while Stitch watched.

That evening, Nani, Lilo's older sister, came home from work. She and Lilo watched Rover play tug-of-war with the kitchen rug. They laughed at everything Rover did. They didn't pay any attention to Stitch.

The next morning, Stitch tried to act like Rover. He hid Lilo's shoes and chewed the kitchen rug. But that only made Lilo angry. "You need a time-out," she told Stitch. "Go to our room while I take Rover for a walk."

Stitch waited until Lilo and Rover were gone. Then he hurried outside and ran towards town. When Lilo and Rover came home, she wondered why Stitch wasn't there. Lilo asked Nani and David if they had seen him. Before they could answer, Cobra Bubbles called. He was a social worker that Lilo and Nani knew.

"You need to hide Stitch," Cobra told Lilo. "Two scientists are looking for him."

"But I don't know where Stitch is!" Lilo said.

"Well, I suggest you find him before the scientists do," Cobra said.

Lilo and Nani looked for Stitch. "Stitch has been acting weird all day," Lilo told Nani. "His badness level was way up. He acted just like Rover!"

Suddenly, Lilo knew where Stitch had gone. "I bet Stitch went to the animal shelter to watch the puppies!"

When Lilo and Nani arrived, Stitch was there. "Stitch learning to be cute like puppy," he explained.

"Stitch, I like you just the way you are," Lilo answered. "Now, let's go home!" But when they started to leave, they saw the scientists.

Nani spotted two dusters in the cupboard. She tied them on to Stitch so he looked like a long-haired puppy. Lilo put a leash on Stitch, and they walked out, past the scientists.

Just then, Cobra Bubbles and David drove up. "Hey!" David called. "We just saw an alien heading out to sea. We'll take you there." The scientists jumped into the car, and Cobra Bubbles and David sped off. Stitch was safe!

Bambi
The Winter Trail

One winter morning, Bambi was dozing in the wood when he heard a thumping sound nearby. "C'mon, Bambi!" his bunny friend Thumper cried. "It's a perfect day for playing."

Bambi followed Thumper through the forest. The sky was blue and the ground covered in a blanket of new snow.

"Look at these tracks!" Thumper said excitedly. He pointed to a line of footprints in the snow. "Who do you suppose they belong to?" Bambi didn't know, so they decided to follow the trail. They soon came to a tree.

"Wake up, Friend Owl!" called Thumper.

"Have you been out walking?" Bambi asked.

"Now why would I do that?" Friend Owl replied. "My wings take me everywhere."

Bambi and Thumper continued on. Next, they spotted a raccoon sitting next to a tree, his mouth full of red berries. "Hello, Mr Raccoon," Bambi said shyly. "Did you happen to see who made these tracks in the snow?"

The raccoon shook his head and began tapping the tree. "I know!" Thumper cried. "He thinks we should ask the woodpeckers."

Soon, Bambi and Thumper had found the woodpecker family. "Did you make the tracks in the snow?" Thumper called up to the birds.

"No, we've been here all day," the mother bird answered.

"If the tracks don't belong to the woodpeckers or the raccoon and they don't belong to Friend Owl, whose can they be?" Bambi asked.

"I don't know," Thumper replied, frustrated.

They soon reached the end of the trail, and the tracks led all the way to a snowy bush, where a family of quail were resting.

"Did you make these tracks?" Thumper asked.

"Why, yes," Mrs Quail answered. "Friend Owl told me about this wonderful bush. So this morning, my babies and I walked all the way over here."

Thumper and Bambi happily joined the quail family for a snack. Soon, it was time for the friends to go home. They'd spent all day following the trail. When they turned to leave, a big surprise was waiting for them – their mothers! Bambi bounded over to his mother and stretched his nose up for a kiss.

"How'd ya find us?" Thumper asked.

Thumper's mother looked down at the tracks in the snow.

"You followed our trail!" Bambi cried. His mother nodded.

"Now, let's follow it back home," Bambi's mother said. So that's just what they did.

THE LION KING

Why Worry?

Zazu didn't know what to do with Timon and Pumbaa! Ever since they had come to the Pride Lands, he'd been trying to find the perfect jobs for them.

"Zazu," said Simba, "I think you should forget it. Timon and Pumbaa are used to taking life as it comes. *Hakuna matata –* no worries – that's their philosophy."

"Well, it's certainly not mine!" said Zazu.

That afternoon, the hornbill told Timon and Pumbaa that they would be in charge of watching the cubs while the lionesses went off to hunt. "No problem!" said Timon.

"Can we go to the water hole by ourselves?" asked Kiara, Simba's daughter.

"Sure," said Timon. "Have fun!"

"Do we have to take a nap?" wondered another cub.

"Not if you don't want to," said Pumbaa.

The cubs thought Timon and Pumba were the best babysitters on Earth. But Zazu didn't. He was furious.

"Aw, Zazu," said Timon. "Loosen up!"

"Things are loose enough around here as it is." Zazu sniffed. "Too loose, if you ask me."

The next day, Zazu put Timon and Pumbaa in charge of clearing the brushes around the water hole. As they uprooted each plant, they found an insect feast in the soil underneath. Pretty soon they were stuffed. It was time for a nap.

"What's this?" shouted Zazu. "Sleeping on the job?"

"Don't get your feathers in a ruffle," replied Timon. "What is it with you, anyway? You seem kind of tense all the time."

"Tense? Of course I'm tense!" Zazu shouted. "I'm Simba's right-hand man. It's up to me to see that the kingdom is in perfect order!"

Pumbaa spoke up. "And you do a very good job of it too."

"Thank you," said Zazu.

"But," added Timon, "what good is an ordered kingdom if you never stop to enjoy it?"

Zazu admitted that Timon had a point. The other members of the kingdom always seemed to head in the other direction every time they saw Zazu coming. Maybe he was too hard on everyone, including himself.

"Gentlemen," Zazu said. "I finally have the perfect job for you. I'm making you the ministers of *hakuna matata*. You are in charge of keeping things from getting too serious around here."

Simba was delighted when he found out. "Zazu, you're a genius!" he said.

"Thank you, sire," said Zazu. "I always said there was something special about those two!"

Buzz Off

The toys were excited. Bonnie was going to the park with Woody, Jessie and Dolly. The others were looking forward to a day of fun. But Jessie was worried. "Keep an eye on Buzz," she told her friends. "I think he may have a loose wire."

Bonnie rushed in and grabbed her bag. "Buzz, you're in charge now," she said as she left.

The peas began bouncing on their shelf. "Wait! This looks dangerous," said Buzz.

Just then, Slinky slipped from the shelf, causing the Aliens and peas to fall too! They tumbled on top of Buzz. Buzz stood up and looked around. "Donde esta mi nave?"

"Oh great," Hamm sighed. "He's switched into Spanish mode again."

Rex tried to look in Buzz's back panel, but the space ranger dodged him! The toys tried to catch him, but Buzz grabbed a curtain from the dollhouse and held it up like a bullfighter's cape. Hamm ran to tackle his friend, but he skidded and.... *CRASH!* Hamm slid right into the bookshelf and a book fell onto Buzz's head! After a moment, Buzz pushed the book away.

"Buzz, are you okay?" Rex cried.

"Buzz, are you okay?" Buzz repeated.

Hamm whispered to Buttercup, "He must have gotten knocked into Repeat Mode!"

The toys were worried. Jessie had asked them to take care of Buzz! They had to fix Buzz before Jessie and Bonnie returned.

"We're gonna have to jiggle his wires," Hamm sighed.

The toys pulled Buzz onto the bed, then Rex jumped. *Boing!* Buzz flew right off the bed and landed on the floor! Then the toys heard the car pull into the driveway.

"Hurry!" Hamm shouted. Rex undid Buzz's back panel and stared at the wires. He didn't know which one to fix! There was a noise outside and the toys went limp just as Bonnie's mother walked in, put down Bonnie's bag and left again. Jessie climbed out. "Buzz, are you okay?" she asked.

"Oh, he's fine," Trixie propped Buzz into a sitting position. But he fell over with a thunk.

"It's not my fault!" Rex wailed. "There are too many wires!"

Jessie laughed, then she whacked Buzz on the back. Buzz blinked and looked at his friends. "Do I have something on my face?" he asked. The other toys sighed with relief. Buzz was back to normal!

Minutes later, Bonnie arrived. Everything was the way she had left it. "Thanks for looking after everyone, Buzz. I knew this place would be okay with you in charge!"

Hanukkah Fun

"Happy Hanukkah, Pooh Bear!" Roo exclaimed as he opened the door for his first guest. It was the first night of Hanukkah, and Roo and Kanga were having all their friends over to participate in some Hanukkah customs.

"Happy Hanukkah, Roo!" Pooh replied. Just then a delicious smell wafted by his nose. "Something smells yummy!" Pooh cried.

Kanga was making little potato pancakes called *latkes*, a special Hanukkah treat. "Try to be patient, Pooh," Kanga said with a smile. "We'll have these latkes a little bit later."

Before long, Piglet, Eeyore, Rabbit, Tigger and Owl had also arrived and it was time to light the Menorah, a candleholder that could hold nine candles.

"First," Kanga explained, "we light this centre candle, called the *shammosh*. Then, we use the shammosh to light one other candle for the first night of Hanukkah."

Tigger noticed that there weren't any candles in the other seven candle holders of the Menorah. "When do we light the other candles?" he asked Kanga.

"Well, Tigger," Kanga said, "Hanukkah lasts for eight nights. So tomorrow, on the second night, we will light two candles with the shammosh. On the third night, we will light three candles, and so on . . . until, on the eighth night, we will light all the candles!"

Everyone watched the candles burning. Then Pooh said, "Um, Kanga? Is it a little bit later . . . now?"

Kanga understood: Pooh was hungry for a latke! Kanga brought the potato pancakes to the table and everyone enjoyed the delicious treats.

When they were all eaten, Roo said, "Now let's play *dreidel*!" He got out a four-sided, clay spinning top. Kanga made a pile of sweets, nuts and pennies in the centre of the floor. She also gave a little pile of goodies to each guest.

Roo explained the rules, then each player took turns spinning the dreidel. Depending on what side the dreidel landed on, the player might win more treats from the centre pile, or lose treats from their own pile and have to add them to the centre pile.

"This is fun!" Piglet exclaimed. "And to think: there are seven *more* nights of Hanukkah!"

"Hey, Mama," said Roo, "there are eight of us and eight nights of Hanukkah. Can our friends come over every night of Hanukkah, and take turns lighting the Menorah?"

Everyone, including Kanga, thought that was a wonderful idea.

So that was exactly what they did.

DISNEY·PIXAR
MONSTERS, INC.

Bedtime for Billy

Mike the one-eyed monster and his friend, Sulley, were excited about their evening. They were monster-sitting for Mike's nephew, Billy. Billy's mother told her son to be good, and he said that he would.

"Everything will be fine, Sis," said Mike. "Sulley and I will take good care of the little guy. You don't have to worry about a thing."

Billy's parents kissed him good-bye and hopped in the car. The three monsters went inside and ate pizza and popcorn while they watched classic movies like Gross Encounters of the Kid Kind. After the movies were over, the three monsters listened to music, sang and danced. Billy and Mike even had a video-game contest! The night flew by and soon it was bedtime.

"It's time for some shut-eye, Buddy," said Mike with a yawn. But putting Billy to bed wasn't going to be that easy. There was one very important detail that Billy's mother had forgotten to tell her monster-sitters. Billy was scared of the dark!

"Aaaaaaahhhhh!!!!" screamed Billy.

"Wh-wh-what is it?" shouted Mike as he and Sulley ran back into the bedroom.

"There's a kid hiding in the c-closet . . ." stammered Billy. "It wants to g-get me!"

Mike and Sulley searched for human children. They checked the whole room, once with the lights on and twice with the lights off.

"There aren't any kids in the closet," said Mike.

"All clear under the bed," announced Sulley.

"See, there's nothing to worry about," Mike said. "You can go to sleep now."

But Billy was still frightened. Mike and Sulley quickly realised they had to come up with another plan. How could they show Billy that children weren't scary?

"I've got it!" exclaimed Mike. "The scrapbook!"

"You're a genius, Mikey!" declared Sulley.

The three monsters looked through the scrapbook. It was filled with photographs of monsters with children, newspaper clippings of them together and laugh reports.

"See, Billy," said Mike. "Human kids are not dangerous, and they love to have fun just like you."

"And they help us!" added Sulley. "Their laughter powers our city!"

"You know, Billy, sometimes human kids get scared of us," said Mike. "But once they see that we're funny and friendly, they realise there's no reason to be scared of monsters."

Billy soon fell fast asleep as Mike and Sulley watched from the doorway. "Another job well done, Mike," said Sulley.

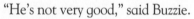

"Hey, Hey, We're the Vultures!"

"Nothing exciting ever happens around here," Buzzie complained to his vulture singing buddies.

"That's not true," said Flaps. "What about that fight we had with the tiger Shere Khan last week?"

"Blimey, you're right," said Ziggy. "That was pretty exciting."

"But what are we gonna do now?" asked Buzzie.

"Let's sing," suggested Ziggy.

"Hey, good idea!" said the other three vultures.

"Only one problem," said Dizzy. "We need a tenor."

"Awww, you're right," said Ziggy. "That little Man-cub fellow, Mowgli, would have been a great tenor. Too bad he left the jungle."

"So, what are we gonna do?" asked Buzzie.

"How 'bout we hold an audition?" suggested Ziggy.

"Good thinking," said Flaps.

So the vultures put the word out in the jungle and, a week later, there was a line of animals ready to try out for the group.

"Name?" Buzzie asked the first applicant.

"Coconut," the monkey replied.

"All right, Coconut, let's hear ya sing," said Flaps.

Coconut shrieked for a few minutes, and the four vultures huddled together.

"He's not very good," said Buzzie.

"And he's a monkey," added Flaps.

"Next!" said Dizzy.

The vultures auditioned a lemur, two sloths, a wolf, a hippo, a toad and an elephant. None seemed like the right fit. Finally, the last animal stepped up.

"Name?" asked Buzzie.

"Name's Lucky," said the vulture. "Hey, aren't you the four fellows that helped that little Man-cub scare away that tiger Shere Khan?"

"Yeah," said Buzzie. "We are."

"Then I guess you four might be called 'lucky' yourselves!" cried Lucky. He began to laugh at his own joke.

"Go ahead and sing," said Ziggy, rolling his eyes.

Lucky sang for a few minutes and the four vultures huddled together.

"He's not bad," said Dizzy.

"Plus, he's a vulture," said Ziggy.

"And he's the last one left," pointed out Flaps. That settled it.

"You're hired!" the vultures sang.

"See, told you I was Lucky!" cried the vulture.

"But only with auditions," said Dizzy.

"Yeah," said Buzzie. "When we meet Shere Khan again, we'll see how lucky you really are!"

Tinker Bell's Bedtime Story

"Shove over!"

"No. You shove over."

The Raccoon Twins were at it again. Peter Pan knew the bickering wouldn't stop until one of the boys had pushed the other out of the hammock.

"Hey!" Cubby yelled. The twins had tumbled out and landed right on top of the bear-suited boy.

Peter sighed. Every evening had ended like this ever since Wendy left.

As the tussle grew, Peter had an idea. He went to look for Tinker Bell.

"Say, Tink," Peter said when he found her, "how'd you like to be the new mother to all of us boys?"

Tink looked at Peter as if he was crazy.

"Aw, c'mon," Peter said. "You've seen the guys since Wendy left. They're fighting something awful. They need someone to tuck them in at night and tell them a bedtime story."

Tink was silent for a moment.

"I guess I could ask Wendy to come back," Peter said, looking at Tinker Bell slyly.

That did it. The last thing Tink wanted was for Wendy to return! The little fairy flew into the hideout and shook a finger at the Lost Boys.

"Gosh, Tink. What is it?" Slightly sat up, straightening his fox ears.

"Tink is going to tell us a bedtime story," said Peter.

The boys settled down. "Go ahead, Tink," Peter smiled. His plan was working perfectly!

Tink sat down and crossed her arms over her chest. She began to jingle.

"Once upon a time," Peter translated, "there was a beautiful fairy who, against her better judgement, lived with a pack of dirty, unruly, silly boys. And the dirtiest, unruliest and silliest of them all was Peter Pa– hey!" Peter interrupted his translation. "That's not nice, Tink!"

Tinker Bell jingled spitefully at him. "Okay," Peter said with a sigh, "I know it's your story. Go ahead." Tink continued and Peter translated, "One day, as the lovely Tinker Bell was minding her own business, the very smelly and unpleasant Peter Pan – *Tink*! – asked her to tell a bedtime story. Well, Tinker Bell didn't know any bedtime stories, so she went to fetch Captain Hook, so *he* could tell one."

With that, Tinker Bell flew out of the window.

"Tink! Tink, come back!" Peter cried. Tinker Bell returned and hovered in the window, jingling with laughter. "That was a dirty trick!" Peter scolded. "And besides, that's no way to tell a bedtime story." He sat down next to the boys' beds. "You have to do it like Wendy did. Like this."

Now it was Tink's turn to smile. While Peter told a bedtime story, and the Lost Boys drifted off to sleep, Tink curled up in her own little bed and closed her eyes. Her plan had worked perfectly!

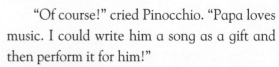

Pinocchio
The Greatest Gift

Pinocchio was the luckiest boy in the world – and he knew it. No longer a wooden puppet, at last he was a real, live boy! And Pinocchio knew he owed it all to Geppetto for believing in him.

"I wish I could give Papa something in return," Pinocchio said to himself one day.

Pinocchio didn't have any money, so he decided to make a gift for Geppetto.

"Perhaps I should use Papa's tools and carve a present for him out of wood!" said Pinocchio.

So, one afternoon, while Geppetto was out, Pinocchio sat down at the woodworking bench. The only problem was, Pinocchio did not know the first thing about woodworking.

"That looks dangerous," said Pinocchio, eyeing a chisel. "I don't think Papa would want me to use that on my own." He decided he needed another gift idea. "I know!" he said. "Maybe I can cook something for Papa!"

Pinocchio went over to the hearth, where Geppetto did all of the cooking.

But he soon realized that he didn't know how to cook either. "And Papa is always telling me to stay a safe distance away from the fire," he reminded himself.

Pinocchio looked around the little house and spotted Geppetto's accordion sitting on the table.

"Of course!" cried Pinocchio. "Papa loves music. I could write him a song as a gift and then perform it for him!"

So Pinocchio picked up the accordion and began to play. But the sounds that came out were . . . well . . . just awful!

"Hmph," Pinocchio said in frustration. "I don't know how to play the accordion or write a song." He put the accordion down and stood in the middle of the room. Tears were welling up in poor little Pinocchio's eyes when Geppetto came in through the front door.

"My dear boy," Geppetto said, hurrying to Pinocchio's side, "what is the matter?"

Through his tears, Pinocchio explained how he had wanted to make a gift to show Geppetto how much he appreciated everything his father had done for him.

As Geppetto listened, his look of worry softened into a smile, and then *his* eyes welled up with tears. "My son," he said, "don't you know that you, and you alone, are the greatest gift a father could ever want?"

"I am?" Pinocchio asked.

"You are," replied Geppetto.

"Well, in that case," said Pinocchio with a sly grin as he hugged his papa, "you're welcome!"

Then Geppetto picked up the accordion and they sang and danced all the rest of the day.

THE INCREDIBLES

A Job for the Incredibles!

Mr Incredible, his wife Elastigirl and their children Violet and Dash had just defeated a deadly robot created by Syndrome.

Syndrome's real name was Buddy, and as a boy he'd wanted to be Mr Incredible's sidekick. When Mr Incredible told Buddy that Supers were born, not made, Buddy had vowed to prove him wrong.

Syndrome had created an Omnidroid robot that only he could defeat. He sent the robot to the city and turned up at the last moment to 'save the day' – but his plan had gone wrong. The robot had turned against him, and the Incredibles had saved the city instead. Syndrome was angry.

Later, when the Incredibles went home, they found a new sitter had come for their youngest child, Jack-Jack – it was Syndrome!

"You stole my future," said Syndrome. "I'm returning the favour! Don't worry, I'll be a good mentor... and in time, who knows? He might make a good sidekick!"

Syndrome blasted a hole in the roof and flew off with Jack-Jack towards his waiting jet. But Jack-Jack was upset. He began to cry and wail. Then he began to transform using Super powers! Suddenly Syndrome was no longer holding a sweet baby, but a flaming monster! Jack-Jack tore through Syndrome's rocket boots. Syndrome quickly dropped him and raced for his nearby jet.

Mr Incredible and Elastigirl were shocked. Until now, they thought Jack-Jack didn't have any Super powers!

Mr Incredible used his strength to throw Elastigirl into the air. She caught Jack-Jack and then stretched out into a parachute to bring him safely back to the ground.

"This isn't the end of it!" Syndrome raged. But he was wrong. Mr Incredible picked up a car and threw it at the jet. Syndrome's cape got caught in one of the engines and with one last yell, he was gone. As the jet exploded, Vi protected her family with a force field – the Incredibles were safe.

"That's my girl," said Elastigirl.

The Incredibles returned to their undercover life. But fitting in was just a little easier now. Vi was more confident and Dash was allowed to use a little of his Super speed by running on the school team.

But as the Super family left school sports day, the ground began to rumble. A monstrous machine broke out of the earth, with a menacing figure riding on top of it. It was time for the family to put on their masks and change into their Super suits. This was a job for the Incredibles.

December
15

Mike's Dog Problem

It was business as usual at the new Monsters, Inc. Mike Wazowski was one of the top Laugh Collectors. He told funny jokes and made children giggle a lot, but lately, he was having trouble on the job.

"Oh, no, this kid has a dog!" Mike groaned as he read the paperwork for his next assignment. Mike was terrified of dogs, but no one else knew. He was too embarrassed to say anything.

Mike was pacing the Laugh Floor, trying to come up with a good excuse to skip work, when his friend Sulley arrived.

"What are you waiting for, buddy?" asked Sulley.

Mike couldn't think of an excuse, so reluctantly he walked into the boy's bedroom He saw the dog straight away and jumped up on a stool to get away from it . . . but this was a playful dog. It ran up to the stool and sat in front of Mike, who got so nervous he couldn't remember his jokes!

The boy didn't laugh at all, and Mike was very upset. He just couldn't relax when dogs were around. He would have to go back to work without any laughs.

The next day, Mike was assigned to the same room because he hadn't collected enough laughs. Sulley noticed that Mike didn't want to go, so he snuck in behind him to find out why.

Once inside, Mike tried to tell a joke – but he was so nervous that he froze with fear.

Watching from outside, Sulley suddenly realised that his friend was afraid of dogs! That day after work, he asked Mike about it.

"I feel like a giant chew toy when I'm near them, like any second they might bite me!" cried Mike.

"Don't worry, pal," Sulley said. He then taught Mike all about dogs.

They read stories and watched videos together about friendly dogs. "Remember Mike," Sulley said. "Even though dogs slobber, have big teeth and make loud noises, that doesn't mean they're scary."

The next day, Mike and Sulley went to a room with a dog. Mike remembered what Sulley had taught him – to stay calm and let the dog sniff him. He took a deep breath. The dog bounded over and sniffed Mike, who tried to relax. The dog was friendly and Mike began to feel comfortable. Soon he was telling one joke after another! Thanks to Sulley's help, Mike became the top Laugh Collector again – and he even grew to like dogs.

"Maybe I'll get a dog," declared Mike.

"Maybe you should start with a hamster," Sulley said with a chuckle.

New Friends

In South America, Carl was sitting inside his house. He had flown it there with thousands of balloons tied to it. He had promised his wife, Ellie, that he would take her to Paradise Falls one day, but sadly she had passed away. Carl kept his promise but he felt sad. That is, until he looked through Ellie's adventure book. It was full of pictures of their life together. Carl had realized their life had been the true adventure.

A boy named Russell had accidentally come along for the ride. They'd met a strange, big bird called Kevin and a talking dog named Dug. A pack of dogs were trying to catch Kevin. Their leader, the explorer Charles Muntz, wanted to capture the bird. Russell was angry at Carl. Carl had promised to protect Kevin, but he had let the bird go in order to save his house from a fire.

Suddenly, Carl heard something. He hurried outside and saw Russell gripping a bunch of balloons. "I'm gonna help Kevin, even if you won't!" Russell cried.

"No!" Carl shouted. He had to help Russell, but the house wouldn't move. The balloons had lost too much air. He had an idea. He began throwing things out of the house to make it lighter. Carl realized he didn't need the things – Russell was more important!

Carl was on his way, but then he heard a knock at the door. It was Dug. Together they set out to rescue Russell. Then they saw the boy being lowered out of Charles' airship! Carl grabbed the garden hose and, using it like a rope, he swung over to the airship and saved Russell.

Once Russell was safe, Carl and Dug went back for Kevin. They set the bird free, but suddenly Muntz appeared with a sword! Carl fought him and finally escaped. He made it back to the house when *BANG!* The balloons began to pop.

The house plunged downwards and landed on top of Charles' airship. As Carl fell out of the house, Muntz ran inside to grab Kevin. Carl knew he had to save his friends – the house was about to fall off the edge of the airship. Carl told Russell and Dug to hold onto Kevin, then he waved a big bar of chocolate – Kevin loved chocolate. The big bird jumped onto the airship, saving Russell and Dug at the same time. Muntz's foot got caught in some balloons, and he drifted away.

"Sorry about your house," Russell told Carl as they watched it disappear into the clouds.

"You know," said Carl, "it's just a house."

It didn't seem as important to him, now that he had friends. They climbed aboard the airship – it was time to go home.

Where Mowgli Belongs

Mowgli the Man-cub had lived in the jungle his whole life. Bagheera the panther had found Mowgli and taken him to Mother Wolf – he grew up happy in the jungle. But everything changed when Mowgli was ten years old. Shere Khan, the man-eating tiger, heard about Mowgli and came looking for him. The wolves agreed Bagheera should take the boy back to the Man-village where he would be safe. So Bagheera and Mowgli set off on their long journey. Mowgli was angry. He didn't want to leave his home in the jungle.

Along the way, Mowgli encountered a python who wanted to swallow him up, a parade of very noisy elephants and the King of the Apes – who wanted to know how to make fire. Mowgli also made a friend, Baloo the bear.

But when Baloo tried to tell Mowgli he needed to go to the Manvillage, Mowgli ran away. It wasn't long before Shere Khan found Mowgli. The tiger gave a loud roar. He leapt at Mowgli, taking the Man-cub by surprise!

But Baloo arrived and fought with Shere Khan. Baloo was knocked onto the ground and Mowgli was terrified that he wasn't going to wake up.

But Baloo did wake up! Mowgli laughed and threw his arms round the big bear's neck.

Suddenly, a lightning bolt struck a nearby tree, which burst into flames. Shere Khan was terrified! Fire was the only thing that scared him.

Seeing his chance to get back at the tiger, Mowgli picked up a burning branch. The Man-cub tied the branch to the tiger's tail. Shere Khan screamed as he tried to get it off. Then he fled into the jungle – never to be seen again!

The three friends carried on towards the Man-village.

Suddenly, they heard someone singing across the river. Mowgli peered through the trees and saw a young girl kneeling by the river.

"Isn't she pretty!" cried Mowgli, climbing a tree to have a closer look.

The girl turned and smiled. Mowgli shyly smiled back. When she began to walk off towards the Man-village, Mowgli ran to join her.

Baloo and Bagheera felt very sad that their young friend was leaving. But they knew he would now be happy and safe. "It's where he belongs," said Bagheera. "Come on Baloo, let's get back to where we belong."

And so the two friends headed slowly back towards the jungle, singing happily.

Having a Ball!

"**T**en days until Santa!" the spotted puppies barked, bouncing into one another as they tumbled down the hall.

"Ten days until presents!" Penny barked.

"And ten days until Christmas dinner!" Rolly added.

"Ten days to stay out of trouble!" Pongo said with a smile.

"Do you puppies know what comes before Santa and dinner and presents?" Perdita asked.

"Umm. . . stockings?" Lucky asked.

"No, before that," she said.

Patch wasn't sure. He sat down on the hall rug to think.

"We have to decorate and sing carols," Perdita said, wagging her tail. At that very moment, Roger and Anita threw open the door to the study and invited all the dogs inside.

Patch blinked. He couldn't believe his eyes. "What's a tree doing in the house?"

"Just watch." Perdy gave Patch a quick lick.

While the dogs looked on, Roger and Anita began to decorate the tree. They hung lights and angels, snowmen and tinsel. Of all the decorations, Patch liked the glittering glass balls best. Balls were one of his favourite things! He could not take his eyes off them.

When the tree was ready, Anita brought in cocoa and dog biscuits. Munching on a biscuit in front of the fire, Patch didn't think the evening could get any better. Then Roger sat down at the piano, and everyone began to sing.

Patch howled along with the others, but he could not stop looking at the balls on the tree. A large red one was hanging near the floor.

Patch reached over and gave the ball a pat with his front paw. It swung merrily above him. Looking at his reflection, Patch started to laugh. His nose looked huge!

"What are you doing?" Penny stopped singing to see what was so funny. Then Freckles joined them, then Lucky. The puppies took turns knocking the ball and watching it sway, then – *crash*! – it fell to the floor, shattering.

The singing stopped. Poor Patch was sure the special evening was ruined.

"Oh, dear." Anita scooped the puppies out from under the tree. "Careful, now," she said. "Those balls aren't for playing with."

While Roger swept up the glass, Patch cowered. He knew he was in trouble.

"Maybe I should give you all one gift early," Anita said with a grin. Patch couldn't believe his luck. Instead of a firm talking-to, each puppy got to rip open a small package. Patch tore off the paper. Inside was a brand-new red rubber ball!

MICKEY MOUSE
CLUBHOUSE

Look Before You Leap!

Mickey and Goofy were enjoying a game of chess, when something soared through the window and landed in the middle of the chessboard! The two friends looked carefully at something that looked right back at them. It was green. It had webbed feet. It said, "Ribbit, ribbit." It was a frog – a very jumpy frog. Goofy tried to grab it. *PLOP!* The frog leaped out of Goofy's hands and right into the kitchen sink.

"You should look before you leap!" Mickey said to the frog. All of the excitement made Goofy hungry. He decided to make lunch. Just then, the frog took a giant leap right towards Goofy's sandwich! SQUISH!

"Stop!" Mickey cried.

"You really should look before you leap," Goofy said to the frog. "And I should look before I bite!" Goofy carried the frog outside.

"Hold on tight," Mickey said. "He's pretty slippery." Goofy yelped as the frog leaped right towards Daisy's painting! SPLAT!

"You should look before you leap!" Daisy said as the paint splattered everywhere.

"I think we should help our friend the frog find a nice, safe pond," Mickey said. "Then he can leap without causing any trouble."

The frog jumped up and down in agreement. Then he hopped down Main Street with Mickey and Goofy following behind him. He took a great big leap and landed right inside Minnie's goldfish bowl! SPLASH! The big wave made the goldfish fly right out. Minnie gently put the goldfish back into its bowl.

"I don't know if we'll ever find a pond for froggie. We need some help!" Goofy sighed.

"Oh, Toodles!" Mickey called. "The net is the right tool for this job."

They held the frog safely in the net. "He seems sad," Goofy said. Mickey agreed. Then he looked ahead and saw something that made him smile. "I think we've found just the right place!"

The friends walked down the street towards a fountain. Carefully, Mickey placed the net on the ground. The frog hopped out and landed with a SWOOSH! right next to another frog!

"Ribbit, ribbit," he said.

"Ribbit, ribbit," she replied.

"Maybe we didn't find a pond," said Mickey, "but we did find a good place for him to splash and leap. And a friend for him, too."

Later, Mickey and Goofy got back to their game of chess. "C'mon, Mickey," Goofy said, "you haven't made a move in a long time."

"I know, I know," replied Mickey. "I just want to make sure I look carefully before I leap!"

DUMBO

The Show Must Go On

The wind whistled around the Big Top, pulling the canvas tent Dumbo was holding out of reach of his small trunk. "I'll get it," Dumbo's mother said as the tent flapped over their heads.

If the weather hadn't been so terrible, Dumbo thought, he could have flown up to grab the edge of the tent. But the whipping wind was too much, even for Dumbo's wing-like ears.

At last, standing on her back legs, Mrs Jumbo caught the canvas in her trunk. She pulled it taut and let the roustabouts tie it off. But Dumbo noticed several new rips in the fabric.

"Quit your clowning!" the Ringmaster barked at the clowns. He noticed the rips too. He ordered the clowns to sew them up. "The repairs must be finished by showtime!"

Dumbo felt terrible. All the circus performers, animals and roustabouts were working hard in the storm. He had gone and made even more work, by letting the canvas get torn. And now the Ringmaster's mood was as foul as the weather!

Just then Dumbo noticed another blast of cold air whirl the Ringmaster's black top hat off his head.

"That does it!" the Ringmaster shouted. "There will be no show tonight!"

Dumbo could not believe his ears. The announcement was even enough to wake Timothy Q. Mouse from his nap in a nearby bale of hay.

"No show? I can't believe it!" Timothy cried. The rest of the circus folk couldn't believe it either. They silently continued to set up.

"What a fuss over a hat." Timothy shook his head. "The show must go on."

Dumbo nodded. Then something caught his eye. The Ringmaster's hat was caught on the flagpole, high over the Big Top. Perhaps he could get it for him.

Bravely, Dumbo took off. The wind was strong, but he tucked his head down and flapped his ears hard. When the wind calmed for a moment, the small elephant saw his chance. He grabbed the top hat and flew quickly to the ground.

Shyly, Dumbo held out the hat to the Ringmaster.

"Thank you, Dumbo." The Ringmaster took his hat gratefully. He looked around at all the people and animals still hard at work. He looked a little embarrassed. Then, as he placed the hat on his head, he shouted, "The show must go on!"

Everyone cheered.

"What'd I tell ya?" Timothy asked, winking at Dumbo.

Old Man Octopus

"You're it!" Nemo tagged Sheldon, who was hiding next to a mollusc.

"Aw, man!" Sheldon swished his tail. "I'm going to get you next time, Nemo."

"Only if you can find me," Nemo teased. Then he called louder, "Ollie, ollie, all swim free!" The rest of the fish who were playing hide-and-seek returned to the giant barnacle they were using as base. When they were all there, Sheldon began to count again.

Nemo swam away, scanning the reef for a good hiding spot. Sheldon would be out to get him for sure. Nemo swam past a large empty abalone shell. "Too easy," he muttered. He darted into an anemone. "Way too obvious." Finally he came to a dark cave in the coral. "Too dark," he shivered, looking into the spooky opening. "It'll be perfect."

Mustering his courage, Nemo swam inside. At first he couldn't see anything. Then, as his eyes adjusted to the dark, Nemo saw a large eye open on the cave wall. What could it be?

Another eye opened. Then the entire wall began to move.

"O-O-Old Man Octopus!" Nemo stammered as eight long arms oozed off the cave wall. Nemo and his friends told stories about Old Man Octopus at sleepovers. In the stories Old Man Octopus sneaked up on little fish and gave them a terrible scare.

"S-sorry to disturb you, sir." Nemo swam towards the cave entrance. Then he noticed something amazing. The octopus's arms were changing colour . . . and texture! Instead of matching the brown bumpy cave wall, now they looked more like the reddish coral at the bottom of the cave.

"You didn't disturb me, boy. Tell me what brings you to this corner of the reef?" The octopus's voice was slow and kind, and Nemo's fear melted away.

"Hide-and-seek, sir," Nemo answered politely. "But I wouldn't need a cave if I could camouflage myself like you!"

Old Man Octopus laughed. "Hide-and-seek, eh? One of my favourites. The camouflage does come in handy, but nothing beats a cloud of ink when you want to make a break for the base!"

"You can shoot ink clouds too?" Nemo was so excited he forgot to be quiet.

"I hear you, Nemo!" Sheldon shouted.

"Are you ready to swim for it?" Old Man Octopus whispered with a wink.

Nemo nodded. He high-fived one of Old Man Octopus's tentacles. Then in a burst of inky blackness he darted out of the cave, past Sheldon, and all the way back to the barnacle base. Safe!

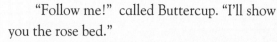

Starry Night

Guess what?" Bonnie looked excitedly at her toys. "We're camping out!" Bonnie announced happily.

A while later, Bonnie and her toys were in her garden. Bonnie unpacked the toys and arranged them inside a tent.

"Now, let's have a picnic!" Bonnie passed out toy food and toy plates.

"Bonnie!" the girl's mother called out. "Dinnertime!"

"I've got to go and eat my dinner. But I'll be back," Bonnie told the toys.

Left alone in the tent, the toys began to explore. "This is a right comfortable spot," Jessie said, admiring Bonnie's sleeping bag.

"Yes, the accommodations are quite satisfactory," Mr Pricklepants agreed.

"Well, shine my spurs!" Woody cried, noticing a camping lantern. He turned it on, and a warm glow lit up the tent. "Let's have a sing-along," Woody suggested. Soon all the toys were singing. Then they decided to head outside. They wanted to explore.

"Look!" Buttercup said. "The stars are coming out!"

Buzz smiled. "That is the Big Dipper – seven stars that form a ladle shape."

Jessie hopped on Bullseye. "I'm gonna look around the yard!" she shouted.

"Follow me!" called Buttercup. "I'll show you the rose bed."

Trixie turned to the other toys. "Who wants to play freeze tag?" But before anyone could answer, she tapped Rex with her horn. The rest of the toys began running away as Trixie chased after them.

"I'm wiped out," Hamm said a little later.

"How about a shadow-puppet show?" said Mr Pricklepants.

"Good idea," Woody said, leading all the toys inside the tent. The toys used Bonnie's torch to create shadow puppets on the wall.

"A sleepover wouldn't be complete without a scary story," Mr Potato Head said. He clicked off the torch. "There was a toy in a forest. The forest was dark. Very dark."

"Just like now!" Rex exclaimed.

"Suddenly there were footsteps," Mr Potato Head said. The toys heard the sound of someone running. Mr Potato Head continued. "A monster was coming –"

"Ahhh! " Rex shrieked as a huge shadow loomed over the tent. The toys all flopped over and went still. The tent flap opened up...

"I'm back!" Bonnie said, smiling at her toys. She brought the toys outside and gave each one a marshmallow on a twig.

Mater Saves Christmas

One morning in Radiator Springs, Mater arrived at Flo's V8 Café with his letter to Santa Car! All the townsfolk had written one. Just as Mater was dropping his letter in the post box, Chick Hicks, one of Lightning's rivals, started to tease Mater, saying Santa Car didn't exist. Then the Sheriff raced up to them with some bad news. All the fuel from the area had been stolen!

The townsfolk were shocked. Without fuel, the post vans couldn't deliver letters to Santa Car! But Mater wouldn't give up. He decided to deliver the letters to the North Pole himself.

But Flo's V8 Café had also been robbed of petrol! Luckily, Fillmore gave Mater some of his homemade fuel. Finally, Mater was ready to leave! But Lightning was worried about his friend. He couldn't let him go by himself!

"Mater, I'm coming with you," he said, and Luigi and Guido gave him snow tyres.

"North Pole, here we come!" cried Mater.

Back in town, Sheriff came up with a plan to find the fuel thieves. Luigi and Guido would be scouts. The friends pooled together their remaining fuel to keep the look-outs going.

Lightning and Mater finally arrived at the North Pole. Lightning stared in wonder. "Santa Car is real!" the race car said.

But Santa Car had some bad news. His reindeer snowmobiles had been stolen!

Just then, Mater remembered Chick acting strangely at Flo's. "Chick Hicks took your reindeer!" he cried. He realized Chick wanted the top-secret flying fuel the reindeer used. Chick would do anything to win a race! Santa Car filled Mater's tank with the top-secret fuel.

Meanwhile, in Radiator Springs, Luigi and Guido had been cornered by Chick and his gang. "Ha! You're too late, boys!" Chick shouted. "I'll fly around the track and never lose to Lightning McQueen again! And you know the best part? No more Christmas! If I can't have presents, no one can!"

Suddenly, the air was filled with the sound of jingling bells. Then, Mater soared over the hill, towing Lightning and Santa Car. Chick raced away, flying just above the ground. Lightning flew after him. Santa Car had filled his tank with the magic fuel too!

Chick was no match for Lightning, and the thief spun out of control. "Tow him straight to jail," said Doc.

Back in town, the Radiator Springs gang celebrated with Santa Car and his reindeer snowmobiles. Everyone cheered. Mater had saved Christmas!

Happy Christmas Pooh!

Just a few more hours to go until Christmas! Outside, big snowflakes were falling. Inside it was warm and cosy. Everything seemed ready, but Pooh wasn't satisfied. He was thinking about what he might have forgotten, when there was a knock at the door.

When he opened it, he found himself face to face... with a snowman!

The snowman's voice seemed strangely familiar to Pooh. The creature stood in front of the fire and began to melt....

Then Pooh discovered with surprise that it was his friend Piglet! He had been covered in snow on his walk to Pooh's house.

That was when Pooh realised he had forgotten to get presents for his friends! Piglet seemed a little disappointed, then he went back home to wrap his Christmas presents.

Pooh watched him heading off in the snow. Though Pooh didn't know how to sort out his mistake, he knew someone who would....

Pooh arrived with frozen paws at the house of his friend Christopher Robin. The little boy happily invited him in.

Pooh saw the stockings hanging on the fireplace and, intrigued, asked him, "Are you drying them?"

"No, Pooh... Father Christmas will leave his presents there," the little boy explained.

"Oh! My presents, that's right... I forgot them!" exclaimed Pooh. "And I don't have any stockings either!"

But Christopher Robin was a good friend – he gave Pooh a stocking for each of his friends in the Hundred Acre Wood.

Pooh hurried off to put the stockings outside of his friends' homes, with a little note saying "From Pooh".

When the bear arrived home, he was exhausted. He settled down in his armchair in front of the fire. He was pleased his friends now had stockings, but he still didn't know what he could give them himself. He closed his eyes and fell asleep.

The next morning, Pooh was woken by his friends. Oh no! He still didn't have any presents for them!

Pooh invited his friends in and was preparing to apologize to them... but they all started thanking him!

Each of them had found a special use for the stocking Pooh had left at their house: a vegetable holder for Rabbit, a stone pouch for Gopher, a warm layer for Eeyore and a hat for Piglet. Pooh was happy – he had realized that Christmas really was magical! Happy Christmas, Pooh!

A Merry Christmas

"**M**erry Christmas!" Ebenezer Scrooge crowed as he watched the Cratchit children open the gifts he'd brought.

"A teddy bear!" Tiny Tim exclaimed. His sister had a new doll, and his brother was busy playing with a new train set.

"And there's another present too," Scrooge said with a twinkle in his eye. "I'll be right back." A moment later, he reappeared, carrying a big package wrapped in red paper and tied with a giant green bow.

The children ripped off the paper and squealed in delight.

"Father, it's a sledge!" they cheered.

"I can see that," Bob Cratchit replied, looking up from the turkey he was carving. Scrooge had brought the turkey over that very morning.

"Can we go sledging? Can we? Can we?" the children chorused.

"Of course," Cratchit replied. "But not until after dinner."

"And dinner is ready right now," Mrs Cratchit said.

"Dinner!" the children shouted as they scrambled to their seats at the table.

Mrs Cratchit sat down at the table. "I can't remember when we've had such a feast, Mr Scrooge," she said happily. "Thank you."

Scrooge raised his glass in the air. "That's what Christmas is all about," he said warmly. "Happiness and goodwill."

Everyone clinked glasses, then got busy eating.

"Now, how about that sledging?" Mr Cratchit said when they had eaten.

Minutes later, everyone was wrapped up. Scrooge pulled the children all through town, singing Christmas carols at the top of his lungs.

"Why is everyone staring at Mr Scrooge?" Tiny Tim whispered to his father.

Mr Cratchit smiled down at his son. "Because they like him," he said.

"I like him too," Tiny Tim said, as Scrooge pulled the sledge to the top of a hill. Everyone climbed off to look at the steep slope.

Scrooge picked up the sledge and walked several paces away from the top of the hill. Then, taking a running start, he jumped onto the sledge and raced to the bottom.

"Whoopeeee!" he cried.

Then Scrooge pulled the sledge back up the hill. "Who's next?" he asked, panting.

"Me!" Tiny Tim shouted. Everyone else got a few turns too.

Later, as he pulled the children back to their house, Scrooge felt warm despite the chill in the air. This was the merriest Christmas he could remember.

A Winter's Tale

One bright, sunny January day, Winnie the Pooh was trudging through the Hundred-Acre Wood on his way to visit his good friend Piglet. Piglet was ill in bed with the sniffles. Overnight it had snowed heavily, and the woods were blanketed in beautiful, fluffy snow.

"Poor Piglet," Pooh said with a sigh. "What a shame he can't come outside to play in this lovely snow." His boots crunched on for a few more steps, and then the bear of very little brain came up with a perfectly wonderful idea. "I know!" he exclaimed. "I will bring some snow to Piglet!" He scooped up a mittenful of snow and formed a snowball. He dropped it into his pocket, and then he made another, and then another. Soon he had three snowballs in each pocket, and another on top of his head, underneath his hat. He hurried on to Piglet's house. When he was nearly there, he passed Tigger, Rabbit, Roo and Eeyore, heading the other way.

"Hello, Pooh!" called Roo. "Come and build a snowman with us!"

"I'm sorry, but I can't," said Pooh wistfully. "You see, I am bringing some snowballs to Piglet, who is sick in bed with the sniffles." He said goodbye and hurried on his way.

Piglet was indeed not well, but he was very happy to see his friend. "Hello, Booh," he said snuffily. "I'b glad you cabe. *Ah-choo!*"

"Poor Piglet," said Pooh. "I'll make tea." He was just putting the kettle on when a large drop of icy water rolled out from underneath his hat and down his nose. This reminded Pooh of something.

"I brought you a present, Piglet!" he cried, snatching off his hat. But there was nothing there. Puzzled, Pooh ran to his jacket, which he had hung on a hook near the door. There were no snowballs in either of the pockets! But there was a sizeable puddle of water on the floor underneath Pooh's coat.

"I don't understand it!" Pooh remarked, scratching his head. "I brought you some snowballs, but they seem to have disappeared."

"Oh d-d-d-dear," Piglet said with a sigh. "Well, thanks for thinkig aboud be. I do wish I could go outside and blay. Could you bull back the curtains so that I can see the snow?"

Pooh hopped up and did what his friend had asked. Both of them gasped when they looked outside.

There, just below Piglet's window, Tigger, Rabbit, Eeyore and Roo had built a beautiful snowman, just for Piglet!

"Oh, friends are wonderbul!" Piglet said happily. "*Ah-choo!*"

Disney·PIXAR
MONSTERS, INC.

The Last Laugh

"Feeling funny today?" Sulley asked Mike on the Laugh Floor one morning.

Mike smiled. "You bet!"

Just then, laughter filled the Floor, catching Mike off guard. A group of employees were standing around another monster.

"Who's the comedian?" Mike asked.

"Stan, our newest recruit," Sulley replied. "I'll introduce you."

"Good morning!" Stan said when he saw Sulley.

"Hey, there's someone I'd like you to meet," Sulley turned to Mike. "Mike Wazowski, this is Stanley Stanford. And Mike here is our top Laugh Collector."

Mike and Stan shook hands. "What were you guys laughing about before?" Mike asked.

"I was just telling them about the time I met the Abominable Snowman and his mother. I said to him, 'Hey, Mr Snowman, where's your mother from?' And he said, 'Alaska.' And I said, 'Hey, don't bother. I'll ask her myself!'"

Everyone burst out laughing all over again – everyone except Mike, who couldn't help feeling green with envy. Mike felt like his position as best scarer was being challenged!

"Hey, good one, Stan," Mike said when the laughter had died down. "But have you heard the one about the skeleton who decided not to go to the party?" All eyes turned to Mike. "He had no body to go with!" Mike exclaimed. Everyone laughed. He was back on top!

But Stan had another joke. "That's funny, Mike," he said. "Have you heard the one about the big elephant that wouldn't stop charging? The only way to stop him was to take away his credit card!" Now everyone was laughing at Stan again. Mike knew this was joke war. As the jokes came fast and furious, the employees gathered around the two jokesters.

The joke-off carried on until, in a moment of panic, Mike's mind went blank! He began to jump up and down, hoping to jump-start his brain. Then, in one of his panicky little jumps, Mike landed on the edge of a wheeled trolly.

"Waaaaaaah!" Mike cried as the dolly took off, rolling across the room and carrying him with it! The employees watched as Mike rolled wildly across the Laugh Floor. They fell down, laughing their heads off! When Mike landed in a pile of cardboard boxes, the joke-off was over, and Mike was the winner. "You're a funny guy, Mike Wazowski," Stan said.

Mike smiled. Stan wasn't such a bad guy, after all. And with two hilarious monsters on the laugh team, thought Mike, just imagine all the laugh energy they could collect!

The Cosiest Carriage

One day O'Malley took Duchess and her kittens down to the junkyard to visit O'Malley's old and dear friend, Scat Cat.

Scat Cat lived in a broken-down carriage that had once been very grand indeed. But the wheels had fallen apart long ago, and the cushions were shredded.

To top it all off, there was an huge hole right in the middle of the worn, tattered roof.

Still, as far as Scat Cat was concerned, his home was perfect. "I feel free here," he told the kittens. "I can come and go as I please. And when I stretch out on the cushions at night, I look up and there are the stars, a-twinklin' and a-winkin' back at me!"

The kittens had a grand time playing with Scat Cat in the junkyard. But they were glad to return to the soft pillows, cosy blankets and warm milk waiting for them back at Madame Bonfamille's mansion.

But a few days later, who should appear at Madame's doorstep but Scat Cat himself. "You'll never believe it," he said. "I went into town to stretch my legs, and when I got back... poof! The carriage was gone!"

"Well, naturally," said Duchess, "you will have to stay with us! I'm sure Madame would be delighted to have you as our guest."

But after only one night, Scat Cat began to feel sad. Everything at Madame Bonfamille's happened according to a schedule. Scat Cat missed doing as he pleased.

"But you know what I miss most?" Scat Cat told O'Malley and the kittens. "My old carriage. What I wouldn't give to be able to look up at the sky and count the twinklin' stars..."

The kittens decided to help Scat Cat. For a while, Madame had been complaining about her old carriage. So, Berlioz climbed into it and began clawing at the old cushions. Toulouse and Marie joined him, and soon, the cushions looked just like the ones in Scat Cat's old carriage!

Finally, Toulouse came crashing down through the carriage roof, making a huge hole. "Oh, my!" exclaimed a voice. The kittens turned, and there was Madame. She surveyed the damage... and smiled! "At last I have an excuse to buy a new carriage," she said. "Let's take this one out to the junkyard at once."

"I don't believe it!" cried Scat Cat, when the kittens led him to his new home, back in the junkyard. "It's purr-fect! How can I ever thank you?" he asked the kittens.

"It was our pleasure," said Berlioz. He flexed his claws. "It's not every day we're thanked for clawing something to pieces!"

Disney · PIXAR

Showtime!

After Andy's toys had settled into their new home in Bonnie's room, Dolly said she had a plan to help everyone get to know one another better. "Let's have a talent show!"

All the toys were excited. But as everyone else started practising, Buzz stood by himself. His friends all seemed to know what to do, but he wasn't sure. He wanted to do something truly spectacular – something that would impress Jessie.

Buzz noticed Hamm and Buttercup working on their comedy routine. Buzz knew Jessie loved a good joke. Grabbing Woody's hat, he shouted, "Howdy partners, I'm Sheriff Woody. Did you know there's a snake in my boot?"

"I don't know about sounding like Woody," said Hamm with a smirk, "but you definitely sound wooden."

Buzz wasn't listening, though. He'd noticed that Mr Pricklepants and the Aliens were doing a play. "Jessie loves to watch plays!" Buzz thought to himself, hurrying over. The Aliens were very excited about their show, which Mr Pricklepants was directing. "There are plenty of parts," Mr Pricklepants said encouragingly. "We're doing Romeo and Juliet!" But Buzz wanted to change the play so it was set in space! Mr Pricklepants wasn't keen.

Then Buzz noticed Rex, who was acting out scenes from his favourite Buzz Lightyear video game with Trixie. Buzz decided there was something missing from their act – him! The dinosaurs were thrilled. "Wait till Jessie sees me do this!" Buzz smiled to himself. But Rex and Trixie just stared – these moves weren't what Buzz did in the game.

"Hey, guys! Time to start the show!" shouted Dolly. Oh no! Buzz still hadn't decided what to do!

Then, up on the stage, Bullseye turned on the music. A lively tune filled the room... and suddenly, Buzz's whole body shook. It was as if the music was taking over his body! Unable to control himself, Buzz started dancing. He couldn't stop! He danced straight to Jessie.

Jessie grinned. She knew exactly what had happened – the music had switched Buzz into his Spanish Mode! "It's okay, Buzz," she whispered. "Just go with it!"

Buzz smiled shyly back at Jessie. "Um, well then," he said. "May I have this dance?"

When Jessie nodded, the two danced across the stage and smiled at each other. All their friends cheered. When the music ended, Buzz and Jessie took a bow together. Buzz was beaming. He'd finally impressed Jessie, and discovered a talent he never knew he had!

Disney
the Fox and the Hound

Tod's Homecoming

Tod the fox wanted to show his fox friend Vixey where he grew up. He took her to the top of a hill where they could look down on a beautiful valley.

"I grew up on Widow Tweed's farm," said Tod, pointing with his paw at a farm nestled in the valley. "She took care of me when I was just a cub.

"And that's my best friend Copper," Tod said, pointing to a handsome hound. "Copper lives at Amos Slade's farm. His house is right next door to Mrs Tweed's."

As the two foxes watched, Widow Tweed, Amos Slade, and Amos's cranky old dog, Chief, climbed into an old banger. With a puff of smoke, they drove off.

But Copper was still at home. He was near the fence, snoozing under an old barrel.

"Let's go visit Copper," said Tod.

"Not me!" Vixey declared. "I'm a fox, and I'm not fond of hounds. I'll catch some fish for our dinner. See you later."

Alone, Tod scampered down the hill, excited about seeing his old pal. But, when he got there, he spotted a strange man sneaking into Amos Slade's henhouse.

"Wake up, Copper!" yelled Tod. "A chicken thief is raiding the henhouse!"

Copper woke with a start and leaped into action. But the rope around his neck held him back.

"You'll have to stop that chicken thief yourself!" cried Copper.

"But I can't stop him alone!" Tod replied.

"We'll help," someone chirped. Tod looked up and saw Dinky the Sparrow and Boomer the Woodpecker sitting on the fence.

"Let's go!" said Tod.

Tod burst into the henhouse first. The thief was there, holding a squawking chicken in either hand.

Tod bit the man in the ankle.

"Ouch!" howled the thief.

Boomer flew through the window and pecked at the chicken snatcher's head. The thief dropped the chickens and covered his head.

Meanwhile, Dinky untied the knot that held Copper. Now, Copper was free – and angry too! Barking, he charged at the burglar.

Eggs flying, the chicken snatcher screamed and ran. As he raced down the road, Dinky and Boomer flitted around his head, pecking him until he was out of sight. The fox and the hound trotted back to the farm.

"Good to see you, Tod," said Copper, wagging his tail. "What brings you here?"

"I just stopped by for a quiet visit," Tod replied.

"It was real quiet, all right!" said Copper.

Countdown to Midnight!

"No sleep till midnight!" Lilo and Stitch chanted, bouncing up and down on Lilo's bed. It was New Year's Eve, and Nani had agreed to let them stay up late.

"Okay, okay." Nani held her hands out. "It's only five o'clock now. Don't wear yourselves out. You still have seven hours until the new year."

Lilo and Stitch looked at each other. Wear themselves out? Impossible! "Look, Stitch," Lilo said, looking as serious as possible. "We only have seven hours. What do you want to do first?"

"Surfing!" Stitch cried.

"Sunset surfing it is!" Lilo gave the little alien a high five before turning to Nani. "Okay?" she asked sweetly.

Nani shook her head again. I must be nuts, she thought. "I'll go get my suit." She sighed.

The three surfed until sundown. Then they headed for home.

"So, what's next?" Lilo asked Stitch.

Stitch smacked his lips. "Dinner!"

"Don't worry," Lilo said. "We'll cook."

"And I'll clean," Nani muttered.

When they got home, Nani lay down on the couch with her arm over her eyes. Five hours until bedtime. She switched on the TV and tried to ignore the crashing noises coming from the kitchen.

"Ta-da!" Lilo emerged with a huge plate of something steaming and cheesy.

"What is it?" Nani asked cautiously.

"Pizza, Stitch-style!" Lilo said. "With anchovies, peanut butter and fruit cocktail!"

Nani cringed. "Don't worry, Nani," said Lilo. "We left the toothpaste on the side this time. Plus, there's a milkshake for dessert!"

The three ate the gooey mess while Lilo and Stitch discussed what was next.

"How about that milkshake?" Nani suggested before Lilo could come up with a noisier, messier or more dangerous idea.

Stitch grabbed the blender and dumped the milkshake on his head. Nani shooed the two into the living room and began to tackle the mess in the kitchen.

The washing-up took forever. Nani could not figure out how they'd managed to use so many pots and pans. She was still elbow deep in suds when her eyes grew wide with alarm. Something was wrong. It was too quiet! Nani rushed into the living room. Lilo and Stitch were sound asleep! Nani looked at her watch.

"Five-four-three-two-one," Nani counted down. "Happy New Year," she said softly, as she covered the pair with a blanket.

She smiled as she looked at the clock. It was only 10pm!